I0749216

THE UNIVERSE BLINKED

Written by

ESSEL MACBETH

Edited by M.K.V.P Macbeth

Grosvenor House
Publishing Limited

This book is published by
Grosvenor House Publishing Ltd
Link House
140 The Broadway, Tolworth, Surrey, KT6 7HT.
www.grosvenorhousepublishing.co.uk

A CIP record for this book
is available from the British Library

ISBN 978-1-80381-996-9

DEDICATED TO THE MEMORY OF
'JOEY'

My inspiration

CHAPTER ONE

Space, a dark lonely place; nothing to focus on but the blackness of the universe itself. A few stars shining against a velvet background, the odd meteor shower, and just occasionally a nebula in all its glorious colours. Further into the vast infinity maybe, a supernova sparked life in the cosmos.

For Sol Nussar, Commander of the Clariziane patrol fleet, none of it seemed real, so he couldn't confirm or deny what he saw. The solitude made him question everything. His small one-man spaceship had been drifting for days; it could have been longer, but he'd lost all track of time. He was sure of seeing something out there in the darkness of space, but his mind refused to believe it. He was alone; he shouldn't be, but he was. It frightened him to be uncertain of his surroundings or even what was happening. Everything was wrong, and he couldn't put it right.

Suffering from severe dehydration didn't help the hallucinations Nussar was experiencing, unable to tell reality from sheer fantasy. The on-board computer appeared to function normally with no hint of a malfunction in the system, but still he assumed it was incorrect. The diagnostics were telling him otherwise, so either the ship's scanners were on the blink, or his eyes were deceiving him. Nussar needed sleep badly, but he had to stay awake. This was too important to miss. He was desperate to stay alert, maintain a vigil, to keep watching the scanners, waiting for a sign of life to appear, anything really to tell him he wasn't going mad.

The ship's equipment continued to play tricks on his mind, tricks that made Nussar question the reality of his situation. Something was out there in the dark void of deep space, then it wasn't, then it was again – only for it to disappear altogether. Nussar kept up the vigil, wanting confirmation of his sanity if nothing else, a sign of life to tell him he was not alone. But nothing. Distraught and exhausted beyond belief, the weariness of his plight made him reflect on the strange events leading up to the time when he'd suddenly found himself alone.

Where was the rest of his fleet? A 20-strong squadron of spaceships crisscrossing the galaxy, maintaining law and order and calm.

This was Nussar's fourth patrol, and for the most part nothing had been unusual as he and his fleet kept formation. But in an instant, it had all gone. He couldn't understand how a whole fleet of spaceships could disappear before his eyes into the depths of space. Those depths were now closing in on Nussar, to the point where he questioned his own existence, asking himself if this was just a nightmare and he would wake up soon.

The intercom remained silent, except for a strange crackling sound that was unfamiliar to him. He couldn't ask for help; no-one was there to answer the call. He had tried to call his fleet again and again, but it wasn't there. Yet it should be. *Where was it? Where was he?* Nussar had no answers to his madness.

The silence continued.

Suddenly the scanners came alive again, the monitor showing the strange object that had haunted him for days. An object far greater than his own ship, at least a hundred times larger. But as quickly as it appeared, it was gone, and the scanners fell silent once more.

The waiting went on. Another day passed, and Nussar's mind wandered again, along the lines of fantasy. *Or was it reality after all?* In his current state of mind, he just didn't have the ability to make such a decision. Over and over, he questioned his own thoughts, battling the anguish inside.

Who could he turn to? Perhaps his other self? Nussar didn't know. The hallucinations returned as the exhaustion took its toll on his body, and he began to see images all around his tiny cockpit, nameless faces taunting him. He argued with them, asking impossible questions he wouldn't like the answers to.

It was becoming too much to bear; he surely couldn't take much more. To be sure of some normality, he checked the ship's components one by one, looking for a possible fault in the works, a short circuit that might be giving out the wrong information... anything to give him the answers he wanted. Unless he'd missed something, it was a hopeless task. A waste of time and energy he didn't have. He did it anyway, then checked and rechecked countless times. The results were always the same.

Not for the first time, Nussar's thoughts drifted again to his fleet. Some of the other pilots were friends of his. *Were they still alive? Or dead?* Trying to recall the events once more was painful and everything blurred into oblivion, a distant memory almost too unbelievable to comprehend. He prayed his friends were still alive and safe somewhere. Knowing the answer would ease his anxiety if not the insanity of the aloneness. Suddenly the universe had become an unforgiving void, a huge abyss he couldn't climb out of, and he could do nothing to stop himself falling further.

The ship was beginning to lose power. The computer sparked again, the scanners barely functioning. Nussar couldn't plot a course home even if he wanted to. The life support was draining; it was just a matter of time before the oxygen was spent. He guessed going insane with the nightmare wouldn't matter then.

The last check of the control system wasn't good news for Nussar. The main computer input panel had finally burnt out and he had no way to repair it. All data was now lost, so he had no record of where home was, or how to get back there. He sank back into the headrest more despondent than ever, perhaps death would be a better option. Nussar stayed seated at his post. *Where could he go anyway?*

Watching the blank screen hour after hour, day after day, took Nussar to the brink. His eyes were heavy, his head dropping, sleep would come soon. A sudden jerk and he sat up straight, afraid to sleep in case he missed something vital. His lungs were telling him the air was getting thin, the oxygen was almost out. Within minutes his head was dropping again, and this time Nussar couldn't fight the fatigue. He slumped back, closing his eyes, reluctantly at first. Then sleep finally took over as he slipped down in his seat.

The shoulder harness pulled tight over his not so pristine white uniform jumpsuit, but he was unaware of what was happening. What little life was left in the controls blinked on and off. The early warning signal lit up, then flashed intermittently on the monitor, before giving out completely. The system was shutting down. But Nussar didn't see it.

A huge intergalactic spaceship appeared in close proximity to Nussar. The vastly more sophisticated spaceship, many times the size of his ship, drew closer and observed for several minutes before attempting to make contact.

Nussar did not answer. He couldn't. The intercom system, along with everything else, was dead, the power gone or burnt out. And he was asleep anyway.

The occupants of the larger ship were intrigued at the tiny size of the craft. They were perplexed by the silence, but more so the fact that this small ship had no distinguishing symbols on the outer hull, and judging by the primitive drive propulsion was not equipped for deep hyperspace travel. Yet there it was, drifting aimlessly in uncharted space on the edge of the galaxy, light years from any civilized colony.

It posed no threat at that size; the concern was that a much larger mothership might be close by and likely to be hostile.

Yet long-range scanning showed nothing in that sector or even beyond, all of which was a complete mystery.

They would need to tread carefully, so again contact was attempted on all known frequencies, but there was no response. Nussar's on-board systems, now drained of power, meant he would not receive a message.

The Earth space rescue hospital ship, Retriever-2, was on an urgent mission across the galaxy. And having already stopped to pick up another small spaceship with no occupant, time was critical.

*

Gram Valmak, Captain of Retriever-2, found himself with a dilemma. There was no more time to waste, but he had been informed of a single occupant aboard the small ship, apparently in a serious condition and in need of medical assistance. The captain had already broken company policy when he'd picked up another unmanned ship, so saw no harm taking another aboard.

It was vitally important that Retriever-2 answered the distress call swiftly, as a planet in the Cenarus system – Kangis-3 – had asked for urgent assistance. Although it was a previously unknown planet, it had issued a request for help, though it was still days away. The mission could not be delayed any further. If the stranger survived, they would return him and his ship to his home planet after the mission.

*

Nussar remained oblivious to his surroundings, sleep being more important, his only comfort. Suddenly he awoke, having felt a huge jolt as his ship was being buffeted by an external force. He had no idea what was happening and was angry with himself for falling asleep.

About to leap out of his seat, the shoulder harness stopped him. As he let it fly off, he wondered what he had missed. Stranger still, the air was different, and he could now breathe more easily. Rubbing his eyes, he tried to focus on the panels in front of him, but everything was gone, burnt out. *No change there*, he thought. Nothing worked yet he was moving. Something was happening. He tried to stand, but his legs were weak from sitting so long.

When he finally managed to stagger to the porthole, afraid to look but needing to know what was going on, Nussar was horrified. His mind did not want to believe his eyes. Something had engulfed his ship.

The stars were no longer shining against the blackness. All he could see was grey bulkheads; he had been swallowed up by some sort of mechanical monster. A taunted mind played havoc with reality. *Was it an illusion, or something more sinister, something beyond his comprehension?*

Nussar had waited so long to find someone to help, but now the solitude had been replaced by an even more fiendish nightmare, one he couldn't cope with. He collapsed, unconscious, his mind unable to take any more of this insanity.

*

On the bridge, Captain Valmak ordered Retriever-2 to proceed without further delay to Kangis-3. He then instructed the medical staff to take great care of their visitor and keep him updated with any progress. The captain was all too aware that as the universe was very volatile at present, any ill-treatment of other beings might be interpreted as an act of war.

Recent attacks by unknown space pirates were frightening enough without causing an intergalactic confrontation. That said, his authority often stretched the rule book to its limits. Nothing fazed the captain; it was all part of the job.

In hangar deck two, security guards were instructed to take no chances. Captain's orders. They stood close to the airlock as the medics accessed Nussar's ship.

Once inside, they found Nussar's unconscious body slumped in a heap. His life hanging in the balance, he was rushed to the hospital and straight into the isolation ward. Nussar only stirred momentarily, drifting in and out of consciousness, mumbling incoherently. But the medics couldn't make out what he was saying.

Back on the bridge Captain Valmak instructed his second-in-command to get a preliminary update on the stranger as soon as possible. Knowing who he was would be a start. Adam King took that to mean straight away, knowing that his captain liked prompt answers. He just wasn't sure his boss was going to get the answers he wanted.

Nussar, now in the isolation ward, was undergoing a thorough examination and immediately put on a drip. Doctor Summers recognized dehydration was a major factor in this poor man's condition. She did not appreciate the captain demanding the medics take great care of the patient; the instruction was uncalled for. She and her hospital staff always treated every patient with the utmost care and attention. *Why was Captain Valmak being so offensive this time?* His attitude seemed to have changed in the last few hours, but she brushed her concerns aside. The captain was way down her list of priorities. The stranger needed constant monitoring.

There were questions on everyone's mind concerning the stranger. If it hadn't been for the advanced warning scanners, Retriever-2 would have smashed right into Nussar's small ship at maximum hyper-speed and perhaps passed it without even noticing its destruction. After all, it was an insignificant little spaceship, according to Captain Valmak, that shouldn't be there in the first place. Meanwhile, Retriever-2 continued its journey on full alert in case a mothership did suddenly appear in the sector. This was turning out to be a tricky situation.

Valmak was riding his luck and risking intergalactic hostility by picking up unauthorised people and removing them from their place of origin without advance notification from Mission HQ. He hadn't the time to wait for a reply, but he couldn't just leave the stranger there to die. It was not in his nature, even if he didn't show his good side often. He still had reservations about this alien but didn't know why. Something just didn't feel right, and the whole episode was disturbing Valmak; there was a nasty niggling at the back of his mind.

At the last calculation, Kangis-3 was still a full day away, so the captain suggested a briefing with his senior officers to discuss the alien and the mission ahead. Perhaps his crew could help put his doubts to bed.

He was first into the conference room, followed by King hotfooting it back from the hospital.

"Well?" said Valmak. "What news?"

"Not much, sir, and not good. The alien was barely breathing when he came aboard, and apparently very dehydrated. Doctor Summers is not too happy with you. Don't know why," said King, slightly out of breath from rushing back for the impromptu meeting.

"I do. Did she say anything else about the alien? His name, perhaps?"

"No, sir, he is sedated for now. She said the next few hours would be critical."

"Thank you, King." Valmak sat at the table with a worried look on his face that suggested he was far from happy.

"What is the problem, Captain?"

"I don't know, King. I think this alien is going to be a headache. Who is he? Where did he come from? I want answers." Valmak slammed his fist angrily down on the table.

"Good question, Captain. He couldn't reach this far into deep space in that small ship, that much we do know," replied King. "There must be a mothership out there somewhere. I'm more concerned to why the long-range scanners have failed to pick it up."

"That's what troubles me, King, so where is it?"

Moments later, Senior Officer Gordon Kursal entered the conference room.

"Ah, come and sit down, Kursal," Valmak instructed.

The other man approached the table, adjusted his uniform, and sat down next to King, whom he acknowledged with a nod.

"Have you managed to inspect the alien ship?" asked Valmak. He needed immediate answers; this alien's arrival was bugging him.

"Which one, sir?" asked Kursal. He had been going over both alien ships, so wanted to be sure what information the captain wanted.

"You know which one, Kursal," snapped Valmak. "Don't try my patience."

"Ok, well not much to tell yet. The ship, as we know, is very primitive and not capable of deep space travel."

"Anything else?" Valmak was impatient that Kursal wasn't telling him much.

"It has no markings on the outer hull to identify it, so no help there, sir."

"Okay, what about the inside. Are the on-board systems able to tell us who this guy is?" Valmak was visibly frustrated by the lack of information and wanted to slam the table again, but the first time had really hurt – not that he let on.

"That is going to take time, sir. It appears that all the systems are burnt out. The oxygen supply was almost depleted, so he wouldn't have lasted much longer. The engineering crew are in there now and repairs are ongoing. We can't access the computer until then."

Captain Valmak paced the room several times, disappointed with the lack of data surrounding the alien, who he was growing to dislike more with every second. *Why did he feel such animosity towards him? Why did the alien make him feel so fearful?*

"So, at the moment you're saying we have nothing on him." Valmak sat down.

"In a nutshell, yes, sir," replied Kursal.

"That was a rhetorical question, Kursal."

"Sorry, Captain." Kursal decided it would be best to keep his comments to himself from now on. The captain's mood was not going to improve.

"What worries me," interrupted King, "is that this ship is like nothing I've ever seen before. I do think we need to be wary. We don't know how why the alien is here, and is it connected to the other alien ship?"

"I agree we must be wary. That's why the guards are outside the hospital, I hope," said Valmak.

Kursal stayed quiet. He was more concerned how the alien would react when he woke up.

"Are we looking at an unknown race of people, sir? He has strange markings on his forehead, and I've never seen anything like that before," asked King. "After all, this whole sector for the most part is uncharted. We are merely passing through."

"Anything is possible," replied Valmak unconvinced. "I'm concerned about his sudden appearance. It's too convenient. I have a bad feeling about it."

There was genuine fear in the captain's voice; he had never been so anxious about any alien. He was a man of total confidence and had been a captain of an elite space rescue ship for many years. *Why was this mission so different?*

Neither of his officers could give him the answers he wanted.

"Okay, we'll leave it until he is conscious. How are we doing with Kangis-3? Have you discovered anything about it?" he asked.

"We don't even know where it is, sir. We are heading for the Cenarus system from where the signal came. But our data says no inhabitable planets exist there," said Kursal, offering what little information he had.

"I find that unbelievable. Double check the data," demanded Valmak. He didn't want mysteries of that nature.

He decided to end the meeting for now, as they were getting nowhere.

"King, can you go and make sure the security I ordered is stationed outside the hospital, and tell them to be discreet. Doctor Summers isn't too pleased with me now."

"Right away, sir," said King, and left to carry out his orders.

As Kursal got up to leave, he turned back to the captain. "You don't think the alien might be one of those space pirates we've been hearing about, do you, sir?"

When Valmak didn't reply, Kursal left and shut the door behind him.

The one thing worrying the captain was that they might have inadvertently picked up a ship belonging to pirates. But he was certain that the alien on board was more sinister than any space pirates.

*

In the hospital isolation ward Doctor Summers kept a vigil at Nussar's bedside, constantly monitoring his vital signs and regularly checking the intravenous drip. Physically he was hanging in there, and she hoped sedating him would give his body time to recover. Getting fluids into him was all-important. Even though she wasn't up on alien anatomy as much as she might like, she surmised that all species needed fluids.

The one problem was that his neurological readouts were a concern; his brain pattern was alarmingly erratic. Something was going on inside his head – maybe it was simply nightmares, but she didn't know for sure. Whatever had happened to this poor man must have been too traumatic for his mind to deal with. She refused to leave his side, watching him sleep, willing him to pull through.

Hour after hour Doctor Summers watched over Nussar, taking the time to document his condition, as she did with all her critical patients. Some hours later, the readouts indicated that his vital signs were improving, so the intravenous drip was taking effect at last.

How he had managed to become so dehydrated was a mystery, but it was a relief to see him responding so well. Looking at his dishevelled state, Doctor Summers wondered how long he had been adrift in space. She was convinced that had to be a factor in his mental state.

She wanted to know so much about him. Pushing his shoulder-length hair back off his face, the ridges on his forehead felt quite prominent – *and rather cute*, she thought inappropriately. Cute for an alien, and very handsome looking with his bronzed skin.

A further scan showed his brain pattern had levelled off to within normal guidelines… whatever normal was for an alien. It was merely guesswork again, but it was a sure sign he was in a lot less distress. Now it was a question of how the patient would react to his surroundings when he woke.

*

With several hours before Retriever-2 reached the supposed location of Kangis-3, Captain Valmak attempted to find out for himself about the mysterious planet. Being told no such planet existed in the Cenarus system was not acceptable to him. He wanted definitive answers and wanted them immediately. Mission HQ back on Earth were not forthcoming with information. Maybe they knew so little as well. It was strange. The data had to be wrong.

Try as he might, Valmak repeatedly hit a dead end in his search for information. Nothing, it seemed, had ever been recorded about Kangis-3 in this system or any other, which deepened the mystery even more. But Valmak hated mysteries, believing there was an answer to all things. Inside he was fuming, his anger rising to intense levels.

The ship's memory banks were no help at all. All he had from Mission HQ was a distress signal coming from the outer limits of the galaxy, which named the planet and requested urgent assistance. Nothing else. Kangis-3, as far as Valmak could recall, was not part of any alliance affiliated to Mission HQ, yet had still asked for help. And of course, the bureaucrats back on Earth had said yes. He surmised that was all down to profit, no other reason.

Sitting alone in the conference room in deep contemplation, Valmak's thoughts returned to the alien on board. His presence was too convenient, and the captain felt sure there had to be a link to the mystery planet.

Valmak hadn't moved since King and Kursal left, and now the dark, niggling thoughts were getting worse, a black ominous cloud looming over him. The alien was obviously up to no good, Valmak decided, and he was determined to find out what was going on. *Maybe the alien was the advance party for the space pirates, or an invasion*, he thought.

He had to know, but the more Valmak sat there alone, the more it added to his stress. He didn't know he had so much hatred in him. His demeanour was changing and, worse still, he didn't realise.

Retriever-2 had been given no choice about responding to the SOS call, as it had come from Earth Mission HQ when they were on their way home. Valmak wished he hadn't stopped to pick up the alien, or indeed the other spaceship, which was also causing problems. But it was the alien who terrified the captain by his mere presence, and nothing could ease his anxious mind.

*

Doctor Summers had finally left Nussar's side. Although he was now stable, he was not quite out of the woods and still needed a lot of care. She sat down at her desk, tired and badly in need of sleep – a luxury that would have to wait.

She proceeded to document Nussar's condition for the records. The extra paperwork was time-consuming, but she knew it had to be done.

Nussar stirred a few times and mumbled a few incoherent words, but nothing which made much sense to Summers or the other medics who came to try and persuade her to take a break. When she tried to engage with her patient, though, it was to no avail. It appears he was trying to communicate with someone. *Had he not been alone?* She surmised that seemed logical, having heard the circumstances of his arrival.

Captain Valmak had already called the hospital several times for an update on the alien's condition, which was beginning to annoy her. His obsession did not make any sense to the doctor. Valmak, she felt, was behaving well out of character – and it was being noticed by the crew. Her answer was always the same – no change – and she was determined she wasn't going to tell him any different until she was ready, and the patient was awake.

By the time Doctor Summers completed all her paperwork, her patient was starting to stir. She looked across the room just in time to see him attempting to pull the intravenous needle out of his arm.

"No, no, no, don't do that!" she said loudly, rushing over and managing to stop him. "It's fine, just stay calm. I'm here to help you."

She spoke gently so she did not alarm him further. "I'm so glad you're awake. I've been very worried about you. Can you talk?" she asked softly.

Nussar didn't answer. He was trying to focus on his surroundings. It looked nothing like his ship, and it certainly wasn't home either.

"Can you tell me your name?"

A gentle hand on his shoulder ensured he stayed where he was. And a smile from the speaker went some way to relax

Nussar, though he was still slightly confused and unsure where he was.

Who is she? he wondered. Surveying the room, all he could see were white walls from floor to ceiling, a couple of empty beds next to him, and strange equipment everywhere – some of it attached to him.

This wasn't right; he shouldn't be here! But he was too weak to move. The strange woman poured a glass of water and offered it to him. Nussar's mouth was very dry, so he hesitantly took the glass, and a friendly nod from the woman persuaded him to take a sip. He relaxed a little. This strange woman standing over him appeared kind and welcoming, but he had no idea who she was. All Nussar could focus on were her piercing blue eyes and golden blonde hair falling over her shoulders. She was dressed in white, like the rest of the room.

She was certainly a vision of beauty in his eyes, but then he had a horrible thought: *it could all be a dream, and he hadn't woken up yet.*

"Do you understand me? Can you tell me your name?" she asked again, her soft words not at all threatening.

Nussar understood her but still couldn't reply. Everything was so strange and unfamiliar, he felt intimidated. It was clear to him she was an alien, which was troubling. *Was he a prisoner? What was going on? Where was his ship? And what had happened to his fleet, his friends?* Questions rattled round his head so much that it hurt. *Would this alien woman give him the answers?*

Doctor Summers smiled at Nussar again, still hoping for a response. She knew he was bound to be disorientated and confused by his new surroundings.

"I'm Doctor Niko Summers, and this is a hospital aboard the Earth space rescue ship Retriever-2." She hoped he would relax enough to respond.

"Where is my ship?" Nussar asked, finally able to speak. He was more concerned about his ship than his own welfare.

"It's here. Don't worry, your ship is in safe hands. Please tell me your name, I need to call you something."

He liked her smile; she seemed nice. "Nussar..." he stuttered, almost forgetting his own name for a moment. "Commander Sol Nussar," he added nervously, and still wary.

"That's a good start, Sol. Where are you from?" Her voice calm and soft, she didn't want to push him too hard, but answers were needed to help him get back home.

Nussar didn't feel afraid of her. "Clarizia," he replied.

Then Nussar remembered his friends. *Were they here, too?*

"My friends, where are my friends?" He looked genuinely worried. "Have you got my friends, are they safe?"

"You were alone when we picked you up," she told him. "Don't you remember, Sol?"

She knew her answers were likely to unnerve him, but the truth was best.

Visibly shaken, Nussar couldn't understand how that could be right. His fleet couldn't have just vanished! Then he recalled that it had. *If that was the truth, whose truth was it?* Certainly not his.

"Forgive me, Sol, but I must ask. Where is Clarizia? What star system is your home planet?"

Clarizia was not a place she was familiar with, but she was worried that he still seemed very confused.

"Star system?" said Nussar, stunned by the question. "I-I don't know..."

If she didn't know where they were, he sure as hell didn't. Now he really was scared.

Doctor Summers decided he'd be better to rest again, and at least now she had something to tell the captain which would keep him happy for a while.

Nussar took another sip of water before lying back and closing his eyes. He was sure he would wake up on his home planet, in his own bed, soon. This was not the real world.

*

Captain Valmak was still alone in the conference room, baffled by the alien in their midst, the niggling doubts remaining. Doctors Summers had relayed the alien's name and home planet, but he didn't believe it. It didn't seem plausible in the captain's eyes. The alien was obviously lying, hiding his true identity. But for what reason?

As the supposed location of the distress signal from Kangis-3 was almost upon them, that would have to take priority. The captain had to push the nagging doubts to the back of his mind to deal with the rescue mission.

Kangis-3 was not yet showing on the long-range scanners, but he hoped it would soon, then they could get the mission done and they could all go home.

In the meantime, Captain Valmak made the sudden decision to visit the hospital, perhaps get some answers now that the alien was awake. He had to get the dreadful thoughts of doom out of his head somehow, and he was sure the alien held the key.

Doctor Summers was pleased things had calmed down in the hospital. Now that everything was finally running smoothly, she could relax and take a break… until she saw Captain Valmak walk through the door.

She jumped up. "Captain, if you want answers, you're going to have to wait," she snapped at him.

"Just tell me if I can speak to the alien," he replied bluntly, having no time for pleasantries.

"You cannot interrogate him." She was adamant. Sol was her patient and still under her care.

"Look, Doctor, I need answers, certain information from the alien. What he said to you makes no sense—"

"Only to you, I suspect," said the doctor, interrupting him.

"He isn't telling us the truth." Captain Valmak exercised his senior rank by standing firmly. He wasn't budging.

"He isn't saying much because he has only just woken up. Give the poor man a chance," she said, hoping for leniency. He is very vulnerable. His mind underwent a traumatic experience, and I don't know the full extent or what happened to him out there. It must have been bad."

But Captain Valmak wasn't shifting. "I want to speak to him, now."

Doctor Summers glared at him. He was being unreasonable and trying her patience. "But Captain—"

"No buts, Doctor. Go and see if he is awake and able to talk."

She was reluctant. Whatever the captain thought, her diagnosis was correct, and she was certain Sol was telling the truth. But the captain wanted answers and he was not going away.

Doctor Summers was apprehensive about his request but relented… with conditions.

"Very well, Captain, but if I say stop, you stop."

He nodded, but privately he had no intention of doing that.

Nussar was sitting up in bed, watching the doctor talking to the strange man in uniform. He then realised he wasn't wearing his own uniform and wondered who had undressed him.

He didn't like the man in uniform; he seemed aggressive and unfriendly to the doctor. And Nussar liked her. As the pair approached his bedside, he became more nervous.

"Sol, this is our captain, Gram Valmak, he would like to talk to you. Okay?" said Doctor Summers, giving him a smile to reassure him he was in safe hands.

Nussar nodded, though he still felt wary around this man.

"Commander Nussar, my doctor informs me you are from the planet Clarizia, is that correct?" Valmak loomed over him and spoke in a cool, threatening manner.

He replied quietly, "Yes, but—"

"And what star system is that?"

Nussar felt even more uneasy. *What sort of question was that?* He struggled for words. "I-I don't know."

"You don't know where you come from? I find that—"

Doctor Summers put a hand on the captain's arm. She wasn't going to tolerate any aggressive behaviour.

"I don't know anything," Nussar managed. "I'm lost. My spaceship ran into trouble, then I got separated from my fleet. I don't know where my friends are." He was becoming agitated and confused. He didn't know what was real anymore, it was just too much to take in. *Could these people really help him? Would they?* The man in uniform wouldn't, Nussar was sure. He felt vulnerable and helpless, especially with no clothes on and no means of escape.

"One more question, Commander Nussar. How did you arrive in this sector, and what is your purpose?" It was two questions, but Captain Valmak wanted answers.

Nussar felt as if he was under arrest and being interrogated like a criminal.

"Please, just help me get home." He was frightened. If this was a dream, it was turning into a nightmare. *And if it was real, how was he going to escape?*

Captain Valmak ignored his plea as irrelevant. He could not believe a thing the alien said whether his words sounded plausible or not. Those niggling doubts about the alien emerged again, and fears of imminent danger would not leave him alone. The captain's judgement was already clouded, and this alien was the cause.

Doctor Summers had seen enough. Her patient was clearly distressed by all the questioning; he was shaking, with panic in his eyes.

"Okay, that's it, Captain, he needs to rest. You must leave. I insist.

Valmak could clearly see from her demeanour that she meant it, and he turned to leave. Before he did, he whispered in her ear, "I want to know everything about him, everything he says. Understand, Doctor Summers?"

The captain stormed angrily out of the hospital, annoyed that he hadn't managed to get answers. Passing the guards, he warned them to stay alert and, if necessary, enter the hospital to keep an eye on the alien.

Doctor Summers was anxious about her patient's wellbeing. The captain had been very harsh on him, and there had been absolutely no need for the last remark. She was certain that Sol was no threat to anyone and was puzzled by the captain's appalling behaviour. Something was biting him today.

Nussar fell back on his pillow, tired, afraid, and unsure of what to do. His super hearing meant he had heard what the captain said. Every word. This man in the strange uniform didn't like or trust him, so he would need to be very careful.

"Why doesn't your captain like me?" he asked, as the doctor was about to leave the room.

"He doesn't know you, Sol. But you can talk to me anytime in confidence. Now rest." She smiled again to reassure him.

The captain seemed to wind everyone up the wrong way lately, so she hoped Sol would talk to her more openly.

For now, though, he had too much to absorb. He was none the wiser about his surroundings or even where he might be. This strange spaceship that had swallowed him up was more than he could stomach, and he had questions of his own. *Why didn't the captain say anything about Nussar's fleet?* They had to be out there somewhere close by. *What were these aliens hiding from him?* He prayed the fleet was safe. He would find a way to get back to them just as soon as he got his strength – and his uniform – back.

*

Captain Valmak arrived back on the bridge after being absent for hours. When he noticed a couple of crew missing from their stations, he was even angrier than before. The helm operator, Will Straten, informed him they had taken off to the science deck after receiving a call. He looked across the bridge to King, at his station.

"Don't ask me what it's about, Captain. They just left without saying a word," said King.

Argent shrugged his shoulders at the captain to indicate he knew nothing either.

After enquiring how much longer it was to Kangis-3, Valmak then disappeared, and Straten turned to his monitoring. He had no idea of the answer, but the captain was in a bad mood. Somebody was about to get a roasting, he guessed.

*

For the last few days, the science team had been busily collecting and analysing data from the long-range scanners. Gathering information was vitally important and part of their job, as defined by mission HQ, and the research helped to map the many galaxies on their long voyage through space. So much data poured in, and because much of the universe was uncharted, it became a time-consuming task for the team. The latest figures were matched up perfectly with already known star systems, then catalogued and put in the archives for when they returned to Earth.

The most recent data, though, was causing raised eyebrows. For some reason, the data did not match with any known star system, and an inexplicable piece of data had been thrown up that didn't sit right with the team.

Senior Officer Cal Bartok arrived from the bridge to check what the problem was, feeling sure his men must have got something wrong. They could have told him over the intercom, but verification was needed before the work could be catalogued. An unusual anomaly had occurred which didn't make sense. It came from the same sector where the alien had been picked up, but with so much data to catalogue it had only just been discovered.

"Right, what's all the fuss about?" asked Bartok, scanning the room for clues but only seeing a desk full of printed star charts, which to his mind looked rather messy.

Tom Phasner was on hand. "Can you take a look at this data, sir?" he said, handing the readout to Bartok and pointing to the monitor already set up for him.

Bartok read over the paperwork then looked at the monitor, then back to the readout. He saw the discrepancy immediately and was puzzled that the figures were not matching up when they should. *It's odd*, he thought. *The findings had to be wrong.*

According to the data, a star had been visible a second earlier, but in the next readout it had disappeared.

Without looking up, he asked, "Have you cross-checked attachments to the data to be sure?"

"Yes, sir, we did. That's why I called you," replied Phasner. "What do you make of it, sir?"

"Well, I would say stars don't just disappear. You need to go through all the data again, recheck all incoming information around the time, and find the mistake. I cannot sign this off until you do," said Bartok, handing back the paperwork.

"I did, sir. Several times. There is no error." Phasner was confident he'd done everything correctly.

Bartok scanned the data again. Maybe there was something to explain the anomaly, a slight inconsistency that even he had missed. The information was there, but it was wrong. *How?* he thought.

"Sir, I was wondering if this might be connected in some way to the sudden surge in the ship's power earlier. It happened at the same time as this weird distortion," said Phasner. He noticed that the rest of the science team were staying out of the way, leaving him to answer their superior. Nobody wanted the blame if a mistake had been made.

"So, why did the computer fail to register such a huge error?"

"Don't know, sir. I did check the computer for a malfunction just in case, but there was nothing," replied Phasner.

Bartok continued to study the data, puzzled by the conflicting readouts. He agreed that there had been a variation in the ship's main power supply, but he had been assured by the engineering crew that it quickly corrected itself. So, it had been dismissed as a simple blip in the system.

"That doesn't answer the question about the disappearing star," he said.

"No, sir," agreed Phasner.

"So, what did happen? What's your opinion of this, Phasner?" Bartok doubted there was an answer, or one that was believable, but he couldn't sign off the work either way.

Phasner was reluctant to reply, hesitant that he might be laughed at. He had a theory that had sounded ludicrous when he'd mentioned it to the others. And he guessed that's why they were staying out of the way.

His theory certainly wasn't based on science, and he said as much.

"Right now, Phasner, I will take your theory. We need something to go on, and something I can relate to the captain."

"Yes, sir. Well, my opinion is... my theory is... the universe blinked," he finally managed. "I believe it somehow caused a rift in space momentarily, and the star was then sucked in." He waited for a response, or maybe a laugh at his suggestion.

But Bartok looked stunned by his explanation. He did not deem it funny, but unlikely.

"Are you telling me a wormhole was formed?" asked Bartok, rolling his eyes at the improbability.

"I don't know about that, sir, but I think a rift in the space time continuum would account for such an anomaly. I know it's only theoretical, but nothing else fits with the scientific analysis."

"Hence your theory that the universe blinked."

"Yes, sir," said Phasner with more confidence.

Bartok wasn't buying it; there had to be a different explanation. He only believed in hard facts, in black and white, concrete scientific evidence, so he couldn't give this information to the captain. He accepted that Phasner wasn't as stupid as he'd first thought, and at least the man had a theory.

On leaving, Bartok issued one request. "Check again, to be sure. And while you're at it, delve further into the alien and examine all sectors surrounding the area where we picked him up. If you find anything, let me know immediately."

"Yes, sir. What exactly are we looking for?" asked Phasner.

"A mothership, for a start." Bartok handed back the readout and left.

He was starting to wonder if the captain's suspicions about the alien had some basis. He had his own gut feeling now that the alien might present a problem.

*

In the hospital, Doctor Summers was busy preparing the sick bay and collecting all the necessary equipment she thought might be needed when they reached Kangis-3. As she'd not yet received any information and wasn't sure what to expect, she packed enough to cover all eventualities. *Better to have more than enough*, she thought.

The only patient in the hospital was Sol. Her other patients, who'd had minor work-related injuries, had been treated quickly and resumed their duties – all except Nely Meki. The helm operator, who always had some non-existent illness, was a real hypochondriac but she always treated him with sympathy.

Doctor Summers kept an eye on Sol, checking on him constantly, though it was more for her own benefit. Since she'd moved him out of isolation, he had responded remarkably well to treatment and even seemed to like the hospital food.

She smiled at him as he looked in her direction. Both she and Captain Valmak clearly had strong feelings about the alien – but those feelings were completely different. She was a little afraid why she felt this way about a complete stranger, an alien. But none of the men on Retriever-2 stirred her emotions like this.

Total concentration was needed for the upcoming rescue mission, and Doctor Summers was fully aware of its importance. Having finished the preparations, she decided to sit with Sol and reassure him she wouldn't be away for too long. She also took the chance to return his uniform, which was newly laundered and pristine white again.

Sol was very grateful. He enjoyed the company of this charming and beautiful woman, who listened to everything he had to say.

As they chatted, Doctor Summers enjoyed finding out about his life – none of which she was going to repeat to the captain. They felt a real connection and were both willing to explore it.

CHAPTER TWO

Captain Valmak retired to his private quarters for a few quiet moments of peace and solitude to clear his head, or so he hoped. The imminent arrival of Kangis-3 weighed heavily on his shoulders, but so did this alien Sol Nussar. That problem was not going to resolve itself anytime soon. If only he could dispose of the alien's presence, it would go a long way to easing the stress and anxiety burning inside him.

He had to put all evil thoughts straight in the bin. He hated himself, but still couldn't fight the dreadful thoughts.

The alien was a complete mystery. No information could be found on him, and Valmak disliked not knowing. He had a fear that he and his entire crew were in mortal danger. *But was it the alien, or Kangis-3 – or both – that caused him the most stress?* He couldn't even answer his own question.

With still no more information regarding their arrival on Kangis-3, Valmak was worried that they were too late for a rescue or, worse still, they were heading into a trap. There was no basis for his feelings, just a terrible premonition that would not leave him.

Since the first and only distress call from Kangis-3, there had been no other contact, according to Earth mission HQ. No further information, no further contact with Earth, other than being told that answering the call was vital for intergalactic relations.

Valmak did not do well with being alone with his thoughts; it just made him worse. He desperately tried to fight against the bad vibes, but the more he thought about the mission and the alien, the worse he felt. Anger, fear, frustration, and hatred all just came together, and he felt as though his head was bursting.

It had been three days since the SOS message had asked for urgent assistance. Retriever-2, as the nearest ship, had been ordered to respond even though they were on their way back to Earth for a well-earned rest. The ship and its crew had not seen home in almost six years.

Now everyone was becoming tense, worried that the notorious space pirates had reappeared. It was a distinct possibility, and the fact that there had been no reports of them operating in this sector to date did nothing to ease the fear.

*

Gordon Kursal stood close to the helm controls, just behind Paul Aztac who was busy monitoring their course to what they assumed would be Kangis-3. Second-in-command Adam King sat at his station, working on a strategy in readiness for the mission. He was drawing up a Plan-B, as they had to be prepared for any scenario. He wondered about the captain's absence; the man didn't seem to be focused of late and certainly wasn't helping the situation.

King enjoyed working with Kursal, who was always a loyal dedicated officer, and he felt they had held the fort well.

Maintaining his stance on the bridge, Kursal was focusing on the large viewing screen, anticipating the appearance of Kangis-3 at any moment. This being uncharted space, very little was known about the sector, and although long-range probes constantly relayed data back to aid the voyage, the ship was in many ways going in blind. It was hoped that at some point soon they would receive a call from Kangis-3 – a sign perhaps that they were still alive, or even to explain what the problem was. However, the intercom stayed silent.

Kursal always enjoyed the peace and tranquillity of silent space. There was a certain serenity not matched anywhere else.

He stood watching, staring at the blackness. Space appeared so empty; it was like watching a screen of nothingness. Then suddenly it wasn't.

He blinked hard. For a second he thought he had seen something, a strange shape flickering at the edge of the viewing screen. *Was it simply gathering dust?* Unsure, he stared more intently at whatever it was disappearing, then returning. No, it wasn't space dust; the shape was too uniform. It needed to be investigated.

Leaning over Aztac at the helm, Kursal pressed the magnification to maximum. If something was out there, he wanted a better look.

"Is everything ok, sir?" asked Aztac, startled by his sudden action.

Kursal didn't reply, his eyes staying glued to the viewing screen. Nothing. *Had he been wrong?* He was confused. *Had his eyes deceived him?*

"Reduce magnification," he requested, saying nothing of his concerns.

As Aztac complied, a small planet appeared in the distance, which he surmised had to be Kangis-3 at last.

"Sir, I believe we have a visual on the planet," Aztac announced.

"Inform Captain Valmak," ordered Kursal.

King left his seat to look. "About time," he commented.

Kursal continued to watch the viewing screen. It was clear apart from the planet approaching. He surmised he must have just stared at the screen too long and his eyes were tired, making him imagine something that wasn't there.

This tour of duty was taking its toll on him, and suddenly he felt physically sick and unsteady on his feet. The thought of losing control of his mental state scared him. There couldn't be anything out there; it was impossible.

Besides, he thought, *the computer would surely have registered an anomaly*. But his mind was still telling him that something unspecified was out there, and it wasn't natural.

He remained standing, almost to attention, watching the viewing screen. His stomach felt queasy, and he didn't feel so good.

For a split second he thought he saw it again, whatever it was, in the opposite corner of the screen. But no, he was mistaken. The nausea wasn't helping; he couldn't remember the last time his stomach had felt so bad, but it was probably linked to the extreme fatigue of doing a sixteen-hour shift without a break.

This time he was certain. "Aztac, full viewing power, now!" he ordered loudly.

Aztac obeyed and hit the switch immediately. Nothing was there except Kangis-3 and a few thousand stars.

"Are we looking for anything in particular, sir?" he asked, puzzled by Kursal's strange behaviour.

"No, no, I just thought I saw... It doesn't matter." He felt stupid, and even more sick.

"Kursal, are you alright?" asked King, looking around to find him unsteady on his feet and holding the back of Aztac's seat for support.

Kursal didn't reply. He couldn't right then. It was ludicrous to suspect anything was out there, floating in space, lurking in plain sight. Whatever he'd thought was there had appeared to be very close to the planet, but he wasn't sure if it had any bearing on the situation. He wasn't sure of himself, and it made him tense.

Moments later, Captain Valmak entered the bridge. Instantly he noticed the uncomfortable looks and could see by Kursal's face he was off colour.

"Something wrong, Kursal?" he asked with a concern he didn't normally show.

Averting his eyes from the viewing screen, Kursal replied, "Not sure, sir. I mean, I don't know, sir." His voice faltered.

"Explain," said the captain.

"It was... it was something on the screen... or at least I thought it was. I'm not sure." *How could he explain what he did or didn't see?*

"What did this something look like?" questioned Valmak. His senior officer was making no sense.

"I don't know, sir. I must have been wrong." Again, his voice faltered. "I-I don't feel so good, Captain." In fact, he was feeling decidedly sick and wanted to throw up. He was sure there was an entity lurking out there in space, but logic said otherwise.

"Go to the hospital, you look awful. Get Doctor Forester to check you over, then report back. I want all hands-on deck for this mission."

"Yes, sir." Kursal quickly exited the bridge before he did throw up.

Valmak needed his crew alert and fit, but he did realise everyone was exhausted due to double shifts and being so long away from home. It was, though, what they'd signed up for at the academy. *And if he couldn't relax, why should they?* This was their last mission, Valmak told himself over and over, it was the only way to get through it.

Kursal made his way along to the hospital, thinking about his behaviour on the bridge and how stupid he had been. The nausea was easing slightly but he still didn't feel good about the whole episode. He regarded himself as a level-headed, rational officer, so this behaviour was totally out of character.

Nearing the hospital entrance, he saw the armed guards standing outside, then he suddenly realised what the captain had said to him. *Why had he to report to Doctor Forester?* he wondered. Surely the medic would too busy to see patients, as he was occupied doing his research – not that anyone knew exactly what he did. He was always disappearing into his lab and for the last two years had been very secretive about his work.

Had the captain suddenly become forgetful about Forester? The captain's behaviour had been worse than anyone's lately. Some of the crew had remarked on it, though no-one dared say anything official.

On arrival in the hospital reception, he could see no sign of Doctor Forester. Kursal remembered he'd not actually seen the medic for almost a week, but it was a rather large spaceship, so it was easy to get lost if one wanted to.

He soon spotted Doctor Summers at her desk. At least she would be more pleasing to the eye.

"Got a moment, Doctor?" he asked.

Doctor Summers looked up, happy to see someone. Sol had fallen asleep a while ago, so the room was very quiet, and she had taken the opportunity to relax while the other medics enjoyed some time off.

"Kursal, what's the problem?" She could see he appeared a bit stressed and ashen faced as he sat down at the desk.

"I'm not sure. I think I've been hallucinating, seeing things that aren't really there or even should be. It made me feel strangely nauseous. I was supposed to see Doctor Forester," he explained. "Where is he?"

"Good question," she replied. "That man is a law unto himself. He hasn't put a single shift in for days. I've not seen him at all."

Kursal buried his face in his hands then gave his face a good rub to try and snap out of it.

Watching him, the doctor could see he was exhausted from overwork. They all were; it was the nature of the job.

"Stay there, Kursal. I'll get my kit, then we'll see what the problem is. Though I suspect sleep would be beneficial, right?"

He lifted his head and watched her elegantly glide across the room. To him, she was a picture of beauty, and he'd wanted to ask her out so many times but had always bottled out.

Instead of saying what he really wanted to say, he simply asked, "I see the guards outside. Not giving you any trouble, are they?"

Doctor Summers returned with her medical bag and laid several instruments on the desk. "No trouble, but I wish they weren't there. Our beloved captain doesn't trust our visitor yet."

"He does have a point, though, Doctor. We know nothing about him."

"Well, I don't agree with the captain," she replied. "Sol is no threat."

"First name terms then?" he said a little cheekily.

"Enough. You know nothing," she snapped back.

She knew enough about Sol to realise he was genuine, friendly, intelligent, and very chatty. She loved his company, but she was keeping that to herself for now. It was no business of anyone else's.

Kursal didn't respond. He was more concerned about what she was doing to him, but he did see her point. The alien wasn't going anywhere, as he was still laid up in bed.

After a few initial tests on her patient, the doctor concluded Kursal was reasonably fit, but guessed he was just fatigued. His stress levels were slightly abnormal, and his blood pressure elevated, but otherwise his signs were all good.

Putting the instruments away, she asked the obvious. "So, what exactly is the problem?"

"I don't know, Doctor. Really."

"Then tell me what happened to bring you here." This wasn't the Gordon Kursal she knew, and she was concerned about his mental state.

"Well, I thought I saw something while I was watching the viewing screen, but no-one else on the bridge noticed it. They were all too busy. And the computers didn't pick it up. Then I saw it again before it vanished a second time. I thought I was going mad, Doctor. That's when I felt nauseous."

"Do you want something to settle your stomach?"

"I'll be fine, thanks… I think." He wasn't sure.

"It does sound strange, but look, I can't find anything seriously wrong that a good long vacation wouldn't fix." She gave him one of her lovely smiles.

"Then I'm not going mad?"

"Can't answer that one," she replied jokingly.

"Thanks, Doctor Summers, I appreciate you taking the time." He felt relieved in one sense, but it still didn't answer his concerns, and the nagging doubts in his head persisted. He was more certain than ever that he had seen something, but he just didn't know what he had seen and, worse still, why no-one else had seen it.

Before getting up to leave, Kursal glanced towards the sleeping alien. He wasn't in the isolation ward, as per protocol on all aliens, but Doctor Summers was quick to inform him it wasn't necessary. Sol was making good progress in his recovery, she said, and so long as he was left alone, his mind would also heal.

It appeared to Kursal that the doctor chatted a great deal with her patient, but the alien probably wasn't saying anything of significance and was holding back the real reason he was there. Doctor Summers just couldn't see it, but an alien in their midst at such a crucial time was suspicious.

Kursal was starting to think like the captain; it wasn't healthy. He had to drop these thoughts before he did actually go mad. And besides, the captain wanted him back on the bridge immediately.

"Well, I better get back then, if you deem me fit for duty, Doctor."

"I do, so get out of here," she said, smiling at him again.

"Thanks again, Doctor, for listening to me."

"That's alright, any time. Just... just take it easy, and don't let the captain run you into the ground," she frowned with concern.

They all knew the captain was extremely hard on the crew, but Kursal felt a glimmer of hope that perhaps she did care a little about him. Perhaps when the mission was over, he would pluck up the courage to ask her out. Until then, he would just have to dream about it.

Getting to the exit, Kursal couldn't see the guards anywhere. He called back to Doctor Summers, "The guards are not at their posts. You didn't get them to clock off, did you, Doctor?"

"Certainly not!" she replied, angry that he'd assumed she was responsible. Secretly, she was glad they had gone. Guards at the hospital entrance was a stupid idea and totally unnecessary.

"Sorry, I'll find out where they are before I leave," Kursal said.

Minutes later he returned. The guards were back at their posts, having been given a dressing down for going on a walkabout for no other reason than sheer boredom. They obviously deemed the job unnecessary, too.

"Sorry, Doctor, but if the captain orders a guard here then they must stay. The alien still has a lot of explaining to do."

Doctor Summers became defensive. "Well, tell them to stay out of my way. The captain is wrong, very wrong. Besides, he is still my patient, and I am in charge of this hospital. You might want to remind the captain of that."

Kursal left abruptly. He wasn't going to win that argument, and he guessed he'd blown his chances by upsetting her like that. His stomach felt easier, his head not so.

Walking back along the corridors, he battled to get control of his composure before arriving on the bridge.

Entering the bridge to resume his duties, Kursal felt all eyes on him and hoped he hadn't made a total fool of himself earlier. He quickly took to his station, doing his best to block out the incident, and a quick glance at the viewing screen showed that Retriever-2 was orbiting Kangis-3.

Captain Valmak looked round in his direction. "What did Doctor Forester have to say?" he asked.

"He wasn't there. Doctor Summers hasn't seen him in a while."

"So, how are you?"

"Okay, I guess, sir. Doctor Summers says I'm fit for duty."

"Good, get on with your work then," the captain replied bluntly, clearly not wanting to engage in conversation. He had too much on his mind.

Kursal sat at his station, not letting on how he really felt. Not wanting to be there, he kept his eyes averted from the viewing screen and promptly checked for data in front of him. There would be a lot to catch up on in his absence.

Scanning through the monitors, he was puzzled. Nothing was available, and there had been no data registered while he had been in the hospital.

Turning to the communications officer Denny Argent, he asked, "Have we established contact yet?"

"No, sir, we keep getting interference on the intercom. I can't pinpoint where it's coming from yet. I'll keep trying," said Argent, who was just as baffled by the lack of contact.

Captain Valmak listened intently from his command seat, pondering the next move. Their orders were very specific: without direct contact, they should not descend to the planet. They could not risk lives at any cost, but without contact they had nothing.

Argent broke the silence again. "I've tried every known frequency, sir. Still no reply from the planet, just that weird static noise."

At the helm, Will Straten managed to compute the approximate location of the static. "It seems to be emanating from the planet's surface, sir."

That's strange, thought Valmak. *Why would anyone be blocking the signal with static if they wanted help?* That ominous feeling crept back into his head. Something was very off with this mission; nothing was going to plan. He wanted to be in and out swiftly and head home. But he needed to stay calm and focused, or at least appear to be. It wasn't easy.

"Time is of the essence," he announced suddenly. "Time for action. Kursal, instruct the shuttle crews to prepare for launch and wait for my presence."

Adam King looked round at the captain, startled at his decision.

"Sir, we have to adhere to protocol. If we can't make contact, is it wise to go down there?" As second-in-command, he felt it his duty to state the regulations.

Valmak, however, ignored him. This was not the time for protocol, and in the captain's mind the regulations were too strict.

"Helm, anything on the atmosphere yet?" Valmak asked.

"Data just coming through, Captain," said Straten. "Oxygen levels only just acceptable, but I'm getting a strange reading. An unknown element in the air. I would suggest protective gear, that's if you're thinking of going down there, Captain."

Valmak noticed a distinct air of defiance in the voices of his crew, but he chose to ignore it and turned back to King.

"What else do we have?"

"Nothing, sir. I mean literally nothing. The computer readout is indicating no life on the planet at all. Again, sir, I would suggest—"

"Yes, yes, I know what you think we should do, King. Noted for the record," Valmak interrupted sharply.

King didn't like his captain's response and wasn't happy with the situation, but he said no more. The captain was violating all company regulations but had never done anything like this before. The man was behaving so irrationally that King was genuinely worried his captain was heading for a breakdown. He didn't know how much longer he could allow it to go on.

Valmak slumped back in his control seat, reviewing the facts, or lack of them. *No life down there, but they had static. That meant something, but what?* Questions went round and round in his head, but with no answers. That same feeling of foreboding loomed over him, now more intensely than ever. *What the hell had happened down there?* he wondered. If the planet and its people had been attacked, there was no evidence of raiders in the vicinity, though it was possible they would be long gone.

Travelling through this sector of the galaxy, Retriever-2 had met no opposition; it was as if nobody else existed in the universe. Valmak thought that seemed odd, but he opted for another approach before making a final decision.

"Argent, do we still have the recording of the distress signal?"

Listening to it again might help him.

"Yes, sir, mission HQ sent us the full message. Do you want me to play it back?"

Valmak responded with a nod. Argent pressed the button and put it on speaker, hoping it was clear enough, but it had been sketchy at best when they had received it.

"Chief Counsellor Argor speaking... someone please help us... we are under attack... something is attacking us... please help us... we need medical assistance... help us, the people of Kangis-3..."

"That's enough," said Valmak. His mind was made up.

"Sir, what did he mean, under attack from something?" asked Argent. It seemed an odd thing to say, *something* not *someone.*

But there was no reply from Valmak. He was silent, considering his next move, knowing King would not like his decision.

To him, there had been genuine fear in the voice on the message. *But was it a ploy? Could he take that chance?*

Their main objective was to assist all who asked for help, including giving medical assistance, so Valmak felt they had no choice but to investigate. Something was urging him to go. He had never disobeyed company policy before, but the sudden change in his demeanour meant he couldn't walk away from this.

Besides, going to Kangis-3 had been a direct order from mission HQ in the first place, and that order had not been rescinded. So, if anything went wrong, he could blame HQ.

As it had taken Retriever-2 almost three days to reach its destination, it was a possibility that they might not find any survivors. But if something dreadful had happened here, the mystery had to be solved.

Valmak knew not everyone was in agreement; King was dead against it. He also knew there was little chance of anyone being alive, so they would not get the answers they wanted. But Valmak was not going to change his mind, whatever King said.

Argent spoke out, still monitoring, doing his job, "The interference has suddenly stopped, Captain, but I still can't get any response."

The bridge crew waited on a response from the captain, but he appeared to be staring into space, weighing up the options. There was a real danger to life if they descended to the surface. If they did, there was no going back, and the crew had to see it through.

Finally, King asked, "Well, Captain, do we, or don't we?"

Suddenly Valmak stood up and declared his intentions. "Right, Kursal, tell the shuttle crews it's go. You're going with the party. King, I need you here to take control of the situation and keep us updated at all times. Understood?"

"Yes, sir, but can I just say—"

"No, King, you cannot," interrupted Valmak.

King was livid at the put-down and shaken by the captain's behaviour towards him. Surely his conduct could not go unchecked much longer. King made a mental note to do something about it.

For the first time in his life, Valmak felt scared, and all his years of experience did not help his mental state. What he was doing was totally out of character and there was no basis for his decision. Inner demons controlled his thoughts, urging him to see the mission out, but he failed to recognise the consequences of his actions.

Outwardly the crew always saw a forceful, decisive, and confident captain, normally a stickler for rules and regulations.

But emotionally he was falling apart, breaking all the protocols and throwing the rule book out of the window. This was a dangerous mission, and Valmak was determined to face the danger head-on, regardless of the outcome. His own fears had to take a back seat. He realised he was doing the wrong thing but justified his actions because he believed he was doing it for the right reasons – his reasons.

Giving one last instruction before exiting the bridge, Valmak said, "King, have Doctor Forester bring extra medical supplies to the shuttles, in case we do find survivors."

He then hurried to reach the hangar deck. *The faster he dealt with this mission, the better,* he thought.

The bridge crew were left bewildered by the captain's erratic behaviour.

"What do you make of that, Kursal?" asked King.

"Don't ask me, I can't make him out," replied Kursal, getting up to leave. "I better follow our leader, I guess. You best get a hold of Doctor Forester pronto. I have a feeling he's still in hiding. Try the lab."

"Sure. Are you going to be alright to do this?" King was worried that his fellow officer was still looking a bit peaky.

"I'll be fine."

"Okay, good luck," said King, secretly glad he wasn't going down to the surface.

Kursal looked one more time at the viewing screen before leaving the bridge. He was frightened of seeing something, but his subconscious told him to face his fears. Thankfully, he did not see anything untoward, and a wave of relief came over him as he raced along the corridor.

*

King, now in temporary charge of the bridge, was still seething at the treatment he had received and was beginning to hate the captain's attitude to the job. For now, he knew he had to put it out of his mind, as there were more important matters to deal with.

Firstly, he asked Straten to be extra vigilant, monitor absolutely everything, and place the ship on maximum alert. Then, to assist Straten, he called for another helm crew to the bridge. The more eyes the better.

The crew needed to carry out their usual tasks, so King requested Tom Phasner and Senior Officer Cal Bartok to begin the job of re-examining all data regarding the current mission, particularly leading up to the time a few weeks earlier when they had taken in the empty spaceship, and the alien they had on board. *There was a slight chance Captain Valmak was right about the stranger's presence, but did it tie in with the alien spaceship they had picked up?* King thought not, but he needed to be sure.

Bartok informed King of Phasner's theory that a rift in the universe had occurred, which sounded so ludicrous it might even be true. King had read up on wormholes at the training academy, as a hypothetical connection between the space-time continuum. While it had only been conjecture at the time, King could not rule anything out, but he would prefer a simpler explanation. If anyone could find a solution to their problems, he knew it was Phasner and Bartok – the ship's best science officers to ever leave the academy, with top marks. King deemed them a credit to Retriever-2, even if the captain didn't always appreciate them.

Phasner's theory of a rift in the universe causing it to blink might have some bearing on the circumstances. And while the captain was off the bridge, King made the decision to investigate the matter fully.

*

In hangar deck two the spaceship picked up weeks earlier was still being thoroughly examined, although without any success. Harry Staten and Dominic Casey had been assigned the task of finding out as much as possible about it.

Retriever-2 had come across the abandoned ship back in the delta quadrant, but there were no signs of attack on it, no clue as to who it belonged, and no markings, as with Nussar's ship. The two craft were of similar size, but this mysterious ship had what appeared to be hyperdrive technology, though that had not yet been confirmed. It had taken Staten and Casey three days to find a way into the sleek black ship which, looking at the seating, would accommodate three crew. It was obviously of alien origin, but its sophisticated advanced engineering meant they had no idea how to actually operate it.

It had been one of Captain Valmak's daft ideas to pick up a strange spaceship without realising the consequences of his actions. At that time Retriever-2 had been on its way home to Earth, and everyone had been keen to return to loved ones after a long tour of duty.

Even though they were first class engineers, Casey and Straten finally had to admit defeat. They had learnt nothing about the ship's origin, who it belonged to, where it had come from, what had happened to the crew, or why the ship had been locked. Casey decided they should sign off the work with the recommendation to take it back to Earth where maybe the scientists would have better luck.

"You okay with that decision, Straten?"

"I guess so, Casey. Do we just leave it here then?"

"Do you want to put it in the lost property? Because I don't." They laughed, but both still had reservations. Taking an alien ship back to Earth might be construed as space piracy, but that would be down to the captain to explain – not their problem.

*

On arrival in hangar deck one, Valmak was quick to brief the shuttle pilots Peter Tranal and Eric Sorisin what was expected of them. Both nodded in response, fully aware of their duties and the possible dangers ahead. They regarded this a routine mission, nothing more. Having carried out countless rescue missions in the last six years, this one didn't seem any different to before.

Valmak, though, was on edge. He had to get this right or his job was on the line.

Kursal entered the hanger with two more crew and three medics, instructing them to suit up and help load the supplies on board. Valmak, already in his protective suit, watched to ensure everything was loaded correctly, then he noticed that the extra medical equipment he'd requested had not arrived. That put him in a worse mood; he hated incompetence.

"Sorisin, where is Doctor Forester? He should be here by now." Valmak didn't want a delay in the launch.

"Doctor Summers called just before you arrived, sir. She said she would bring the equipment here herself," Sorisin replied.

Valmak was frustrated. He didn't want to face Doctor Summers right now or want her anywhere near this mission. Deeming it too dangerous for her, he wanted Forester.

Moments later Doctor Summers rushed through the sliding doors, laden with the supplies he'd ordered.

"Where is Doctor Forester?" the captain snapped, waving his arms in disgust at the man's unacceptable absence.

"I don't have a clue," she told him. "No-one has seen him for days apparently. He's probably hiding in his bloody laboratory, but I couldn't get an answer. Right now, Captain, I really don't care." She was livid that the captain didn't offer to relieve her of some of the boxes of supplies.

Valmak, on the other hand, couldn't be bothered to reply. He could see she was still angry with him. *So what?* he thought. He made a mental note to reprimand Forester when he got back, though. The man's disciplinary record was lacking the high standard he demanded from all his crew.

After checking he had everything on board to his satisfaction, Valmak looked across the hangar. Kursal was already suited, but so was Doctor Summers, which he hadn't anticipated, as there were three medics available.

"Doctor, surely you don't intend going?" he asked.

"Stupid question, Captain. Protocol states clearly that a doctor is required on every mission."

"So, who is looking after the alien?"

"The alien has a name, Captain, and apparently your guards are there." She made no effort to hide her anger that he was asking stupid questions.

"Well, I hope he behaves himself," came his terse reply.

The pilots entered their designated shuttles, strapped themselves into their seats, and started preliminary procedures in readiness for take-off. There were five crew to each shuttle, and within minutes the outer hangar doors opened then both shuttles cruised out.

"Have you calculated the proximity of our landing?" asked Valmak. They had to be precise, even though they did not have an exact location.

"Yes, sir, but we have a problem. The on-board instruments are suddenly going haywire," said Sorisin. "The computer is unable to pinpoint the precise location of our landing, and I fear it's going to be a very bumpy ride."

"Correct it then, man!" demanded Valmak furiously.

"I can't, sir. Where we land is down to guesswork."

"Where is the interference coming from?"

"Unsure, sir. The computers appear useless at present, so hold on," replied Sorisin nervously.

"Maintain an open channel with the other shuttle," snapped Valmak. Losing contact with them was not an option.

"Sorry again, but contact is patchy. It keeps breaking up, probably due to the dense atmosphere."

Sorisin's nerves were getting the better of him, and Valmak wasn't feeling any better. This was turning into a disaster. A wave of panic swept over the captain, telling him to abort the operation, but panic was not a good enough reason to turn back. They had to go on.

Sorisin was right about the bumpy ride. The shuttle was buffeted by extreme turbulence, and he had to use all his expertise to maintain control, particularly as his co-pilot was less than useless it seemed. He hoped his friend Peter had more luck as they came down to a heavy landing.

"Thank goodness for that," sighed Doctor Summers, relieved they'd made it.

Sorisin had no clue where the other shuttle had landed, or if indeed it had. But he said nothing to Valmak, as the man was clearly already on a short fuse.

"Can you get through to the ship, Sorisin? Inform them we have landed safely and await further instructions," said Valmak, relieved they'd made the landing.

"No good, sir. Communication with them is also out. We're on our own." His reply didn't go down well with the crew, who all looked suddenly very nervous.

"What about Tranel's shuttle then?" the captain asked.

Sorisin checked. No reply. It was not a good sign.

Ignoring the worried looks around the shuttle, Valmak had no intention of going back yet. Reluctantly he made his way to the airlock and was first out of the exit, taking in a lungful of air... then suddenly wishing he hadn't. The air was foul, almost toxic. He slammed his visor down, realising he should have done that first.

Moving away from the shuttle proved difficult underfoot. The soft, black soil was littered with boulders, which were obviously part of the terrain but somehow didn't look natural. Scanning the horizon, he saw no sign of life, and there were no structures to suggest any kind of civilization existed here. None of it felt real but Valmak couldn't make out why.

As the crew emerged from the shuttle to join him, he urged Sorisin to try again to contact the other shuttle crew and find out their location. There was certainly no sign of them nearby. But Sorisin had no luck on his helmet radio, and Valmak grew angrier at the situation, wondering what they had let themselves in for.

Doctor Summers looked around at the desolation, then stepped close to Sorisin and said quietly, "Don't worry, we'll find them."

Her comforting words helped to calm him a little. Sorisin didn't mind admitting he was scared; he'd never felt this way before.

The captain had no time for sympathy, though. He had his own problems. His emotions were running riot in his head, and he was experiencing the same feelings the alien had given him, heightening his anxiety even further.

The party continued at a slow pace, hoping to spot the other crew or some sign of life, but all they saw was a barren environment; a terrain covered with boulders, hampering their every stride. The soft soil wasn't helping, as their boots were sinking in with each step, yet the heavy boulders sat on the surface without sinking. The whole environment wasn't natural looking.

They pushed on, but it was clear that vital clues to the mysterious people of Kangis-3 were lacking. *Where were they?* This was a desolate planet. Maybe the ship's computers had been correct after all and there was nothing here, just a deserted piece of rock.

Suddenly it hit Valmak that they might have walked into a trap – the one thing he didn't need. *Could the space pirates be operating again?*

As a dark, sinister-looking mountain range came into view, he dropped down to touch the black soil and sensed a much stronger air of evil. This was a depressing place to lose one's bearings, and he wondered how much further they should proceed.

Doctor Summers was struggling to trudge through the soil and boulders just to keep up with the captain. Avoiding the boulders was bad enough, but sinking with every step was harder, and she called after him to ask what he made of the soil. But he didn't reply. Instead, he stopped abruptly to look around in every direction, scanning the view, his mind racing.

"Captain, what is it?" she asked, eventually catching him up.

"It's all wrong, Doctor, all wrong," he announced.

"What do you mean?" She was puzzled by his remark.

"This entire planet is wrong. It doesn't feel right, it doesn't look right, I don't think it's even Kangis-3."

"But how—?" Doctor Summers was stunned. *What did he mean?* she wondered. *How did he know if it was Kangis-3 or not?* This was unexplored space until now, so the captain couldn't know for sure. He was acting stranger than ever, and she was convinced he needed a break more than anyone.

"I don't like this awful silence, Captain. Surely there can't be anyone alive here, if they were even here in the first place." The doctor felt genuinely concerned for their safety. This was not a good place to be.

"That's it," he declared.

"What?"

"Look around, Doctor. If the people of Kangis-3 were attacked by someone or something, where are the bodies? Where are the buildings, the cities? There is absolutely nothing to suggest a civilization exists here."

Now that he was beginning to make some sense, Doctor Summers had to agree with her captain. But at that point they both suddenly realised they were alone. Sorisin and the other crew were nowhere in sight, and there was still no sign of the other shuttle and its crew.

"I don't like this, Captain, where are they?" Summers did not scare easily, but the mood had definitely taken a turn for the worse.

They both called out several times, but the haunting silence hung in the air. They couldn't even be sure their helmet radios were working, so Valmak took a chance, lifted his visor, and yelled out. Nothing.

"What happened to them, Captain? I was sure they were right behind me," she said.

Glancing down, she pulled Valmak's arm and pointed to their boots. The black soil was drying hard, so they would be weighed down if they stayed any longer.

Valmak nodded in agreement, but suddenly lost his bearings. *Which way should they go?* His eyes searched about for clues, but the mountain range was no help as it had somehow disappeared. Then he spotted something more mysterious.

"What is that?" he said, pointing to the ground close to their boots. A trail of white, glistening slime settled on the surface.

"Slug tracks?" suggested Doctor Summers.

"If it is, it's a bloody big slug. I think we have to head back, find the others, locate the other shuttle, and get the hell off this rock."

"Oh, yes please," she said, for once in full agreement. "Which way, Captain?"

"This way, I think. Yes, let's go." Valmak led the way, hoping he was right.

Heading back, they avoided the huge trail of slime, but couldn't understand why they heard nothing or saw what had made the trail. They called out several times, lifting their visors in short bursts, but there was still no response.

The others couldn't have gone far, thought Valmak, *but why did they stray off?* He would be demanding answers when they got back.

Doctor Summers was still trying to call out in all directions. Suddenly she let out a scream in sheer panic. "Captain, where did that come from?"

Valmak turned, concerned by her scream, and saw a thick blanket of fog descend in front of them. Their visibility was suddenly non-existent.

"What the—?" He had no words to describe it. "We have to go," he said. As the fog was edging closer, he took her arm to guide and steady her over the boulders.

Stumbling a few times, unable to see the ground at all, they both prayed they were heading in the right direction.

There was no way of telling, and all the while there was the fear of what had made the trail of slime. Something was alive down here, and Valmak thought the fog must be a connection.

Doctor Summers started to panic; they couldn't see the shuttle yet. The captain was still holding onto her arm, and she gladly accepted his assistance, but it wasn't helping her fear. She didn't realise he was feeling a hundred times worse, as he didn't let on.

"Are we even going in the right direction, Captain?"

"Just keep going. We'll make it," he replied, sounding confident.

Strangely, ahead of them the fog was thinning out, and a vague outline of something appeared in front of them.

"Is that the shuttle?" she asked hopefully.

Valmak tried to focus on what was ahead of them, but then he froze abruptly in his tracks, pulling the doctor back with him.

"What now?" she cried out.

The outline wasn't the shuttle. It couldn't be. The shape wasn't stable, appearing to pulsate, and was quite large. Valmak knew they were in real danger. Something ahead made him fear for them both.

"Captain—?"

"Quiet, Doctor, don't speak." *Silence was the best option*, guessed Valmak, *at least until he was sure of what they were dealing with.*

They remained silent for a while, Valmak still holding the doctor by the arm, until the fog cleared enough that they could see the outline of the shuttle. With a sigh of relief, they moved slowly forward.

Suddenly, the captain drew back in horror. He could see a dark, indescribable shadow lurking in the distance. Huge in size, and still appearing to change shape, it seemed similar to what he had seen moments earlier. He couldn't tell what it was, but he felt an air of evil descend on them.

Whatever it was moved away from the shuttle, then disappeared completely.

"What's wrong, Captain? Did you see something?" Doctor Summers hadn't seen anything, but she could see something had obviously scared the captain.

They raced towards the shuttle, still trudging through the black soil, safety not far away. It occurred briefly to Valmak that it was odd the shuttle hadn't sunk in the soil, but he was just relieved it was there.

As he rushed to the airlock, desperate to get inside, he was unaware that he had let Doctor Summers' arm go. As the doors of the shuttle opened, he heard her scream behind him.

"Christ, what now?" he muttered.

Going back outside, he found her frozen to the spot, staring at a ghastly sight at her feet. She was trying hard not to vomit inside her helmet, pushing to get her visor up quickly as Valmak leaned over her to see what she was looking at.

He was aghast at the sight of the badly mutilated body of one of the crew, and realised he must have rushed past it in his haste to get the airlock open. A sickening repulsion swept over the captain, realising it was he who had brought the crew here. This was all down to him.

He grabbed Doctor Summers and pulled her inside the airlock. "Get inside and lock the doors, don't go anywhere," he instructed, his voice shaking with emotion. "I'll be back."

Her whole body shook as she tried to stop him leaving. "No, Captain, don't go," she pleaded.

"No arguments, Doctor. I have to check this out and find the others." He closed the outer door and prayed that just for once she would do as she was told. "Bloody hysterical woman," he muttered to himself, remembering he hadn't wanted her on the mission in the first place.

The grisly sight lying yards from the shuttle sickened Valmak, but he needed to know who the body belonged to. Two diagonal white stripes on the ripped uniform confirmed it was either Tranel or Sorisin, but he couldn't tell which.

Something had attacked the man violently, mutilating and shredding apart the body, its protective suit and helmet a useless defence.

Searching the surrounding area, Valmak saw the same white slime glistening. Some was on the body, and it was obviously fresh. He feared for the lives of the other crew but couldn't understand why he had heard nothing. *Had none of them cried out for help?*

Valmak felt guilty. He'd been convinced danger lurked on this planet, so he shouldn't have come. But now he had no choice but to find the others... or their bodies. Venturing round the side of the shuttle, he gave a gasp of disbelief when he found another body – mutilated in the same way – then another close by, both covered in slime.

What was causing such atrocity? he asked himself. Now he wanted to vomit. It was a sight no-one should see.

Moving further away from the shuttle, but keeping it firmly in sight, Valmak began searching around the vicinity when he spotted the other shuttle close by. It hadn't landed too far away after all; they just hadn't seen it.

But when he reached the other shuttle, Valmak spotted more bodies, all murdered in the same way. It was such a barbaric act to do this to a rescue team sent to save lives. Valmak could only identify each body by the ranks on their suits. There were eight in total, only one so unrecognisable he assumed it to be the last member of his crew.

Seeing no point in hanging around any longer, he decided he better get back to Doctor Summers. Getting off this planet alive now looked doubtful, but he was determined not to be the next victim.

Quickly reaching the shuttle, Valmak spotted slime dripping down the sides of the craft. The thing, whatever it was, had come back!

Hurriedly he opened the airlock, trying not to touch the slime in case it was hazardous, then he rushed inside and sealed the outer doors.

Doctor Summers had never been so happy to see him alive. She was still shaking. "Captain, I'm so relieved to see you, did you find the others?"

"No time to talk," he replied brusquely. "We have to go."

"I heard something outside, I'm sure it was trying to get in. What was it?" She'd been sitting in the shuttle alone, scared for the captain's life, but he didn't seem too concerned about her.

"Please, Captain, tell me what's going on."

"Okay, it's been here. That thing, whatever it is, has been here, all over the shuttle, probably trying to get in."

"What!" She was stunned at his bluntness.

Valmak didn't say more but prepared for lift-off. They were going to have to manage the controls between them.

Ignoring her pleas to explain what had happened, he concentrated on starting the lift-off procedures. He couldn't deal with her emotions as well as his own; he was already struggling to cope with what had happened. This was proving to be a nightmare, yet they were still awake! He just wanted to escape.

Suddenly a banging on the outer hull alerted them.

"It's back!" cried out Valmak, unable to hide his fear that the thing would get into the shuttle. Lift-off had to be now!

But Doctor Summers had heard something else; a different noise. "Stop, Captain! Stop!" She raced to the airlock.

"Don't open the bloody doors!" he screamed.

She ignored him and opened the airlock to see Gordon Kursal standing there, bloodied, shaking uncontrollably. The man staggered inside, speechless, barely able to focus, but clearly frightened beyond belief.

Doctor Summers sat him down and strapped him in. "Kursal, are you alright?" she asked. "What happened to you?"

His helmet was missing, and he had superficial wounds on his face. But he didn't answer, unable to speak. Words were there but wouldn't come out. He was obviously in shock.

"Now can we go?" shouted Valmak, angry at the doctor's rash decision to open the doors.

"What about the others, Captain?" she asked, wrapping a blanket round Kursal.

"Dead," he replied abruptly. "They're all dead." Still fuming at her reckless action, he saw no reason to soften the truth.

She staggered back into her seat at his shock announcement, fumbling to strap herself in. She sat in silence, leaving Valmak to pilot alone while her mind went into overdrive. A glance toward Kursal suggested he had seen the horror, but now he was traumatised, either he couldn't or wouldn't speak. The poor man was pale, his eyes refusing to focus on his surroundings.

What had happened on the surface? What of the poor crew? The captain should never have taken them down there. Everyone knew there was always an element of danger on any mission, but this had gone far beyond that. The biggest question on her mind now, though, was how the three of them had made it back alive when the others didn't.

As her mind whirled with questions, she kept watch on Kursal, motionless in his seat, eyes glazed over, his expression completely blank. The poor man was not in a good place.

Valmak called out to Kursal to assist in piloting the shuttle, as the ride back was still as bumpy, but the injured man didn't even acknowledge his name. Doctor Summers shook her head, telling the captain to forget it.

"Can you co-pilot then?" he asked.

"I'll try." She sat down next to Valmak and followed his instructions, but co-piloting was not one of her skills.

"See if you can contact the ship. Tell them we are returning minus one shuttle and eight crew."

That she could do. "They're going to ask questions, Captain, so what do I say?"

"Just say we're on our way back." Valmak was in no mood for questions at that point. Piloting the shuttle took all his concentration, as it was something he hadn't done in a very long time.

Doctor Summers eventually got through to the ship, but not until they left the dense atmosphere. After confirming their return, she left her seat to try and comfort Kursal. None of them wanted to speak of the horror they had left behind. Retriever-2 was a hospital rescue ship, so they had not been prepared for this kind of danger. But then, nobody was.

As Valmak piloted them back to the ship in total silence, he realised that his initial suspicions about Kangis-3 had been spot on. However, being proved right gave him no comfort. Eight valuable crew were dead, and he had led them straight into a death trap – that plagued him.

Part of him was angry he had allowed such a thing to happen, but inner demons had surfaced that played a major role in his behaviour. The trouble was he didn't know how to put it right. And he wasn't sure he really wanted to.

CHAPTER THREE

Inside the hangar deck, Valmak remained seated in total silence, waiting for the outer bulkhead doors to close. A few minutes passed before full air pressure was restored, and his mind whirled as it went over the events. How was he going to write this one up? It was going to take some explaining to mission HQ how he had lost so many crew. He feared a reprimand or, worse, a suspension from duty. Yet he hadn't wanted this mission in the first place; like the rest of the crew, he had just wanted to go home.

A click of the intercom suddenly jerked Valmak into action. It was time to leave the shuttle. Slowly and very reluctantly, he got up and moved towards the exit without speaking to the doctor or acknowledging Kursal. The injured man wouldn't have responded anyway.

King was waiting for Valmak as he stepped out. "What happened, Captain?" he asked. "We lost contact with you almost immediately. Scanners were blocked out and the computers useless."

"Really?" Valmak wasn't in a talkative mood.

King thought the captain was a bit offhand with his response, but nevertheless persisted. "What is that on the shuttle?" he exclaimed. "And where is the other shuttle?"

He had so many questions, but Valmak was not the least bit interested.

"If you are so concerned about the other shuttle, King, go down there yourself and bloody retrieve it." Valmak was about to walk off when he suddenly announced, "I want that stuff analysed."

He pointed to the dry slime on the side of the shuttle. "Then get a detail down here to sanitize the place, including the protective gear. After that, get back to the bridge and start scanning the entire planet surface."

King was stunned by Valmak's harsh tone; he'd never heard such vehemence before, and for a second he was not sure how to respond.

"Just in case I didn't make myself clear, there is a thing down there, a creature on the loose. It killed eight crew – no, seven."

He corrected himself, suddenly realising that if Kursal was alive, then whose was the other body?

"Get to it, man," he demanded, then he stormed out of the hangar.

King didn't know what to make of the captain's aggressive attitude, but dealing with him was undoubtedly going to be a problem. He turned to look at the state of the shuttle just as Doctor Summers emerged, struggling to get Kursal to even put one foot in front of the other. King was horrified to see his colleague in such a distressed state. The man appeared totally withdrawn from reality.

"Doctor Summers, are you alright?" King asked, taking Kursal's other arm to help guide him.

"I'm fine, King, thank you," she said.

"What happened to Kursal? He looks in a bad way."

Kursal failed to acknowledge the outside world, and when King looked him in the eye, there was nothing there but a blank stare.

"I don't actually know the details yet," the doctor replied, "as we got separated. I need to get him straight to the hospital."

"Ok, I'll help you. What's biting the captain anyway?"

"You might well ask."

At that moment Valmak returned to the hangar entrance. "King," he shouted, "when you're finished nursemaiding, find Doctor Forester and inform him that I demand his presence."

Valmak was furious with just about everyone, and even more with himself for allowing such a tragedy. He was exhausted, fearful of what he'd done and anxious about future decisions.

Although it went against all company policies, though, he wasn't leaving until the monster on the planet surface was hunted down and destroyed. The dead crew had to be avenged.

That was his ship's only mission now.

*

When Doctor Summers reached the hospital, she summoned a medic to assist her with Kursal, and King left them to head back to his post. *Somebody had to keep an eye on the captain*, he thought.

Kursal was totally compliant, allowing the medic to help him to a bed in the isolation ward. He still hadn't said a word and didn't look likely to. A decision to sedate him wasn't easy but the best option.

Doctor Summers hated to see the man so unresponsive. Kursal was normally a strong-willed, confident officer, so his condition was alarming. She only hoped that time would ease his recovery. Whatever he had seen must have been so traumatic that his mind refused to accept it.

What she'd seen had been horrific enough, but she had to keep things together for the sake of the patients, and the crew in general. It looked like they were a doctor down again, and as three medics had lost their lives, she was short-staffed. If she got hold of Forester before the captain, the man was going to get a roasting from her. His persistent absence from his normal duties was out of order.

Spotting Sol out of bed, dressed in his uniform and hovering in the background, Doctor Summers shook her head at him, waving him away for now.

He was doing fine thankfully, so it was Kursal who needed attention right now. She did, however, give him a quick smile just to let him know she was still there for him... just not now.

Sol understood the gesture and stayed back, though it was not really what he wanted. He felt she looked like she needed two strong arms wrapped round her to comfort her.

*

On the bridge, Valmak was back in charge, and he immediately instructed the helm crew to maintain a standard orbit above Kangis-3. Puzzled by the order, they nevertheless obeyed.

"Begin scanning the planet surface," he ordered. "I want every sector searched thoroughly."

With the dense atmosphere, it was unlikely the scanners could penetrate enough to register anything, but Valmak was determined that Retriever-2 was not going anywhere until he found what he wanted – justice.

"What are we actually looking for, Captain?" asked Senior Helm Officer Paul Aztac.

"Anything that moves." Valmak didn't go into detail, but the crew were about to find out more.

"Argent, send a message to Earth mission HQ. Report that we have lost seven crew. Mission was a failure. Are continuing to investigate."

Argent was stunned for a second; surely that couldn't be right. They were on their way home, and everyone was looking forward to a very long vacation.

Gathering his wits, he made the call in a subdued manner. The rest of the bridge crew were silent in disbelief. They hadn't realised the true extent of what happened because there had been no communication with the groups on the planet surface.

What was the captain up to? they wondered. *Surely, they should be heading to Earth?*

With scanning of Kangis-3 complete, Aztac computed the data before relaying it to Valmak.

"No sign of life, Captain, no anomalies. In fact, we have nothing of significance on the monitors. No lifeforms or any living organisms registered."

Valmak ordered them to continue checking, as the search had to go on until evidence was found. The computers had to be wrong. Something down there was alive and dangerous, and he could not allow this creature to go unpunished.

The helm crew were pretty much certain they would discover nothing, but unfortunately their captain appeared hell bent on pursing the unknown. They understood why, though. Valuable crew were dead – some of them friends – but they were concerned about staying around if there was a threat of more deaths.

Following orders, they started another sweep of the planet while Valmak sat silently waiting for information. His eyes stayed glued to the viewing screen, watching Kangis-3, his mind in overdrive. With the sophisticated monitoring system and the best computer hardware that mission HQ had installed in the hospital ships, he couldn't understand how they were unable to track the creature. The computers had failed to register a single entity on the surface, but Valmak could not – would not – believe the data.

He thought again about the inhabitants of Kangis-3: *were they real or not? Where did the distress call really come from?* The more Valmak thought about it, the more he was convinced this mission had been a trap all along. He blamed mission HQ for that, as Retriever-2 should not have answered the call. There was the possibility it could have involved space pirates, but Valmak dismissed that idea. It didn't feel like their work.

Watching his crew working hard for him, Valmak wished he could shake off the irritating notion that something was missing from the equation, some details were lacking. He knew he had to solve the problem, but the lack of data was hampering his efforts.

Suddenly a certain Commander Nussar popped into his head, reminding Valmak of his suspicions that the alien was connected to the recent events. In Valmak's mind, Nussar was responsible for the bad occurrences, and he blamed him for the deaths of his crew.

Valmak refused to blame himself for anything. He couldn't see how his mind was changing and creating another personality. But he was sure of dark connotations below the surface concerning the alien. Maybe it was time to question Nussar again, to see if he could provide answers. He also wanted to check on Kursal. Although the man had appeared to be in a bad way, this was not the time to lose a senior officer, and he wanted him back on duty.

A snap decision from Valmak had him leaving the bridge without a single word to the crew and heading to the hospital. The crew looked round at each other, taken aback at the captain's sudden departure. His actions were worrying them, but their loyalty was never in question. In his absence, they continued the search of Kangis-3, sector by sector, searching for clues to give them closure for the tragic loss of the crew. If only Valmak had been a bit more forthcoming about the circumstances on the surface, the crew might have understood better why he was behaving so out of character. However, he was reluctant to explain how the men had died, and that was hurting the most.

The search went on, intensifying with each sweep, but each time, the results were the same. Nothing to report. The crew were getting desperate for answers, to have something to tell him when the captain returned.

Science Officer Tom Phasner arrived onto the bridge, keen to access a different computer to do his own research. He had been busy attempting to find answers to the anomaly that had occurred earlier, as the scientific analysis of the distortion in space was still unexplained. He could find no logical solution to account for the fluctuations experienced in the galaxy. His own hypothesis that the universe blinked, thus causing the disruption, was still the only explanation he could come up with.

He had decided to put his theory to the captain, but Valmak was clearly absent from his post. Cal Bartok was no help, eventually telling him the idea was a non-starter.

So Phasner decided to use the bridge computer to try and prove his theory. He hoped Kursal's station would supply him with the extra data. However, if he found the answers and his theory was true, he had no idea what the consequences would be or how they would deal with it.

He had several questions for the bridge crew, but they were all busy with their own problems and suggested he go back to his own station and do some real work. Although he was still convinced, he had something, it was going to be hard getting anyone to believe him. He left the bridge, hiding his disappointment that both the computer and the crew had been no help at all.

Retriever-2 continued standard orbit, now scanning the southern hemisphere. The atmosphere had changed; it was very thin now, not the same density as before. A planet could not change its atmospheric conditions, the computers agreed, yet the monitors said otherwise. It was about the only fact the monitors did register.

Kangis-3 was proving to be a complete mystery. How could it block all probes so that scans could not penetrate the surface. The planet was beginning to scare the crew; they wanted to leave orbit and head home.

Their loyalty to their captain and to the ship had never wavered in six years, but something was telling them that evil surrounded Kangis-3 and they should not stay a moment longer.

*

Four white walls stared back at Sol. The same walls that had once terrified him now held comfort, and the thoughts of madness and loneliness no longer haunted him. He felt more at ease with himself. He was eternally grateful for his rescuers, particularly a certain very beautiful and enchanting doctor whom he had become attached to.

From the moment he had wakened in the hospital and seen that vision of beauty, he had known there was a definite spark between them. And he was certain of it when he fully came to his senses. She had helped him through a difficult time, but Sol very much wanted the chance to explore a meaningful relationship, daring to hope she would feel the same.

He had no-one back home on Clarizia for whom he felt such emotion. Oddly enough, he didn't even care if he never saw his home planet again. Yet that feeling made him anxious for the future. *Would he be allowed to stay aboard this monstrous vessel, which was beginning to feel like home? What did he have to go back for?*

So far, Sol hadn't left the hospital at all. He'd wanted to, but the guards outside the door had prevented him from leaving. Thoughts of disloyalty to his missing fleet came into his head. He was sad for them, torn between two worlds, which worried him deeply, yet this was all out of his hands. He realised it was something he had to live with.

For the time being Sol waited patiently for Doctor Summers to finish attending her duties. He missed her warm, friendly smile and her softly spoken voice. She was still in the isolation ward where he'd been on arrival. He'd watched her come in supporting a man who didn't appear to be in a good way.

*

Doctor Summers stayed in isolation with Kursal for some time while the remaining medics rushed around doing their best to assist. His vital signs were of grave concern and his mental state even worse. His condition was similar to Sol's when he'd first come on board, and Doctor Summers was quick to recognise his symptoms. Keeping him sedated was vital. Physically he was fine and no more could be done.

She had just sat down at the bedside a matter of minutes when she heard a voice calling out for immediate assistance. Once again, she silently cursed the whereabouts of Doctor Forester, who had still to show his face. His duties were piling up, and he had apparently ignored all calls to turn up to the hospital or even report to the captain.

Coming out of the isolation ward, Doctor Summers was greeted by a distressing sight.

"What happened to him?" she asked, recognising the injured officer – just – as Charles Denton from engineering.

As two other officers helped him in, Denton was screaming with the pain to his face and chest, his uniform burnt away.

"Malfunction in engineering, Doctor. Charles caught the blast full on."

"Get him straight into isolation," she instructed, calling for some of her staff to assist.

Then she remembered medics were in short supply now. Having lost three senior staff on Kangis-3, everyone else was having to do double shifts just to keep on top of the work.

They went into the isolation ward and closed the door. After assisting the doctor with the injured man, who was pretty messed up, the two officers left.

Sol stayed in the background, watching. He knew by now he had to allow the doctor to do her job, but he heard things and wondered what was going on. *Was there trouble aboard this ship?* Injuries appeared to be regular. Something terrible had happened on another deck, he knew that much.

They were orbiting a planet, but it wasn't his planet sadly, and several men were dead. Even with the isolation door closed, Sol heard everything the crew were saying and could just about listen into the conversation. They were trying to calm the injured man, giving him powerful pain relief before peeling his uniform off without taking more skin away.

Sol hadn't told anyone about his super hearing, not even the doctor, and he thought it best to stay quiet about it for now. They wouldn't understand, and he knew the captain didn't trust him anyway.

He sat on his bed and just listened. There was much to learn; this was indeed a strange race of people.

For what seemed like hours, Doctor Summers and a couple of medics attended Denton's wounds, as the burns were severe. He was still in a great deal of pain and in danger of going into shock, so sedating him was the best option. It felt as if this was becoming a habit for the doctor as she glanced across to see Kursal laid in the next bed.

For a moment, she couldn't help thinking about Forester and his whereabouts. He wasn't being fair on her or the other staff. They had lost another doctor, Ken Marland, three years earlier. His death had been recorded as natural causes, although that had been presumed but not verified. Summers remained dubious about the circumstances of his death, but whatever the case it had left Retriever-2 short of a doctor for the rest of the mission.

Now, with Forester not around, she was alone and starting to feel the pressure. *Yet how could they lose a crew member aboard a spaceship?*

Finally stabilizing Denton's condition, Doctors Summers emerged from the isolation ward, leaving a junior medic to monitor his condition while another medic watched Kursal. Exhausted, she sat down at her desk to rest. Paperwork was piling up, but she shoved it to one side.

Then came a familiar voice. "Niko."

She looked up to see Sol standing there, unable to stay away any longer. He could see she was tired and stressed from the endless work, her emotions boiling over for all sorts of reasons.

Sol realised she was at breaking point, and he was angry that the captain would make her work so hard. He put a hand on her shoulder to comfort her.

Knowing it was there giving her the feeling that at least one person cared about her.

"Thank you, Sol," she said.

"You must not concern yourself with every little problem on this ship," he told her, trying to soothe her fractured nerves.

She hadn't yet mentioned the trip to Kangis-3, but he was aware that something awful had happened though he hadn't quite worked out exactly what. Niko didn't seem to want to talk about it.

Sol wished he knew where he was in the galaxy. This place was far too dangerous for his liking.

"Sol, it's kind of you to think of me, but right now you are a patient who should be resting." She smiled up at him.

In response, he lifted the doctor to her feet and hugged her.

Trying not to react, she knew her own feelings were genuine, but she was unsure how she should or could act on them. They both sensed they had a real connection; the look in their eyes said it all.

Doctor Summers had to push her personal life to the back of her mind, though. She had duties to attend to, but she did allow Sol to sit on the edge of her desk. His presence was a comfort and somehow gave her the strength to carry on.

There was no way she could sleep until another doctor was on duty, so she put another call out for Doctor Forester to be found and report to the hospital.

Staying with her, Sol held her hand to offer comfort, and she did nothing to discourage him, even though it was wrong. She was not likely to be court-martialled out in space – at least that's what she told herself. But Valmak would have other ideas for sure. Deciding it was best to keep things under wraps, she gently pulled her hand away and started on the paperwork.

Suddenly the outer door of the hospital opened, and Sol jumped up from the desk as soon as he heard the captain's voice call out for Doctor Summers.

"Sol, make yourself scarce," she told him quietly. "I'll talk to you later."

He did so promptly, not wanting a confrontation with a man who clearly hated him, and Doctor Summers rose from her chair, straightened her white coat, and brushed back her hair over her shoulders. She dreaded to think what she looked like after such a long shift.

Captain Valmak entered the hospital with a stern look on his face. There was no alien about, but also no guards at the hospital entrance. He wanted to know why.

"Where are the guards? I ordered them to stay put!" he yelled at her angrily.

"I commandeered them for hospital duties," she told him. "In case you hadn't noticed, Captain, we are very short-staffed."

He decided not to reply to that; she did have a point. "Well, is everything alright here? How is Kursal?"

"He is under sedation and will remain so for the time being," she replied.

Valmak looked through the window of the isolation ward. "Who is the other patient?" he asked.

"Charles Denton, he's also sedated. Severe burns. Accident in engineering apparently."

Valmak didn't enquire any further about Denton. As far as he was concerned, the man should have been more careful at his work.

"I want Kursal back on duty as soon as possible," he announced without a shred of emotion.

"Not a chance, Captain," she told him bluntly. "He won't be going anywhere any time soon. Look, whatever he saw on Kangis-3 traumatised him so much that his mind disconnected from the real world. I can't predict how he will react if I bring him round. That's why he is staying in an induced coma for now."

Valmak was clearly unhappy with the situation. Although he understood what the doctor was telling him, he really needed Kursal back. But she was adamant the officer was going nowhere.

"Okay, what about the alien then?" he asked, fearing he was on the loose somewhere.

"I've told you before, he has a name, and Sol is just fine. I'm more concerned about the whereabouts of Doctor Forester. Have you found him yet?"

"No." Valmak was still puzzled by his absence.

"Well, it's a good job I asked personnel to locate him and inform me when they find him. We cannot operate the hospital with only one doctor."

"What was he doing last?" Valmak asked her. "Can you remember?"

"No idea."

The truth was that Doctor Forester had always been very secretive about his work, and no-one had a clue what his research was all about.

"He shouldn't have let his work interfere with his medical duties," she added. "Have you tried his private quarters? He may have left a clue lying around."

"Okay, I'll check it out, Doctor. Meanwhile I want to talk to this Nussar guy."

"Really, Captain, is that necessary?" she said, getting defensive again. The captain's attitude towards Sol had no merit; he wasn't a threat, and he'd done nothing wrong except get lost in space.

"He appears well enough to me," replied Valmak, spotting the alien wandering about at the far end of the hospital.

"Captain, listen to me—" she pleaded, grabbing his arm to stop him. "What's he done to you? Nothing. Captain, you have to let this go."

But her response only further angered Valmak. *How could she possibly defend the alien?* he thought. *The alien was dangerous.*

"Look, trouble started when he came aboard, and I don't like it. I don't like him." Valmak was adamant, but also vicious with his answer. "I will talk to him right now. That goddamn alien has some explaining to do. I want answers, and I want the truth."

Sol could hear every word Valmak said about him but pretended not to. He didn't understand why the captain hated him so much. He'd done nothing but be polite, and all he'd got in return was anger and suspicion. *The captain's actions were not logical*, thought Sol. *How could he get the captain to believe him?*

Doctor Summers pulled Valmak back a second time.

"Please, Captain, don't do this. He is still vulnerable mentally. Give him a chance." She had genuine concern for her patient and his well-being. Sol was on a strange spaceship a long way from home, scared, and helpless.

But her concern didn't alter a thing for Valmak. "Don't get involved, Doctor Summers, I'm warning you. Now, I will talk to him... alone."

Doctor Summers stood rooted to the spot, wondering whether the captain had just threatened her or not. The man was so aggressive, and she was convinced his behaviour meant he was not rational in his thinking. This last mission was beginning to take its toll on the crew, but the captain was losing the plot completely.

As the only doctor on Retriever-2, she had a decision to make – one she didn't want to. She decided for now to stay in the background and keep an eye on the captain and his behaviour.

Valmak made his way toward the alien with a purposeful stride. He could see Sol examining phials on the shelf along the back wall, then he started flicking through sensitive documents in a folder on another shelf. Valmak was furious. *What was he doing? What was so fascinating?* To Valmak, the behaviour was suspicious, and he had no business looking or touching anything. He was definitely up to something; possibly spying right under their noses. *Why was the doctor allowing the alien free access to the hospital?* This was unacceptable.

"Commander Nussar!" called Valmak, as he marched up to him.

Even though he'd heard the footsteps and knew the captain was coming, Sol almost dropped the folder. It was the harshness of Valmak's loud voice that startled him and was so frightening.

"Nussar, I want some answers from you." Valmak came straight to the point, as he hadn't time to waste with this alien.

Sol didn't say anything; he didn't know what he should say.

"I want to know why you lied to us when you came aboard my ship. Answer me."

"Lie?" Sol was confused at such an accusation.

"Yes, lie." Valmak stood close, imposing his authority over the slightly shorter Sol, intimidating him.

Sol could only stutter for several seconds, trying to get words out, attempting to find the right words to please the captain. He didn't understand the accusation as he had been completely honest.

But Valmak took his silence as guilt. He was certain the alien was hiding something.

"Nussar, if you are so reluctant to tell me the truth, perhaps I should give you a few facts. Maybe that will jog your memory." Valmak took no notice of the fact Sol was struggling to speak and making no sense at all.

The captain paced round him just to demonstrate who was in charge, while Sol stood scared, intimidated by Valmak's stance. His eyes searched for Doctors Summers, hoping she would rescue him, explain everything to the captain, and make him see sense.

But Doctor Summers had been called away when she heard Denton waken from his sedation, screaming with pain.

Meanwhile, Valmak was relentless. "My crew ran the information you gave us through our computers—" he pushed his face right into Sol's face "—but the planet Clarizia does not exist. Your little spaceship is not equipped for hyperdrive, so explain to me how you got here. Where is your mothership?"

Sol was visibly shaken and nervous. *What could he say?* He stepped back, staggering against the wall as fear ran through his veins.

"No, no, you are mistaken, Captain. My world does exist. I am from Clarizia, believe me."

"No, Commander Nussar, it does not. We checked our records thoroughly. Our computers verified no such planet, and our computers are never wrong. Now, admit the truth, damn you. You're a space pirate, admit it."

Sol shook his head in response, but Valmak edged even closer, backing him tight to the wall so he couldn't escape. His mind raced with uncertainty then suddenly he stared into oblivion, blocking out Valmak's voice. He couldn't take any more.

Valmak would not let go. This alien was guilty, and he would have the truth one way or other. He ranted at Sol, shouting in his face the whole time.

Sol cried out for help, but Valmak didn't care and refused to let him go.

"Please, please stop. I live on Clarizia, it is my home, you must believe me. I need to get home," Sol stuttered again, his voice cracking under the intense pressure.

"Admit it, Nussar. Admit you're lying. Tell me who you really are right now!" demanded Valmak furiously. He'd had enough of this whimpering alien and refused to back off.

Sol couldn't reply. He opened his mouth, but words wouldn't come out. He tried to recollect the events since setting off from his home planet. He and his fleet had set off from Clarizia on a routine patrol mission, but it was never completed as he'd become separated from the fleet. Now he was lost in this unknown galaxy and unsure of anything since. *What had he stumbled on?* These people were not that friendly after all; in fact, they were decidedly hostile. He had nowhere to go but inside his own mind.

"Nussar! Nussar!" Valmak grabbed him by the shoulders and shook him hard, pushing for a response.

At that moment, Sol collapsed on the floor, mumbling incoherently. He was gone, withdrawn once more from reality, his mind the safest place to be.

Doctor Summers came out of the isolation ward to see Sol lying on the floor, with the captain standing over him.

"What have you done? Did you hit him?" she screamed, rushing immediately to Sol's side. "I told you not to interrogate him, Captain. He wasn't ready for it." She couldn't believe how heartless Valmak had become. "Help me get him up and into the ward."

But Valmak didn't want contact with the alien, so he didn't move.

"For God's sake, Captain, help me." She was furious. "What did you say to him?"

"Just a few home truths, like that his home planet doesn't exist." There was no passion in the captain's voice as he replied. In his mind, the alien's condition was none of his concern.

Getting Sol into bed, Doctor Summers finally turned to her captain. "Now, you get the hell out of my hospital and never come near here again." She was so angry her face was bright red.

Telling someone their home planet didn't exist wasn't the right course of action and certainly didn't help future diplomatic relations. *What had the captain been thinking?*

Valmak, though, had no regrets. He left without saying a word, only sorry that he hadn't got any answers.

Sol lay, still unresponsive, his eyes open but not looking at anything, while Doctor Summers settled him as best she could. Her mind was in turmoil. *How could anyone do such a despicable act? It was brutal.* She'd lost all respect for the captain. He was not a rational man. Maybe the captain was the next patient she would need to treat. He certainly had no idea what he'd done and had made no attempt to apologise. Now she might never know what had really happened to Sol.

Settling down to sit with Sol, Doctor Summers looked up suddenly to see Valmak coming back. She rushed to the door. No way was he coming into the isolation ward.

"What did I just say to you?" she snapped. "Get out."

"I want to explain why he is a fake," said Valmak, still trying to justify his actions.

"He is not a fake." She held her ground at the door, determined the captain would not get in.

"Look, he had to be told the truth, but he just didn't want to face up to it. How do you know he's not faking now, Doctor?"

Summers shook her head in disbelief, finding it hard to hide her anger. He had no right to be in the hospital, and she couldn't believe she had allowed him inside in the first place.

"Get out, Captain. You have no jurisdiction here, or do I have to cite regulations to you?"

Seeing that she meant what she said, Captain Valmak left for a second time. Nevertheless, he felt no compassion for the alien; he was a fake and a danger to the ship, and no way was he going to get away with it.

In the captain's mind he was completely in the right, whatever the doctor thought.

Glancing back into the hospital, he saw the doctor sit down at the alien's bedside and hold his hand. Immediately he wondered if there was more to their relationship.

Still determined, he decided to check the patient's records on the way out. He didn't care about privacy, he just wanted answers. There was a possibility he had a criminal on his ship, and that would take priority over Doctor Summers' concerns. He knew the regulations, too.

*

Doctor Summers remained at Sol's bedside while keeping an eye on Kursal and Denton in the next two beds, both still sedated. Denton seemed a lot calmer now thanks to the extra pain relief. The captain didn't ask about either of the men; he didn't seem to care.

As she watched Sol, tears trickled down her cheeks, her anger turning to sadness. Sol was a genuine, kind man, who had simply got lost in the depths of space and only wanted help and comfort. Instead, he'd got nothing but hostility. He didn't deserve this. Her feelings for him ran deep and would never waver. She would not leave him in his hour of need.

*

As Captain Valmak passed the doctor's station, he stopped to see if there were any clues left lying around. He cursed under his breath when he realised the alien's file was not there. He'd have to leave it for now, but he would be back.

As he turned to leave, the intercom bleeped repeatedly. Valmak looked around for a medic to answer it, but nobody responded. It bleeped again, and Valmak thumped the switch. "What?"

"Ah, Captain. Personnel here. We have confirmed Doctor Forester is not on-board Retriever-2. Internal probes checked for his DNA signature, and it is not registering. Doctor Summers wished to be informed."

Valmak switched off the intercom, stunned by the report. *How could that be?* Suddenly he thought about the extra body he'd found on Kangis-3. *Could it have been Forester? It seemed likely, but how had he got down there in the first place?* The man had been absent from his post for several days, but that didn't answer the question.

The situation over Kangis-3 seemed to be escalating, and he could do nothing to stop it.

Valmak was about to leave again when the intercom bleeped a second time. This time it was King calling from the bridge.

"Captain, we have detected an entity of sorts. Or at least we think we have."

"Well, have you or haven't you, King? Make up your mind." Valmak was in no mood for the man's indecision.

"Yes, sir. I mean it isn't a constant, but definitely a positive trace on the planet's surface." He sounded hesitant.

Valmak picked up on the uncertainty. "You're being a bit vague, King. Explain."

"It's just that whatever it is keeps disappearing, and we don't know what to make of it."

"Is it there now?" asked Valmak.

"Yes, sir."

"I'm on my way."

Valmak left in a hurry, forgetting to relay the other message to Doctor Summers.

CHAPTER FOUR

Captain Valmak frantically rushed along the corridors to the bridge, desperate to know more details. *Was this the breakthrough he needed?* He was certain danger was still lurking in their midst, and in his head, he was planning his next course of action. Whatever was on the planet surface was alien, hostile, and murderous, so it had to be dealt with, although it wasn't going to be easy.

He was already thinking about what he was going to say to mission HQ about the loss of company property – one shuttle, which he was not going back for – and the loss of seven crew under his command. The big problem he had was that Retriever-2 was a hospital ship, not a battle cruiser. It had little in the way of fire power, and they had nothing much to defend themselves with.

Valmak was determined to deal with the mystery of Kangis-3 and its murdering resident, but he just didn't know how. He was certain Retriever-2 had been led into a trap, and he wanted to know why. *Why pretend to need assistance? Was it the crew or the hospital ship itself that was the real target? Kangis-3 had no civilization, so why bring them to this awful place?* Valmak had so many questions burning into his brain that he pushed aside his concerns about the alien on board. His fate would be dealt with later.

Immediately entering the bridge, Valmak looked straight at the viewing screen, but Kangis-3 wasn't showing. *Had they left orbit without informing him?* Then he saw something which he could only describe as space dust. *But was it?*

King approached the captain from his station.

"What's going on, King?"

"Sir, we are monitoring from a higher orbit above the planet. The trace we picked up moved position to the upper atmosphere, then small particles broke away into space," King explained.

"So, is it space dust or something else?" Valmak demanded.

"Unsure, so I thought it wise to take the ship to a safe distance."

Valmak for once nodded in agreement with his first officer. He continued to watch the screen, thinking how the space dust reminded him of the eerie fog they'd encountered on the surface. There had to be a connection.

King could sense the captain had other plans, but he decided to remind him that their job was done.

"Sir, I have to remind you our mission is over. We should return to Earth."

"May I remind you, King, the mission is over when I say it is." Valmak looked appalled at the suggestion they should leave. "We will investigate the deaths of the crew, and I want you to find out why Doctor Forester is not on board. How did he get off the ship?"

King returned to his station and said nothing. It was his duty to point out the facts, whether the captain liked them or not, but he decided to secretly note the exchange in the ship's log in case it was needed in the future. He predicted a court martial on their return to Earth, as there were higher authorities to deal with this.

Several hours passed in silence, nothing out of the ordinary occurred on the bridge, and the crew continued to monitor the planet surface as the captain had instructed. The small area of supposed space dust lingered, seemingly harmless.

Valmak sat in his control seat, watching, waiting. Aztac and Straten at the helm were keeping a safe orbit, and King was at his station, quietly fuming at his captain. *Why was Valmak behaving in such a manner? The ship was just sitting there when they could be on their way home.* King felt deeply for the dead crew, but hanging around would not bring them back.

Suddenly the space dust altered its appearance, turning almost transparent only to reappear much denser again and closer to the ship. Helm went into full alert, attempting to get an analysis. Whatever it was, it shouldn't be able to change like that. Valmak came to the conclusion it was not space dust, but some kind of entity with a mind of its own.

Cal Bartok joined the bridge crew, taking over Kursal's position, and quickly completed a sweep of the space dust. It turned out to be something he had not anticipated.

"Captain, computer analysis suggests the space dust is actually a single life form."

Valmak gave a strained look at the viewing screen. *How could life exist like that in deep space?*

"More data, sir," said Bartok. "Its size varies by the second, but density remains constant."

"It has density?" questioned Valmak.

"Apparently so, sir," replied Bartok.

Valmak sensed an eerie presence as he had when that damned alien came aboard. He just could not get him out of his head, everything revolved around him; the alien had to be connected to what was going on.

"Maintain position, full alert, helm. Be ready for anything," ordered Valmak. He couldn't take a chance with the space dust. Whatever was out there had intelligence, not unlike the mist on Kangis-3, and that had proved deadly. He was sure there was a connection. *But was it the same?*

"I need more data, men. Give me facts, give me something," he announced. "And move us further away. We need distance between us and that thing."

Retriever-2 backed off, but the mist moved too, matching the ship's course precisely.

"It appears to follow us, Captain," said Aztac, as he unsuccessfully attempted to manoeuvre the ship out of harm's way.

"King, do you have anything?" asked Valmak.

"No, sir, nothing," replied King. His monitors registered nothing on the mist at all.

At that point Valmak knew his ship was in trouble. If this entity had intelligence, it wouldn't go round the universe destroying other intelligence. It would thrive on it like a sponge, soaking up as much data as it could, eventually sucking the life out of its victim in the process. He wanted to believe the space dust was the same as the deadly mist on Kangis-3, but he couldn't connect why it needed to murder and mutilate other life. That part had no logic to it, so this had to be different.

The crew were waiting on him, relying on him for answers, but he had none and that was the problem. Valmak knew his own actions had been erratic of late, but now he had to be decisive and find a way to destroy this lifeform before it destroyed the ship. Then he might get his life back on track, or at least partially. There was also a certain alien to get rid of.

For the time being he had to come up with a plan before more lives were lost.

"King, get Phasner to the bridge immediately. His intellect might be needed." Valmak had an idea of a plan.

"Yes, sir, right away," replied King, thinking the captain might have a shred of sanity in him yet.

Aztac and Straten remained vigilant at the helm, waiting to see what the space dust was going to do next. They had no idea what to expect, though, this was way above their pay grade. Aztac was getting nervous, and Straten kept wiping his sweaty palms on his uniform.

The tension was getting to all of them when suddenly the dust made a move, spreading itself across space, covering a vast area, then drew itself back in for no apparent reason.

"What's it doing?" cried Aztac.

"Probably waiting to see what we do," said Straten.

"I want to know what its intentions are," replied Aztac.

"Stay alert, men," ordered Valmak, then issued a very strange request. "Aztac, switch your monitor to maximum beam and position it towards the planet surface."

"Sir?" Aztac was puzzled.

"Yes. You have the location of our shuttle, and you will find eight bodies close by. I want every one of them identified."

Aztac complied but didn't understand. It seemed odd to be asking about dead bodies when the crew were struggling with the living.

Valmak was playing for time, hoping if the dust did have intelligence, it might be distracted. Aztac was sure his captain had a plan, because if he didn't, they were all in trouble.

Denny Argent was constantly busy with communications, but suddenly he received a distressing message – one Valmak would not like.

"Captain, I have an important message from Earth mission HQ. They say Retriever-4 is in trouble. They are under attack by unknown aliens, and we are requested to assist them immediately."

"They what—?" Now Valmak was puzzled.

"I thought Retriever-4 wasn't in operation," said King, just in case the captain had forgotten.

"That's what they said, Captain. Should I reply?" asked Argent.

"Inform mission HQ that our mission to Kangis-3 is not complete. We are unable to assist at this present time."

"Yes, sir."

"Then find out where the other rescue ships are," added Valmak, before turning his attention back to the viewing screen. He had enough to handle without adding to his stress levels.

Argent was soon back with a reply. "Captain, Retriever-1 is back on Earth for extensive repairs, and Retriever-3 has disappeared. Mission HQ cannot make contact. We are the only rescue ship able to assist."

That wasn't in Valmak's plan at all.

"Try to contact Retriever-4 and tell them to hold out as best they can, we cannot assist at the moment." Valmak was determined not to leave here without answers.

"But, sir, surely—"

"Do you have a problem with your hearing?" snapped Valmak.

"No, sir." Argent obeyed the order, but he wasn't happy about it.

"Aztac, have you that data yet?" Valmak was getting impatient. Time was short.

"Just coming in, sir. Computer about to analyse."

Valmak paced the bridge, anxiously awaiting the results, all the while thinking of a plan.

King decided it was time to speak up. "Captain, shouldn't we assist Retriever-4? They may need urgent help."

Valmak ignored the question. They were surely too far away to be any good now, and it was far too important to deal with the problem at hand. He also had an inkling that whatever lifeform was out there would not let his ship go very easily. He had no choice but to stay.

King realised the only thing he could do was again document the captain's response in the ship's log.

Valmak was fully aware that whatever happened from then on was wholly his responsibility, and his alone. With seven crew dead, another missing, a mystery alien aboard giving him grief, and now an intelligent lifeform outside that appeared to have a mind of its own, it all weighed heavily on his shoulders. Going by the book simply wasn't an option. Mission HQ should never have sent Retriever-2 and its crew on this rescue when they were overdue for vacation time.

For now, though, Valmak had to push his fears into the background. This situation needed leadership. At times he felt he was going mad, and maybe he was, but this was not the time to torment himself. In his mind he was standing up for his crew. His priority was to protect the crew at all costs and get them home – eventually.

Aztac swivelled round in his seat to alert the captain of his findings.

"Sir, analysis complete. The probes located the eight bodies, and the computer has confirmed the DNA profile from seven are that of the crew. The eighth one, however, is alien of unknown origin. No other details available."

Valmak acknowledged the information with a nod. So much for his theory the extra body was Doctor Forester. *But if the medic wasn't on the surface and not on the ship, then where was he?* It made Valmak angry that he had no answer to how Forester had managed to disappear from the ship undetected. *What was the man doing? What was he up to?* Valmak was determined to find out.

He turned to Argent again. "Have you managed to contact Retriever-4 yet?"

"Yes, sir. They say danger has passed, no details on that, but they are seriously crippled. They think they have enough power to make it back to Earth."

"Good. What about Retriever-3, have they answered the call sign?"

"No, sir, no response at all. We have no idea where they are either."

"Keep trying," said Valmak. That left him free to deal with the imminent danger which he knew was coming.

The crew were showing signs of tiredness, exhausted by the long shifts they were doing. Every one of them really wanted to go home, and hopefully he would get them there. They just had to be patient.

When Tom Phasner entered the bridge, Valmak summoned him over to a corner where they spoke privately for several minutes. King watched them, wondering what the captain was up to. He couldn't hear what they were saying, but Phasner was nodding in agreement. The exchange further angered King.

After all, he was the first officer and yet the captain was excluding him.

While they were whispering, helm crew Aztac and Straten observed the so-called space dust make a move, stretching out again across the blackness, and this time expanding even more than before. Then it appeared to edge closer to the ship.

Valmak saw what was happening from the corner of the bridge.

"Back off! Back off!" he yelled suddenly. "Take any defensive action necessary. We need a little more time," he said.

Retriever-2 moved further away from the planet, but the mist followed. Valmak was banking on the move. This alien intelligence wanted something, and he was sure it was about to make a move on the ship. Valmak had assumed the intelligence disguised in the mist existed purely as an energy source. If that was true, it was very likely looking for another source of power to replenish itself and expand in size. It needed, wanted to grow.

Phasner put forward several theories to his captain, which Valmak took on board. They concluded that the mist was probably waiting to pounce and was assessing the ship's defence. It was after one thing – the main energy banks; the life-force of Retriever-2. That much they agreed on.

Valmak had the sense to realise he did not have the scientific acumen needed, but he was sure Phasner had and understood this strange phenomenon lurking in space.

The captain wanted to believe the mist was the same as he'd seen on Kangis-3; it was eerie-looking and deadly. But Phasner did not think so. He felt this was something completely different. An entity purely existing without a body was not beyond the realms of reality. The two men continued to debate several ideas, all the while keeping an eye on the viewing screen.

While Valmak was busy in discussion with Phasner, more data was received, this time from the planet surface. Bartok attempted to decipher the readout as quickly as he could, as it might be vital. He had sent a probe to the surface earlier in an effort to get answers about this mysterious planet, but he was alarmed to discover the results. Something was still down there... alive. A trace of a lifeform registered pulsating energy off the scale.

A further scan proved the initial data correct, but he was startled by the next set of information and had to look twice at his monitor in case he was reading it wrong. The captain was not going to like his discovery, but it seemed the mist outside the ship had a similar genome sequence as the lifeform on the planet.

Bartok surmised there had to be a connection but struggled to get his head round the fact that the mist had DNA in the first place. *So much for being space dust*, he thought. This was much more, but it was still not logical to Bartok, and he could only speculate how such a lifeform could really exist this way. To his mind the fundamental basis of all life, carbon-based or otherwise, would surely need to be more than mist. *Or*, he wondered, *had this alien entity found a way to live on a higher degree of existence? Was that really possible?*

The new data was confusing Bartok more than ever, and he had no idea how he was going to explain it to the captain.

The helm still had eyes on the mist as it came closer still. It seemed to be teasing them, provoking the ship to take action.

Although the crew wanted to, the captain appeared to be against any form of action, ignoring the danger. King in particular was concerned as he watched the captain, then spotted Bartok hovering around wanting to speak to Valmak. It seemed urgent.

Bartok now had evidence that the mist was low on energy. His mind was suddenly clear; he knew what its intentions were.

Having finished his discussions with Phasner, Valmak knew now that if they tried to destroy this entity, they would simply be feeding it. The mist wanted them to do just that, so it was time to put a plan of action into place. They needed to find a weakness that would impact on the entity itself.

It wanted an energy source to feed its hunger, but Valmak planned to exploit that greed by giving it too much power. It was a huge risk – one that Phasner and his captain had discussed in depth. They had finally formulated a very intricate plan, but if it failed, they were all dead. If they did nothing, though, they guessed there would be the same result.

Valmak turned to see his bridge crew staring at him instead of monitoring the situation as he had ordered.

"Why is everybody not keeping an eye on the viewing screen?" he yelled.

Swiftly the helm crew swivelled round, afraid that a reprimand was coming.

"Bartok, talk to me. I see you hovering there," said Valmak.

Bartok did his best to explain his findings, thinking the captain would dismiss them as complete rubbish, but Valmak was actually not surprised. His discussions with Phasner meant they were on the same wavelength.

Valmak was, however, disturbed that the thing on the planet was still lurking about and that the mist was connected to it in some way. It proved his theory right – not Phasner's – but gave him no satisfaction.

Before any action could be taken, the mist suddenly opened up again, stretching itself out and, without warning, lunged at the ship. Everyone was taken by surprise, and Retriever-2 was hit with such tremendous force that it rocked violently. Several minutes elapsed before the crew staggered back to their feet – some with minor injuries.

Valmak had expected the action.

"Aztac, reverse engines, maximum power!" he shouted as they got back to their seats. "Put some distance between us and that thing," he said. He realised the ship couldn't outrun the mist, but he was banking on it having the intelligence to think it had won.

"No good, sir, it matches our course and speed exactly. It's like it's anticipating our every move."

Valmak was relying on this. He needed it to follow, to make it come after them. He also needed time for Phasner to put their plan into action.

King wasn't sure what Valmak was playing at. His actions seemed reckless and dangerous, and he'd already recorded in the ship's log that Captain Valmak was acting totally irresponsibly. His problem was, though, he had no ideas of his own to override the captain. They were all in danger.

"Here it comes again, Captain!" cried Aztac.

"Prepare for impact, everyone," said Valmak.

Seconds later the ship rocked again, this time more violently. Many sections were blacked out for several seconds before auxiliary power kicked in.

Valmak scrambled to his feet, having taken a knock to the head. Blood trickled down his face from a gash over his right eye. He felt slightly dazed for a moment, ignoring the blood dripping on his uniform. Grit and determination, and probably a touch of stubbornness, helped him focus quickly.

"Captain!" screamed King. "We can't take this."

Valmak refused to back down; this was the only way. He had to do this for the sake of the crew and the ship.

Bartok was back at his station to check for damage to the ship. Everyone wanted to know what was going on, but he couldn't say because he wasn't sure himself.

Valmak interrupted him, needing to know if Phasner had completed his task. But King was not giving up his resistance.

"Captain, we cannot sustain this attack much longer. We're not equipped for it. This is a hospital ship, not a bloody battleship." King was livid with his superior officer, and he pleaded several times before Valmak finally looked up from the monitor.

"Volatile emotions, Mister King, and an insatiable appetite," he declared confidently.

"What the—?" King spat out, astounded by such nonsense.

Aztac and Straten looked round, equally dumbfounded. The captain had lost the plot for sure. But before they had a chance to speak, the ship was hit again with such force that parts of the outer hull buckled under pressure.

Aztac picked himself up again, this time with a bloody nose and sore ribs. Straten struggled to his feet, nursing a suspected broken arm. He was in a lot of pain.

"Sir, do you want to tell me what's going on? Because if you're saying that mist out there has feelings, I'm not buying it," said King, anger overriding his fear.

It was ludicrous, the captain was mad, and he wanted to say as much but had to bite his tongue. Approaching Valmak, King got right into his face.

"Sir, this is crazy. We'll all be killed." His voice was intense with anger. *Would he need to take control of the ship and relieve Valmak of his command?* He was seriously thinking about it.

"King, you have to trust me. Now get back to your station."

Reluctantly King obeyed but wondered how long he could allow this behaviour to go on.

Meanwhile Valmak went straight back to the computer to monitor the progress.

"Sir is there something I can help you with?" asked Bartok, confused by his captain's actions.

"Stay focused, Bartok," Valmak said, almost in a calm, soothing manner, and certainly not in the way he had spoken to King.

Bartok, still worried, watched the captain as he was analysing the data on the monitor. This was a bizarre situation, and he didn't know what to do.

"Come on, come on," muttered Valmak, waiting for something to happen.

At that precise moment, the mist made a decisive and impossible move – anticipated by Valmak – to seep through solid metal and enter the outer hull of the ship on several decks. Once inside, it began to reassemble itself in its original form – a highly intelligent entity in pure energy form. It wanted one thing – the energy source on the ship. It had become desperate for a new source to replenish itself. That would allow it to grow even stronger and bigger. It was as if it had an insatiable appetite that could not be fulfilled.

"Captain, the mist has entered decks six, nine, and twelve," reported Straten, now more afraid than ever and scared they were doing nothing.

"Clear those sections immediately. No-one engages with the mist," announced Valmak, as he kept up the surveillance on the monitor. He prayed the entity did what it was supposed to do.

"Captain, decks six, nine, and twelve are where the ship's power cells are stored," said King, worried this was not going to end well.

"Yes, I know, King. Stay with it," said Valmak.

He watched the entity as it started to do exactly what he wanted it to. His plan was working, as it went in search of the biggest source of power on Retriever-2 – the power cells located in the main computer packs spread over the three decks. The power cells controlled everything on the ship, including life support.

As Valmak had calculated, the intelligence of this lifeform was driven by greed. The more it absorbed, the more it craved. He now hoped Phasner had the time to do his job, because the entity was tapping into the power as Valmak had predicted.

King and the other bridge crew were afraid of Valmak's behaviour, as his actions went against all logic. They were all unaware of his motives, therefore unable to comprehend his lunatic conduct. Although his actions were terrifying, however, not one of the crewmen said anything. The threat of insubordination and a court martial, if they ever got back to Earth, wasn't something they wanted on their records.

King had already tried but failed, so he had instead documented his feelings in the log. Over the last six years the entire crew had relied on Captain Valmak and trusted him implicitly. His steadfast leadership had never been in question – until now.

No-one could understand how they had got into this predicament. After all, they were just a hospital ship, and the bridge crew were simply pilots taking Retriever-2 through space to wherever it was needed. Most of the other crew were connected in some way with the hospital. None of them were cut out for this sort of mission, and they sensed it might be their last one, destined never to see home again.

The entity was quick to locate what it wanted. Relentless to its own end, it lustfully continued to drain the power cells that Retriever-2 needed to stay alive.

King switched his monitor so he could see what was happening. Each power cell drained until it reached zero.

"Sir, do you realise what will happen to us?" he cried out in despair. "Why are you allowing it?"

"Keep monitoring, King, and stay calm," said Valmak, ignoring his pleas. "Bartok, when I say so, switch all computer storage cells on every deck into the main energy supply banks."

"No, sir!" shouted King. "That will only help to feed this thing." He rose to his feet in a fury. He couldn't allow it.

"Sit down, King, unless you want to be relieved of duty." Valmak was determined to see the plan through to the end.

Bartok was about to speak up as well, but Valmak had other ideas. "Are you ready, Bartok?" he asked.

Bartok nodded, sweating profusely at the thought of dying.

"This is the final part. Now trust me," said Valmak.

Bartok wanted to, but it was hard to believe in his captain anymore. King looked across to him, just as despondent, and shook his head. He couldn't help.

"Ready, Bartok, NOW!" said Valmak loudly.

Bartok hit the switch; all remaining power cells were diverted. He was scared this might well be his last action in life, and the looks on the faces of the other bridge crew staring back at him said it all. He felt it was all his fault that they were doomed. If dying wasn't bad enough, he had to feel guilty as well.

As predicted, the entity took the bait. The extra energy surge was too much temptation. The energy gave it more power, more intelligence, and even more greed, but that greed became too much to handle.

It was soon apparent that the entity had expanded beyond the capacity of the power cells' perimeters. It needed to move out to gain additional space to grow and in turn absorb more and more pure energy. Yet it wouldn't release the flow surging into its very being. An insatiable hunger couldn't allow it to let go.

The surge continued.

"Power draining fast, Captain. Down to thirty percent," King told Valmak, who acknowledged his words with a wave of his hand.

Valmak went back to the monitor. "Is the energy still flowing?"

"Yes, sir, but—"

"Just keep an eye on the readout," he instructed, still hoping his plan would work. It had to.

Phasner appeared back on the bridge and nodded to Valmak, as if to acknowledge job done. Moments later, one of the instrument panels in front of Straten sparked wildly, followed by a puff of smoke, then the circuitry went dead. Helm had no control of the ship now.

"Complete burnout, Captain. We are powerless," said Straten, wincing. The pain from his broken arm was making him nauseous and he felt like passing out.

Zymotz was there for him. "Hang in there, Will," he said.

Straten nodded. Zymotz had his back, but he didn't have the pain.

Valmak continued his observation at the monitor. It was obvious the entity was struggling, having trouble digesting the continuous flow of energy. It was suddenly fighting for its own survival, something it was not familiar with. But all the intelligence in the universe couldn't make the entity see sense, and it couldn't deal with its own greed. It needed – wanted – room to expand. That was essential, paramount to its very existence. Its own selfish greed kept soaking up the energy supply, more than it could sustain in its current capacity, yet it still refused to let go of what it craved. Soon the entity would be all-powerful.

Lights all over the ship flickered on and off. The power was almost gone. Valmak thought it would all soon be over one way or the other.

"Captain, power to the main memory banks is at critical levels. They will completely burn out soon. We cannot lose the memory banks."

King kept pressuring Valmak with his reports, desperate for the captain to stop this futile act. But even though Valmak was listening, there was no response. The captain stood in silence, palms sweating, anxious that the entity should burn itself to a crisp before it burnt the ship to a cinder. All eyes were on Valmak waiting for him to say something, to do something constructive to save their lives.

The captain watched as the ship's energy source was almost gone. It seemed he'd done all he could, but it just wasn't enough. Power to Retriever-2 was barely enough for them to limp back to Earth, if they even survived.

A small explosion behind one of the monitors blew out the panelling, smoke billowed out, then a small electrical fire started, sparks flying in every direction, smoke filling the bridge.

"Get that fire under control!" demanded Valmak.

"Wish someone would get him under control," came a whisper from King.

"Do you have something to say, King?"

"No, sir," King replied.

Computers burnt out all over the ship on every deck, except in the hospital, which was using auxiliary power that Phasner had diverted per the captain's instructions.

Valmak hadn't said anything to his bridge crew, thinking the entity might sense a trick. He needed everyone to play their part perfectly.

"That's it, Captain, all power gone. Every deck, including life support, gone. We have nothing left. I hope you're happy now." King had never felt so scared of dying. He really wanted to thump the captain but knew that wouldn't achieve anything.

Valmak scanned round the bridge, seeing every monitor and computer screen blank. Wondering if the plan had worked or not, he waved Phasner over.

"Do what you have to," Valmak told him quietly.

Phasner went to one of the monitors and keyed in a sequence of numbers. Thirty seconds later, minimal power returned to the bridge. Just enough, it seemed, for Valmak to check what the entity was doing. *Was it still lurking in the machinery?*

He prayed not.

King turned to his monitor, as did the helm crew.

"What just happened?" asked Bartok, stunned for a moment.

King tried to locate the signature of the entity, but he only had limited access to the computer.

"Someone please tell me what is going on?" asked Bartok again.

Phasner was busy computing, his monitor working fine.

"Has it gone?" asked Valmak.

"I can't find a trace of it anywhere," he reported.

"Well done, Phasner," said Valmak, pleased he hadn't blown them all up.

Phasner, meanwhile, started to reconnect some of the main circuitry.

"So have we destroyed it, whatever it was?" asked Aztac, letting out a sigh of relief.

"I want confirmation first," ordered Valmak, deciding it was too soon for celebrations.

"But, sir, there is barely enough power to do a thorough search," questioned Bartok. "And most of the circuits are burnt out." He wasn't sure what the captain expected them to do with nothing working.

As he spoke, the air-conditioning kicked in, sucking out the remaining smoke.

Valmak was feeling a little more confident. "There is enough power in the reserve chamber to allow the burnt-out sections to be repaired. Get it done as soon as possible."

Puzzled faces looked round at each other, then at the captain, wanting an explanation from him.

"Okay," he said. "I had Phasner bypass some of the circuits, allowing enough power to be diverted to the reserve chamber. So, we have power."

A wave of sheer relief came over the bridge. Nevertheless, they were absolutely stunned. The reserve chamber hadn't been used in two years.

"Well, you could have bloody told us, Captain," yelled King, fuming that he hadn't been in on the secret. He was, though, relieved that the captain wasn't entirely mad after all.

"Sorry," Valmak replied. "I couldn't say in case the entity realised what we were doing."

Now they needed to turn their attention to the clean-up.

"Use the power to make repairs, Bartok, and see to it that the memory banks are secured first. We mustn't lose them. I want output at once."

"Yes, sir, right away," announced the crew almost in unison, realising their captain had known exactly what he was doing all along.

Valmak left the bridge to allow the crew to get on with the repairs. When he returned, he told Straten to go to the hospital and have his arm attended to.

"Phasner," he went on, "double check as soon as you can that we have eliminated the intruder."

"Yes, sir, I'm on it," said Phasner.

As he left the helm, he instructed, "And then find out why that mist had a similar DNA to Doctor Forester. There has to be an error. I want it double-checked, so see to it, King. Work with Bartok if necessary."

CHAPTER FIVE

Captain Valmak found a quiet haven in his private quarters to contemplate everything that had happened. He'd put his ship and the entire crew at risk, but he'd got lucky. That realisation didn't make him feel any better.

He still had so many unanswered questions, but he just wasn't sure he would ever get them. Kangis-3 was a strange planet, and certainly not a good place to revisit. He felt he had to, though, or there would be no peace of mind for him.

According to the data received, something was still alive on the planet's surface. Valmak wanted revenge for his crew, but that emotion had subsided slightly. He supposed being on the verge of death put things into perspective.

His thoughts drifted to Gordon Kursal, wondering what the man had seen down there to make him completely withdraw into himself. Whatever it was must have been so grotesque. *How was he going to get information out of him now?* Valmak didn't know, but he couldn't let it go. Too many questions raced through his head. Having held himself together for the crew in a crisis, it now got the better of him.

The sinister thoughts returned. He was convinced evil lurked nearby, too close for comfort, and he still blamed that alien Commander Nussar for everything. Life aboard Retriever-2 had been running smoothly, the ship on its way home, until Nussar turned up.

Valmak couldn't help his thoughts, and hatred rose to the surface again. He was sure of one thing, though. Returning to the surface of the planet had to be a priority, and he had to take another look at the dead bodies. They might have missed vital clues, and he had to solve the murders. He couldn't go home with that on his record.

There was also a concern about the slimy slug trail. *Was there really a slug prowling around searching for prey? Was that what Kursal had actually seen?* It was a distinct possibility.

Returning to the surface presented a big problem, Valmak knew. They would have to be diligent, but Retriever-2 had limited weapons because it was a hospital ship. All they had were hand-held phasic guns, which were not powerful enough to do any real damage, but the Retriever class rescue ships were not allowed to carry anything else. Nevertheless, Valmak was determined to be fully prepared this time. He would not lose any more men.

The mist in space did look the same as on the surface, Valmak was sure of that. *But how was it possible for it to rise up from the surface to attack the ship? What was the connection with Forester?* Valmak remembered Bartok telling him that the entity had a similar genome sequence to Doctor Forester. *But how could that be?* Valmak thought it very unlikely to travel across the galaxy and find a similar DNA on a dead planet which now was being occupied by a giant, murdering slug – if indeed it was a slug.

He was desperate for answers, but he would not find them in his quarters. Perhaps Doctor Forester's notes needed further scrutiny. Perhaps the medic had left some of his research in his quarters – something, anything to explain his disappearance.

He was angry with himself for allowing Forester's prolonged absence from the hospital. Now it was time to find evidence about what he'd been up to and how he'd managed to get off the ship without alerting security. Valmak was more determined than ever to return to Kangis-3.

Entering Doctor Forester's quarters, Valmak scanned round the room for obvious clues. The place was a complete mess, probably due to the attack on Retriever-2 when the ship had been violently rocked sideways. The floor was cluttered with papers and files, but nothing stood out.

The captain knelt down among the papers and lifted several files, going through them one by one. Nothing of any relevance stood out and the rest he didn't understand, science not being his strong point. Then he lifted a file with the heading 'MOLECULAR CELL RESTRUCTURE'.

"What's all that about?" he muttered to himself.

Skimming through the pages, he saw lots of symbols and equations, stuff that meant very little to Valmak. Then he spotted a file beneath the first one. It had one title, 'TELEPORTATION'.

"Now that's a word I do understand." He took the two files, hoping that Doctor Summers might be able to understand them better then him, even though he wasn't her favourite person at the moment.

*

The hospital had been extremely hectic with injuries coming in, mainly from the attack, so it was proving to be a crazy time for Doctor Summers. She soon realised she had to recruit more non-medical crew to assist her, and even train some of them on first aid procedures.

Will Straten had insisted she just strap up his broken arm so he could get back to the bridge to help out. And most of the other treatments were just minor cuts and bruises. Doctor Summers delegated as much as she could and dealt with the more serious ones herself.

When the place finally quietened down and most of the crew returned to duty, there was just the clean-up to do. The emergency area was a mess, with bloodied swabs, gauze wrappings, and bandages. One of the orderlies offered to do it, for which she was most grateful, leaving her to concentrate on the most serious patients.

Gordon Kursal was still unresponsive, but at least she had been able to bring him out of the coma. He still remained in a dazed state, occasionally muttering something which sounded to Doctor Summers like the name Forester. As that didn't make sense, she assumed she must have misheard.

Charles Denton's burns were healing fine, and she was able to reassure him that the scars were not so bad. He was now sitting up and alert.

A pile of medical records littered her desk relating to the patients that had just been treated. *Had there really been that many?* She sat down to gather her thoughts and take a well-earned break.

"Doctor Summers, would you like a cup of tea?" came a voice from behind her. It was Carol Harding, one of the crew roped in to help.

"Yes please," smiled the doctor, grateful that someone was thinking about her. Sleep was what she really needed, having forgotten what that was really like, but a cup of tea would be nice.

Personnel checked in again, asking if she had received the message concerning Doctor Forester. She hadn't, but now she knew he was officially reported missing – presumed dead. She felt nothing but contempt for the man, as he had left her in the lurch in the middle of a crisis to pursue his worthless research. *How could he do that to her with Doctor Marland passing away early in the voyage?* She still wondered about the circumstances of the other man's death, but she had to let her doubts go.

Eventually her thoughts drifted towards the isolation ward once more and to the one patient she really cared for, the one patient she wanted to help but couldn't. Sol lay motionless; his eyes were open, yet he responded to no-one. His mind was confused and refused to connect with his surroundings. The only thing in his mind was his own madness, shutting everything else out, believing all outside thoughts were irrelevant. Sol's innermost conscience told him to stay there, and he would be safe. There was nothing he needed from the outside; Captain Valmak had made sure of it. Sol was in his own world, and it was beautiful.

Doctor Summers eventually got to her feet and went to the isolation ward for the umpteenth time. Sol's condition was unlikely to change any time soon, but she took every opportunity to sit and talk to him in the hope of a response. At his bedside, tears pricked the back of her eyes. Shedding tears for someone who might never know was hard, and she felt remorse, sadness, and even anger at times. She had allowed the brutal questioning that had sent Sol over the edge, but her bitterness was toward the captain. What Valmak had said and done to Sol was not worth this. Her patient was so vulnerable, so far away from his home, and now he had nothing.

The lights in isolation were dimmed slightly, giving the impression of calmer, more soothing surroundings for Sol. She kept hoping for even a faint response, and maybe in time he would.

Doctor Summers left Sol's bedside and stood on the other side of the glass, still watching him for some time. Within minutes she was lost in her thoughts. Nothing mattered at that precise moment but the man she realised she had fallen in love with. Yet she couldn't tell anyone; it wouldn't achieve anything but perhaps get her struck off. Tears began to flow freely down her cheeks, and she felt so emotional but drained of energy. If only she could do more for her patient, anything to pull him back to reality.

Suddenly a voice called out in the distance, and she quickly wiped her tears away. Valmak appeared and stood next to her at the isolation window.

"Hello, Doctor, I understand you've had a busy time." He was clearly trying to strike up a friendly conversation, but he was the last person she wanted to see. She recalled telling him to stay away, but obviously he hadn't listened.

"How is he?" the captain asked.

"What do you care?" came back her reply. There was annoyance in her voice as she tried to choke back tears without Valmak noticing.

He changed the subject. "I went to Doctor Forester's quarters and came across these files." He handed them to her. "I thought you might be able to make sense of them better than me. They might give a clue as to what he was up to."

Reluctantly Doctor Summers opened the first file. *A quick glance wouldn't hurt*, she supposed.

"Molecular cell restructure?" she said, stunned at the heading.

"Yes, exactly. Unfortunately, not my area of expertise."

Doctor Summers looked at the other file, but she wasn't really interested in either of them. "I'll take a look later," she said.

"Thank you, Doctor." His attempt at politeness wasn't washing with her, so he turned his attention to the alien he hated so much and went to enter his room.

Doctor Summers swiftly followed him, determined never to leave him alone with Sol again.

The patient was staring at the ceiling, and Valmak wondered if the alien was even aware of his presence.

"Don't try anything, Captain," said Doctor Summers sternly.

Valmak briefly questioned himself as to whether he was wrong about the alien. *Was he really lost in space? Could he have harmed anyone? Yes, he could.* That haunting sense of evil swept over the captain again, a gut feeling that this Nussar guy was a threat, not just to him but to the very existence of all life. *But why?* He was just one alien with funny ridges across his forehead and didn't look much different otherwise.

It wasn't that Valmak simply didn't like him, but that he was genuinely afraid about the future. And that sense of foreboding refused to leave him – no matter how hard he tried. It was as if the alien had an unseen power over the captain.

Doctor Summers hovered close by, taking Sol's hand to check his pulse, but really just wanting to touch him and let him know she was there.

"When we get back to Earth, could the experts help him?" asked Valmak, breaking the strained silence.

The doctor shook her head. 'Another damn fool question.'

Valmak decided he better leave, then suddenly remembered that his own crewman, Gordon Kursal, was still a patient.

"How is Kursal?"

She looked at Valmak solemnly without answering.

"I need him back, Doctor."

"Then you will have to wait, Captain," she told him firmly. "He was so traumatised – in much the same way as Sol – that his mind won't allow the outside world in. Until he does, he won't be going anywhere."

"You refer to the alien by his first name," commented Valmak, sounding suspicious.

"You know nothing, Captain, so just go."

Valmak realised there was little else he could do. "Well, if there is anything you need—"

Doctor Summers glared at him with anger in her eyes. She didn't want him there any longer.

"—then just say, Doctor," he went on. "Anything you need, and if you find anything in the files let me know." Valmak knew if he apologised, she probably wouldn't believe him, so it was best he just left.

When he'd gone Doctor Summers pulled up a chair and sat beside Sol. If there was the slightest chance of bringing him back to reality, she would be there for him. Holding his hand firmly, she talked to him in a soft voice about all the things they could do together, places they would visit, even going to Earth.

She had already decided this would be her last tour of duty. When she got home, she was resigning from the company and taking a very long vacation. And she wanted Sol to be there with her.

Sol, though, was still staring at the ceiling, his eyes open, staring up but seeing nothing. It was simply part of the outside world he wanted nothing to do with.

*

Repairs to Retriever-2 were near completion and the ship was now fully functional, with any cosmetic details put on the back burner for the time being. Nobody wanted to stay longer than necessary. While the ship had been motionless, it would have been an easy target for space pirates, which had been a concern for everyone. Now they wanted to go home, and the crew were feeling more relaxed at the prospect of seeing their families again.

However, no sooner had the communication system been reconnected than Earth mission HQ made contact with another matter of priority. Valmak, now present on the bridge, received the order himself but chose to ignore it. He replied that the ship was non-operational for the time being and could not assist anyone. He had his own agenda first.

Maintaining a steady orbit above Kangis-3, final repairs now complete, the crew assumed Captain Valmak would give the order to head for Earth. A long vacation was looking good, and many were making plans for their arrival.

Valmak, though, had other ideas, and made it absolutely clear to his crew they were going nowhere until the mystery of Kangis-3 had been solved, along with the disappearance of Doctor Forester and finding the murderers of seven crew. They still had no idea the identity of the eighth body.

The captain also had to decide what to do about the alien on board and the strange spaceship they had picked up. He had a lot to think about.

King was not happy with the captain's announcement, and he approached the control seat to reason with him.

"Captain, the crew are exhausted. They have worked hard on the repairs and thought they were heading back to Earth.

Six years in space is a long tour of duty. Why don't we just go home?" he pleaded, hoping to find a shred of decency in the captain.

Valmak saw the concern all over his face and knew the crew wanted to go home. It's what they'd worked hard for, but it didn't make a bit of difference. He had to pursue this course of action.

"We arrived at a planet which I am certain is not Kangis-3," he replied.

"What do you mean, sir?" King asked, confused by the captain's words.

"I believe the distress signal was a fake to lure us to this worthless planet. The question is why. Some grotesque lifeform down there murdered seven crew. Good crew. I want answers, King. I want justice." Valmak was forceful in his statement; he was determined.

"Is it justice you want, Captain, or revenge for something? Please, the crew have had enough, we all want to go home," he pleaded again.

"Go back to your station, King, this is not for negotiation. We have a mission to complete."

King could see that the captain was more determined than ever to follow a destructive path. Angry and dispirited, he returned to his station fuming, logging comments into the memory banks, wondering if all this effort was worthwhile. Something told him they would never make it back to Earth if Valmak didn't back down.

The captain ordered an extensive search of all sectors of the planet surface. He needed to know the exact location of the lifeform the computer had detected earlier. He assumed this single entity to be the slug creature but didn't know what else to call it. Having a familial match to Doctor Forester's DNA in the mist had to be a connection, but it was a disturbing one and totally illogical in Valmak's mind. In the light of the files he had found in Forester's quarters, he felt compelled to investigate.

He had no choice, but he would not go back down to the surface without being prepared. Once again Valmak called upon the expertise of Phasner and asked him if it was possible to re-calibrate the phasic guns to deliver a more deadly charge. The weapons hadn't been out of the armoury for quite some time, almost four years. There had been no cause to use them until now, but if ever a back-up plan was needed, this was it.

Phasner stood close to Valmak as he sat in his control seat and listened carefully to his captain and what he proposed.

"You do realise, sir, we are breaking every code in the book?" he said. "Not to mention what the company will do to us when we get home."

"I do, Phasner, and thank you for pointing it out. Will you do it anyway?" asked Valmak.

"Yes, sir," said Phasner immediately. There was no question about his loyalty to a senior rank.

"Good man, see to it and let me know when you have finished."

"Right away, Captain. Just how powerful do you want these phasic guns to be?"

"Deadly powerful." Valmak looked his officer in the eyes. "Do you understand?"

"I do, sir." Phasner left the bridge in no doubt what he had to do.

Valmak's next request stunned the entire crew, not least King, who sat quietly at his station livid with the captain's outrageous behaviour. A ship-wide announcement was made requesting volunteers to descend to the surface once more, but only if they had a strong stomach for the sight they would encounter. It then became apparent to everyone why Retriever-2 had not left orbit.

King naturally declined. He had no intention of leaving the ship, which was just as well, as it turned out Valmak wanted him on the bridge, pointing out he was second-in-command. *Not that it made any difference*, King thought. *When it came to his opinions, Valmak ignored them all.*

To King's surprise, several crew members came forward for what he viewed as a suicide mission. But some were friends of the dead crew, and they were with the captain one hundred percent without question.

Valmak proceeded to brief the volunteer crew what was expected of them, and he was relieved when none of them backed out. He was glad that he was not going alone. There was a good possibility they could bring the abandoned shuttle back, which would at least save him from one charge.

Before leaving the bridge, Valmak received yet another message from mission HQ.

"Sir, we are requested to return to Earth without further delay. Direct orders from the top," said Argent, relaying the message word for word and hoping the captain would comply this time.

"Inform mission HQ we have..." he paused for a second. "Tell them we have not completed our mission."

Argent hesitated, reluctant to do so, while King had to bite his tongue and once again note his feelings in the log, afraid to take direct action against his superior officer.

"When you have done that, Argent, cut all communication with mission HQ until further notice."

"Sir?"

"Just do it, man, we are not going home until the job is complete."

With that Valmak hurriedly left the bridge, eager to meet up with the volunteer crew. He hoped they could handle the difficult situation he was about to put them in.

*

Best friends Alec Zymotz and Nely Meki, normally helm officers, were preparing themselves for the task ahead. Having received the co-ordinates of the landed shuttle, they laid out a course for the planet surface. Meki, being his usual jittery self, was nervous. This was not his idea of fun, but his friend

Zymotz had volunteered him to join the party. For a moment he had even questioned their friendship and just hoped it was worth it.

Valmak sat at the back of the shuttle, fiddling with his phasic gun. He had put his trust in Phasner to make a better weapon and hoped it would be enough. He was just as frightened as the others, but he was eager to get to the surface. He had one thing on his mind: murder.

King had been right about him; he was out for revenge. But Valmak could not control his wayward thoughts and knew he had to do this.

The other shuttle crew, Carol Harding and Joe Whiting, sat in complete silence, reflecting on their own lives. This was a perilous task; it might even be their last. Harding, for her part, had volunteered against the wishes of Doctor Summers, but she had soon realised that working in the hospital was not for her, even though her brother Darryl had had some medical training. She'd signed up for action, not nursemaiding.

The shuttle landed smoothly, with none of the turbulence of the first descent. Valmak rose to his feet and peered out of the porthole to see the outline of those ominous black mountains. He knew they were in the right sector. He was more terrified than the crew right then but couldn't show it. They needed him to be strong and totally focussed.

Zymotz indicated he was ready to open the airlock, and all the crew were suited up in readiness. Whiting and Harding were keen to get the mission over, while Meki followed at the rear, always the reluctant one. Seconds later, they all stood outside, their heavy boots sinking in the black sand.

"Everyone, have your phasic guns set to maximum," said Valmak. They nodded, helmets on and quickly checking their radios.

"I want no heroes. We stay together at all times. Under no circumstances go it alone, understood?" he barked.

"Yes, sir," they all replied.

"And stay away from the slimy tracks," added Valmak.

A mist lingered over the horizon to the west of the mountain range, making Valmak wary. He would keep an eye on it.

As they slowly crunched their way over the rugged terrain, he realised that some of the boulders looked too uniform in shape. Previously Valmak had thought they were merely debris from long ago buildings, but now he discounted it. Nothing had ever existed on this desolate piece of rock. The atmosphere was too polluted.

With the mist far away in the distance, they had a clear view all round, and Valmak prayed the mist stayed away.

Soon the second shuttle was located, approximately thirty metres from their landing spot. On approach, Valmak prompted his crew to stay alert. He was sure they wouldn't like the next part.

"Okay, everyone, there are bodies around the shuttle. I want them examined."

"Really?" asked Meki. He definitely hadn't signed up for this.

"What are we looking for, sir?" asked Whiting.

"You'll know when you see it," replied Valmak, but privately he didn't know himself. "The other bodies are a short distance that way," he added, pointing eastward.

"Stay in pairs," he reminded them.

Suddenly he felt more concerned about facing the slug. It was here, that evil presence lingering in the air. But he hadn't told the crew about it, and for that he felt guilty.

Zymotz and Whiting went in search of their crew, while Meki and Harding followed close behind. Valmak kept watch on the surrounding area, keeping an eye on the mist. If it moved closer, they were in trouble. He also kept an eye on his crew, not wanting them to stray too far.

Before long they found the bodies of their friends, lying half sunk in the black soil. The captain hadn't been very forthcoming with the details, but this was worse than they had expected, and they felt physically sick at the sight. The mutilation was horrific, as if a rabid creature had run amok, clawing them to death and shredding their suits in the process. They hadn't stood a chance.

Searching the immediate area, they found nothing to tell them what had really happened.

Returning to Valmak, Zymotz said, "Thanks for that, Captain, we really needed to see that."

"Sorry, I know it was difficult," said Valmak. "Did you find any clues?"

"Nothing, sir," said Whiting.

"Okay, I want you to collect soil samples and anything else you deem relevant." All the while he was speaking, Valmak kept looking round, expecting trouble.

Half of him wanted something to happen, the other half was scared beyond belief. "Meki, Harding, check the other bodies and take samples as well, but be quick about it."

Although they thought it was a pointless exercise, they promptly did as they were asked, then returned.

"Captain, we checked all the bodies. Nothing really to report, except that we found a body that doesn't belong to our crew, it's—" said Meki.

"Yes, an alien," interrupted Valmak.

"How did you kn—?" asked Meki, before he was interrupted a second time.

"Never mind. Did you get samples?"

"Yes, sir."

"And from the alien?" Valmak wanted some for analysis.

"Yes, Captain, I got that," confirmed Harding, relieved to be back.

As Zymotz and Whiting returned with their samples, Valmak was still focussed on the landscape. He'd been watching the mist the entire time and was sure it was moving.

"Well done, everyone," said Valmak, pleased to see them all back safely. "Now, let's get out of here."

The crew were in full agreement.

"Zymotz, you and Whiting take all the samples and get airborne. We'll pilot the other shuttle; it isn't too far," he told them.

Zymotz and Whiting wasted no time in getting into the air, glad to be away. Meanwhile, Valmak led Meki and Harding to the other shuttle. Although he still wanted revenge, he was happy to leave this desolate place. Maybe there was nothing else he could do.

They were within a few feet of the shuttle when suddenly the mist dropped out of nowhere and they were instantly blinded.

"Captain, what the hell just happened?" yelled Meki. He knew Valmak was in front of him, but Harding wasn't sure of her whereabouts.

Valmak knew straight away that 'it' was back. "Guns ready!" he said loudly. "We have company."

As Harding went into complete panic mode and started screaming hysterically, Valmak stumbled in the direction of her screams and grabbed her arm.

"Quiet, Harding, get a hold of yourself. Focus." He was brutal as he dragged her along til they bumped into the shuttle. Another bump and Meki was safely there. Behind them came a loud, crunching sound, as the cracking of boulders drew closer.

"Captain, what is that?" cried Meki. He was terrified and sure he hadn't signed up for this shit, whatever it was.

"Stay alert, back to the shuttle, and have your guns ready, maximum power. Got it?" Valmak was still holding Harding, who was shaking all over. "Harding, you can do this. Answer me," he urged.

"Yes, yes, sir. I think so." She tried to calm down, but it was difficult to breathe properly inside her helmet.

"Good. Have your gun ready, ok?"

"Yes, sir," she said, her grip on her gun shaky.

"Stay focused," said Valmak, feeling the tension they were experiencing.

He hadn't told them everything, but he wasn't sure exactly what to expect himself. Valmak was determined to get this murderous slug creature once and for all and had no qualms about killing this thing, whatever it was. It went against all the rules he had honoured to keep, and it went against company policy, but right now that didn't matter to him. All reasoning left his body on hearing that eerie crunching sound coming out of the mist.

The unearthly sound was almost upon them, but they could not see a thing. Valmak knew the mist would clear and show them what they were up against. Then a strange gurgling noise echoed all around, like nothing they had ever heard before.

"Get ready," whispered Valmak. "Harding, are you ready?" He wanted to be sure she could do this deed.

"I think so, Captain," she quivered.

"Good, on my mark I want you to fire and keep firing. Don't stop."

With only feet away, the mist mysteriously thinned out without warning. Suddenly a shape was visible, a huge, grotesque, blob-like creature, about five feet high and expanding about six feet across, pulsating as it moved. Strange tentacles waved in the air with what could only be described as hands with claws.

Valmak and his two crew shrunk back in horror at the hideous sight. Meki was trembling out of control, and Harding froze on the spot. Slightly more focused, but only just, the captain prodded them to point their guns.

Then he gave the order. "Shoot!" he shouted.

In seconds, three high-powered laser beams hit the mass simultaneously, causing it to squeal. It was an odd sound as it felt pain as never before, recoiling on itself. It was obvious they were hurting it, so Valmak was relentless.

"Keep firing, but watch out for those tentacles," he warned, watching the claw-like hands getting too close for comfort.

Meki and Harding obeyed their captain but only out of fear. They did not want to be the next victims, and those claws looked lethal.

The blob mass began shrinking further, getting smaller with each blast of their phasic guns. Suddenly a scream from the blob shocked them into stopping for a second.

A croaky voice yelled out, "Stop, you're killing me. Stop."

"What the—!" Aghast at what he thought he'd heard, Meki froze.

Harding lowered her gun. "What was that?" she cried out.

"Help me, help me..." the croaky voice rang out again. It was definitely coming from within the mass as it continued to shrink.

Valmak vaguely thought he recognised the voice. Although slightly distorted with the croakiness, he could have sworn it was Doctor Forester's.

"It's not possible. It can't be," he muttered. "It's just a giant killing slug."

He had to finish it off, because if it recovered it would surely finish them off.

"Keep firing, you two, we have to destroy this monster," he told them.

Meki and Harding raised their guns again. But the mass shrieked louder in agony, shrinking even further, its tentacles withdrawing into its body. Again, it cried out for mercy.

"Stop! Stop!" The croaky voice was weakening by the second, becoming much fainter. "Please stop," it said.

"I think it's dying, Captain," Meki said, still shooting into the heart of the mass.

Harding didn't stop either. She too was sure she recognised the voice, having worked with Doctor Forester in his lab once or twice. But seeing the hideous blob up close and coming at her in a menacing manner didn't prevent her finishing the job. She didn't like Forester anyway; he was rather creepy for her.

Meki kept firing until his phasic gun went dead. "Out of charge, Captain."

"Same here, sir," said Harding.

Then Valmak's also went dead.

By then the blob was motionless, a small mass of dead cells a mere twenty centimetres across. The mist had miraculously disappeared, too, and that air of evil had gone.

The three of them slumped back against the hull of the shuttle, staring at the sight. Meki thought, *What the hell did we just do?*

Harding fell to her knees, sinking into the soil, doing her best not to vomit inside her helmet. Meki put a glove on her shoulder for comfort.

"What just happened, Captain?" he asked.

Valmak wasn't sure. *Had he managed to rid his mind of the evil for good?* He hoped so.

"Is it dead?" asked Harding, in tears. The release of emotional tension was too much for her.

"Think so," said Valmak.

"Please tell me you heard it cry out, Captain," spluttered Harding. "Just tell me what we heard, because right now I don't want to believe it."

Valmak was speechless for once, struggling with his own emotional stress. *Had he really heard Doctor Forester in that mass? Was it him metamorphosed?*

"I–I heard something," was all he could say.

"Well, I definitely heard a voice," said Meki, as he helped Harding to her feet.

It was some minutes before they could gather their thoughts and focus. They had committed murder of an alien species, although they were not sure if that was okay to save their own lives. Valmak was sure it wasn't in the rule book, so it probably was a crime.

"Can we go home now?" asked Harding. She was not up to this kind of action and would not be volunteering again.

Valmak nodded. "We have to take the remains of that thing back for analysis."

"Is it safe to touch?" asked Meki.

"Well, I'm not picking it up," said Harding.

"Meki, go and get the shuttle prepped for take-off. Harding, you bring me one of the containers from the shuttle, then we can go."

Valmak felt a wave of relief that they had all survived this time. He'd got lucky again, but there was still a pang of guilt at what he'd done. There was more to this than killing a slug. That haunting voice they'd heard had been disturbing, and he struggled to get it out of his head. They'd all heard it, and still they'd killed it. They'd had no option. Valmak had assumed he would feel better and be able to rid the demons from his head. But he did not.

Cautiously he picked up the small mass, which was smouldering a bit from the intense laser beams. His hands were trembling, frightened the creature might suddenly move.

Harding opened the container for him. "Oh Christ, Captain, what are we doing?"

"What we have to. Let's get inside and back to the ship."

*

An expression of pain, then a grimace, suggested to Doctor Summers that Sol was having a nightmare. He was obviously agitated by the bad dreams and restless, but it wasn't the first one he'd had. Sol was battling to release his inner demons, but the emotional stress he was under was not letting up. Doctor Summers would have given anything to know what was going on inside his head. She talked to him endlessly, hoping the words would trigger his mind into reality. And she held his hand, not wanting to leave his side, praying that a tightening of his hand would indicate some recognition. But there was nothing.

Sol refused to communicate. His mind was his sanctuary, and he couldn't leave it. He did hear the soft voice of the woman he loved, but to acknowledge it meant leaving his inner sanctum, and he didn't want that reality, only his own.

That way he could block out the bad memories which Captain Valmak had given him.

Over and over Sol acted out his thoughts, answering his own questions, punishing himself for the wrong answers, then the nightmares would start again. *What was the right answer?* In his nightmarish state, anger, bitterness, and fear were the only emotions he could feel, bubbling up beneath the surface to the point where he had to yell out loud to release the anxiety.

The latest episode startled Doctor Summers, who momentarily dozed next to him, still holding his hand. But Sol went calm again, back into his world, while she kept up the vigil, refusing to give in. She would never give up on him.

When Kursal woke from his comatose state, it was one less worry for the medic. But he refused to speak and was unable to relate what he had seen on Kangis-3. Like Sol, the trauma had had a devastating effect on the mind. Doctor Summers could only hope Kursal's mind would heal slowly, and he would come round to the living, as there was nothing else, she could do for him.

Her main focus was Sol, and yet it seemed she couldn't do any more for him either. *How could she love a man who couldn't love her back?* It was heart-breaking. Nevertheless, she stayed with Sol. Nothing was going to move her.

*

While Valmak had been occupied on the planet surface, Phasner had been busy trying to unlock the personal files belonging to Doctor Forester, and he'd discovered some startling facts. Unfortunately, some of the data had been wiped clean and was irretrievable, but Phasner had enough data to piece together that the doctor had been dabbling in secret experiments in his laboratory, messing with DNA and certain genetic codes of living organisms. Unfortunately, he couldn't discover which organisms, as Forester had deliberately wiped those tapes. Phasner could only guess what he had stumbled on and wondered if maybe Forester had had an accident with his experiments.

Having seen the file on 'HUMAN CELL TISSUE', following the discovery of the second 'MOLECULAR CELL RESTRUCTURE', Phasner was convinced that Forester was as eccentric as everyone believed. But he decided this work was taking it to a whole new level; it was complete science fiction. To Phasner's mind, the man was a nutcase, meddling in something he shouldn't have.

Phasner discussed in detail his findings with Valmak on his return, and when they compared notes with what the captain told him of his encounter on the surface, the pieces started to fit together. Analysis of all the samples collected would confirm his theory. *The burning question, though, was why? Had an experiment really gone wrong for Forester, or had he done it deliberately?* None of the evidence explained how he had got to the planet without anyone realising he was missing.

Valmak vowed new protocols would be put in place regarding all personnel logging in on a daily basis. No-one was going missing again on his watch.

Phasner still had to work out the mystery of the deadly mist that had nearly destroyed the ship. That was confirmed as Forester's DNA, but again those particular tapes had been wiped clean. It was all conjecture for Phasner. He couldn't be sure it had been accidental, or if Forester had created an intelligent mist to attack the ship in a bid to destroy all evidence of his work by draining the ship's power, which in turn would destroy the memory banks. That would have left Retriever-2 unable to operate or even find a way home. Phasner thought it was a distinct possibility. He did agree with Valmak that they might never find the answers, so Phasner decided to leave the file open and walk away from the investigation for now. He had other duties to deal with.

Valmak arrived back on the bridge to a skeleton crew. King had ordered some of them to take a break, as they had all earned it, but he had stayed along with Denny Argent. He didn't like anyone else fiddling about with his station, so he sat glued to his monitors, listening for information and generally eavesdropping on any conversation going on in space.

He was still picking up messages from Earth mission HQ demanding Retriever-2 return to Earth with immediate effect. It seemed they were now in breach of company policy, theft of company property – e.g. one space rescue hospital ship – and violating several direct orders. As a result, a warrant for their arrest had been issued.

Argent wasn't sure what to do with the message, but he decided not to inform Valmak just yet. It wouldn't change things, as they were all in deep trouble. He guessed no promotions were coming their way now, as all the years of service meant nothing to the money-hungry company bosses.

Not long after that message, Argent picked up a faint sound which he recognised straight away. He tried to pinpoint its location and once he had it, he spoke to Valmak.

"Captain, I have picked something up on the long-range scanners. I believe it is a distress beacon from Retriever-3."

Valmak was surprised, having assumed the ship had been lost forever.

"Can you make contact with them, Argent?"

"No, sir, not yet. But I should say the distress beacon is automatic and has probably been emitting a signal for quite some time. And, sir, it's coming from the delta quadrant."

"What's it doing there?" Valmak was confused.

King was quick to answer. "Maybe answering a distress signal like we did, Captain."

"That is very possible, sir," added Argent.

Valmak agreed with his crew; something was definitely luring spaceships into a trap. He was pleased he had dealt with the slug creature, but that obviously wasn't the cause with Retriever-3. *Were they really in trouble, or was Retriever-2 being led into another trap?* He had a difficult decision to make.

"Should we at least investigate, sir?" asked Argent.

Valmak was still thinking. He had promised the crew they were going home, even if it meant he faced a court martial.

"How long will it take us to reach them?" he enquired.

"Less than a day, at hyper speed... that's if we can maintain that sir. Repairs were difficult, as we did have substantial damage," said King, pointing out the possible delays.

"Okay, we go, if only to find out why they went off grid. They may well need our help. I want the bridge crew back and at full alert," said Valmak.

"Captain, I think I have to point something out," said Argent, thinking this was not the best time to mention mission HQ.

"What is it, Argent? And it better be good," Valmak replied.

"Well, sir, apparently we are in breach of company policy, committed theft of company property, and we have been ordered back to Earth immediately," explained Argent, waiting for a possible backlash from the captain for holding back news.

"Anything else?" asked Valmak.

"Yes, sir, we're all under arrest for violating company protocol and disregarding direct orders."

"I guess that about covers everything, Captain," said King. They certainly couldn't throw anything else at them.

Valmak didn't think too long before he made his decision. He was fed up dealing with the bureaucrats on Earth who knew nothing of what was going on.

"We go. A retriever ship is in need of assistance. Is everyone agreed?" he asked.

The bridge crew and most of the ship were in agreement. Retriever-3 would do the same for them if required, so this was important to them.

Crew members all over the ship returned to work as Retriever-2 proceeded at maximum speed in the direction of the distress beacon which was still emitting its signal.

Valmak thanked them for returning to duty promptly. Once they had been made aware of the situation, there had been no question that Captain Valmak was making the right call.

"King, make sure that Carol Harding takes a little extra time off. She didn't handle the mission to Kangis-3 too well," said Valmak, taking to his control seat.

"Yes, sir. I also took the liberty of sending Straten back to the hospital to get his arm set properly," replied King.

"Good work, King."

King was slightly shocked that the captain appeared calmer and less offensive in his manner. He seemed to genuinely care about the crew, which was a welcome change. He didn't know how long it would last.

Valmak wanted every crew member to be aware of protocol being ignored by this mission, and that they would all effectively be under arrest. Anyone wishing not to take part could have it entered in the log. He hoped they would not face charges on their return to Earth, but this was the best he could do for them. He intended to take full responsibility himself.

"Helm, I want to know as soon as we get visual," he announced, breaking the silence on the bridge after many hours of travelling across space.

"Yes, Captain," replied Aztac. "I am scanning each sector as we approach it."

Valmak nodded. From his control seat he pondered over their actions as a crew, heading further and further away from Earth. There was only a slim chance anyone was still alive on Retriever-3, and heading for the notorious delta quadrant was not a prospect he relished. *What if they were to meet space pirates?* He knew he was asking a great deal from the crew.

He decided on another conversation with Phasner, whose skills were needed. The phasic guns were again being brought out, every last one. Valmak wanted them further modified and fully charged for action. He had a dreadful premonition that the guns would be needed for their defence. This time it was a premonition that didn't involve a certain alien, but these were desperate times and Valmak wanted to be prepared for whatever was coming.

The bridge crew were all busy monitoring the viewing screen or computing incoming data. Even King was exceptionally quiet in his work, not giving the captain grief about doing the right thing and doing everything by the book. Valmak was relieved that at least there was calm for now. They were a good crew, knowing exactly what had to be done, although he didn't tell them often enough how good they were.

Suddenly the silence was broken. "Captain, we have picked up a trace directly ahead," announced Zymotz.

Valmak leapt to his feet, eager to see. "Adjust monitors, full magnification now," he said.

They all watched the viewing screen, waiting for something to appear.

"Retriever-3! Captain, it's Retriever-3," said Zymotz excitedly.

"Can you detect any life signs?" asked Valmak. "I want confirmation."

"None at present, sir, but still searching. It does appear to be crippled."

"Argent, try calling them," said Valmak.

"Sir." Argent was on it immediately. He got no response, then tried again, but still nothing.

"There is evidence of attack, Captain," relayed Zymotz. As the ship drew closer, the damage became apparent.

"No response on the intercom," said Argent, as he turned his head to see that Retriever-3 was indeed in bad shape. A gaping hole could be seen in the bulkhead near the main decks three and four, which housed the communication section.

"What could have done that?" said King, now standing closer to the viewing screen. It was a scene of devastation floating in space.

"Obviously someone has no respect for a hospital ship," said Valmak. They stared in disbelief, wondering how anyone could do this to a rescue ship.

"Report is back, sir. Long-range scanners say no life signs at all," reported Aztac in a more subdued manner.

"Captain, there were four hundred and six crew and passengers aboard Retriever-3," King told him. One of them was his brother Tom, a first-rate engineer.

"I'm sorry, King," said Valmak, with genuine compassion in his voice for once. He had met the younger brother many years before and been convinced he was destined to go far.

Silence followed on the bridge for a few moments; the grief was immense.

"Sir, we must go aboard to investigate," said King. He needed to know if his brother was alive or not.

"Is that the right thing to do, King?" queried Valmak.

"Probably not, sir," he admitted.

But without any hesitation Valmak agreed. "Ok, King, we'll go check it out. We all need answers."

"Thank you, sir. I would like to volunteer for this mission."

Valmak knew he couldn't refuse his first officer, who needed to do this, if only for his brother.

"Go. Select your crew, but weapon up and take no chances. I can't lose any more men," said Valmak.

"Captain, I do believe you care," King replied almost flippantly.

The captain frowned. "Get out of here, King, before I change my mind."

"Yes, sir."

King swiftly left the bridge, eager to find out what had happened to Retriever-3 but scared for his brother. The last thing he'd said to his parents six years earlier was that he would take care of his little brother. But without warning Tom had been assigned to Retriever-3 while he'd remained on Retriever-2, and they had not seen each other since.

"Helm, manoeuvre us into position, check oxygen supply on Retriever-3 hasn't been compromised, then activate the airlock system. When you've done that, relay all data to King and his team," said Valmak.

"Right away, sir," replied Aztac.

"Monitor our crew all the way, and do not lose them," added Valmak. He had real concern this was not going to end well. That feeling of death came over him again and he could not shake it off. But it was something he couldn't share with his crew and just had to deal with himself.

*

Passing through the airlock to the adjoining ship, King and his two crew entered the lower section of Retriever-3. The gaping hole luckily was on the portside, and King hoped the inner bulkhead was still intact. Receiving data from Aztac told them the air supply was sufficient, so they flipped their visors up.

"Okay, guys, stay alert," said King. "Have your weapons ready. Computers said no life, but I'm not so sure." He was eager to know what had happened, his brother at the forefront of his mind.

Michele Torrence and Steve Brown accompanied King into a long corridor which would lead them to the main part of the hospital. Reaching the intersection, they suddenly stopped dead in their tracks. A gruesome sight awaited them. Dead bodies lay everywhere; bloody carnage was the only way to describe such a horrific scene.

"Oh my god!" screamed Torrence. She hadn't expected to be confronted with death in such a grisly way, and suddenly her feet were frozen to the floor, and she couldn't move forward.

King edged closer to the bodies. Even with the blood-splattered clothing, it was evident by the uniforms that this was the crew. Their uniforms had been ripped open, exposing a sickening sight of mutilation, bodies torn apart – possibly while they had still been alive. It was a massacre beyond belief.

King felt sick to his stomach at the horror. *What of his brother? How would he deal with his loss, and how could he tell his mum and dad?* He looked both ways of the intersection, and everywhere bodies lay in the corridors. No wonder Retriever-3 had gone offline; they were already dead.

Brown approached one of the bodies and knelt down to examine it for clues. "King, I think you better take a look at this."

"Really, Brown, you want me to get closer?" King was already feeling queasy.

"Just look, sir." Brown had completed a few shifts in the hospital and knew what he was looking at, having read several manuals Doctor Summers had insisted he study. "This body is missing all its vital organs," he announced.

"What?"

"I'm guessing the others will be much the same." Brown got up and checked the next body a few feet away, then another. "Yep, same here, sir. Vital organs all missing." Brown ventured further along the corridor, bodies of the crew everywhere, all the same. It didn't make sense to him.

"Why didn't they put up a fight?" he asked, not really expecting a reply.

King finally pulled himself together, doing his best not to gag at the sight. He was a senior officer and had a job to do. He just prayed his brother was not among the dead, but he didn't hold out much hope of finding him alive.

Looking round, he shouted to Torrence, who was still too afraid to move an inch. He had to snap her out of it.

"Torrence, get here now!" he ordered.

She followed Brown and King, very reluctantly, passing body after body, all mutilated, the corridors covered with blood.

"How far do we have to go, sir?" she managed, unsure how much further she could go.

"We have to get to the main computer deck. We need the memory bank disks," King replied. "I need you two to check anything out of the ordinary, something that might help us."

"And what we're looking at isn't out of the ordinary?" yelled Torrence.

"Then you stay here while we investigate, ok?" King was trying to be sympathetic, but they had to press on. He didn't want to be here any longer than necessary.

"I'm not staying here alone," she said, and pushed on with them. It was the lesser of two evils.

Eventually arriving on the main computer deck, Brown extracted all the memory disks which could be analysed later.

King had gone ahead, saying he needed to check something out, while Torrence was still lagging behind. She was just about managing to take it all in when she noticed something out of place and called Brown back.

"This body is different, Brown, come and take a look."

He went back, thinking she might be overreacting. "What is it, Torrence?"

She pointed down to the body she was standing over. "This body is not human, and it is intact. No missing organs."

"That is strange," he agreed.

"Didn't Captain Valmak say an alien had been found on Kangis-3?" she asked.

"Yes, so what's your point?" Brown was slow on the uptake.

"Well, this scene is different to what the captain described."

"He described it to you?" Brown was surprised.

"No, silly, it's in the logs. Don't you read them? Never mind. This is different, and this alien could be connected with Kangis-3."

"It's a bit of a stretch, Torrence. We're light years from Kangis-3, so how can it be connected?" It didn't make sense to him.

"I don't know," she replied. "I don't have all the answers."

"Okay, I agree it's not right, so take tissue samples and the science lab can investigate."

"So, I get the good jobs, do I?" she replied.

"Just do it, Torrence." Brown exercised his seniority, although he was certain it was a job he didn't want to do either.

King returned moments later, having surveyed as much as his stomach allowed him. He'd gathered the data he wanted.

"Did you find out anything, sir?" asked Brown.

Suddenly King noticed Torrence doing something to one of the bodies. "What the hell is she doing?"

"Taking samples, sir. It's an alien body, so I thought we should—"

"Yes, yes, quite. Good man," said King. "Are you sure she is up to it?" he added.

"So long as she doesn't puke on the samples, she'll be fine. What did you find, sir?"

"I went to the bridge to access the main computer scanners. Ship's log says there were only three hundred and fifty-five bodies aboard this ship. That doesn't say what happened to the other fifty-one, if we discount the alien body, of course." King suddenly thought about his brother. *Could he have escaped?* He hoped so.

"Can we leave now sir?"

"Yes, let's get off this death ship," King agreed.

*

Back safely on Retriever-2, King reported his findings straight away to Valmak, who listened intently. The captain wasn't surprised with such news; that sense of death was constantly in his head and was a sign of something about to happen.

"Brown has taken the memory disks to be analysed, but I'm not sure if they can tell us anything. And I sent the alien tissue samples to the lab for testing," King reported.

"Well done, King. I have a feeling the DNA of this alien will match the dead alien on Kangis-3."

"How do you know that sir?" King was puzzled. The captain was behaving weirdly again.

"I just know, King, trust me," he replied.

"Torrence didn't handle it too well – none of us did actually. I relieved her of duty for now."

Valmak agreed, but he started thinking nasty thoughts again, becoming detached from normality. He had no control.

"So, what now, sir?" King asked, unaware how his captain was feeling. "Sir, what now?" he asked again.

Valmak snapped back. "For once, King, I have no idea."

"What about going home?"

"Yes, home," said Valmak. "Mission HQ are demanding our immediate return, so let's go home and face the music."

"Yes, sir. What about our arrest, though?"

"I will sort it, King. None of the crew will be held accountable for my actions."

King was grateful that the captain was showing compassion and wished it was something he did more often. "So how do we tell them about Retriever-3?" He thought it was a valid question, as they would need to make a report at least.

Valmak, though, didn't have the answers. His problems were stacking up on Retriever-2. Now they had unknown aliens stalking the galaxy, murdering and stealing body parts. It was bizarre. *How could they stop it by going home? And could they live with themselves if they did?* He stood on the bridge in silence for several minutes, trying to work out the mystery and what to do about it.

"Captain… Captain, what are you thinking?" asked King. The captain's expression suggested he was somewhere else other than on the bridge.

"Spare parts!" announced Valmak loudly.

"Say again?" said King, stunned. The bridge crew looked round at the captain's sudden outburst.

"Spare parts, King, it's the only explanation," repeated Valmak, convinced he had the answer.

"You've lost me, Captain. I have no idea what you are talking about."

"Get with it, King. Think, man," Valmak snapped. "Somebody is harvesting vital body parts for transplanting."

King nodded. "Makes sense, I guess, but barbaric in these times."

"Yes, I agree. If only we knew who."

"Space pirates?" asked King.

"No, this is not their doing. It doesn't fit with everything the pirates have done before."

"So, who then?" asked King, hoping the captain might have the answer.

"That I don't know, King. So, what do we do now?"

"Sir?"

"Go home like we agreed, or stay and hunt down these savages?"

"Well, Captain," King sighed. "We're damned if we do, and damned if we don't."

"Stay?" asked Valmak.

"Stay, Captain." For once King was in agreement that it was the right thing to do. Besides, he desperately wanted to find out what happened to his brother, so the company could whistle for their return. The crew would have to wait a little longer before they saw home again.

*

Alone in his quarters once more, Valmak wanted to study the data on Doctor Forester in private. He was in no doubt the man had meddled with the natural order of things, but how and why remained a complete mystery. So much of Forester's work was incomplete due to the missing files and other sensitive information he'd wiped clean from the memory banks.

The mist that had attacked the ship had definitely been Forester's doing; DNA proved that beyond a doubt. But the mist hadn't managed to wipe everything clean, and there were still incomplete files, one mentioning Doctor Ken Marland which Valmak thought very strange. Marland had had no dealings with Forester, as far as he could recall, unless he was trying to hide evidence of something.

Valmak remembered there had been some suspicion at the time over Marland's death. *Was Forester involved? Was he trying to cover his tracks?* Valmak struggled to get his head round the fact that Forester had felt the need to experiment on himself. *What was the man trying to achieve?* It certainly wasn't immortality. It changed his physical being at a molecular level. *Was that meant to happen, or had he got it wrong?*

Perhaps Forester wanted a higher level of intelligence and ended up with something at the wrong end of the scale, the captain mused. He'd used the mist to destroy the ship and all the files he hadn't yet deleted, but Valmak had thwarted him.

In the end, the captain put the file down then entered into the ship's log: 'Doctor Karlton Forester, missing in action, presumed dead.' No way was he going to mention a slug. *Who would believe him?*

Extreme fatigue finally took over and Valmak fell asleep, rest long overdue. Before long, nightmares returned, and impending doom filled his dreams. The alien on board had caused so much stress and grief. *Why did he pick him up in the first place?* He should have left him behind. *Was he really connected with the evil foreboding that plagued Valmak's waking hours? Was he also connected to the mysterious alien spaceship they'd picked up?*

There was so much hurt in his dreams, and Kangis-3 played a big part. Retriever-2 had definitely not finished with that evil planet.

CHAPTER SIX

The burning sun began to set over the horizon, the heat remaining intense, and there was to be no let-up as nightfall approached. Nights were as hot as the days and getting worse. The temperature of the sun increased daily, and the people of Naasook had to escape their planet or perish in the blistering conditions. They were running out of time.

The slaves dragged their weary feet as they were whipped back to their cells to spend another sweltering night in appalling conditions, hungry, in agony, and dehydrated. Their captors had little compassion for their wellbeing, and it mattered not to them that the slaves were suffering. They didn't care that the workers had been all day in the exhausting heat, toiling under arduous conditions against their will, just as long as their captors didn't have to do the work themselves. The Naasooks were a lazy race of beings, but they were also going to die if the work wasn't completed.

The sun took its toll on the slaves every day, and even the fittest of men would succumb to the conditions eventually. The tyrannical guards locked up the last few stragglers in their cells and left them to the night, knowing some would possibly not make it until morning. It was unfortunate but inevitable.

"The schedule is falling further behind, Qrotei. We must do something about it," said one of the guards. A tall lean man, Oston was sweating profusely from the humidity of the evening.

His sidekick – a tiny hunchback, malformed soon after birth – simply waved his arm in the air. "What can we do to step up the production? The task is getting harder each day." He finished winding up his whip and thrust it inside his belt.

"The grandmaster will be displeased when he finds out."

"Yes, Oston," agreed Qrotei. "But we must have more slaves to do the work. Fifteen slaves died today, and more are sick. These inferior aliens cannot survive the intensity of the sun's rays for very long."

Oston agreed with his little friend, who had to run to keep up, his dwarfed legs taking twice as many steps.

"What are we going to do?" asked Qrotei, as they wearily walked away from the slave camp to take refuge in the cooler confines of their homes.

"I will think of something, Qrotei. Let's get out of the heat first." Oston was aware that a hundred or more aliens had arrived on Naasook that day, but they were not yet conditioned to work, as the brainwashing was taking longer than usual. He didn't know why.

The process, though, had to be speeded up, and extra workers were urgently needed to build the spaceships they needed. Oston suggested they should visit the high priest Zumus that very evening to make a report on the growing crisis. It was in all their interests if they wanted to escape this planet.

Qrotei agreed and they arranged to meet later that evening. Zumus was less grumpy when it got cooler after dark, albeit only marginally.

That evening, arriving at the palatial home of high priest Zumus, Oston banged on the heavy door and waited. Qrotei was still negotiating the many steps, his short legs not good for climbing.

"I hope he is in a good mood," said Qrotei, panting heavily as he reached the top step.

Finally, Zumus appeared at the door.

"Ah, Oston – and Qrotei, I see." Zumus couldn't disguise the fact that he disliked Qrotei intensely, regarding him as an under breed of the Naasook race.

Qrotei was always made to feel inadequate by Zumus, but he couldn't help the way he was. He nodded to Oston and descended the steps to wait for his friend at the bottom. He wondered why he'd even bothered going up.

Oston went inside. "I wish you wouldn't show such resentment to Qrotei, high priest," he said, defending his friend. "He does have feelings, despite his physical disability."

Zumus didn't care. He escorted Oston into a luxurious anteroom of his home, set atop the crest of a small mountain on the edge of the city. Outside, Qrotei sat on the bottom step, exhausted by the heat and the twenty or so steps he had just scaled and descended.

Oston followed Zumus into another room – one more fitting, it seemed, for a high priest. Surrounded by sheer opulence, there were gold encrusted busts of all the high priests preceding Zumus. One day he hoped to have his image immortalised, but unfortunately it would not be on this planet. Naasook was doomed, and all the priceless gems, gold, and platinum would not save their home. Once the spaceships were built, the Naasooks would escape the deadly sun and take all their possessions with them to a new world.

"Tell me, Oston, why do you hang around that hideous little being Qrotei? He should have been killed at birth. We cannot keep breeding inferior hunchback monsters like him. What will become of our status in the galaxy?" Zumus was brutal with his words, always quick to make nasty aspersions about the lower ranks.

"He's my friend," said Oston. "And we won't have any status at all if the work schedule isn't stepped up. The ships will not be completed on time. We need more slaves, and we need them now."

"Oh." Zumus was not pleased with the news. It sounded serious, but it didn't stop him reaching out for the jewelled covered jug to pour himself a goblet of wine. He had a dreadful thirst; doing nothing all day was tiring in this heat.

"You will join me in a drink, Oston?"

Oston nodded and took a goblet, thankful for a satisfying indulgence not normally offered to lower ranks like himself.

"Now, tell me why you disturbed me tonight." Zumus sank into his soft chair, thinking how comfortable it felt. The solid gold armrest gleamed in the artificial lighting.

"It's like I said, your excellency, the schedule is falling behind further every day. Slaves are dying in huge numbers. They cannot stand the sun's rays for any length of time, so we need new prisoners urgently. Beings that can tolerate the deadly rays." Oston pleaded his case earnestly.

"And what do you want from me?" asked Zumus lazily, reaching out to fill his goblet with more wine.

"More slaves, now!" Oston announced loudly, forgetting where he was for a moment. It was not appropriate to raise one's voice to the high priest of Naasook.

Zumus drank some of his wine while mulling over the problem. "This is really your responsibility, Oston," Zumus reminded him. "How far behind schedule are we exactly?" he asked.

"Six days, your excellency, and it will be worse tomorrow."

Zumus jumped up – probably the most exercise he had had all day – and slammed his goblet down in a temper, splashing the wine over the table. "Six days? It was only two days last week. How can you let it get out of control?" He was furious with Oston. "You must step up production," he added.

"I cannot help the slaves dying. We must rush the process on the new prisoners, and we will need many more. Please, your excellency, I must have more slaves," pleaded Oston again.

Zumus nodded. He knew Oston was right, but he wasn't happy that he would have to do something about it. The Naasooks were a notoriously lazy race of people and Zumus was no exception.

"Very well. I will speak to the grandmaster," he said.

"Tonight?"

"Yes, yes tonight, Oston. Now go." He was growing impatient.

"You will send out the robot ships immediately then?" Oston persisted.

"Go, Oston. Leave it with me." He waved the man away, tired of his presence.

Oston departed hurriedly, descending the steps to meet up with Qrotei.

"What did he say?" asked his friend.

"He will speak with the grandmaster tonight."

"Then the robot ships will go out again?" asked Qrotei.

"Guess so. Let's go home. It's been a long day."

*

Zumus entered the grandmaster's inner chamber, deep inside the mountain where it was cooler. Zumus didn't visit too often, as the grandmaster was old and didn't always like to be disturbed in his inner sanctum. He remained mostly in semi-darkness, much preferring to stay in the shadows. No-one even knew his true identity or what he looked like. Apparently, no-one could ever remember seeing him.

Having requested an audience with his eminence, Zumus relayed the problem in detail. The grandmaster remained seated in a corner of the room, dressed in a black hooded cloak. Zumus couldn't see him but knew he was there.

The grandmaster said very little but was aware what had to be done. He only had ten robot spaceships left to use – ones the Naasooks had purloined from another race many centuries ago. But the problem was that the robots were obsolete; working but primitive.

The grandmaster, though, was confident they would deliver. He moved slowly from his seat to a panel in the wall and into a control room housing a huge computer complex. Switching the machines on, lights flashed into action and another switch activated the robot spaceships already in orbit. A new flight path was programmed, and the robots immediately responded, leaving their dormant chambers to take control of their ships.

The grandmaster suddenly became weary as he made his way back to his seat. He was feeling every one of his hundred and sixty years, fearing he would not live to see a new world for his people. He sat down and closed his eyes.

The robots left orbit with a destination unknown, their mission to seek out and capture aliens to become slaves. It didn't seem to concern the Naasooks that they would die if they didn't leave their home planet. They were lazy, slothful, and didn't want to do the construction themselves. But captured alien prisoners couldn't last very long under the scorching rays of the sun that was pulling their planet towards it.

Naasook was burning up, but the Naasooks were desperate to survive. Unfortunately, thousands of years of indolence as a way of life had inhibited the growth of any kind of industry. They just didn't want to do the work themselves, so slaves were needed to build spaceships for them to escape. It was how they survived.

*

On the bridge of Retriever-2 Valmak stood to attention by his control seat, suddenly watching the viewing screen, waiting impatiently for something to appear. He wanted action. The pursuit of the perpetrators who had killed the crew of Retriever-3, and the despicable act of removing the victims' vital organs, could not go unpunished. He wanted justice, but that task weighed heavily on Valmak's shoulders. The crew had agreed not to go home as planned, not until the murderers were found and dealt with. Their captain was determined not to fail.

All communication with Earth mission HQ was severed, though Argent kept a line open to know what was happening. He needed to know for himself but didn't tell the captain, who was not interested in anything the authorities had to say.

Retriever-2 had a new mission; one they were going to carry out no matter what. But Valmak realised their biggest problem was their limited weapons. Phasic guns were not ideal to fight space pirates or any other hostile confrontation, so something more powerful was needed. Valmak set Tom Phasner and other officers a task of designing and constructing a weapon that would make their ship battle-ready – or at least allow them to defend themselves.

Phasner had a plan, but it required robbing materials from just about every deck on the ship, so he drafted in several crew to assist him. His idea of a phasic blast, able to fire from the ship, seemed the only option. His plan was full of risk, but it might just save their lives.

Staying alert was vital, so helm crew changed every few hours to make sure no-one became fatigued. Every sector of space was scanned and logged into the computer's memory banks. It might be needed to chart their way home.

Hours soon turned into days as the search went on. Sooner or later Retriever-2 would run into aliens somewhere. *But would they find the space pirates the intergalactic authorities were hunting? Or was there another enemy they had to deal with?*

Valmak wanted answers and he wanted results. He had to redeem himself before going back to Earth to face the authorities and knew he couldn't run forever.

Cal Bartok sat at the station previously occupied by Gordon Kursal and was promptly given the task of reviewing and cataloguing all data regarding Doctor Forester. It was something Valmak couldn't quite let go, and he hoped Bartok would find something he'd missed.

Bartok took the job on, continuing for many hours, using every permutation available to find a solution. Each time the computer failed to completely analyse the input, insisting there was insufficient data to draw any logical conclusion. All tissue samples had been examined several times, even the dead blob matter Valmak had brought back. The DNA was

Doctor Forester's, without a doubt, but they already knew that. The big problem was the computer calculations refused to acknowledge that a blob had any bearing on the proceedings.

Bartok thought it very strange that the computer was unable to make logical deduction. The science of molecular transformation did not compute as a genuine hypothesis, so the computer rejected it.

Eventually he presented everything he had – and it wasn't much – to the captain. They decided to log it all into the memory banks and put the problem to bed for now.

Valmak still had an inkling that Forester was guilty of Marland's death. He wondered if Marland had found out what Forester was up to. It was a likely scenario, but there just wasn't the evidence to back it up.

It didn't matter anymore. Retriever-2 had other priorities now. Bartok turned his attention to assisting the helm crew mapping space, recording star clusters, nebulae, and searching the galaxy for space pirates.

*

Into the eighth day of their search, Alec Zymotz at the helm suddenly picked up a positive trace on their viewing screen. Not sure what it was, he wanted a better look, so enlarged the picture to maximum, computing its course in the process. It was then he alerted Valmak to take a look.

"What is it?" asked the captain, coming down from his control seat to the viewing screen.

As the trace approached, Zymotz realised it was more than a single body. "Captain, several spaceships on a direct course to us."

"Confirmed, sir," added Meki, springing into action. "Computer says they are of alien origin."

"Can we get an exact flight path?" asked Valmak, not comfortable that several ships were heading their way.

"According to the computer, the ships are on a collision course with Retriever-2. They're coming straight for us, sir," warned Zymotz. The crew started to get edgy at the thought of a confrontation. They were not ready for it.

"How many ships are there?" asked Valmak.

"Ten, sir," said Zymotz. "All in formation" he added.

"Should we hail them, sir?" asked Argent.

"Yes, request their intentions and advise them to change their heading."

King remained at his station, attempting to analyse the strange ships to get an angle on their identity, but he wasn't having much luck.

Anxious moments went by while Argent tried to establish a link with the oncoming ships. "No response, Captain. No reply, but I'm receiving a weird sound coming through the intercom system. It's causing interference on all channels, and I can't stop it.

"Switch everything off, Argent. They obviously don't want to play ball." Valmak didn't care for the lack of communication, which suggested hostile to him. Suddenly that evil sense of foreboding crept back into his head. He'd managed to block it for a while, but now it was back worse than before.

"Captain, I have completed a scan of the alien ships," said Bartok.

"Do we know who they are?" he asked.

"No, sir, but this is strange. All ten ships are on autopilot and, get this, there's a single robotic lifeform aboard each ship."

Valmak looked round at Bartok, stunned. "Robots?"

"Yes, sir, the scans suggest they are not that sophisticated – probably the reason the ships are on autopilot. But that's only my theory."

Staring back at the viewing screen, Valmak seemed perplexed. "A fleet of robot ships? What the hell would they be up to, I wonder?"

It was a rhetorical question, and no-one attempted to answer.

"Orders, sir?" asked Meki.

But Argent butted in before he could answer. "Captain, we have a major problem."

"What is it?" asked Valmak, worried by the escalating situation. He suddenly wasn't feeling quite as courageous as he'd first thought.

"I switched everything off like you said, sir, but that weird sound is still coming through. It's a humming sound coming directly from the alien ships. It's going all round the ship."

This wasn't something Valmak had anticipated and was beyond weird. *What could it possibly mean? There was danger,* he knew that for certain, *but could he handle ten approaching alien ships who obviously weren't in a talkative mood?*

"Sir, reports are coming in from all decks. Some of the crew are acting strangely, like they're in a trance," announced Argent.

Valmak realised these robot ships were hostile and now showing their hand. "See what you can do to block it out, but stay alert," he commanded.

Bartok was scanning the robot ships in search of more data, to perhaps find a weakness they could exploit. His hearing had not yet been affected by the strange humming sound, but he still had to act fast, as he could see the helm crew were not as alert as they should be.

After a quick study of the probe, Bartok had an inkling of what it was all about, but there was no time to lose. "Earplugs!" he announced loudly.

Valmak and King looked at him as if he had suddenly lost his marbles.

"What are you on about, Bartok?" King asked abruptly.

"Explain yourself, Bartok, we don't have a lot of time," said Valmak.

"The sound coming through, I think it might be a form of induced hypnosis. The robots wouldn't be affected by it. And if we're all paralysed, they could simply attack us. Why else would the crew start behaving weirdly? It has to be, Captain."

Valmak couldn't work out how the officer had arrived at such an incredulous logic, but it did make sense.

"And the earplugs?" he asked.

"To block out the sound. We have ample supply on board that have never been used, enough for everyone. We have to distribute them to the crew immediately."

"He's right, Captain, we must act," said King, starting to feel strange.

"Issue the order now," agreed Valmak.

"Sir, the robot ships have taken control of all communications throughout the ship," said Argent. "They are overriding the system to enhance the sound, so the intercoms won't work."

"Ok, go with Bartok. We'll do it the old-fashioned way. Get the earplugs to every deck as soon as possible," ordered Valmak, then turned to the helm. They needed a little more time to distribute the equipment. "Full reverse speed at once. Let's put some distance between us," he said.

But helm did not respond. Meki sat at his station staring into oblivion, as did Zymotz, both having succumbed to the hypnotic sound.

King, struggling to stay alert, launched his body across the bridge to hit the controls. Retriever-2 suddenly jerked then shot into reverse, leaving the robot ships in the distance. The humming sound faded slightly, and King staggered to his feet, still a bit lightheaded, and sure he had just cracked a rib on landing badly on the floor along with everyone else.

"Are you ok, sir?" he asked, as Valmak got back to his feet.

"I'm fine," said Valmak, thinking the engine might need recalibrating. That reverse had been just a bit too jerky for his liking.

King picked Zymotz up from the floor and gave him a good shake to wake him from the trance, while Valmak helped Meki up.

"What happened?" said Meki. "I don't feel so good."

"Me, too," said Zymotz.

"You'll both be alright," King assured them. "Back to your stations."

Valmak wasn't sure why he hadn't been as affected as the others. Possibly his advancing years had some bearing on his hearing, more than he wished to admit, but he was nevertheless grateful. Maybe getting old did have its benefits.

"Are you alright, King?" asked Valmak, concerned his first officer was in pain.

"I think I bust a rib, but yes, I'm ok, sir."

The robot ships failed to respond immediately to Retriever-2, as a sudden reverse had not been in their calculations. But just as quickly they re-adjusted their flight path and matched speed, closing in fast.

Paul Aztac arrived on the bridge. "Earplugs, Captain," he said, handing them over without delay.

The robot ships were gaining fast, and whatever their intentions Valmak was certain they were going to be in for one hell of a surprise. He was determined they were not going to take his ship.

He had a plan, which was going to require volunteers, and he wanted Phasner present. If ever he needed a computer expert, it was him. For some reason Phasner seemed to understand and connect with his captain. But the plan was intricate, and they had to get it right first time.

In total silence, per Valmak's instructions, it was proving difficult to relay messages on the bridge. But he managed to signal his intentions for a gradual reduction in speed to allow the robot ships to come alongside.

King prayed the captain knew what he was doing, as some of his decisions lately had been suspect to say the least.

Using one of the monitors at Bartok's station, Valmak pulled out the normally obsolete touch keyboard below the computer and reverted to old-fashioned communications to let his crew know exactly what to do. Typing in his request as quickly as two fingers would allow, Valmak got his message through.

King was astounded the captain could actually type. It was an outdated mode of contact but nevertheless effective. The man never ceased to amaze him. *How could he ever doubt his ability as a captain?*

Now with only one airlock operational out of six – the others disabled for the time being – it was the start of Valmak's daring plan. *Having only one access point to deal with would make things easier*, he thought.

It wasn't long before the first robot ship locked on and opened its doors. Air quality had already equalised, so it was obvious the crew were wanted alive. A robot stood at the entrance, assuming that the prisoners would simply walk through the airlock in a hypnotic trance and take their position aboard the alien ship, which had enough seats for twenty men.

Valmak couldn't afford for his bold and risky plan to go wrong. The alternative didn't bear thinking about.

Phasner volunteered to do the first run and took a handful of crew with him to make it look authentic. They were understandably frightened of the consequences and nervous about what they'd actually volunteered for. But Phasner had a more positive attitude to the mission. He was confident his scientific brain could pull it off, so long as Bartok was correct in his analysis that the robots had limited mental capacity and were unable to operate independently.

Entering the docked robot ship, Phasner led the way, walking slowly and stiffly to mimic a trance, while the crew followed behind in single file as they had been instructed. As Phasner passed the robot, it made no move, so now he had to act fast.

Once behind the robot, he turned and violently slammed it into the bulkhead. A quick blast from his hidden phasic gun and the robot went down noisily, smoking and sparking. It tried to get up but couldn't. To make sure, Phasner reached over and twisted its head aggressively until it detached from the body.

"Shit! That was too easy," he muttered. Taking out his earplugs for a second, he signalled for the others to do the same.

"Okay, guys, dispose of this heap of junk back inside its ship and report back to the captain. I'm going inside to take a look."

"Will you be alright?" asked one of them.

"Yes, now hurry, the captain needs to know. Then get back here ready for the next one." Phasner waved them away while the remaining officer carried the disassembled robot back inside. "And put your earplugs back in," he reminded them.

Heading for the control section, Phasner hoped he would be able to understand the alien workings, otherwise they were in trouble. To his surprise he found the system rather rudimentary; the creators of these machines had put very little in the way of safeguarding in the systems. *It was primitive*, Phasner thought, *almost ancient*. The creators had obviously not expected resistance.

His task was simple, and he quickly adjusted the system to register a full quota of prisoners. Before he had time to congratulate himself, he heard the airlock closing. He hadn't realised it would close automatically, so he had to run fast and only got out by the skin of his teeth before the robot ship disembarked.

Valmak was already waiting for Phasner, eager to know he was safe. He was also no longer wearing earplugs.

"The hypnotic sound has gone," he explained. "So how did it go?"

"Piece of cake, sir. The robots and their ships are ancient technology, nothing to worry about," he said with confidence.

"Well done, you will make an excellent senior officer, Phasner."

"Thank you, sir, that means a lot. I've put the robot ship on autopilot again and hope it will take itself back to its home planet."

"Good man. Were there any weapons aboard?" asked Valmak. Any extra fire power would come in very handy.

"None at all, but I guess they assumed it wasn't necessary."

"Right, can you quickly instruct the crew what to do at the controls? I need you back on the bridge."

"I think so, sir. It's not rocket science," said Phasner.

"One more thing. Did you manage to find out where they had come from?"

"No, sir, not enough time."

"Ok. Back on the bridge as soon as then."

Valmak was extremely pleased the plan had worked. As he left Phasner at the airlock, the crew were waiting for his instructions. He pointed out to them to be swift, reminding them that the airlock would close without warning, so they would only have seconds to get out.

One by one the robot ships were dealt with swiftly and effortlessly. All ten ships, now on autopilot, soon regrouped in formation and departed at great velocity. Monitoring them from the bridge, everyone was relieved that a crisis had been averted.

Valmak was quietly annoyed with himself for allowing the ships to leave, but at least the robots had been destroyed. Maybe now they could relax a little. He really needed a break after this. Retriever-2 should have gone home.

The quiet was suddenly shattered by King announcing a startling piece of news. "Captain, the last crewman didn't get out of the robot ship before the doors closed on him."

Valmak's heart sank. "Who is it?" he asked.

"Steve Brown from engineering."

Phasner shot round from his station. "We can't leave him behind, Captain," he said. "We'd be sentencing him to death."

"He's right, sir, we can't leave him," added King.

For once Valmak was in full agreement with his first officer. Without hesitation he issued the order. "Lay in the co-ordinates, don't let that fleet disappear from view. Maximum hyperdrive, helm."

"Already done, sir," said Zymotz. He hadn't waited for the order. He was doing it whatever the captain said.

"Argent, if that hypnotic sound returns, inform me immediately, though I suspect it won't."

"Yes, sir," said Argent.

As Retriever-2 went in pursuit of the robot ships, keeping a safe distance was not an option anymore. A crewman's life was at stake.

They pursued relentlessly, but gaining on them was not happening as fast as they wished. For supposedly ancient ships, they were faster than predicted. Retriever-2 was one of the fastest intergalactic rescue ships in the galaxy, but it was not making much ground.

Valmak, however, made a promise to himself that he would not lose any more crew. This was important to him.

He sat in his control seat contemplating what his next move would be. Chasing robots across the galaxy had not been in the plan, but now there was no choice. He wasn't even sure what he could do when Retriever-2 finally tracked them to their home planet.

He watched King at his station, obviously struggling with grief over his brother being missing, perhaps dead. Every now and then the man winced in pain. His ribs were still sore, but he refused to visit the hospital for pain relief, as he wanted to remain at his station. Despite his many disagreements with the man, Valmak admired his dedication to duty.

The helm crew, Zymotz and Meki, were busy monitoring, watching the viewing screen, and maintaining maximum velocity in pursuit. Bartok was off the bridge with Phasner, busy with their plans. He hoped they could come up with something for their defence.

Everyone was busy except the captain, and his mind drifted to other things, questions that were eating away at him. He couldn't fathom the mysteries of the universe, nor could he understand why it mattered so much to him. *Perhaps it was time to retire*, he thought. Then again, as soon as he set foot back on Earth, he would be slapped in cuffs for sure. It was a daunting thought he didn't wish to explore right then.

Suddenly Nussar popped back into his head. The captain still had a great deal of resentment toward the alien. The mystery surrounding Nussar only heightened Valmak's fear for the future, and he still didn't like having him on board. The real question was what to do with him after Retriever-2 completed its mission.

Then there was the strange alien spaceship they had picked up. *It had been an unauthorised pick-up, so should he maybe dump Nussar in it and cast it adrift before returning to Earth?* It would solve his problem, but he wasn't sure he would get away with it.

Valmak was abruptly brought back to the bridge.

"Captain—" Zymotz called out a second time, disturbing his train of thought.

"Yes, what is it?" he asked. Looking up to the viewing screen, he saw a distant trace which he assumed was the robot fleet.

"Not absolutely sure, sir. We are still in pursuit of the robots, but something weird just happened," said Zymotz.

Meki, next to him, was trying to compute the anomaly with no success. King moved closer to the helm for a look.

"We can't make it out, sir, but look at the stars directly ahead," said Zymotz.

"What are we looking for?" asked King.

"There—" Zymotz pointed. "Don't you see it?"

"Yes, some of the stars are not aligned," agreed King.

Valmak still didn't know what he was looking at.

"There is a distortion in space," said Zymotz. "But it just appeared out of nowhere," he added.

"Ok, I can see a deviation now," admitted Valmak. "So, what's causing it?"

"Don't know yet, Captain. I'm still trying to compute the anomaly," offered Meki.

"Well, keep scanning. Log everything, but don't lose the robots," Valmak ordered.

At that moment Meki made a shock announcement. "We just lost the robot ships, sir. They simply disappeared from view." He kept punching keys at his station in a futile attempt to regain their position.

"How can that be?" questioned King.

"He's right, sir. The robot ships are no longer registering on long-range scanners. They've simply gone," confirmed Zymotz.

"Increase velocity now. Take a reading from their last known position and get them back," ordered Valmak, furious at the thought of losing the fleet. He smelt a rat, fearing this might be another trap, but they had to stay on the robot ships' tail.

"We're already at maximum, sir," confirmed Zymotz. "Full hyperdrive in operation."

"Activate the solardrive then," snapped Valmak.

"Captain, that is dangerous. We could overshoot them without even realising," warned King.

"Thank you, King, get back to your station. Zymotz, analyse the distortion or whatever it is. We need to know what we're up against."

The captain's demeanour had suddenly changed. He no longer cared about right or wrong as revenge rose up, boiling over in his brain, leaving him unable to control his behaviour. He wanted that robot fleet no matter what.

King returned to his station, angry at the captain again. *Why was the man blowing hot and cold all the time?*

Zymotz activated the solardrive. It was something he had never done before, as it was not a good manoeuvre at any time. However, it made no difference. The robot ships failed to appear.

"How could they disappear in an instant?" Valmak wanted to know.

No-one answered at that moment, they were too stunned at being outwitted by disassembled robots inside ships controlled on autopilot.

"Captain, I can't get anything to explain the distortion, but we're going to either hit it or pass through any second," said Zymotz.

"Any trace of the robots yet?"

"No, sir, all scans just bounce back at us."

With some trepidation Retriever-2 headed straight into the distorted area of space. The crew assumed they were simply going to pass through it without any deviation, but very abruptly the ship caught everyone off balance by rocking sideways and literally bouncing off an invisible barrier.

Bodies went flying across the ship. On the bridge Meki went crashing into a section of panelling and knocked himself out. Zymotz went over the top of his station, crashing heavily to the floor. Valmak hit the deck hard, banging his head and, although dazed, managed to stagger to his feet. King and Argent, both picked themselves up gingerly. King's ribs were hurting him even more. *Probably cracked another one*, he thought.

"Is everyone alright?" Valmak asked eventually.

King went over to Meki, but he was still out cold. Argent managed back to his station and sat down to check that the controls were still intact.

"Somebody please tell me what just happened." Valmak was livid they had been caught off guard so easily. He felt a lump developing on his forehead and ignored a small trickle of blood running down his cheek.

King assisted Meki as he came round on the floor. "Stay there for a second, Meki, just get your bearings," King suggested. The man was still very groggy.

"King, I want a full analysis immediately," said Valmak. He wasn't interested in nursemaiding right now.

But King wasn't leaving Meki until the medics arrived. "If you want answers, Captain, I can only give you my opinion right now."

"And what is that?" Valmak replied angrily, clearly unhappy with King's attitude.

"My opinion, Captain, is that the distortion was actually an invisible force field to stop us pursuing the robots."

"Well, it bloody worked." Valmak was irritated. They had no chance of chasing the robots now, and another crewman had been lost. That hurt him more than anything.

Zymotz finally stumbled back to his station to check for damage but saw that his friend was hurt. "Are you alright, Nely?"

"Protocol, Zymotz," Valmak snapped. First names were not allowed on the bridge.

Zymotz ignored the order and checked his readings. "No major damage sustained, Captain," he said, disgruntled at being ticked off.

To his horror he noticed a flashing warning light on the panel in front of him. It wasn't a good sign. The reverse switch had been hit. Cancelling it swiftly, he realised he must have hit it when he had been thrown over his station. Retriever-2 operating both hyperdrive and solardrive at maximum velocity was not good news. The question was how far in reverse Retriever-2 had travelled.

"Captain, we have a major problem," he said.

Valmak didn't reply. He was studying the viewing screen. Something was amiss; the star system they were travelling in was all wrong. King noticed it, too, having left Meki with a medic who had rushed in seconds earlier.

"I don't recognise that configuration," he frowned.

"Neither do I," replied Valmak, "and I know most of them."

"Sorry, sir, I accidentally hit the reverse when I fell." Zymotz felt so guilty; the crew didn't need this on top of everything going on. "But that's not the worst of it, sir," he went on.

"How can it get any worse?" asked Valmak angrily. He realised his plan was falling apart and there was no back-up.

"Go ahead, Zymotz," said King, sounding a lot calmer than the captain. He realised it had just been an unfortunate accident.

"With both hyperdrive and solardrive activated, I can't calculate our position. Especially when we have no idea where we are."

As Valmak pondered the next move, Meki, who was showing signs of concussion, left with the medic.

"You better follow them and get those ribs checked out," the captain told King. "And that's an order."

For once King was happy to leave the bridge. He felt undermined all the time, and the captain didn't appear to bother about feelings – caring one minute, then biting his head off the next. He just couldn't make the man out.

When they'd left, Valmak ordered Argent to recall Bartok and Phasner to the bridge. They were needed to calculate the time Retriever-2 had been in reverse at twice the normal velocity, and to plot a course back.

"Zymotz, you will work with them to find the solution. After all, it's your fault we're in this mess." He didn't bother to hide his anger at the man.

"Yes, sir. Sorry, sir," apologised Zymotz. Privately, he thought his captain was being very harsh, particularly as he had ordered the solardrive when hyperdrive was still in operation in the first place. It went against normal procedure and against company policy.

It seemed that Valmak had broken so many rules lately and just expected the crew to go along with it. Zymotz decided not to harbour bad feelings, as he was more concerned with his friend. The panelling across the bridge definitely looked rather worse for wear, so it was no wonder his friend had been knocked out.

Valmak maintained his stance in his control seat, watching his crew, waiting for answers from Bartok and Phasner. All he could think of was chasing the robots back to their home planet. Retriever-2 needed to intercept them before it was discovered that the robots had been destroyed.

It might be construed as an act of violence, another violation of the rules, but he justified himself that it had been in self-defence. He feared there was little chance of saving his officer Steve Brown, but the dark side that controlled his mind questioned what was one life when he was trying to save a whole ship.

Bartok and Phasner struggled to find any solution to their predicament, unable to match the star system they were in with the star charts in the memory banks. Nothing matched and they couldn't understand why. They admitted they were actually lost, but the captain refused to accept it and ordered them to continue checking.

Meanwhile he continued to stare at the viewing screen, noting every single star formation in his head. He had seen this once before but didn't know where. Then, decision made, he rose from his seat.

"Keep checking the data, men, I need answers. Let me know when you find the solution. I have something to take care of." With that, Valmak hastily left the bridge.

"What was all that about?" asked Bartok.

"Don't ask me, I only work here," said Argent flippantly. He'd given up trying to understand the captain a long time ago.

Zymotz looked at Bartok and shrugged his shoulders.

Fifteen minutes after leaving the bridge, King returned with Meki, who took his station immediately.

"Nely are you alright?" whispered Zymotz.

"I've got a headache," he admitted. "The doctor says I'm fine, but I think she's wrong."

"You always think the worst, but I'm glad to have you back."

"Thanks, Alec."

King sat down at his station gingerly. Three cracked ribs were no fun, and he hoped the painkillers kicked in soon, but the doctor said she couldn't do much else. Besides, he could see she had enough on her plate with so many crew being treated.

*

Valmak headed directly to the hangar deck where Nussar's spaceship was stored. He was certain the answers he wanted must lie inside the alien craft. On his instructions the engineering maintenance team had been working round the clock to restore the ship to full working order, no matter how primitive it was.

Initially he had assumed he could send Nussar home soon after. But as that didn't happen, he was now hoping to retrieve any data from the craft's on-board system.

The need to understand the alien was paramount to Valmak, but he really wasn't sure why he was there. Something had drawn him to the hangar deck, and his gut instinct was telling him that the star charts were the key.

Being in such close proximity to Nussar's ship made Valmak feel worse than before. So much hatred ran through his veins and evil in his head, it was no wonder he had trouble focusing on his own crew.

Climbing into the ship Valmak soon realised just how primitive the technology was. But the maintenance team had done a good job. The burnt-out circuits had been replaced and reconnected to the main computer system, while a new monitor screen had been put in, courtesy of the company. Valmak didn't know yet how he would explain that particular expense.

Only one file was of interest to Valmak and luckily, he found what he wanted straight away. Accessing the ancient computer was easier than he'd expected, and as star charts appeared on the monitor, he hurriedly flicked through each one until he found the exact one – a star system identical to the one they were in right now.

For a moment Valmak was stunned to know he had been right, but that sixth sense he had suddenly acquired had brought him to the alien ship to seek out the truth. This galaxy was Nussar's home. He had hoped to be wrong, but the facts were there.

Before leaving he scanned the other files. Having done so, things were beginning to make sense about Nussar and his strange presence on Retriever-2. Valmak didn't like what he'd found, but he returned promptly to the bridge with the newly obtained data.

Bartok and Phasner were still trying to calculate a way home, but it was proving impossible. The computer kept coming up with the same conclusion every time, that they were totally lost in a galaxy unknown to them. And the computer could not compute the unknown.

As soon as Valmak entered the bridge Bartok was quick to give him the bad news.

"Captain, we cannot plot a course back. This star system, according to the computer records, does not exist."

But Valmak wasn't surprised. "That's fine, Bartok. I have better news. Interesting facts I managed to retrieve from Nussar's ship," he announced almost smugly.

"You did? I mean, does it help us at all?" Bartok was confused why the captain had gone to the alien ship. *Surely it couldn't have any bearing on their own problem?* he thought.

"Not sure yet, but I have to tell you this star system we're in right now does exist."

The astonished looks from everyone on the bridge said it all. Valmak drew in a deep breath as he prepared to give them the news.

Before he could, King stood up to speak. "Please tell me you haven't lost your faculties, Captain."

"I will disregard that remark, King," Valmak responded harshly.

King realised he was pushing his luck, but with the captain's behaviour being so erratic, he couldn't be sure of anything.

"So, what have you found, sir?" asked Phasner.

"Remember when Nussar first came aboard—"

They nodded, wondering where this was leading.

Valmak turned to Phasner. "Wasn't it you who came up with the hypothesis about a rift in the universe?"

"Yes, but only as a theory," said Phasner hesitantly, worried he was going to get the blame for something.

"Well, how about this for a theory? We went into reverse at an incalculable velocity, and Retriever-2 passed through that rift – the same rift Nussar came through. In doing so, it caused a possible time warp, and/or we entered an alternate universe."

"Wow!" was all Phasner could say. His theory hadn't gone that far, and he was amazed the captain had thought that one out on his own, especially at his age.

Words were sinking in slowly, painfully even, as the crew wondered if this could really have happened to them. They all looked at the viewing screen, wondering not where they were – but when.

Meki, in particular, appeared more alarmed than the others. He struggled to understand what Valmak was telling them.

"Sir, could you just run that by me again? Exactly what are you saying?"

Bartok abruptly stepped in. "The captain is saying we crashed through the space time continuum and we're probably not going home. Is that clear enough for you?" he snapped. His anger wasn't really directed at Meki but the fact that Retriever-2 was stranded in the unknown.

"Easy, easy, Bartok," soothed Valmak. "This is a lot to take in, and its only conjecture. Look, we have to work together to find a solution. For now, don't go losing it with each other."

For once in his lifetime Valmak was calm, rational, and in full control. His mood had changed again. He was responsible for his crew, and he had to get them home.

"So, how did you know about the star system, Captain?" King asked, wondering how Valmak had managed to find it out on his own.

"It's on the computer system in Nussar's spaceship, but just don't ask how I knew. I haven't fathomed it all out myself."

"So, Nussar was telling the truth all along. Clarizia does exist?" asked King, still slightly bemused by the captain's intelligence upgrade.

"Yes." Valmak actually surprised himself by admitting he was wrong. He pointed to the viewing screen. "That small planet in the distance, bottom left corner, is Clarizia, just before it disappeared a millennium ago."

Meki slipped off his seat in disbelief while Zymotz opened his mouth but couldn't speak. King couldn't comprehend the extent of his statement or how he had come by such information. Bartok didn't want to believe a single word; it was ludicrous. Phasner was beginning to see the light, but only just.

"Let me get this straight," said Phasner. "We came through a rift in the universe, possibly the same way Nussar came through to us, but an alternative universe with a different timeline?"

Valmak nodded. It sort of made sense the way Phasner put it.

"So where in the bloody universe are we then?" Bartok, normally very level-headed and calm in a crisis, was beginning to feel anxious and not taking the news well.

"If I'm right, Bartok," replied Valmak, more sure of his facts now, "we are in another universe. This one is not ours." He tried to make the situation sound as straightforward as he could, and of all the crew he thought Bartok would be the one to understand, but it was obvious the man was struggling.

"Look, men, I don't have all the answers yet, but everything I've said makes sense with the star system out there right now.

This isn't our universe. It's another dimension, which would account for the timeline variation."

"Yes, but... but a thousand years, that can't be right, Captain," said Bartok. "If this Clarizia is a thousand years ago and they have space travel technology, surely that makes them far more superior to us."

Suddenly the bridge was silent. *Was any of it true? Had they become stranded in someone else's backyard a millennium away from Earth?* It was hard to accept the facts. Valmak realised he might have opened a can of worms.

Zymotz finally gathered his wits. "I'm really sorry, guys, it's all my fault. We wouldn't be in this mess if I hadn't—"

"Enough!" Valmak said, determined nobody was to blame for their predicament. "Now listen, is it not possible to recreate the same circumstances, the same velocity, the exact conditions in reverse, and possibly pass back through this rift and return to our own universe?" Valmak thought it was a good question. "Well?" He was waiting for answers.

"What direction do we take?" asked King.

"And how do we know where the rift is?" asked Bartok, not convinced about the whole idea.

"Simply retrace our journey using the computer files. You were still mapping the universe, I hope," said Valmak. "It shouldn't be that difficult, should it, Bartok?"

"I just don't know if it's feasible," he replied.

"Do you want to stay here?" argued King. This would not be his favourite destination for a holiday.

"I think we should give it a go, Captain," said Phasner.

"I say we try," agreed Zymotz.

"Me, too," added Meki.

King nodded in agreement.

"Okay, I'm in," said Bartok reluctantly.

"Then get to work on the computations, men," ordered Valmak, satisfied that at least they were all in agreement.

“But about Nussar, Captain,” asked King. “Do we take him home first?”

Valmak looked up to the viewing screen. “That’s his home,” he agreed. “We have to send him back.” Privately, he wanted to get the damn alien off his ship and maybe things could return to normal.

“And what of the small detail that his planet allegedly disappears. How much do we tell him?”

Valmak thought about it. “We don’t.” The alien wouldn’t believe it anyway. Besides, it wasn’t their problem.

CHAPTER SEVEN

Standing outside the hospital, Valmak hesitated for a moment, reluctant to go in. He wasn't welcome there; Doctor Summers had made that very clear. He accepted he hadn't made life easy for her, but he only admitted that to himself. Now he had vital information on Nussar and thought she would at least be pleased at the prospect of sending the alien home. He wanted him off his ship as soon as possible, certain that all the animosity against them would disappear.

Valmak was sick of the bad vibes. The sense of danger and death had only occurred after Nussar came aboard. The alien had been bad news from the start. The strange sixth sense he experienced was something Valmak was certain he had never encountered before, and it was unnerving. There was something mysterious about Nussar that pushed him to the limit, his very presence intimidated him. The alien had to leave Retriever-2, no argument.

Valmak hated himself for the way he felt, knowing it wasn't his normal behaviour. Suddenly he drifted away in his mind and was reminded of his own brother, murdered by unknown aliens many years before he joined the military rescue academy. It had left the captain resentful of all aliens.

He questioned whether he had applied for the right job back then, but it was all he had ever wanted to do. Piloting an intergalactic hospital rescue ship had always been his dream job, and until recently he'd had twenty-five years' service with an impeccable record. Now, though, he had been reduced to breaking company policy, there was a warrant out for his arrest, an unwelcome alien was aboard the ship, and they were marooned on the wrong side of who knew where. *What more could go wrong?*

He went into the hospital, stepping over medical files strewn across the floor alongside broken phials and used dressings. He knew the ship had been knocked about a bit when they had hit the force field, but nothing had been cleaned up and the hospital was a complete mess. Doctor Summers never allowed it to get so untidy.

He turned around, looking for the orderlies to speak to, but it was unusually quiet. As he was about to call out, Doctor Summers came out of isolation and approached her desk, which was just as cluttered as the floor.

"I thought I told you to stay away from the hospital, Captain," she said. "What part of that did you not understand?"

He had been right; she was not happy to see him. He ignored the frosty greeting. "What's been going on here, the place is a mess?"

Doctor Summers looked at him sternly. She couldn't believe he had the cheek to even ask that question.

"All this mess is your fault, Captain, the result of whatever you did with the ship. I have been overrun with multiple injuries. I even reset Will Straten's arm when he took another bad fall." She was angry and about to walk off, but added, "And just in case you forgot, I am the only doctor on this ship. The mess will be cleared up soon, but the orderlies are still attending patients alongside the medics."

Valmak was sorry he had asked. She was obviously still bitter over his intrusion into hospital business. He gave out a loud sigh, exasperated at her bad mood.

"What do you want, Captain? I'm extremely busy." She made it quite clear in her voice she didn't want him there.

"I have news concerning Nussar, but it's good news, before you bite my head off."

Doctor Summers was surprised and wondered what could have changed. Until now the captain had never said a good word about Sol.

"We're on route to the planet Clarizia, Nussar's home planet. We're going to take him home." He said it with a smile, thinking she would be pleased.

But in a split-second Doctors Summers felt her heart sink. She didn't want Sol to go home, and she was sure he didn't want too either. "I thought you said—"

"Never mind what I said. It appears we sort of took a wrong turning and arrived very close to Clarizia. We won't be long before we reach his home." Valmak was surprised to see a despondent look in her eyes. *He couldn't think why – or maybe he did know.*

"So how is he?" Valmak thought he better ask.

"Believe it or not, there's been some improvement. He has started to respond to my voice. But" she made it clear, "not enough to move him."

Valmak was relieved not to be the cause of the alien's mental state, but it didn't change what he had to do.

"What about Kursal?" he asked.

"Apart from falling out of bed when you rocked the ship on its side, not much change." Doctor Summers didn't mention that she was extremely concerned for Kursal's health. His readings were off the chart, and she couldn't stabilise him. He wasn't recovering any time soon.

"I want you to try and explain to Nussar that he's going home. The news would be better coming from you anyway. His ship is fully functional."

"I don't think so, Captain. He is barely able to understand his surroundings. It's just not a good idea."

"Sorry, Doctor Summers, he has to go home. Then we can concentrate on finding a way of getting home ourselves." Valmak was not going to budge on the matter; the alien had to go.

Doctor Summers tried to fight her emotions and give a real reason to keep Sol aboard Retriever-2. Then she questioned his last statement.

"What did you mean just now?"

"I wasn't kidding. We're lost, and I haven't told the entire crew yet. We're stranded one thousand years in the past, but unfortunately, it's not our past."

"You're talking nonsense as usual, Captain," she snapped. "I don't have time for this." She turned to walk away, deciding he sounded crazier than ever. "Just go, Captain."

Valmak called out after her. She needed to listen. "Look, we haven't established the exact period of time, and Clarizia might suddenly vanish. History suggests something is going on and that the planet's disappearance causes a catastrophic chain of events. We just don't know what or when."

Doctor Summers stopped suddenly and turned back. "Well, that's it then. We cannot send Sol back now. He might not have a home to go back to." She was so angry tears rolled down her face. She knew that becoming emotionally involved with her patient broke the rules, but she couldn't help herself. "I can't allow you to do this, Captain. Rule number one of the company policy is to protect the innocent. You cannot send him back; it might be to his death."

"He has to go back to his own race," Valmak insisted, ignoring the tears. He had a duty to perform. "Get him ready!" he snapped in her face, then turned and walked away, treading over the mess. "And get the orderlies to clear this bloody mess up. It's a disgrace."

His remarks made her feel worse, but she was furious at the captain for being so heartless. That anger was enough to spur her into action. She could not let Sol go without knowing for sure if it was the right decision.

Valmak had obviously got his information from somewhere, otherwise how could he know about Clariziane history? *Did Sol have to die with his people? Did any of them have to die?*

Was it actually part of history for him to arrive on Retriever-2 in such a manner? Maybe none of it was meant to happen. Doctor Summers was more determined than ever to find out the truth.

Looking across in the direction of the isolation ward where she'd left Sol, she made a promise to herself. She would not give up on the man she loved without a fight. Time was crucial as she raced out of the hospital.

*

On approach to the planet Clarizia, Denny Argent picked up a signal from the surface just as Valmak entered the bridge, still seething from his confrontation with the doctor.

"Do we have contact yet?" he asked in a brusque manner, letting the bridge crew know he was in a bad mood.

"Yes, sir, we received a signal a few minutes ago," confirmed Argent.

"On course to orbit now, Captain," said Meki.

Argent then alerted Valmak that he had the message in full.

"Go ahead, Argent, what do they say?"

"They are quite clear about it, Captain. They demand we leave this sector of space immediately. We are violating their territory."

That wasn't the response Valmak had expected. They were up to no good, and his suspicions about Nussar extended to his people. A dreadful sense of imminent death flashed across his mind. This was the place causing all his grief. There was danger ahead, he was sure.

"Anything else, Argent?" he asked.

"Only that if we don't leave, we will pay the penalty. Their exact words, sir."

"Captain, have we just been threatened?" asked King.

"Sure as hell sounded like it," replied Valmak.

"Not very friendly, sir. Shall I reply?" asked Argent.

Valmak signalled not to for a moment as he tried to work out in his head what these people could be hiding. *Were he and his crew in danger from the Clarizianes? Or was his own paranoia taking control?* It felt like a trap again, and they had just walked straight into it.

"Can we get magnification up?" he asked Zymotz. "I want to see what we're up against."

"No chance, Captain. Every time we try to zoom in, there is interference. We're being blocked by the planet. Computer can't clear it."

Without warning, the viewing screen went blank, all visual gone.

"I guess that's the universal language to say, 'Get lost'," commented Meki.

"Well, they certainly don't want us to know what's going on, Captain," said King. "I believe the next move is ours."

Valmak had a suspicion the Clarizianes were definitely scheming, not wanting intrusion at any cost. They had to find out why.

"Argent are you able to open a channel to speak to them?" asked Valmak.

"I'll try, sir." Seconds later, he announced, "All channels are now open."

Valmak composed himself before speaking; he needed to choose his words carefully. "This is Captain Gram Valmak of the Earth space rescue ship Retriever-2. We come in peace and would like permission to orbit your planet. We have one of your commanders here. Please acknowledge..."

They waited. The silence was frustrating and unnerving for the crew.

"Computer scans say the message was received, Captain," said Argent.

"What are they waiting for?" murmured King.

Several minutes passed before the viewing screen cleared again and a white-haired old man appeared, not unlike Nussar in features. He looked straight at Valmak and for a second stared at him almost with a shocked expression, then he spoke.

"This is Chane Auston of the Clariziane empire. My warning still stands. You must come no closer to our planet. Do not defy us."

Valmak thought it rather strange the man didn't ask about one of their own. *Did Nussar not mean anything to them?*

"Chane Auston, Commander Sol Nussar needs to return home," said Valmak.

"Are you holding him prisoner?" asked Auston.

"No, of course not. We merely wish to send him home," replied Valmak.

"Then send him back alone and leave this galaxy immediately."

Valmak was growing tired of the conversation. He didn't want to be there any longer than he had to, but they were not making it easy.

"I cannot send him alone. He is ill and unable to travel alone."

He couldn't make it any clearer, but the alien seemed offhand, dismissive even. Valmak tried to fathom what he was hiding.

Chane Auston spoke again. "Can we at least speak with the commander?" he asked.

"Again no, that isn't possible at present." There was a pause, and then the viewing screen went blank again for several minutes.

"What are they up to?" asked King but didn't get an answer.

Valmak knew they had to be plotting something, because that evil sense of foreboding surged through his body like never before.

"Captain, what do you reckon?" asked King again. "Are they genuine?"

"I don't think they are, King. I think they're hatching a plot—" Valmak's words were interrupted by the viewing screen clearing once more and Chane Auston reappeared.

Valmak hated the fact they could control the intercom system and the viewing screen at will.

Auston spoke again. "Very well, you leave us no choice. We will send a ship to rendezvous with your ship. Have Commander Nussar ready." He was abrupt in his manner, then he was gone.

"Friendly sort of alien, isn't he?" mocked Zymotz.

"Okay, helm. Cruise in gently and take no risks." Valmak didn't trust the alien one bit.

"I must advise extreme caution, Captain, this might be a trap," said King, then waited to have his head bitten off as usual.

"I totally agree, King. Something is not right here."

King was stunned that the captain had agreed with him. "So, what's the plan, sir?" he asked.

Before Valmak could reply, he spotted Doctor Summers standing in the doorway of the bridge. *How long had she been there?* he wondered. *And how much had she heard?*

Doctor Summers came storming in. "You really are going to send Sol back, aren't you, Captain?"

"I have no choice; he has to go home." Valmak was not used to this sort of confrontation on the bridge. "I thought you of all people would be pleased."

"Well, I'm not, Captain, and you are being heartless. I told you he isn't ready for this." She was livid he had taken little notice of what she had said earlier.

"I don't think you are talking very professionally, Doctor Summers. You're starting to sound irrational, too involved with this patient." Valmak had long expected she had feelings for this alien which were clouding her judgement.

"That's outrageous!" she screamed in his face. Everyone on the bridge could hear the argument.

"I think not, Doctor, and furthermore I don't tell you how to run the hospital, so you don't have a say on the bridge. Get Nussar ready, he is going." Valmak departed for the exit. To his mind, the conversation was over. He was getting rid of

Nussar and then they were leaving this place one way or another.

Doctor Summers ran out after him. "Captain! Captain, you can't do this. It isn't right."

He swung round in the corridor, furious at her persistence. "Look here—" he started.

"No, you look. You have no real evidence to prove your ridiculous theory about this planet. I can't allow you to take Sol, he is still very vulnerable. It would do more harm than good. It goes against the rules." She pleaded her case, becoming very emotional in the process, but it did no good.

"I have had enough of you, Doctor. The alien goes. That's an order. OBEY IT!"

Valmak left her standing in the corridor in tears. She knew the captain had been right about one thing. She was too involved, but she couldn't bear to let Sol go. But she couldn't believe she had allowed herself to fall in love with history – if indeed what Valmak said was true.

Suddenly Doctor Summers knew what had to be done. If the captain had found some information about Sol, surely there had to be more. Wiping away her tears, she rushed off down the opposite corridor. There was someone aboard who would help her in any crisis – the one person she always relied on. She had to be quick and hope no-one missed her in the hospital.

*

The archives were housed in the depths of the main computer storage complex. The entire journey of Retriever-2, endless records, and data were all stored here. Every minor detail was catalogued and deposited ready for the return to Earth.

Doctor Summers entered the archives looking for her friend Mike Dyland.

"Mike, Mike, are you about?" she called out.

Stirring from the narrow aisles came a rather dishevelled looking man with piles of papers, tapes, and disks in his arms, promptly dropping most of the papers onto the floor.

"Niko, this is a nice surprise. What can I do for you?" he asked, giving her a soft kiss on the cheek. "Have you been crying?" He'd put money on the captain having upset her; the man was a heartless sod.

"I'm alright, Mike, really," she told him. "But I need help, and it's urgent."

"Anything for you, Niko," he said trying to scoop up his papers. "It's going to take me ages to put this lot back in order."

Doctor Summers looked down the aisles to see files and tapes on the floor in a total mess. "I see your place is as bad as the hospital."

"Quite. What happened up there?" he asked, putting his work on the table.

"You don't want to know, Mike. Besides, why haven't you put all this data into the computer and dispensed with the paper? It's so old-fashioned."

"I like old-fashioned, thank you. By the way, how is your favourite patient?" Mike was always so grateful for his friend keeping him updated with the ship's affairs. He'd never know what was going on otherwise.

"Sol has made some improvement. He's the reason I'm here."

"Sounds intriguing. How can I help?" Mike was just happy to do something different; his job didn't exactly tax his brain cells.

"What I need to do has to stay between us for now, though. I don't want the captain to know yet. Will you come with me to the hangar deck?"

"Am I going to get into trouble, Niko?" He was curious, but he could do without any trouble. Valmak was forever putting a black mark on his record, and for no reason.

"You won't, trust me. Just tell me you can access the computer aboard Sol's ship. The captain was able to find data about him which had to have come from his ship, but I need more."

"No problem," he replied. They hurried along the corridor, hoping nobody noticed Mike was not at his station. Valmak didn't like him wandering the ship.

"What are you hoping to find, Niko?"

She wasn't sure at that point; it was only a hunch. "I need you to find any data on Sol, his home planet, well, anything really. Can you do it?" she asked earnestly.

Mike suddenly looked wide-eyed at her, as if he had just hit the jackpot. He knew he could trust Niko to keep a secret. As they turned to the last corridor on the approach to the hangar, he told her what he had done.

"I know it's against company policy, but I sent an unauthorised probe out to orbit Clarizia before they blocked all communication."

"How did you know about—? Doesn't matter. What did you find out?" Now Doctor Summers was intrigued. Mike just might have something.

"Well, the probe picked up some very interesting data. Certain facts about what is going on down there."

"Oh Mike, I could kiss you." Doctor Summers couldn't hide her emotion. "So why did you do it, Mike?"

He shrugged his shoulders. "Everyone thinks I'm just an eccentric nutcase, but if I don't do these things, how else do I collect data for the archives?"

Suddenly Doctor Summers could see a light at the end of the tunnel. Maybe Sol had a chance of staying. She was afraid of getting her hopes up, but a small chance was better than none.

"I always have faith in you, Mike, and you are not a nutcase. You have a very clever brain that's wasted down here. So, what did you discover?"

When they reached the hangar deck, they carefully checked to ensure no-one was about.

"I'll have to access Sol's on-board computer system to confirm a few details, then head back. I will explain everything, but the captain isn't going to like what I found out." Mike was actually quite chuffed with himself for using his ingenuity. It was something he was never given credit for.

"Never mind the captain, why did you keep it to yourself?"

He shrugged his shoulders again. "Because no-one asked me til now. They don't talk to me."

"I do," she said, and hugged him. "You should have told me, Mike."

"I didn't want to get you involved, Niko. Who would believe what I found out anyway?"

"Okay, they will listen now, so we have to be quick. I'll stand guard, you check out Sol's ship."

For the first time in her life Doctor Summers was doing something she had never thought she would do, breaking the rules and partaking in a clandestine operation.

Waiting impatiently outside Sol's ship, she was beginning to panic. Time was running out and she was anxious to know what Mike had to say.

Eventually he climbed out of the ship.

"What kept you?" she asked.

"Sorry, that computer was harder than I thought."

"Did you get what you wanted?" she said.

"Yes, let's go. I will tell you on the way."

Mike had found some startling data that even he had trouble digesting. As they hurried back to his room, Doctor Summers listened to every word her friend said.

*

Sol was unsteady on his feet and unsure of his surroundings. Two orderlies dressed him in his uniform and assisted him to leave the isolation ward, but he was reluctant to leave the darkened room. It had become his safe place, his sanctuary from the outside.

The gleaming bright lights and brilliant white walls slowly came into focus, but he wasn't used to them and didn't want to go. *Where was Niko?* He wanted her to be there. She could reassure him.

Valmak was nearby as the orderlies helped Sol along.

"Will he be alright?" asked one.

"Yes, I'm sure," confirmed the captain. "You can leave now. Doctor Summers will be along shortly."

A little puzzled, the orderlies left. The doctor hadn't said anything to them about moving the patient, but they knew better than to disobey the captain.

Valmak had no intention of waiting for the doctor. He couldn't understand why she wasn't there to stop him, but it didn't matter. He took Sol by the arm and led him out of the hospital. Just touching the alien gave Valmak the creeps and his anxiety intensified beyond belief, but he had to do it.

He didn't want to alarm Sol, so spoke quietly. "Commander Nussar, can you hear me? You are going home. You remember home, don't you? Clarizia."

Sol was slightly shocked and responded with a nod then a side look at Valmak, but he didn't seem to get upset. He understood and spoke for the first time in a while.

"Niko is coming with me," he replied. "She said she was coming with me."

Valmak wasn't sure if the alien knew what he was saying, but decided he better play along to keep him calm.

"We must go now. Your friends are coming to collect you, take you home."

"Yes, friends. Where is Niko?" he asked, a little shaken that he couldn't see her.

Valmak had to keep him calm. "She will be here very soon, just keep walking."

They were very close to the hangar deck, and soon the alien would be gone. Valmak wanted his life back and this was the only way. It had to be done.

*

Racing along the corridors, Mike Dyland hadn't done this much exercise in years and suddenly realised how unfit he was. Clutching an important file, he had to get to the hangar deck before it was too late. As he turned the last corner, he heard the hangar doors opening.

Suddenly he spotted the captain holding Sol in the doorway. "Captain! Captain Valmak, wait!" he shouted.

Valmak heard an unfamiliar voice and turned round to see a scruffy crewman rushing toward him. Then he remembered who it was.

"What the hell are you doing here? You are out of order, Dyland."

"Captain, I have important information. Commander Nussar cannot go back to his planet," Mike said, his words rushing out.

"Are you serious, man?" Valmak was furious with the delay. "When I get back, Dyland, you will be arrested for the duration of our journey home."

Mike could see Valmak was determined that Nussar was leaving his ship, no matter what. In the captain's mind, some jumped-up little jerk from the archives was not going to stop him.

"Please, sir, it can't happen. He has to stay," pleaded Mike.

Just then Valmak spotted the doctor approaching, almost out of breath, having been delayed by one of the crew.

"You! I might have known you would have a hand in this, Doctor Summers. What the hell do you think you're playing at? I told you this alien is leaving," Valmak said forcefully.

"Captain, you have to listen to Mike here. It's very important." She saw Sol standing next to the captain, nervously shuffling his feet. Clearly, he didn't know what was happening and was nervous.

"Hello, Sol," she said softly, as she put an arm around him to comfort him.

He smiled back, knowing she wouldn't desert him. Everything would be alright now.

Valmak was beginning to lose his patience with the pair of them. Seeing the doctor and the way she looked at the alien, he knew for sure there was something going on between them.

"I'll have you both arrested for insubordination, just—"

"Arrest yourself, Captain. Now bloody well listen to Mike," screamed the doctor.

Mike looked at her in amazement for standing up for herself against the captain. He prayed he was right with the information or they'd both end up in prison.

"Mike, tell him what you found," she said.

Valmak was seriously not in the mood to listen to anyone. His mind was working against him, and the evil thoughts had full control.

But Mike blocked the entrance to the hangar deck. If Niko could stand up to the tyrant, he decided, then so could he. "Captain, I sent a covert probe into orbit above Clarizia before they shut off all contact."

"On whose authority?" raged Valmak.

"Mine!" butted in Doctor Summers, covering for her friend.

Mike said nothing as she moved Sol out of the way.

"Now listen, Captain, it's important," she urged.

Valmak was fuming. Nothing would thwart his plan. "Go ahead, make it quick," he snapped angrily.

"If we allow Commander Nussar to return home, we change history," Mike told him.

"What? No, no, you're talking rubbish. You know nothing, Dyland. You never did."

"I admit I don't have all the facts, Captain, but it's true. The probe picked up some very interesting conversations from the people there. The Clarizianes don't want Nussar back. They think it's a trick, because he disappeared five years ago."

"No, how can that be?" Valmak was not convinced. They were trying to stop him doing the right thing.

"There is a rift in the universe which is causing multiple disturbances through the galaxy. It might be a second to us, but for the Clarizianes it's been five years since Nussar was lost on a routine patrol. And yes, they are planning something, that's why they don't want outside interference. You have to believe me, Captain."

Valmak was deeply troubled, and not just because Nussar was standing so close to him. Suddenly he felt sick to his stomach, everything was unravelling. His world was falling apart, and his mind struggled to comprehend the complexity of what Dyland was saying. *He was sure the alien had to go, so why were they stopping him?*

"What am I supposed to do?" he asked. "My mission is not complete."

"Listen, Captain, from what I can make out the Clarizianes are going to disappear. I don't have details, but I do know we need to leave now. They plan to be gone very soon, but there are no spaceships built so I can't see how."

Valmak didn't want to believe it. They needed to get home, not get involved with aliens. And yet this one alien had caused him more grief than anything else in his entire life.

"Captain, I'm taking Sol back to the hospital. You and Mike need to establish a plan." Doctor Summers led Sol away, slipping an arm round his waist as she spoke softly to him. "You're going to be fine, Sol, trust me."

He smiled. He liked her words; they were warm and comforting. He felt safe once more. Niko would take good care of him.

Valmak watched as they disappeared round the corner. But Mike hadn't finished with the captain. There was more revealing data that was going to change everything, and the captain wasn't going to like it.

Valmak stood motionless, worried how he could get his life back on track while the alien was still aboard.

Mike knew time was critical, so he had to deliver the news quickly. "Sir, the rift is unstable. It's causing fluctuations in the timeline."

Valmak remained silent. He didn't understand that scientific stuff and believed it even less. He suddenly realised that sense of impending death was upon him again, stronger than before. But whose death he wasn't sure. He was terrified more than ever; he'd lost the ability to make a rational decision.

"Captain. Captain." Mike touched his arm to snap him out of his trance-like state.

"Sorry, Dyland, what did you say?" His mind was away elsewhere.

"I held something back from the doctor, Captain. The timeline keeps shifting and it has thrown up startling data. I have managed to record events that haven't actually happened, but which will."

"You've lost me," admitted Valmak.

"Well, according to the data I received, before the Clarizianes disappeared an unknown spaceship materialised close by." Mike waited for a response.

"Us?" asked Valmak. "You mean Retriever-2 was meant to arrive here?"

Mike nodded. "But I haven't been able to tell if we make it back to our own time, or indeed our own universe."

"I don't accept these facts, Dyland. Are you trying to tell me that according to their history, we were meant to slip through a rift in the universe and end up in a galaxy in a parallel whatever? Ridiculous, man." Valmak looked at Mike with disdain, almost sheer hatred.

But Mike had expected that Valmak would not accept the facts. "I know you don't like me, sir, but you need to read this file." Mike held it out, but Valmak seemed reluctant to touch it. "Please, sir, you must read it. The contents concern you in particular."

Valmak took the file, pausing for a second before opening it, then glanced over the report. A look of shock on his face said it all. He was horrified.

He stared at Mike in total disbelief. "This can't be true, can it?" He didn't want it to be true, but suddenly all the bad vibes and evil foreboding were beginning to make sense.

"Sorry, sir," said Mike, genuinely apologetic. There was nothing else he could say to help the captain. Words could not change the facts. Destiny demanded it.

"Keep this information to yourself," said Valmak, walking away in silence.

The corridors started to blur into one, each intersection negotiated blindly. Several crew passed Valmak in silence, almost scared to confront him. His strange behaviour was now well known among the crew. How their captain could threaten to arrest the only doctor on the ship was unbelievable, even by his standards.

Valmak was aware of his actions, past and present. *But how could he avoid his future?* He read out the data in his head over and over. *Was it really the truth of his future? Could he avoid it? Or even change it?* He had questions with no answers. *What else was there that would define his career?*

He finally found himself standing outside his quarters. There was something very important he had to do before returning to the bridge.

*

Quietly sitting at his control seat, Valmak was alone with his thoughts, trying to work out a plan of action. He found his concentration failing him. He looked around the bridge at his crew – all hard-working men, diligent in every aspect of their work. They were a credit to him. The last six years had been difficult at times. Retriever-2 had taken on the longest tour of duty in its history, and the crew were supposed to be rewarded well on their return. *So how could he tell them what was on his mind?* He couldn't.

The bridge crew, however, sensed something was wrong with their captain. He hadn't said a word since entering the bridge and taking his seat. He had blown up earlier, the crew knew that, but something had happened since, and nobody wanted to ask what.

Valmak's tormented mind was becoming so clouded he couldn't think straight. Somehow, he was going to have to play things by ear. The next move had to come from the Clarizianes.

King watched his captain very closely for several minutes, wanting to speak but afraid of getting his head bitten off. The captain wasn't right, and King really wanted to help. It didn't matter they'd had their differences in the past, this was now. The captain needed his crew behind him... if only he would let them help.

Zymotz broke the silence finally. "Captain, a small spaceship is about to dock."

Then Argent received a transmission. "Sir, it's Chane Auston again. He requests an urgent meeting with you. He says the docked ship will accommodate you. End of message."

Valmak swung round in his seat. "What about Commander Nussar?" he asked, surmising this was the alien's cue to leave.

"He didn't mention Nussar. A bit odd, don't you think, sir?"

King interrupted. "They do want Commander Nussar back, don't they? Only, I get the impression they're not interested in him." Although he didn't get an answer, some of the crew agreed with him but kept quiet.

"Sir, I'm sensing a trap," said King.

"No, no, it's not a trap, King," replied Valmak, though he couldn't tell the crew any different. He had to deal with this mission alone. "Acknowledge the call, tell them I'm on my way."

The tension grew heavy; the crew didn't like the situation one bit. The captain was normally very sceptical in situations like this, but he seemed to be making a rash decision. He was not thinking in his usual logical manner, but nothing about this last mission had been logical or normal. It had been one disaster after another, and they had already lost several officers needlessly.

King decided he was duty bound to point out the risks. "Captain, surely you aren't seriously going down there?"

Valmak rose to his feet. "I have to find out what they want. Continue to monitor the planet as best as you can. Maintain a full alert, that's all."

"But sir—" King was ready to plead his case, perhaps even go with the captain. Somebody had to keep an eye on him.

"Phasner, Bartok," Valmak interrupted, "have you managed to calculate our way home yet?"

"Well, yes and no," said Bartok with some reluctance.

"What he means, Captain, is we're almost there. A few minor tweaks and the odd guess. Just say the word and we'll go." Phasner sounded a little more confident.

"What about the rift in space, have you taken that into account?" Bartok asked. "We can't predict precisely what will happen, sir, that's the guesswork." Truthfully, Bartok was stumped by the problem.

Valmak appeared very lucid for once; he had full confidence in their ability.

"Well done, I know you will get us home. Now, let's go and see what this Chane Auston has to say."

King stared across the bridge to Bartok and Phasner as Valmak departed, but Phasner just waved his arms in the air.

"Did the captain just congratulate us? I don't believe what I just heard."

"Helm, maintain full alert as the captain ordered," said King, as bewildered as the rest of them.

Valmak knew he had left certain matters unfinished. Stopping at the intersection, he hesitated. One corridor led to the hangar deck, the other to the hospital. He wanted to put things right with Doctor Summers. He should never have threatened her with an arrest, but guessed it was too late to mend those bridges. He couldn't involve anyone else in his actions, not now. He had violated several commands from mission HQ, so this mission was on him alone. *Time,* he thought, *to put things right.*

Inside the hangar, a small Clariziane spaceship was waiting, its airlock already open. An alien stepped out. *Almost a clone of Nussar,* Valmak thought, which didn't give him any reassurances.

"Will you please come with me, Captain Valmak?" said the alien, ushering him to enter.

Valmak nodded, wondering why this weird race all had to look the same. He was certain they couldn't be trusted but he played along for now. "Are we not waiting for Commander Nussar?" he asked.

"Later," came the short reply. The alien was completely disinterested in his fellow being, which didn't surprise Valmak at all. He already knew the answer.

Entering the alien ship, another alien turned to look Valmak straight in the eyes. *Another bloody lookalike*, he thought.

The two alien pilots said nothing but turned round to initiate their departure. Valmak's mind was racing as he watched their every move. Of course, he knew it was a trap, but he had come prepared for it – he hoped.

They put him on edge as they kept looking round just to stare at him, it was unnerving. Whatever was going on, the plan had already begun. He had to be vigilant, choose his moment carefully, and somehow gain control of the ship. After that he wasn't sure.

As they passed through the upper atmosphere smoothly, Valmak knew he had to make his move soon. He wanted control of the ship before meeting the mysterious Chane Auston.

All too soon he saw the planet surface below. The sight was not what he was expecting. Something was wrong. There were crumbling buildings as far as the eye could see, devastation everywhere. The Clarizianes could not be living in the ruins; it didn't look right, and it certainly didn't feel right. On the horizon he spotted a strange structure – a building, perhaps. It was intact, so unlike anything else on the surface. It didn't belong there.

"What's that structure ahead?" he asked. Perhaps engaging in conversation, they might lower their guard.

"Our redemption, Captain Valmak. You will be able to join us soon in our salvation," said one.

Valmak didn't like the sound of that. "Join you in what?" Slowly he put his hand inside his suit, gripping the handle of his phasic gun.

"We are to rendezvous with Chane Auston at the departure point. He will explain everything."

Alarm bells went off in Valmak's head. *What was the departure point?* The structure they were heading for held the key, and he was certain he was being kidnapped for something. *Time for action*, he thought, *it was now or never*. The phasic gun was suddenly pointing at the head of the pilot.

"Sit down, please, Captain Valmak. There is no need for weapons." The pilot seemed a little too calm, considering he had a gun pointing at his head.

"We mean you no harm," said the other alien.

Valmak couldn't understand how they could be so relaxed. It was unnerving, but he had to persist. "Tell me right now what that huge structure is before I blow your pathetic alien brain all over the place."

"We will have to tell him, I suppose," the other alien spoke again.

"Tell me what, damn you?" demanded Valmak, prodding the pilot's head with his gun, threatening him further. "Talk!"

They were a little less relaxed with the threat of violence.

"Very well. You are coming with us. You are the image of the ancient messiah who will deliver us into the new world. It is written in the scriptures."

Now the stares made sense, he thought. He looked out of the cockpit window again at the structure and started to put two and two together. This was it. "I'm going nowhere, you alien freaks, and neither are you."

In a split second Valmak shot the pilot point blank in the head, the phasic gun at close range almost blowing the alien's head apart, then he turned the gun on the other one. The ship went into freefall as the pilot slumped over the controls.

Pulling him out of his seat, Valmak grabbed the controls and did his best to steer the ship at the structure. A huge, arc-shaped building with no windows and only one doorway, it wasn't a building in the normal sense. Valmak was sure it had another purpose, something far more sinister. He just hoped the alien ship would have enough of an impact to put it out of action. This was his destiny, the penance for all his past sins.

As the ship plummeted at speed, Valmak struggled with the alien controls, attempting to keep a level descent as best he could. He steered it directly into the heart of the structure, and the impact caused a huge explosion with catastrophic damage. Multiple explosions followed.

The structure crumbled, scattering aliens in every direction. Some didn't escape the initial explosion. Utter chaos ensued as dust, smoke, and flames billowed out from the debris. Valmak was underneath it all.

His mission was complete.

*

The entire crew on the bridge waited impatiently for news, but the viewing screen stayed blank. The Clarizianes still had some control over the communications system, so everyone was twitching with frustration. King wondered how much longer he'd have to wait for Valmak before he was forced to take action.

Suddenly the viewing screen lit up without warning, and the crew witnessed the aftermath of several explosions, clearly visible from space. Zymotz leapt into action to analyse what was happening while Meki attempted to back him up.

Something was beginning to happen. The planet surface started to glow bright orange; it was burning up from the inside.

"I don't like this, King!" yelled Zymotz, working furiously to compute the data. "The planet's core is destabilising. It's going to blow."

At that moment, Mike Dyland charged onto the bridge. "King, we need to leave. Like now!" he yelled.

King looked round, puzzled. "Who the hell are you?" He couldn't put a name to the face at all.

"Damn it, man, do you all want to die? Look at the viewing screen, the planet is about to go. Get the hell out of here before it explodes and lights up the galaxy like a Christmas tree on steroids." Mike couldn't make the situation any clearer, such was the urgency in his voice.

Phasner was the first to react. "Helm, hit that button now," he said.

Zymotz didn't respond immediately. It wasn't a direct order from authority, so he wasn't sure what to do.

King jumped up from his station, startled by what was going on around him. "What about Captain Valmak? We can't go without him," he told them.

"He isn't coming."

The crew were visibly shaken by Mike's abrupt announcement.

"Zymotz, hit that bloody button, for Christ's sake!" yelled Phasner again, suddenly realising the havoc that was about to happen.

"I have! I have!" screamed Zymotz, not wishing to hang around any longer.

Seconds later, Retriever-2 was rocked from side to side with shock waves emanating from the planet as more explosions split it apart. It was glowing white hot now.

Bartok and Phasner crossed their fingers and hoped their calculations were correct. The hyperdrive immediately kicked in – something not normally initiated in a stationary mode, but they had no choice – swiftly followed by the solardrive which was fuelled by the heat of Clarizia as it blew apart. The ship continued to be buffeted by the shock waves, which were strong enough to distort space in its wake.

Retriever-2 left the galaxy at such a velocity that many of the crew passed out. It was several minutes before they started to come round, slightly dazed but alive.

King got up from the floor and then sat down, feeling rather lightheaded. *Where were they? Had they made it back to their own universe?*

"Is everyone okay?" he managed, then realised blood was trickling down his forehead. He didn't need that on top of his sore ribs.

"Okay here," said Zymotz, getting back to his station from where he had landed on the floor. He checked his friend Meki was alright.

"Well, guys, did we, do it?" asked King nervously.

Phasner was already at his station, with Bartok computing their exact location. Helm was also attempting to compute the data, but it was slow coming through.

"I think we have a short somewhere," reported Meki, whose monitor was not working.

Phasner had no problem with his. "It's ours, we're home," he said ecstatically. "The star system, it's ours. We're back in our own time." He couldn't hide how pleased he was that the computations had been spot on.

Cheers went round the bridge. It was such a relief that they almost forgot Valmak.

King turned to Mike again. "Remind me, who are you?"

"I'm Mike Dyland, keeper of the archives," he said.

Meki looked at Zymotz and whispered, "Do we have an archive?"

Zymotz shrugged.

"Something tells me you know what's going on, Dyland. Care to share it with us?" asked King.

"Well, Captain Valmak knew he wasn't coming back—"

"And he still went?" interrupted Argent.

"Let him finish," said King. He badly needed to understand this tragedy.

Mike continued, "The Clarizianes never wanted Commander Nussar back in the first place. Apparently, he disappeared five years ago – that's their timeline, by the way, not ours."

"So how did Captain Valmak feature in all this?" asked King.

"That's where it gets complicated."

"We're all ears," piped up Meki, who was totally confused.

"According to Clariziane history, Captain Valmak was to be the new messiah – being the exact image of their ancient prophet – and lead them into the new world, which was actually their own past."

"But how?" asked Bartok, still trying to work it out.

Mike carried on. "They built a time portal to go back, but their own experiment with time travel is what started the problem. They interfered with the natural timeline that caused the universe to blink, and that caused the rift between our universes. Now the timeline is distorted. The baffling thing is that I was able to record data that hadn't happened, which is causing more problems. The Clarizianes might have perfected time travel, but they had no idea what they were messing with. Fluctuations in our universe are going to happen."

"Well, you've lost me," said Argent, shaking his head.

King had a question. "So, these fluctuations, or distortions in the timeline, can we predict where and when?"

Mike shrugged. "Your guess is as good as mine. There is no way of telling."

"Phasner, you're the expert, what do you think?" asked King.

"I agree with Dyland. We can't predict what the universe is going to do."

"So now what do we do?" asked Bartok. "I mean, can we get home?"

They all looked round at each other for answers.

"We could finish what Captain Valmak started," suggested Phasner. "We can't forget the lives of the crew of Retriever-3."

"Or we could just go home," said Meki, who was sure of what he wanted to do.

King reminded them that they were effectively on the run. "We go home, we will be arrested, court martialled, and thrown into prison."

"The robot ships will be long gone by now, but there is still Retriever-3. That mission is not complete," said Zymotz, adding his view.

"Okay, guys, enough debate," said King finally. "I think we need to take a vote. Go home or continue the mission." He was in charge now and this was a new era. He wanted things to be done differently.

"In that case, I vote go home," said Meki rather sheepishly.

King looked at the others.

"I say we stay and carry out the captain's last orders," said Phasner.

"Me, too," added Bartok.

"Okay, I'm in," said Zymotz.

"What about you, Dyland? And you, Argent? Don't you have an opinion?" asked King.

"I don't want to face a court martial," admitted Argent. He didn't fancy either of the options.

"Neither do I," said Dyland. "I guess we're in."

They all looked at Meki, who couldn't believe that nobody wanted to go home. "Alright, alright," he grumbled, "I'm in. Where else am I going to go?"

"Right, we stay. From this point on, we don't work for the company. So, remove your rank and insignia." King made it absolutely clear where they stood. "We're on our own now."

"Does that mean we don't get paid then?" asked Meki, suddenly worried for his future.

"Shut up, Nely," warned Zymotz. He could see that his friend was going to be a handful.

"First priority, we need to check our supplies – the hydroponic gardens for one. We have to be fully self-sufficient if we stay. There is no going back from here, understand? But whatever we do, we do it together."

They all agreed.

Mike had one request. "I don't want to be keeper of the archives anymore."

"Done!" said King sharply.

Mike looked perplexed. "Really?"

"Really. You will be assigned to another department as soon as we get established. So, let's crack on, guys. Work to be done."

King finally had an air of authority in his voice. He had to do this.

CHAPTER EIGHT

A small, lone spaceship passed silently through the galaxy on a seemingly endless journey. A journey in search of a new future, a new home. Coming out of the darkness, into more darkness, it was proving to be a relentless voyage. Destination unknown. This was an arduous journey that had taken many years, but still had no end in sight.

The spaceship was the last of a fleet of ships belonging to the Avaan people, who had travelled for so long that it had taken its toll on their numbers. Now only one ship and a handful of survivors were left. They were desperate people, afraid of dying alone in the vast emptiness.

The Avaan ship was damaged, limping along, having been battered by a meteor storm. The guidance system was non-operational, with no means of fixing it. And with very little food or water left, things looked bleak for the five Avaans left of their race.

Every other ship in the fleet had succumbed to the harsh conditions of deep space, the occupants forced to drift into oblivion. A mere two hundred and forty Avaans had escaped their planet when invaders came to destroy their idyllic world, leaving it uninhabitable. Avaa had been left a floating mass of contaminated rock.

The fleeing Avaans left behind millions of dead in their world; family, friends, all gone. Still, they were not bitter. That was an unknown concept in their culture. The only objective now was survival, and that was looking doubtful. They didn't want revenge, just to survive and find a new world in which to thrive. That would be the ultimate triumph over the evil barbarians who had come only to destroy the peaceful existence the Avaans had enjoyed for centuries.

With so few of them left, and no way of doing repairs, it felt like the end of their existence. They had no-one to help them, the universe seemed empty of life, and no suitable worlds could be found. Even if they found one, it was questionable whether the damaged ship would be able to land without crashing.

They huddled together for comfort and prayed for a miracle.

*

In the pursuit of an unknown enemy, Retriever-2 continued its journey. The crew were unanimous in their quest – all except Nely Meki, who persisted in letting everyone know. He was still unhappy he would not receive a wage for the last six years. It was a good job his best friend Alec Zymotz kept him under control.

The crew had come to terms with the fact that they would never see Earth again, but the mission had to be completed. So many unanswered questions remained, some of which would never be solved.

Captain Valmak's name was added to the list of brave crew who had lost their lives in the line of duty. The crew were also resigned to the fact that they had lost Steve Brown aboard the robot ships who had covered their tracks so well behind an invisible force field.

But they were determined that Retriever-2 would be better prepared from now on. They were duty bound to carry on and avenge the deaths of the crew of Retriever-3, and their only objective to find out what had happened to the missing crewmen and women.

Valmak had left a message in his quarters, telling the crew to carry on and do the right thing, whatever it took.

He apologised for his irrational behaviour towards the end, saying he had no idea that outside forces would take control of his life. His sacrifice to save the ship was his way of telling the crew to choose their own destiny.

Weeks dragged on into months for the lives of the crew, the universe suddenly devoid of all other life. They searched galaxy after galaxy for the whereabouts of the robot fleet or the planet they came from, or for the criminals who had committed the atrocious act of stealing vital human organs from their victims.

It seemed inevitable that the missing crew would not be found alive, as the journey was taking too long. The only good news was that they hadn't come across the space pirates, despite the length of time Retriever-2 had been travelling.

Many formalities were dispensed with aboard Retriever-2, though Adam King had been elected leader, because someone had to make the important decisions. They were effectively rebels now, deserters from their own planet.

Earth mission HQ persisted in their demands to return the hospital ship, having deemed it stolen property, and a repeated warrant for their arrest fell on deaf ears. The crew were not interested in anything the bureaucratic authorities had to say. The administration was only ever after profit. Without their hospital ship, there would be only losses. The hierarchy back on Earth had no idea what was going on in space, so threatening demands for their arrest only hardened the crew's resolve to continue the search for justice.

A new regime on the ship saw the crew regularly rotate their job titles, each learning a new skill. As a result, everyone got to know colleagues they had barely said hello to in the six previous years. Titles and ranks were dropped, first names preferred, and a slightly more relaxed atmosphere was the norm.

Mike Dyland relished his new role and the freedom. The job of keeping records in the archives, which had now been closed down, had only been his because the late Captain

Valmak had assigned him there soon after leaving Earth. He had taken an instant dislike to Mike so relegated him to the archives where he was subsequently forgotten about.

For years he'd led a quiet, lonely life, doing his job with no interference, but having little contact with the rest of the crew. If it hadn't been for his best friend Niko keeping him informed, he wouldn't have spoken to a single soul.

Now, though, he had acquired new skills, even new friends, and was enjoying good company he'd never experienced before. With Niko's help he'd even smartened himself up and got a haircut. She also made sure everyone knew who he was and what he had done to help save the ship and everyone on it.

There was a sadness on board, though, with the sudden death of Gordon Kursal, who had been a valuable member of the crew for so long. He'd suffered a brain aneurism, then a major stroke, from which he never recovered. The trauma that had tormented him on Kangis-3 had put a great strain on his mind and body. It was a tragic loss to everyone, and now no-one would ever know what he had seen on that dreadful planet.

*

A small speck of unknown origin appeared on the long-range scanners. As it barely registered on the viewing screen, nobody noticed it for quite some time, and computer sensors failed to record it because the size was deemed insignificant. Paul spotted it first and began monitoring the sector for further analysis. He was convinced it was just an asteroid, but his friend Will, next to him at the helm, was not so sure.

A faint trace picked up on the sensors confirmed an object not natural in origin. But it was too small to be what they were looking for – the robot fleet. This was a single object, confirmed prematurely by Will to be a spaceship. He was merely guessing but wanted to show off.

The object wasn't moving much, just drifting really, which ruled out an asteroid. However, the crew had learned to treat everything with suspicion, at least until they were certain what they were dealing with. They trusted no-one.

Anxious minutes passed until Retriever-2 came within a parsec of the object which was now showing clearly on the viewing screen but was still unrecognisable. The size was puzzling the crew, and everyone stood around staring, trying to visualise what it could be.

"What is it?" asked Paul, mostly to himself.

"I still think it's a spaceship," said Will.

"Surely it's too small for a spaceship," remarked Adam.

"It has the configuration of a small ship," Will pointed out.

"Cal are you getting any readings yet?" asked Adam. "We need data fast."

Cal and Tom were working together to download the data as fast as they could. "Computer says a single spaceship," reported Cal.

Will gave Paul a nudge. "See, I told you so," he smirked.

Paul just snapped back, "Don't get big-headed, Will, or I might be forced to break your other arm."

"Cool it, guys," warned Adam. "Stay focused."

"Data suggests it might be crippled, Adam. It's barely moving," Tom reported.

Realising they had to tread carefully, Adam spoke to the helm. "Okay, let's slow down and assess the situation first."

"Should we be stopping at all?" questioned Paul. "We all know what happened the last time."

"Just slow down and maintain a full alert," replied Adam calmly. He didn't envisage any danger, but they didn't want to be too hasty. It was his natural instinct to investigate, as this was the first sighting of anything in months.

Within minutes the small spaceship fully appeared, with Retriever-2 now stationary at a safe distance to allow the crew to study it.

"Well, it's definitely a ship," exclaimed Will, so happy to be right. "But it's size isn't much bigger than Sol's."

Adam agreed on that, but the question was how it had got there.

Tom suddenly had a crazy idea. "Is it possible that, like Sol, it came through another rift in the universe?" he asked, looking around for feedback.

Cal and Adam turned round to look at him. "Are you trying to tempt fate, Tom?" asked Cal.

"Of course not, but it is a possibility, surely." He felt he had a valid point and Adam, though reluctant, had to agree. Certain things were going on in the universe that they didn't understand or even know about.

"Adam, take a look at this," called Paul. "There is significant damage to the outer hull. I suspect it's been hit by a meteor or something."

"That's probably why it isn't going anywhere," Adam said.

"I still say a spaceship that size is not capable of intergalactic travel, so it has to have a mothership." Cal decided there was no other explanation.

"But why, Cal? Sol's ship came through a rift in space, there was no mothership. Maybe this one did the same," explained Tom. His theory was all they had to go on.

Denny, listening to all the debate, decided to add his opinion. "Why don't we try and make contact, Adam?"

"Yes, the occupants might be in distress, injured even," replied Adam.

Denny was quick to open communications as Adam braced himself for their first contact. "This is Adam King, leader of the rescue ship Retriever-2, please acknowledge."

They waited.

Further scans from Cal confirmed there were no weapons aboard of any kind. "It doesn't appear hostile, Adam. No firepower," he added.

"There are five life signs registering," said Tom. He continued scanning the ship for more clues of its origin but started to wonder about its unusual structure. *Could it really have such technology to arrive in hyperspace?* After all, size wasn't everything. It puzzled him deeply.

He was still scanning when suddenly a voice was heard over the intercom, startling the crew for a second.

"This is Ti Glish. We are stranded and in need of assistance."

Silence descended on the bridge. It had been a long time since they'd heard a stranger's voice, and a squeaky one at that.

Tom spoke up. "Well, are we going to answer or not?"

Adam reckoned the voice did not sound in any way intimidating; quite the opposite, in fact.

"What is your problem?" asked Adam finally.

"Our ship was damaged during a meteor shower. Our guidance system is out, and we are hungry."

A few sniggers echoed round the bridge. That certainly wasn't what they had expected.

"Where are you from?" Adam asked again.

"Avaa. We're from the planet Avaa. Please can you help us?"

Adam signalled to Denny to cut the intercom for a moment. "What do you think, guys?" he asked them.

"Sounds genuine to me," said Tom.

The others nodded in agreement. "Its size is no threat to us," said Paul.

Adam made the decision. "We can take you aboard and assess the damage."

"Thank you, thank you," came back a chorus of voices.

Adam looked round the bridge at the crew, who were still smiling at the squeaky voices. "Well, I guess we are technically still a rescue ship," he said. "Tom, you and Cal go and greet our guests, see what they require."

"Sure, Adam. Suppose we better lay on some food for them as well," Tom suggested.

"Good idea, see to it. Just hope they like it," Adam laughed. He couldn't help smirking at how almost childlike the voice had sounded. This could be an interesting encounter.

Tom and Cal hurried along the corridors to the hangar deck to wait for the docking. Tom in particular was eager to see new faces. He didn't feel afraid in any way. He felt a certain bond with the voice, and a feeling of empathy came over him. Besides, like many of the crew, he still had the need to fulfil their vocation in life, to rescue the vulnerable and save lives. It gave them all a purpose to carry on.

On the bridge further checks were still being carried out. Paul was slightly concerned.

"I checked the memory banks, Adam," he said, "but I can't find any record of a planet called Avaa. Should we worry?"

"No, I don't think so," replied Adam. "We hadn't heard of Clarizia until we discovered it in the alternate universe. Nothing surprises me anymore."

"Yes, but it was another dimension. What if this ship did come through a rift? Can we trust the universe not to do it again?" Paul was genuinely concerned. They weren't used to this sort of encounter, and it was difficult to put personal emotions on hold when they entered the unknown.

"Don't read too much into it, Paul," Adam assured him. "I'm sure everything will be alright."

Secretly, though, Adam had his own concerns. The ship was genuinely damaged, and it looked so innocent. *But had he done the right thing?* Suddenly he remembered Captain Valmak's last message: 'Do the right thing, whatever it takes'.

He was sure now.

*

The hospital had been extremely quiet for the last couple of months, so there had been enough time to take stock of priorities, deep clean the entire deck, retrain some of the officers as medics, and generally maintain a sterile environment in case of emergency. That seemed unlikely, as Retriever-2 was unnervingly alone in the universe.

Only Nely visited the hospital on a regular basis, always with his usual nondescript symptoms. Niko tended to him every time, listening to his woes, then having to reassure him he was as fit as the next man. It usually worked and she'd send him off with a smile, knowing he would be back next week with another complaint. Niko was actually glad to be doing something.

Sol was always by her side. His recovery was nothing less than a miracle, but he hadn't yet found the courage to leave the comfort of the hospital. He was doing fine otherwise, and Niko had sat with him for many long hours, coaxing him to make the final hurdle back to reality. It seemed his mental trauma had practically disappeared when Captain Valmak died, as if some kind of uncanny connection had been broken.

It still took some weeks for him to fully accept he would never go home, but as Niko couldn't either, it was another experience they were to share which gave them both strength.

Receiving news that the hospital might be needed shortly, Niko hurried around making preparations and giving the medics last minute instructions. Sol was assisting where he could, and as long as Niko was nearby, he managed very well.

*

As Cal and Tom arrived at the hangar deck, the Avaan ship was already inside. They were both nervous and excited as they prepared to enter.

"Are we ready for this?" asked Cal.

"I'm wondering what they're like, but I guess we're about to find out," Tom replied, as he pressed the button to open the doors.

They entered to a bustle of noise and chatter, which sounded like a hundred of inhabitants, not five. The Avaans were busy unloading some of their belongings, and the commotion was so loud with them all talking at the same time.

Cal and Tom suddenly stopped in their tracks at the sight greeting them.

"What the—?" they said in unison.

Watching the noisy Avaans go in and out of their spaceship at speed was almost unbelievable. They hadn't even noticed Cal and Tom standing watching.

Not one of them over eighteen inches tall, they were swift and agile and appeared to be very excited.

Cal smiled at Tom. "Are they for real?" he said in total astonishment.

Tom thought they were definitely cute in an alien sense. "Hi, guys," he announced.

The Avaans stopped abruptly, frozen for a second as they stared back at the two towering beings looming over them. Tom was a strapping six-foot six-inch giant in their eyes, Cal a mere six foot two.

"Well, that was a show-stopper, Tom," joked Cal.

The Avaans came forward hurriedly, totally unafraid of their hosts' huge size.

"Hello, I am Kanon Garg," said the older looking one. "I thank you for your assistance." He was very polite.

"Well, we're not sure we can do much, but we'll certainly give it a go," replied Tom, deciding to drop to his knees to make things easier for the visitors.

He had never seen aliens quite like these. They were so different, with small, round heads and silvery white skin, completely bald, and huge eyes that swung from side to side on stalks. He wasn't quite sure cute was the right word anymore, but he instantly warmed to their presence as they huddled around him.

"My name is Tom Phasner," he said gently, "and this is my friend Cal Bartok."

Cal nodded. "Hi," he said, still standing.

Kanon Garg pointed to his companions. “This is Ti Glish and his wife Ke Tegan. And that is Xander and his wife Evon.”

“Very pleased to meet you all,” said Tom.

“Pleased to meet you,” they replied in a giggling chorus. Their funny little faces beamed huge smiles as their eyes went in all directions.

Xander stepped closer to Tom. “I am very hungry, have you any spare food for us?”

“I think we can manage that,” said Tom, as he noticed one looking a bit fatigued all of a sudden. “Is everything alright with Ke Tegan?” he asked. She was unsteady and looked in some discomfort.

Ti Glish spoke as he looked at his wife. “She is pregnant.”

“Oh, how pregnant?” asked Tom.

“Very pregnant, Tom Phasner,” replied Ti Glish.

“No, no, it’s just Tom,” he laughed. These visitors were certainly going to cheer everyone up for a while.

“We do have a hospital here if it will help your wife,” Cal pointed out. He was still trying to get used to them meandering round his feet.

“Thank you,” came the chorus again, so enthused by their saviours. They all looked neat in their made-to-measure clothes, what looked like dungarees and tiny black boots – all except Ke Tegan, who was dressed in a full-length robe for her expanding size.

“Well, you just tell us what you need for your ship, and we’ll do our best to help,” offered Cal.

Suddenly Ke Tegan yelled out in pain.

“I think we better get your wife to the hospital, Ti Glish,” urged Tom.

“Yes, yes,” he said, putting his arm round Ke Tegan to support her. “It is time. Will you take us, Just Tom?” He put his tiny fingers on Tom’s arm.

“Of course. Cal will stay and see to your needs.”

“Food, we need food,” pleaded Xander, just in case their hosts had forgotten.

"Xander!" said Evon. "Mind your manners."

"It's alright, we'll sort food out for you," said Cal, warming to the visitors.

As Tom left with Ke Tegan and Ti Glish, Cal radioed through for catering to immediately bring a range of food. He then glanced over the Avaan ship, still puzzling over how they had managed to survive in such cramped conditions. The damage on the outer hull, he decided, would be easy to sort out, but not so the inside. He was keen to know more about the Avaans, why there were so few of them, and how they were so deep into space.

Xander and Evon busied away with their belongings, but Kanon Garg sat down on a case, his advanced years beginning to show.

"Tell me, Kanon Garg, what happened to the rest of your people? Why are you travelling like this?" Cal sat on the floor attempting to make eye contact, which wasn't easy when the little guy's eyes kept swinging round on their tiny stalks.

"This is all that is left of my people. We managed to escape our planet, but many millions did not. Invaders came, murdered everyone, destroyed everything."

"Aliens! Do you know who?" asked Cal.

"No, we did not fight. We had no weapons; had no need for them. We lived a peaceful existence for many centuries. We are on a journey now to find a new world, but alas many of my people died on the way. We have been travelling for many years, and I fear for our survival with so few of us left." Kanon Garg was saddened to tell his story; their survival could not be guaranteed.

Cal suddenly felt deep sympathy for the Avaans. *How could anyone decimate a whole race of people so callously, so violently?* He made a promise to himself that he and the rest of the crew would make sure they stayed safe from now on.

To Xander's delight more crew entered the hangar, laden with food, and he immediately dived in. Cal sat with them while they ate, then, realising he'd missed his meal break, decided to join in. The Avaans were delighted at that. To them it was fun, and they ate a lot for such tiny bodies.

*

Heading for the hospital with two little people in tow was going to feel like a marathon, especially with one about to give birth. So, Tom decided to help in the best way he could and scooped Ke Tegan up into his arms and carried her. She was very grateful, or at least Tom assumed she was. He couldn't tell, as her eyes were rolling about on those tiny little stalks.

Ti Glish, though, wasn't so sure about his wife being so far off the ground. He couldn't watch her while running to keep up with Tom. Suddenly he was at Tom's shoulder.

"What? How did you—?" Tom didn't finish his question.

The look on his face made Ti Glish smile, and he pointed to a button on the belt round his waist. He came to rest on Tom's shoulder. "Now let's go, Just Tom."

Tom carried on walking faster as Ke Tegan began squealing louder.

"Levitation?" he asked Ti Glish, astonished at such incredible technology these tiny aliens possessed.

"Yes, Just Tom, levitation," confirmed Ti Glish.

Tom was sure the little guy just winked at him, but he couldn't know for sure as he didn't appear to have eyelids.

"Hurry, Just Tom."

"Don't worry, we're here," Tom said, reaching the hospital entrance.

Ke Tegan didn't look too good, Tom thought, so he rushed inside and began calling out, "Niko, are you about?"

Two new medics assigned to the hospital for training came rushing over.

"Wow! What have you got there, Tom?" said one.

"Hello, Simone, meet my new friends," said Tom. "Ti Glish," still sitting on his shoulder, "and this is Ke Tegan, who is very pregnant."

"Please look after my wife," said Ti Glish earnestly.

Simone Costin escorted them to a side room while the other medic, Darryl Harding – brother of Carol – rushed off to find Niko. He realised this was going to need expert hands.

Tom put Ke Tegan gently down on the bed, which was obviously way too large for her, and assured her she was in safe hands. She didn't take a lot of notice at that point, as the pain was too intense.

Ti Glish stepped onto the bed to comfort her. "I will stay here, Just Tom. My wife needs me. It is time."

"Ok, Ti Glish, I will check on you later. I have to go now. The doctor will be here soon, and Simone here will take care of everything."

Ti Glish was saddened his big friend was leaving, but suddenly Ke Tegan yelled out. The pain was worse, and she was in distress. The scream alerted Tom as he reached the exit, and he rushed back.

Ti Glish was panicking. "Something is wrong, Just Tom, you must help."

Suddenly Tom was panicking, too. He knew nothing about childbirth, but Simone was holding Ke Tegan. "The doctor is coming, everything will be fine," she soothed.

Sol, with his sensitive hearing, came running to the bedside, but for a second his appearance seemed to alarm Ti Glish. He hadn't expected other aliens to be aboard this huge ship. His looks were strange, and Ti Glish wasn't sure about his presence.

Niko finally arrived from the other end of the hospital and immediately stopped in her tracks as she entered the room. The sight of two little people on the bed wasn't what she had expected.

Ti Glish walked across the bed and looked up at her. "Are you the doctor?"

"Yes, I am," replied Niko, just as Ke Tegan squealed loudly again.

"My wife is in labour. Can you help?" he asked.

"Oh, my word!" gasped Niko, not sure how she was going to handle this one. "Simone, go and lay out all the surgical instruments like I showed you. Darryl, see what you can find that would double as a cot."

Tom was still on hand, but all he could do was comfort Ti Glish who was beginning to panic, fretting over the prospect of being a father. Tom assured him his worries were normal.

Sol had been standing in the background, a little afraid to intrude, but felt he had to say something. "Baby is in trouble," he announced abruptly.

"How do you know that?" Niko asked, already seeing that Ke Tegan was struggling.

"I can hear the heartbeat; it's a bit erratic. Baby needs to come now," said Sol.

Until then, Niko was the only person who knew about his super hearing. She found it incredible but trusted him, nevertheless.

"Well, this is going to be a first," she said, an anxious look on her face. Then she took complete control of the situation. "Tom, out!"

Realising this wasn't the place to be, he quickly departed.

Ti Glish looked sad. "He's my friend," he told Niko.

She reassured him, "He will be back later. Now you need to tell me everything if I'm going to deliver this baby safely."

Simone helped Ke Tegan to get ready, while Ti Glish told Niko what he could.

"Sol, I might need you. Can you stay and help?" asked Niko.

"Of course," he said, happy to be of use. He suddenly felt like a member of the team, which pleased him more than anything.

The medics rushed around gathering whatever equipment they thought might be useful, although it was all oversized. Three more medics came to help, and they all had ideas on how to improvise. Teamwork was essential, but Niko knew she had trained them well.

Sol stayed close by, assisting Niko as he listened very carefully to the baby's heartbeat. He instructed her every move, and it was working well. Sol suddenly realised the reason for the distress – there was another baby! He could hear a faint heartbeat, but it was weak.

Ti Glish and Ke Tegan had had no idea there were twins, and their look of astonishment said it all.

Alerted to the situation, Niko had to work swiftly to deliver the first baby before she could help the second. The medics had managed to put a small cot together and brought extra oxygen in case of emergency.

The first baby arrived in minutes, and Darryl took it away to tend to its needs while Niko and Sol focused on the second. By that stage Ke Tegan was very tired. Simone held her tiny fingers and soothed her, while Ti Glish held her other hand.

Sol was quick in his actions. He had delicate, agile fingers, so Niko allowed him to take the lead. He had no real medical training yet seemed to know exactly what to do.

Half an hour later Ke Tegan, exhausted, gave birth to her second baby. But there was a problem; it wasn't breathing. Niko, though fully trained as a doctor, had little knowledge of childbirth and had no idea how to help with an alien birth.

The situation was quickly becoming stressful for everyone. Sol picked up the tiny, lifeless baby, barely three inches long, turned it upside down and proceeded to gently slap it.

Shocked, Ke Tegan screamed at him, while Ti Glish rose to his feet, panicking at the sight. *What was he doing to their baby?*

Niko gasped in disbelief, putting a hand to her mouth. But seconds later the baby cried out, taking its first breath. It had obviously just needed a little help.

"Sol don't ever do that again. Not without telling me first," Niko told him shakily.

"It's what my people did sometimes. It worked, didn't it?" He smiled.

Niko couldn't fault his efforts, but she was relieved it had been a success. She instructed the medics to take the baby to join its sibling.

"Simone, I want you to stay with the babies and make sure the oxygen levels stay constant," she said. "Clean them up. Darryl, you assist. Thank you for your work, well done."

"Yes, Doctor, of course," said Simone, delighted to tend to the babies. It was amazing to see such tiny lives breathing, laying there side by side in a drawer which she had quickly emptied and lined with a blanket.

Ke Tegan, although exhausted and desperate to sleep, wanted her babies. She needed their closeness to reassure her they were actually alive. But Niko reassured her they were being cared for as a precaution, to make sure they remained stable, and it wouldn't be for long.

Ti Glish, the proud father, couldn't stay put. He was so excited that his eyes were swinging frantically to and fro.

"Thank you, my friend," he told Sol gratefully. Then he floated across the room to the doctor. "What do we have, Doctor, boys or girls?"

Niko looked at him fondly. "I have absolutely no idea." In all her excitement, she hadn't noticed. *And what did she know about alien anatomy anyway?* Something told her she would have to learn fast. "Why don't you go and take a look, Ti Glish?"

Niko and Darryl attended Ke Tegan to ensure she was alright and comfortable, and she soon fell asleep. It was certainly the most excitement the hospital had seen in years, and Niko had a feeling life there was never going to be the same.

Finally leaving the room to allow Ke Tegan to sleep, Darryl asked the doctor if they could have a chat.

"Of course, Darryl, what's the problem?"

"There's no problem, Niko, but that experience will live with me for a long time. Will you train me to be a doctor?" he asked, enthused at the very idea.

Niko was taken aback for a moment, but his words were music to her ears. "Darryl, it would be a pleasure."

"Thank you. I won't let you down," he said. He'd worried that she might not want to teach a burly, six-foot guy with muscles to show off.

"Training starts tomorrow then," she said.

"Do you think the babies are going to be alright?" he asked, concerned for their wellbeing.

"I hope so, Darryl. For a moment there I really had no idea what I was doing."

"You did great, and so did your boyfriend," he added cheekily.

"Don't call him that!" said Niko, an embarrassed look on her face.

"Oh, come on. You two are an item, aren't you?"

"Really, Darryl. Now is not the time to discuss my private life. Now, get things cleared up here," she said, ushering him away. When she reached her desk and sat down, Sol joined her and put his arms around her.

"Thank you, Sol," she whispered. "I couldn't have done that without your help."

He kissed her forehead and gave her comforting hug. "We did good, yes?"

"Yes, we did good." She put her head against his chest, so relieved that it had all turned out okay. Having Sol so close to her meant so much, and with the babies on board this was a new era.

*

Adam arrived in the hospital some hours later, eager to see the reason for all the gossip spreading round the ship. Even he couldn't help but be excited.

"Niko, hi," he said, seeing her at her desk working through a pile of paperwork.

"Hello, Adam. Whatever it is I don't have the time to talk."

"I only wanted to check on our guests," he said with a smile. "I hear we have a new arrival."

"Yes, twins."

"Wow!"

"Exactly. As I said, Adam, no time to talk. Two babies to look after, and anatomy I know nothing about, then a pile of paperwork and reports to be made. On top of that, I need to document the babies' progress."

Adam could clearly see Niko was flustered and taking on too much. She didn't need to put herself through all this.

"Scrap the paperwork, Niko," he told her. "I don't know why you're still making reports. Who are we going to give them to? It doesn't matter anymore. We answer to no-one. The important thing is looking after ourselves. Bin the lot."

She couldn't believe he was serious. "Really?"

"Yes, really, Niko. Make life easier for yourself. Now I'm going to see the proud parents, and of course the babies, if that is alright with you, Doctor Summers," he grinned cheekily.

"Of course, Adam, go ahead." Niko was relieved about the paperwork, but she still felt the need to document certain details. It was important to her to have records. Then again, perhaps a little delegation wouldn't hurt, and she had enough staff now.

Adam popped his head round the corner to mention something important. "Niko, can you not recruit any more medics for a while? Some decks are saying they are short-staffed." He gave her a wink and returned to the new arrivals.

*

On a shift change, Nely and Alec were back at the helm to continue the navigation through the universe, with specific instructions to immediately report any anomalies, no matter how insignificant. What they really wanted was to find life, something to say they were not alone. Picking up the Avaans had been good for morale but that wouldn't last forever.

They couldn't let their guard down for a single moment while the search went on.

As usual, the shift was quiet with nothing to report. The emptiness was unbearable at times, but Retriever-2 pressed on relentlessly.

Nely was just back from the hospital after yet another visit – Niko was sure she would need a whole shelf for his records alone, although she had binned all the records from the last six years as they were no longer required.

He hadn't been the only one to visit the hospital, though, and the mental well-being of the crew was beginning to be of some concern. The idea of spending the rest of their lives roaming the galaxy was starting to take its toll on some of the crew. To know they could never go home wasn't a good feeling, but they'd made their choice and had to live with it.

*

Two weeks had passed since the birth of the Avaan twins, who were doing extremely well and growing a lot faster than humans. Sol's intervention and quick thinking at the birth had not gone unnoticed. And his actions were the talk of the ship, as was his super hearing.

Although he had hoped to keep that quiet, it seemed that no-one minded, and some had even suggested he would make an excellent doctor with the right training. With everyone's approval he was given a new uniform as a Retriever-2 crew member, complete with a white coat – something he wore with pride.

With the twins thriving, the Avaans were eager to leave and continue their own quest to find a new world. But their spaceship was unfortunately proving to be the sticking point. Repairs were taking longer than expected, with spare parts having to be fashioned from whatever materials were aboard Retriever-2 and then miniaturised. It was a hard, complicated task, undertaken by several crew.

The Avaans could not thank their rescuers enough. They would never be able to repay the crew's generosity and friendship, but their bubbly and exuberant manner was infectious and cheered everyone up.

It hadn't gone unnoticed how much they actually ate. Xander in particular had an appetite to compete with any normal sized human.

Some of the crew set about making clothes for the Avaan babies, then decided to do the same for the adults, who had very little in possessions. It was a good way of passing the time, particularly when they had time off, and it took their minds off their own future.

*

Ti Glish missed his new best friend, Just Tom, but he didn't want to leave his wife and babies. They were the proud parents of a girl and a boy, and no-one could dampen his excitement as he and Ke Tegan sat on the bed holding one each.

Kanon Garg was also very happy with life. He spent hours talking with many different crew members, imparting knowledge of the Avaans' way of life. His wisdom and superior intellect provided an insight into how to utilise technology more efficiently. He could see the humans were advanced in many ways, but the Avaans had so much untapped practical science they could use. For small brains, the Avaan intelligence was much more advanced than the humans could ever imagine, so sharing knowledge was indeed beneficial for both. Engineering was getting an upgrade to maximise power output more efficiently, while the Avaans were being given a maintenance course on how to do their own repairs.

Tom was relaxing in his quarters, having a well-earned time-out. He found it hard to unwind when all he could think about were the Avaans and how he was going to miss them. He visited Ti Glish and his family regularly and felt a certain affinity with them – a connection he'd never thought possible, and certainly not with aliens.

He couldn't bear to think about them leaving when their spaceship was fixed and knew Retriever-2 would be a very dull place. Then he hit on an idea, a suggestion he wanted to put to Adam later. A solution that might benefit everyone.

On the bridge, things were beginning to happen at the helm. After several days of mind-sapping monotony, Nely was watching the viewing screen when he noticed something not quite right. As instructed, he was checking for any anomaly, so he alerted Alec next to him to verify his findings.

Straightening himself up in his seat to concentrate, Alec looked at the viewing screen and asked the computer to analyse the data to double check. They waited.

Mike, now on communications duty, was watching the helm and was keen to be involved. "Shall I call Adam to the bridge?" he asked.

"Yes, I think you better, Mike," said Alec.

"What do you make of it, Alec?" asked Nely.

"No idea, my little friend, but I bet it isn't good news," replied Alec, suspicious of their findings.

Adam arrived promptly to the bridge. He'd been checking on the crew, wanting to know if they were happy doing their different duties. Morale was important, and he was determined to keep on top of it.

When he got the call, he realised it was important or the bridge would not have sent for him.

Nely quickly pointed out the star formation in the distance which appeared somewhat distorted. At first it was presumed to be the robots' force field, but that was ruled out. This was clearly different. Retriever-2 cut the hyperdrive and slowed down to take a more studied look at the strange occurrence.

"Ok, guys, exactly what are we looking at? Suggestions please," said Adam, staring at the viewing screen. He could see something not right with the picture, but what he was looking at didn't make sense.

"Not sure what it is, Adam, but something weird is going on out there," commented Nely. He could offer no explanation.

"I've cut engines for now," added Alec.

"Good," said Adam. "So, nobody has any ideas?" he asked again.

He got no reply.

"What do the scanners say then?"

"That's just it, the scanners aren't showing a disturbance at all. And the computer isn't registering anything," said Alec.

"I did suggest giving the computer a kick," said Nely, trying to make light of the situation.

They watched as some of the stars began to warp, then disappear, only to reappear misshapen in an elliptical form. The whole sector of space ahead of them was being twisted out of shape.

"What the hell is going on out there?" Alec was suddenly fearful they were watching the supernatural.

"I really don't get this," said a perplexed Nely.

"What do we do, Adam?" asked Mike. He'd left his station to stand closer to the helm, but getting a better look made no difference to what he was seeing.

"Hell, if I know." Adam was as baffled as the rest of them.

Suddenly Nely spotted one of his dials going crazy. "Will you look at that!" he exclaimed loudly.

Adam leant over the helm to see the timeclock going backwards at speed, then it reversed and went forward in time, before stopping altogether. Nely and Alec began checking their instrument panels and it was soon evident the ship was not responding as it should. They had no control of the helm, even though the computers said everything was normal. They looked at Adam with worried faces.

At that moment Tom rushed onto the bridge. He hadn't been able to relax, thinking about the Avaans, so he had started to monitor the ship's progress from his quarters.

He'd made some startling discoveries that would shake their world to the core.

"Adam, I believe I know what is happening," he announced.

"Go on, Tom, as we're flummoxed here," Adam admitted. Any answer was better than nothing.

"Remember the rift in the universe a few months back, which we thought at the time the Clarizianes might have caused? Well maybe, maybe not. I think somewhere another rift opened up and it is causing fluctuations in the normal timeline. Of course, the original rift might not have closed. My theory is that the universe blinked again, but this time we're caught up in the flux." Tom was certain of his findings, up to a point.

"Anybody buying into this theory?" asked Adam, looking round the bridge. He struggled to understand Tom's philosophy but couldn't discount his idea completely.

Nobody disagreed, though there was a lot of scepticism on the bridge that the universe could do this. *And what was the solution to the problem?* Everyone had doubts they could find an answer.

Nely innocently asked, "Can we not just reverse?"

"Reverse into what?" replied Alec. He felt his friend was always two steps behind everyone else.

Tom had to agree. They couldn't move with the timeline playing havoc with the present, though it wasn't certain if they were in the future or the past at that point.

"What's the timeclock saying now?" he asked.

"We have gone back in time six hours and twenty-one minutes," replied Nely, not sure how they were going to put that right.

"This is serious shit, guys, what are we going to do?" asked Mike.

"I guess we stay put for now," said Adam.

Alec tried a few buttons on his panel. "Don't have a choice, Adam. We can't go anywhere, as we don't have control of the helm. This flux Tom is talking about, I think it wants us to stay."

"So, what are you saying? Are we actually stuck?" Nely's brain was working overtime. He still didn't get it.

"Something like that, Nely," said Tom.

"We need to find a way to seal the rift for good before we go anywhere," said Adam. "It's too dangerous to travel at the moment."

They all agreed with him.

"If we find a way, how will we know where the rift is?" asked Mike from the background.

Adam looked at the viewing screen. "I guess right out there would be a good place to start."

"I'm not liking guesses," whispered Nely, always the pessimist.

His friend wanted to slap him, but that wouldn't solve anything. "Just be quiet, Nely."

As they puzzled over the best course of action, Denny suddenly arrived on the bridge in a hurry. "I thought you might need me; things are going crazy all over the ship," he announced.

"Like what?" asked Adam. As if they hadn't got enough problems.

"Several dials and clocks are not recording correctly. That set off the alarms in engineering, causing malfunctions to register. The crew are trying to work out which are genuine, and which are false alarms."

"Is everything alright down there for now?" Adam wanted to know.

"Just about, but some of the crew are really stressing out."

No doubt, Adam thought. He was stressing over his own leadership qualities. This was bigger than anything he had ever encountered, and he didn't have the answers.

Tom was already at the door, deciding action was needed. "I'll go find Cal and see if we can come up with a plan."

Adam nodded, then turned to the others. "Right, guys, stay alert and keep an eye on whatever is out there. And if you have anything constructive to say, I'm all ears." He climbed into the command seat and waited.

Nely was just about to open his mouth to speak. "Don't you dare," warned Alec.

Nely turned back to his station, annoyed he was always being put down.

*

Relaxing alone on a couch in the hospital, Sol felt a strange premonition suddenly come over him, which made him sit up. For a moment he wasn't sure what to make of it, but for some reason he was drawn to the Avaans. They had recently all left the hospital, babies as well, to set up a makeshift home in one of the empty quarters. They were settling in well, but they knew it wasn't permanent.

Sol liked them around, and it meant he wasn't the only alien on board now. His thoughts told him to seek them out, but he had never ventured outside the hospital yet. It had become his sanctuary for so long, but now he felt he had to go.

Strangely, he knew which direction to go and to which deck, and he knew his hearing would soon pick up their funny little voices. A certain sixth sense told Sol the Avaans were the key to everything. He was sure their superior brains held the solution to the bizarre occurrences, the things that were going wrong, things that were not normal in any sense of the word.

Kanon Garg sat with Ti Glish and Ke Tegan, away from their new babies who were resting. Xander and Evon were close by, all five chatting at the same time, all understanding each other. They were happy. It felt good to be comfortable and well fed, for Xander especially. His appetite was well known all over the ship, so it was a good job Retriever-2 could produce an endless supply.

They were interrupted by a knock at the door, and Sol entered the room, apologetic for the intrusion.

"We need to talk," he said.

"Yes, I know, Sol. I feel it, too," replied Kanon Garg. He was very aware of the happenings.

"Can you help the humans?" Sol asked.

"Possibly, but will they want our help?" questioned Kanon Garg. He thought it presumptuous to assume the humans would accept help.

Sol knew the intellect of Kanon Garg; he was wise and all-knowing, and Sol was sure he already had a plan.

"We must help them," Sol pleaded.

Kanon Garg agreed. "We must find Just Tom and Cal first."

*

Tom, Cal, and Mike – possibly the best brains on Retriever-2 – sat in the conference room, huddled round the computer monitor, going through every permutation they could conjure up to bring about a solution to their predicament. Nothing added up. Each time the computer dashed all hopes of answers. It seemed the computer would not consider dabbling with the laws of science. It was not possible or feasible in any environment. *So how could they consider tinkering with the universe when they didn't fully understand the fundamental law of the natural order of things?* The dynamics would not compute to their satisfaction.

The universe had been tampered with from outside forces, and now all life was being affected. They all knew a parallel universe existed – a different dimension entirely – but if the calculations were not spot on and went wrong in any way, both universes were in danger of colliding, with catastrophic results.

The three men had considered this, but the reality didn't bear thinking about. The rift had to be sealed – they just didn't know how to do it. *And what was stopping the universe from blinking again?* It was a phenomenon they wished they had never experienced in the first place.

Time dragged on and they continued to work, getting tired but refusing to give up. Retriever-2 remained stationary, locked in a state of flux, as the hours passed painfully slowly, and no solution was forthcoming from the conference room.

Adam felt time was not on their side. The dials at the helm were still behaving erratically. He watched the timeclock jump into the future, then weeks into the past, and yet the ship never moved. He could see no way to get the ship free and the crew to safety. Somehow, an outside force was holding them against their will.

But Adam dared not go forward in space, even if they could. The possibility of passing through the rift was unthinkable. *What would they find on the other side? Certainly not home, if that was ever an option. Would they ever get back? Would they cause more chaos in the universe if they stayed?* Adam's mind was full of questions he couldn't answer.

He hadn't heard from Tom and Cal, which was disturbing him even more. And he didn't know what Mike could offer them. But whatever was going on, he suddenly didn't like the idea of leadership. The responsibility weighed too heavily on his shoulders, while the crew were looking to him to do the right thing, solve all the problems, and save the universe.

He tried hard to stay strong, wondering if Captain Valmak had experienced these feelings when in charge. Perhaps that accounted for the man's erratic behaviour, and Adam wished now he hadn't made all those reports about the captain's rash decisions. In the end, Captain Valmak had made the right decision for his crew, but Adam didn't think he could rise to that level.

*

Kanon Garg and Sol reached the conference room, knowing exactly where their friends would be. Sol's sixth sense had heightened beyond his own expectations, and it was matched by Kanon Garg's own intellect. They felt as if they could reach into each other's minds.

"Will they listen to us?" Kanon Garg asked Sol, as they stood outside the door.

"I think they must if they want to survive. You have the knowledge they need."

Kanon Garg nodded.

Sol opened the door and announced abruptly, "We're here to help." He strolled in, forgetting he still had his white coat on, while Kanon Garg floated in beside him and landed on the desk.

All three men sat up quickly with surprised looks on their face.

"And what can we do for you, Doctor Sol?" said Cal in a jokey manner.

"It's what we can do for you," he replied, not understanding human humour at all.

Kanon Garg walked across the desk and looked at the monitor to see what they were working on. "That won't work," he told them with confidence.

"What?" Cal looked back at the monitor, bewildered by his remark.

"Kanon Garg, please explain," said Tom, and Mike moved the monitor round so the little alien could see better.

"These schematics, they won't work," Kanon Garg said again.

"How can you know this?" Cal was eager to know more.

"Please listen to him," said Sol, urging his little friend to continue. "We know the situation; we can help."

The men looked doubtful. *How could two aliens think they had the solution?*

"I believe you have recently constructed a weapon of mass power," said Kanon Garg.

"Yes… but how did you know?"

"I know, Just Tom," was the reply.

"Ok, well, it's a phasic blast of pure energy, able to be fired from the ship. It's been modified but hasn't been tested yet. What about it?" Their attention was now piqued.

"That's alright, but it won't work in its present form. You will need to make alterations. The power supply will need to be reconfigured, then reverse polarity of the phasic ignition mechanism. Then a few other minor adjustments are needed. I can help you with this."

"You?" questioned all three.

Kanon Garg seemed almost excited, his eyes swinging in every direction except frontwards. "Yes, do you not trust me, Just Tom?"

Everyone looked thoughtful. "It's better than anything we've come up with," admitted Mike. "And I for one am starving, tired, and in need of my bed."

"I will explain everything and instruct you," their visitor assured them. "The new modified phasic blast can then be used to seal the rift."

Cal wasn't sure about the idea. The phasic blast had originally been designed to kill, if ever it was needed.

"What if we miss the target?" Tom asked, beginning to be swayed by the little guy.

"Make sure you don't, Just Tom. You have one chance to do this."

"Kanon Garg and I will assist on the modifications," added Sol, eager to be useful.

"Sol, you were a space pilot, now training to be a doctor. How can you understand the science of this?" Cal was not convinced they would not blow themselves up.

"I have knowledge," replied Sol with confidence. He knew more than they realised.

"Ok, I'll compute the schematics you come up with and see what the computer says," Cal agreed.

"Well, I still say it's better than anything we've come up with in the last twenty-odd hours. What have we got to lose?" added Mike.

They all agreed to try.

"One more thing, Kanon Garg, how did you know about our phasic blast?"

"I know many things, Just Tom. More than you realise."

Tom smiled, yet he was astounded by the Avaans' superior power and ingenuity, despite their size. He trusted them beyond a doubt.

Cal set up the computer so Kanon Garg could instruct him on the computations and a unique way to bypass the computer's logical thought process, as that would only impede the outcome. Kanon Garg relayed precisely what Cal and Tom had to do. It was going to be challenging.

Some hours later, it was concluded that the plan could work, but it was risky. Shooting a powerful phasic energy blast into space, when it hadn't been tested, was highly dangerous, no matter how much it had been adapted.

Finally, Cal had the results sitting in front of him. "Ok, it is possible, if Kanon Garg is correct with his schematics—"

"I am," the little alien interrupted.

"I do have to point out, though, there is a chance the fluctuations in the timeline are not guaranteed to stop." Cal warned, "We could make it worse."

"What do you think, Mike?" asked Tom.

Mike was in agreement with the idea. He felt they had no other choice.

"It has to be a unanimous decision, guys, so let's have a show of hands," requested Cal.

"I believe we can do this," said Tom straight away.

"I agree with Tom," added Mike.

Reluctant as he was, Cal had to agree, but he wanted to go over the plans one more time.

Sol, up to this point very much the outsider in the discussion, piped up, "Do you want to sit here and debate it further, or get on and do something about it?"

Tom jumped in. "Sol is right. Let's just go and do it!"

All of them agreed nervously, whatever happened now the decision was made.

"Thank you, guys. I want food, shower, and bed," said Mike. "You lot can do this without me. I've just done a triple shift." Mike waved at them all and left.

"I like Mike," said Kanon Garg, "He mentioned food. I want some." He left, accompanied by Sol, who realised he had been away from the hospital too long and Niko might be worried where he was. He was pleased, proud even to be part of the team.

Cal and Tom just laughed. *How could they all think about food at a time like this?*

*

Adam was getting restless, pacing the bridge, beginning to lose patience – mostly with himself. He felt useless, which only added to his stress. As leader he should have been more hands-on, more involved with Cal and Tom, but he didn't have the acumen for the science part.

Bridge crew members were employed simply as pilots and Adam wished he'd studied better at the academy. He'd only got in by the skin of his teeth, and now he was wondering how he had managed to get to first officer level.

Tom informed Adam of their intention to use the phasic blast machine and rig it to fire at the rift in an attempt to seal it. Adam thought it was a ludicrous idea. *But what did he know?*

Fluctuations in the timeline were still happening at irregular intervals and they had to stop them. There was a real threat of an alien race coming through from a parallel universe to cause even more chaos, so they could not allow the situation to continue. The balance in the universe had to be restored and maintained at all costs.

The crew of Retriever-2 deemed it their responsibility to be guardians of the cosmos. Captain Valmak had died in the parallel universe so that the balance would be restored. The imbalance had probably contributed to his feelings of foreboding and animosity toward Sol, but the captain's destiny had been inevitable.

Now it was up to Adam and his crew to make sure the laws of the natural order of all life were not disrupted again. Adam thought the untested phasic blast was a foolhardy plan, but he bowed to the science officers and the intervention of the aliens. Whether he believed in the plan or not, it didn't matter, so he kept his thoughts to himself.

Alec and Nely were still at their stations, deciding not to let the shift change over. They wanted to see the plan through to the end, one way or the other. They continued to monitor the area of distorted space, assuming it to be the centre of all the mayhem. The timeclock registered seventy-eight hours into the future, but that was likely to change. They dreaded the timeclock moving, having one eye on it all the time.

"Adam how is this going to work?" asked Alec. "I mean if we do succeed, will we stay in the future or slip back to the past?" Alec was only asking what everyone else wanted to know.

"No bloody idea!" came a disgruntled reply.

There was no way of predicting the erratic behaviour if the universe decided to blink again. Who knew where they might end up, if they survived the phasic blast, and Adam didn't mind admitting he was scared.

"Sorry, guys, I don't mean to snap, but the waiting has got me on edge," he said. "Just be ready when Tom gives the order. We only have one shot at this," he reminded them.

"I'm worried the phasic blast will make the rift bigger and we'll get sucked in, then what do we do?" asked Nely. He couldn't see a favourable outcome, but then he never did.

"Kanon Garg assures me it will be like sealing the rift with a strong adhesive. Not his exact words, obviously, but that's my understanding," said Adam, doing his best to allay Nely's fears. "Great, a sticking plaster to repair the universe," muttered Nely under his breath. "Now I'm really worried." Nothing would make him feel any better.

*

Six hours after the phasic blast targeted the rift, it appeared to be holding – much to everyone's surprise. The distortion of space had gone and, according to the scanners, was acting normal – whatever normal was. The crew couldn't be sure of that.

Retriever-2 had been released from the flux, and immediately the hyperdrive had kicked in and the ship sped away at full speed. The need to put some distance between them and that sector was paramount, and everyone on board felt relieved.

There were no guarantees, no way of knowing if the seal would hold, so they weren't hanging around to find out. They feared the danger of another rift opening up at anytime, anywhere. It was a constant threat to their very lives.

The Clarizianes, having caused some of the damage in their own universe with their interference with the natural timeline, could not have realised the chaos they would create in another universe. Experimenting in time travel had proved a futile way of trying to extend their existence. And it had cost them dearly.

Retriever-2 went on its journey several weeks in the past, according to the timeclock, which was always going to be a possibility. It didn't bode well for the natural continuity of life itself, but the crew had to accept it.

At least they were alive.

*

Once things settled down and the ship's routine was as normal as it could be, Tom finally put an idea to the rest of the crew. He wanted the Avaans to stay. Their superior intellect had already proved invaluable, and the improvement to the engines' capacity output had increased by forty percent. Retriever-2 was able to accelerate to a velocity beyond anything on the other rescue ships or even the federation police. So, they had a good chance at least of staying one step ahead of the authorities.

The Avaans imparted such wisdom to the crew, and the longer they stayed the more they were adored. Their unique outlook on life had become the envy of everyone. The new babies were thriving, growing at a faster rate than human babies, and they were active, mobile, and becoming a handful to their parents. Now there was better news when Evon announced she too was pregnant.

Tom's idea of the Avaans staying for a while was put to a vote.

CHAPTER NINE

Out of the darkness came a small fleet of spaceships, with one purpose in mind – death and destruction to the enemy. Nothing else mattered but absolute victory. Standing at the controls of the lead ship was the emperor of the Cynturian race, Yulan – an evil, barbaric murderer of thousands. Leaving devastation in their wake, the Cynturians were beings only bred for war, their goal was total annihilation of anything and anyone in their path. Then they would crown themselves rulers of the galaxy.

Yulan watched and waited for the next prey to appear. It had been many weeks since their last victorious battle, and he was hungry for more blood, ready to take whatever he wanted.

When a lone spaceship approached, heading straight in their direction, Yulan thought it would not involve much of a fight. But it was huge, so perhaps it was time to have a little fun first.

It was soon evident that the solitary ship was one of the Earth space rescue ships. It would be easy prey, and a prize Yulan had craved for a long time. He was determined that when he finally reached Earth itself, he would let the people there know of his superior power.

The rescue ships were allegedly the fastest spaceships in the galaxy, with the most sophisticated technology known. But Yulan deemed his fleet far superior in every way. *Destroy the rescue ships*, he decided, *and nothing could stand in his way to the planet Earth*. Yulan would be famous among his people; his ultimate prize.

The Cynturian fleet was already responsible for laying waste to many civilisations and had no respect for life or the devastation they caused. It was simply a game to be won, going into battle purely for pleasure. Kill anything that moved, kill anything that didn't move.

The detector transmitter in front of Yulan bleeped, meaning the target ship was in range.

"Time, I think, to have some fun with the Earth people, yes?" he laughed.

"Yes, your excellency, we await your orders," said one soldier, dressed in heavy battle armour plating from head to toe, eager for the action to begin.

Yulan's bulging black eyes waited, anticipating the right moment to strike. He ordered his entire fleet into attack formation.

"Fire a warning shot. Let's play with them," he ordered.

*

Aboard Retriever-2, Adam was alerted to a fleet of ships in the distance. Nothing suggested hostile yet, but they couldn't take any chances. They had nothing to defend themselves with, as the phasic blast machine had burnt itself out and was still undergoing repairs. This was not the time to engage in a confrontation.

Retriever-2 slowed its engines to allow the crew to assess the strange fleet of ships. If they were the dreaded space pirates, Adam realised they would be in trouble.

Suddenly and without warning, the lead ship fired on Retriever-2, rocking it sideways. The blast just missed them, but still sent some of the crew flying.

"I guess that was hello," said Paul, at his station once more.

"No damage just missed us," reported Will.

"A warning shot, I presume," said Adam. "Who are they?" he asked.

If the shot was meant to scare them, it definitely caught their attention. Mike was already scanning the images through the computers.

"Cynturian warships, and it looks like we are target practice," he said alarmingly.

"Don't they realise we're a hospital ship?" questioned Denny.

"Probably they do, but that wouldn't mean anything to the Cynturians," replied Mike, getting more data from the memory banks. "They are a race of murderers, notorious throughout the galaxy."

"But a hospital ship?" repeated Denny. "Surely the intergalactic symbol on our hull would tell them not to open fire?"

"Apparently not," said Will, as another warning shot came across the bow of the ship.

Adam watched from the control seat. He'd heard of the Cynturians, but this was not their patch. He guessed Retriever-2 was in big trouble, so evasive action was promptly needed.

"Let's back off, guys. Put some distance between us," he ordered.

Coming up with a defence plan was going to prove difficult when they had no weapons. At that precise moment he hadn't got a clue how they could get out of this situation. Paul hit the reverse and Retriever-2 moved swiftly away to a safe distance. But Adam wondered for how long.

*

Yulan was laughing that the ship was retreating so soon without a fight. They weren't much of a contest, but he would have his prize soon enough. They would not get away.

"Your excellency, you do realise the Earth rescue ships are not armed for combat?" questioned one of his warriors.

Immediately, he regretted speaking up as Yulan turned to him, eyes bulging in anger at the defiance and sheer impudence of his subordinate.

He took his photon-atomiser and pointed it at the warrior, then shot him straight between the eyes.

"Nobody questions the great Yulan, understand?" he raged.

His minions nodded, afraid to say a word to anger him further.

"Clear away the body and get back to the fun," he laughed.

*

As Retriever-2 raced away, Yulan's warships matched their speed. They were not giving up the chase.

"Can we get any more power to the hyperdrive? We need more power!" Adam cried out.

Helm tried but they couldn't break away.

"What if we use the new technology Kanon Garg installed?" asked Paul, remembering they had extra power in reserve thanks to the Avaans.

"What about initiating the solardrive?" said Will. "It would certainly boost the velocity."

"No, look what happened to us the last time," Adam reminded them. That would have to be the last resort.

"Well, if Kanon Garg is correct with his schematics, the solardrive won't be a problem," Tom was quick to point out. He was more confident about Kanon Garg's work than the rest, and he could see it working without the problems Adam expected.

As he finished speaking, several more warning shots came a little too close for comfort. *The Cynturians were merely toying with them, but for how much longer?* Retriever-2 wasn't built for heavy bombardment, only for speed, and it appeared the Cynturians could match that.

"Continue with the retreat, guys, at least until we come up with a plan." Adam wasn't entirely sure he would come up with a solution, but at the same time it would be difficult to stay out of the firing line. He was reluctant to use the new technology which hadn't been tested yet. He had to leave it as a last resort, but he had a feeling it wouldn't be too long before he made that decision.

Kanon Garg suddenly materialised on the bridge, hovering close to Adam. He had sensed danger for his friends.

"What is happening, Adam?" he asked, as he came to rest on the arm of the seat.

"We're under attack, Kanon Garg, and we can't defend ourselves without the phasic blast. We have no other weapons. It's best you stay with your people. I can't say how safe you'll be, I'm afraid." Adam felt genuine remorse for the Avaans, Retriever-2 was no longer a safe haven for them.

But Kanon Garg ignored Adam's request. He felt the ship was in mortal danger and he had to help. His eyes started rolling and swinging every which way, alarmed at the impending threat to their new home. He could not allow it to happen.

Still sitting with Adam, he looked at the viewing screen at the oncoming fleet of warships. Wanting a closer look, he glided across the bridge to study the deadly looking warships. There was something very familiar about them.

"Can you enlarge the picture for me?" he asked the helm crew.

Will magnified the viewing screen, and in an instant Kanon Garg recognised the symbol on the outer hull.

"I know these ships, Adam," he said angrily.

"Are you sure?"

"Yes, I am, Adam. They are the attackers of my world, the barbarians who destroyed the planet." Kanon Garg had never been more sure. "I will never forget what they did."

He started to get furious – something he didn't do often, if ever. He hovered closer to the viewing screen, his little face twisted in anger, turning his skin a bright red as he shook a tiny fist at them.

"Murderers!" he squealed, bitterness choking him, fury at these killers. They had robbed him of his entire family before he'd managed to escape with some of his people. They would pay for their crimes.

He turned back to Adam. "I will help you, Adam, and your people," he declared.

"What can you do?"

"Size isn't everything, Adam. You must trust me."

"It's not that I don't trust you. I do – we all do. I just don't see how you can help us." The genuine concern in Adam's voice spoke volumes to Kanon Garg, but it made no difference.

"I am old, but Ti Glish and Xander will do the mission. You must keep as much distance as you can from these ships, and my people will do the rest."

If there was one thing Adam was sure about it was Kanon Garg's enthusiasm. *How could he doubt him?*

With a touch of a button on his belt, the little alien vanished from the bridge in a flash.

"Hey, where did he go?" Will was stunned. He hadn't seen the Avaans do that little party trick before.

"Close your mouth, Will," smiled Paul. He'd seen it once or twice, but it still amazed him.

"Can we trust them, Adam?" asked Will.

"Do you have a better option?" replied Adam. They had no choice in the circumstances. Whatever the decision, they had to act quick.

"Get ready, incoming attack!" yelled Paul as another blast came in close. This time the ship reeled from the blast shockwaves.

"Too close for comfort; they mean business now. Get us out of here!" shouted Adam. He had no idea what Kanon Garg intended, but he had to give the Avaans time for whatever the plan was. He prayed his faith in them was justified.

*

Kanon Garg quickly explained the situation to Ti Glish and Xander. The mission was dangerous, but the young ones were up for it, no question. It was their way to help the humans who seemed powerless to help themselves. It was also a way to repay their kindness for saving them and giving them a home.

The Avaans were determined to fight, and this time they would succeed in defeating the invaders. Their ancestors had not rebelled against the Cynturians when they had come to destroy their world, because fighting was not in their DNA.

But it was now.

The harshness of travelling the universe for many years had hardened their resolve, and this time they would rise up and fight.

Kanon Garg, however, had concerns for Xander and worried he was not mature enough to be fully aware of the enormity of the mission ahead. He was young and impetuous, even foolhardy at times. Born a year after the Avaans escaped their dying planet, Xander's parents had died early into the journey, and he had generally been allowed to roam freely. There hadn't been much mischief one little boy could get up to aboard the ship.

If only Kanon Garg had known, then how rash he would turn out to be. At least, though, getting married to Evon had calmed him down – a bit.

Kanon Garg gave Ti Glish and Xander a final briefing. "You know exactly what to do?" he asked.

"Yes, we follow the instructions the humans taught us, but in reverse, and then get out fast," said Ti Glish.

"Xander?" Kanon Garg looked at him sternly.

"Yes, I can do this. I will not let my friends down." *Xander was confident but cocky*, thought Kanon Garg. He was too old to move so quickly himself, so he had to allow the young ones to do this.

"Good, then go. Be swift, be safe."

In seconds they were gone, and Kanon Garg returned to the women, Ke Tegan and Evon. They were understandably afraid – Ke Tegan, not wanting her husband to do this perilous mission – but knew they had no choice. If they failed, it would affect their lives as well as that of the humans.

*

Almost in darkness, Ti Glish and Xander arrived in secret aboard one of the warships, having teleported themselves into a tight compartment. Ti Glish hoped his calculations were correct and they were close to the control section – the main framework linking the engines and the bridge controls, where most of the Cynturians were operating.

Kanon Garg had instinctively known where to send them, as his sixth sense was so much sharper than the younger generation. He was slightly off, but they could hear voices and laughter. The Cynturians were mocking the humans and their feeble attempt to escape.

"This is going to be fun," whispered an excited Xander.

"Quiet, Xander, be serious for once."

"Sorry." Xander couldn't help his exuberant nature; it was hard for him to dampen such enthusiasm.

He listened as instructed and watched Ti Glish squeeze between the small gap to reach a tangled mess of cables. The Cynturians weren't very particular about neatness, so there were cables everywhere, intertwined, knotted, and in a complete muddle.

Ti Glish found what he was looking for and swiftly pulled a cable out of the connection.

"Isn't that dangerous, Ti Glish?" asked Xander, watching intently, knowing he would need to do one shortly.

"Of course it is, but not for us."

Locating a second cable, Ti Glish pulled that one out and switched them over before anyone noticed a loss of power.

"Is it done, Ti Glish?"

"Yes," he whispered, trying to negotiate the cables about his feet to reach Xander. "Let's hope Kanon Garg is correct," he said. "Kanon Garg's theory is that the weapon cable switched for the main engine cable will cause a reversal of power to the engines. They will fire and overload the network and blow themselves up."

Ti Glish hoped Xander was paying attention. "Let's get out of here fast," he said.

In an instant they were gone, the Cynturians none the wiser.

Soon they landed aboard another warship to repeat their actions.

"What now, Ti Glish?" asked Xander. His friend was waiting patiently, but Xander wanted to move.

"We wait for a moment. I just want to be sure I've got it right," said Ti Glish.

"I hope they like the surprise," sniggered Xander.

Moments later a huge explosion rocked the warship they had been on. The rigged ship fired its weapon and the feedback from the photon-atomiser exploded violently in the engine section. It had effectively fired on itself with disastrous results – just what Ti Glish had hoped for.

The exploding ship sent shockwaves and debris into space, hitting two other ships in close proximity. One limped off course, unable to maintain its position in the formation, and subsequently smashed into another ship, crippling that one.

Emperor Yulan was raging at the loss of his ships for no apparent reason. The Earth ship hadn't fired, so he couldn't understand what had happened. Then another explosion occurred on another ship as it attempted to fire on Retriever-2, mistakenly thinking it had opened fire first. It failed, blowing the ship apart and taking two more ships in the process.

Yulan erupted. "Get that ship now!" he demanded. "We have wasted enough time playing silly games." He wanted victory at any cost. "Destroy the Earth people and their worthless ship."

His fury was boiling over. So many ships out of action was not acceptable, as he was not used to such losses. The crew of Retriever-2 would pay dearly for this with their lives, he decided.

Ti Glish and Xander found themselves on Yulan's ship and could hear him shouting furiously at his men.

"He is very angry."

"Shall we make him even more bad-tempered?"

"Why not, Xander? It's your turn. I will listen out. Be swift."

Ti Glish watched through a tiny slit in the panelling and saw two huge metal boots stomp across his eyeline. It was Yulan for sure, still spitting anger at his crew. Ti Glish grinned at the evil murdering dictator, hoping he would soon regret his past actions.

Xander struggled through the cables, knowing exactly what he had to do but he just had to get there. He didn't want to teleport that short distance in case he overshot the mark. He knew this would complete the mission.

Ti Glish was growing anxious. He could see Xander fiddling about with the cables, but not what he was doing. He couldn't call to his friend in case Yulan heard them; the emperor was standing too close to the panelling.

Xander was having trouble pulling out the weapons cable. It was stuck. He knew Yulan was soon going to open fire, so he had to hurry, but his tiny hands were not as strong as he'd thought. Finally, it came loose, and he quickly swapped the cables over and signalled to Ti Glish that the job was done.

Ti Glish whispered to him, "Let's go, Xander. Teleport now."

In an instant Ti Glish was gone, assuming Xander was right behind him. But Xander was not. In his haste, and thinking he was free of the cables, he stumbled into them. The more he wriggled to free himself, the worse tangle he got in, until even his hands were caught up.

Unable to reach his belt to press the teleport button, Xander panicked and made so much noise in an effort to free his hands that Yulan was alerted to a strange sound coming from inside the panel at his feet.

In his anger at a delay to firing at Retriever-2, he bent down and ripped off the panel, only to see a tiny alien creature desperately trying to get free.

He began to laugh. "Well, what do we have here?" said Yulan. He suddenly had a vague memory of such a creature in the past. *How could he forget such ugliness?*

Reaching inside the panel, Yulan yanked Xander free and held him aloft to show off to his warriors. "I wonder how we missed killing you, a worthless ugly creature from a race who wouldn't fight. How did you get here then?"

"Not so worthless, I think, you treacherous monster." Xander was smiling, his eyes swaying all over the place in his excitement. But that merely made Yulan's temper so much worse. "Thank you for freeing me," Xander said.

Yulan roared, "You have guts, I'll say that for you for one so small." Yulan swung Xander round in the air by the scruff of his neck. "What shall we do with him, men?" No-one answered.

Xander had had enough anyway. "The debt to my people has been repaid," he giggled, able to reach his belt now. As he pressed to teleport, he squealed in Yulan's face, "You are a murderer, a barbarian, a despicable being, not a very nice person – and by the way, I think you are the ugly one."

Then he was gone.

Yulan couldn't believe what had happened. *How had the tiny alien escaped his grip so easily?* He felt cheated out of his prey, and this could not go unpunished.

"I have had enough!" he screamed. "Fire! Destroy that ship now, I want nothing left of it."

His warriors obeyed, firing every one of the photon-atomisers available. A massive overload surged out of control and the ship blew out from the inside with enormous force.

The devastating effect took several other warships in the huge explosion.

The battle was over. The few enemy ships left retreated without further violence before suddenly self-destructing, the ultimate price for failure.

*

On board Retriever-2, Adam watched with his crew in utter silence as they witnessed the explosions, floating debris, and the total destruction of the Cynturian warships. All the ships had gone in a matter of minutes.

They were stunned, almost disbelieving their own eyes. The fleet had gone, and they were alive. A wave of relief went round the bridge. Adam was grateful they were all safe, but he couldn't fathom just how they had managed to survive a battle they'd had no hand in.

"Well, I saw it, but I don't believe what I saw," said Will, finally breaking the silence.

"You and me both, buddy," added Paul.

"Can I stop shaking now?" asked Mike. He had never seen real action before. This was his first tour of duty, and the archives had always been a safe haven away from everyone. He didn't mind admitting he had been scared for his life, but as far as he was concerned the archives could stay closed. Being with his friends meant so much more.

Moments later, Kanon Garg appeared once more on the bridge next to Adam, who flinched, startled by his sudden appearance and bulging swinging eyes in his face.

"Oh, bloody hell! I wish you wouldn't scare me like that, Kanon Garg."

"Sorry. I didn't mean to alarm you, Adam. I just wanted to make sure you are alright up here."

Adam smiled at him. "We're all fine, thank you. I don't know what to say, because thank you doesn't seem enough. We are all indebted to you for saving our lives."

Suddenly the entire bridge crew stood and applauded the little guy. Kanon Garg was humbled; never had he felt so overwhelmed before. He had never experienced gratitude like this, and it warmed his heart.

"No, it's us who should thank you for our lives. Besides, it was Just Tom and Cal who gave us useful information on mechanics and engineering. We just made good use of it. We were only too pleased to help."

Adam nodded in appreciation. The Avaans had proved to be a great asset to them. They still had unfinished business, but it seemed like a good opportunity to ask the Avaans to stay and join them wherever their journey took them. However, he could offer no guarantee of finding the Avaans a suitable new world, and he couldn't even say what he and the crew were going to do next. At that moment everything seemed pointless. *Were they pursuing justice or running away from the truth? It was a difficult choice.*

For now, everyone on board was happy to have the Avaans for company. They could teach the humans so much, and their antics had everyone in tears of laughter, especially their hide and seek, disappearing at will, popping up just about anywhere. The crew would never doubt their ability or intellect, or their size, again. In many ways the Avaans were more advanced and their technology off the scale than humans. Their naivety was a breath of fresh air.

Ti Glish and Xander were honoured as real heroes, and Xander would relate his exploits to anyone who listened. Kanon Garg realised then that Xander had finally grown up. He would still make mistakes, he was sure, but Kanon Garg could let go of the responsibility he'd taken on when Xander's parents died. He would allow Xander the freedom he deserved, and Evon would keep him in check.

A deadly crisis had been averted, and now peace and harmony prevailed on Retriever-2. The journey, though, had to continue. They didn't know what they would find, but it was time to move on.

Along with the Avaans and Sol, they continued their endless journey into the vast emptiness. Not for the first time, space seemed devoid of life. But it seemed not all was well back on Earth either.

Denny had always kept one line of communication open so he could listen into what was happening back home. But the news was not good. He heard that not only was there a warrant for their arrest, but now federation police were searching the galaxy for them. Worse still, the federation police used heavily armed ships.

Denny let the others know what was being said, and they decided that the Earth authorities would have to find them first if they wanted their ship back. Nely even suggested they should keep it in lieu of their wages. He would not be outdone.

Retriever-2 tried to stay one step ahead of any federation patrols but being labelled criminals and fugitives from their own kind really hurt. Everything they had done had been for the right reasons, but Earth mission HQ just wanted their property back and the crew in custody.

*

Retriever-2 was now a playground for the baby Avaan twins, who weren't really babies any more. Not only were they mobile, walking, and talking, but they found the game of hide and seek exhilarating, having acquired the ability to levitate, vanish, and pop up anywhere on the ship without any aid – something their parents couldn't do. It quite often got them into trouble and stuck in awkward places, but nobody seemed to mind.

Niko was fascinated with the twins' progress and wanted to find out how these little beings evolved to the point of fending for themselves at such an early age. Even humans couldn't do that in the twenty-sixth century. Try as she might, she could find no logical physical explanation for their advanced development, other than that they were far superior and unique. *She would definitely write this one up in the medical books – not that anyone would get to read it*, she thought.

Many more weeks went into the search to find either the robot ships or their creators. Additionally, they wanted to solve the mystery of the missing crew from Retriever-3. Adam still had hopes of his brother being alive, but it was beginning to look less and less likely that he would ever see him again. The search appeared futile, but no-one wanted to ask whether they should give up or not.

There were only so many times one could count the stars before going stir crazy. And the monotony of endless vigils on duty, watching space to the point of sheer boredom, was starting to wear the crew down. They were becoming restless and more despondent at the thought of being alone in the universe, unable to go home, and not able to find a suitable world for the Avaans or themselves. It seemed the universe was fighting against them all the way.

All crew members enjoyed spending time with the Avaans, exchanging views, opinions, and wisdom of their cultures. It broke the monotony and gave everyone down time, helping to ease the pressure of their mundane existence. Several empty quarters were adapted for the Avaans to suit their needs and generally be more comfortable, as befitting their tiny statures.

Four months had passed since the battle with the Cynturian warships, and life wasn't much different on Retriever-2. Still nothing to report, the universe was very quiet. Too quiet.

The crew had somehow evaded all attempts to capture them. Adam thought that was probably because they had journeyed so far that Earth didn't know where to look for them. Retriever-2 was skimming the edges of the known universe and getting away with it by the skin of their teeth.

After a while, though, Adam began to doubt why they continued to run away from the truth and from civilisation altogether. *Who were they kidding?*

They were not the avengers of the galaxy. The truth was they didn't know what else to do. Returning to Earth was never an option; they had been away too long, and the countless charges piling up made a return impossible. They hadn't had the opportunity to tell mission HQ that Captain Valmak had died, as had several crew members in the line of duty. So, the authorities had no idea the traumas the crew had gone through. But the way things were going nobody would ever know.

Adam relaxed all remaining rules on the ship; it was pointless sticking to any kind of protocol or routine. He allowed the crew free time to pursue interests at any time, which was fine. It was also common knowledge that Niko and Sol were a couple, particularly as he had finally moved into her quarters. They couldn't keep it a secret any longer, and Mike made sure of spilling the beans to everyone about his best friend. He was happy for them.

Sol felt at peace, finally coming to terms that he was the last of his race. It in no way deterred his affections for the woman who had saved his life. He loved this new life, and being accepted into the crew made him feel he had a new purpose, one he could excel at.

The hospital had been empty of patients for a while. Only Nely popped in occasionally with the usual ailments, but even he was becoming a less frequent visitor. So, Niko and Sol had plenty of free time to be together.

The Avaans decorating their quarters gave Niko inspiration to do the same with hers. She'd never spent much time there before, as she was always busy in the hospital, but now it was time to turn it into a home for her and Sol. She left Darryl to study alone; he would make an excellent doctor in time.

Niko knew the hospital wouldn't stay empty for long, particularly as Evon was pregnant and due to give birth soon. The Avaans were, it seemed, intent on growing their numbers. Niko had a woman's intuition about Ke Tegan's condition but held off speaking up until she was ready to say. But she knew.

CHAPTER TEN

On the bridge, another shift began in the usual way for Alec and Nely. Sitting at their stations, they watched the viewing screen, monitoring the sector closely, checking and logging all incoming data in case it was needed at a later date, and then generally becoming bored silly with the routine. This shift, however, was going to be different.

They both did all the usual checks and settled back for another quiet session. Everything appeared fine, nothing out of the ordinary. Tom, working away at his station, asked Alec to check a star system that had come into view. He wanted verification of an anomaly that had occurred on his previous shift, as the data wasn't adding up.

"Tell us what we're looking for, Tom, and maybe we can help." Alec was happy to be doing something.

"Just record the star system, log it, and send the data to my computer," Tom replied.

A strange request, Alec thought, *but what the heck. If it broke from the monotony of doing nothing, he wasn't going to argue.*

A couple of minutes later, he had the data recorded. "Ok, Tom, you should have the data on your screen now," he said.

"Thank you," was all Tom said. No explanation.

Nely stared at his friend, who shrugged his shoulders, and they both carried on. But moments later Tom was standing at the helm right next to Alec.

"What now, more stars to count?" suggested Alec sarcastically.

Tom ignored the negative remark. "Can you put up that last star system we just passed?" he asked. Tom's voice seemed more serious, so it had to be important.

"Now, put up the star system from three days ago," he said.

Alec was curious where this was going.

"Ok, now do the same with the star system from a week ago. I've just uploaded it for you."

Even Nely stopped what he was doing to watch Tom and Alec. Something was up, but he just hoped it wasn't bad news.

"Can you tell us what we're looking at?" asked Alec, who couldn't see any connection at that point.

Tom's face suddenly changed; his suspicions confirmed. "Right, Alec, now can you overlap all three systems on the viewing screen?"

"Ok." Alec thought it was a pointless exercise. But as he did, he stared at the viewing screen in utter disbelief. "Bloody hell!" he said.

"They all match," declared Nely. "How can that be?"

"Not just a match, my dear friend. Identical, in fact." Tom wasn't happy that he was right. It meant trouble, serious trouble.

"What does it mean?" asked Alec, trying to fathom the data, worried for a moment that there had been a miscalculation in logging the reports.

"It means it's the same star system each time," Tom responded.

"But how?" Nely struggled to get his head round the data. It was there in front of him but still he didn't believe it.

Tom, though, was certain of his facts. "Basically, guys, we're going round in circles."

"What? No. Sorry, Tom, just run that by me again. I think I misheard you." Nely was always a bit slow to realise the importance of the situation, but the truth was he didn't want to believe what he'd just heard.

"I think – no, believe – the ship is trapped in a time warp. We're caught in some kind of loop, so no wonder the ship is going nowhere. We thought the universe was empty all this time, but we're simply looking at the same sector every few days."

"So, you're saying we are doing the same journey over and over?" Alec asked. It was hard to take in.

"Yes," replied Tom with a grimace.

"Shit! I mean serious shit," said Nely.

"Precisely, guys. Something is wrong. The equilibrium in the universe has been disrupted again. Somebody has caused the imbalance, but where or why I don't know."

Tom had been concerned things were too calm for too long. He wasn't even certain how long the ship had been going round in circles. It could have been weeks, and they'd all become so lazy that they had missed the vital clues.

"What about the timeclock, Nely?"

"Normal, Tom, whatever normal is," replied Nely.

"Could it be the rift again?" asked Alec. He thought it was a genuinely plausible suggestion.

"Maybe the sticking plaster came off," quipped Nely.

Alec looked at him sternly. "Are you deliberately being stupid? Idiot!"

"No, Alec, not an idiot. It's plausible," said Tom. "Nely could have a point."

"See!" Nely replied smugly.

"Now what?" Alec wanted to know. "Why is it always us who has to fix the universe?"

"I suspect we might be the only ones who know about it," admitted Tom, realising they wouldn't get answers by standing there doing nothing. All this time they had thought they were safe.

"Ok, we need a plan," he went on, taking a deep breath, "There is a distinct possibility the imbalance is because someone came through the rift from the parallel universe, and it disrupted the timeline. Look, guys, we have to sort this."

"How?" asked Alec and Nely in unison.

"Someone or something is messing with the laws of nature. We have to stop it."

"You mean visitors through the rift, or even enemies, Tom? We can't do it; we can't fight anymore." Alec was serious. The crew were exhausted.

"I'm not sure we have a choice, Alec. The universe is unstable."

"And we're going nowhere, right?" said Nely.

"Quite. We better go on full alert, so get all crew back to their stations, and inform Adam immediately that we need him on the bridge. And keep an eye on the timeclock. I have a bad feeling about this one."

"Oh joy," muttered Nely.

"Shut up, Nely, now is not the time to be flippant," snapped Alec.

Nely sank into his seat in annoyance. He hated when his friend put him down.

But Alec was already regretting being snappy. "Sorry, Nel," he said seconds later. "I didn't mean it. I'm scared, too. We have no idea what's coming and that worries me."

"It's ok, Alec." They had been friends for too long to fall out over petty words. "Let's get to work then."

"Yeah, maybe put that sticking plaster back on, eh?" said Alec with a wink. Nely nodded with a snigger.

Suddenly without warning, the universe blinked again, but this time it really had something in its eye. The distortion in space was immense and the entire galaxy moved out of place. Then another rift opened up, a huge crack appeared, and stars slipped through. Utter chaos ensued.

The timeline started playing havoc with the on-board timeclock, which went crazy. The fluctuations were worse than before. There was no way to stop the distortions, the crew were powerless to act, and they could only stand and watch the mayhem. The natural order of all life was out of control. All creation was being threatened with its very existence.

The universe appeared to be having another hissy fit. Something was interfering with space and time, trying to manipulate the universe to its own end – something not natural to this world.

In an instant Retriever-2 found itself back to a familiar place, but the crew didn't like it. According to the timeclock, they had gone back six months into the past, and the planet looming directly up ahead was Kangis-3. It had appeared out of nowhere just as the distortions in space began. This was not a good sign.

Adam, now back on the bridge, watched nervously with the others. The very thought of that planet gave him goosebumps. They had lost too many good men on that evil place.

Stranger still, the crew realised this wasn't the right sector for Kangis-3. It shouldn't even be there. The question on everyone's mind was how a planet could travel halfway across the galaxy. None of it made sense, but Adam thought the entire voyage wasn't making sense anymore. He couldn't understand any of it.

Further analysis suggested the planet was maybe not Kangis-3, even though every aspect of it said otherwise. Adam recalled Captain Valmak voicing suspicions about its identity. It made him very uneasy about its reappearance.

This had to be connected to the distortions in the universe, maybe even the cause of them. But at that point Adam was more concerned the ship would become caught in another state of flux. He feared it wouldn't be so easy to escape a second time.

A huge distortion on space registered close by – too close for comfort – and Retriever-2 had no choice but to stop dead. There was no point rushing head on into something they had no control over, and certainly not before the crew could work out a plan of action.

The mere fact this strange planet was beginning to move towards the ship said it wasn't natural and was definitely hostile. It didn't appear to be in any kind of orbit.

Tom reached the conclusion it was being manipulated independently – but how, or by whom, was a mystery. It definitely had something to do with the unnatural occurrences in the universe, of that much, he was sure.

Several probes sent out to gather data confirmed Tom's theory, and there were shocked faces around the bridge.

"It's an artificial planet?" asked Adam. "I mean, it's fake?"

"Yes, a probe did discover that underneath the surface a subterranean world exists. That same probe detected many lifeforms."

"That's weird," frowned Adam. "So why did they hide that fact last time we were here?"

"Good question. And I don't have an answer," replied Tom.

Adam was alarmed at the thought the perpetrators they were looking for might be hiding inside the artificial planet which was heading straight for them. The crew were not prepared for it.

At that precise moment Denny received a distress signal saying assistance was urgently required. "I think it's coming from the planet – a plea for help. A crisis has occurred, and the people need medical help."

Adam wasn't buying it, and neither was Tom. It had to be a trap.

"What shall I do?" asked Denny.

"Hold off, Denny, while we have a think," replied Adam. "Suggestions anybody?" he asked, scanning round the bridge.

Nely kept quiet in case he got slapped down again, Alec had no idea, and Denny and Tom were the same.

Cal walked onto the bridge to be met by silence. He looked round at the men. "What?" he asked. Something was clearly going on, then he saw the planet looming closer on the viewing screen.

"Oh, I get it, another encounter with the mystery planet," he said, recognising it straight away.

"Now if I had said that you lot would have shot me down," quipped Nely, deciding to have his say anyway.

"Well, it's obviously a trap, guys," said Cal. "You can't seriously be considering going down there."

"We don't know yet, Cal, but we have to make a decision. If we don't, the problems going on in the universe will only get worse," Adam told him.

"I agree," said Tom. "That planet is the link to what's happening, I'm sure."

"Is it definitely the Kangis-3 that Doctor Forester was on?" asked Nely.

A sensible question for a change, Alec thought.

"What about those lifeforms inside the planet. They must have been there when the doctor was, surely?" Alec added to Nely's question.

"Possibly, but if so, they might have stayed hidden while Forester was on the rampage as that hideous blob thing," replied Tom, speculating on the reasons.

Adam listened to everyone's point of view. The situation was indeed grave and needed to be resolved, but he just couldn't see how to do it. Whether or not any of them wanted to return to Kangis-3, they had to solve the mystery of the planet, find out who the subterraneans were, or end up becoming lost in the fluctuations. Adam just wondered how much more debate to allow, as time may be limited.

The distortions in space and the fluctuations in the timeline had stagnated for the time being, but there was no way of knowing how long that would last. One thing was certain, Retriever-2 could not stay there forever. The universe was in a volatile state, unstable and unpredictable.

Tom declared that in his view the cause of the disruption in the universe was down to Kangis-3, and it had possibly even been responsible for the second rift appearing. Something had to be done, that much they agreed on.

Adam realised they had to investigate. If the situation wasn't resolved, nobody was coming out of this alive.

Decision taken; Retriever-2 moved into orbit at a safe altitude. To be absolutely sure, Adam wanted to hear the distress call once more.

The crew all listened carefully.

"Anyone notice anything?" asked Adam. He wanted the others to confirm what they'd heard.

"I do," said Cal. "It's a recording. It's identical word for word to the original distress call."

"Exactly!" said Adam enthusiastically.

"So, a decoy?" asked Alec.

"Not sure, Alec, but whoever is inside that planet wants us back there," replied Adam.

"So, it's a trap for us then?" Cal asked.

"I think so," agreed Tom. "Ok, Adam, what do we do?"

"We have to go down to the surface and investigate." Adam tried to sound confident and assertive, but privately he was scared.

"But you just agreed it's a trap. Now you want us to walk straight into it? No way!" Nely was adamant he wasn't going. He didn't like the situation one bit.

Everyone agreed it was a trap and highly dangerous, but Adam pointed out that it was more dangerous not going. He had to convince them they simply had no choice.

"Look, guys, we go, but this time we will be prepared and armed. Plus, that murdering blob isn't there. Karlton Forester is dead." That was the only certainty they had.

"But has it gone, Adam? Don't forget we've gone back in time six months, so who knows what we'll find?" Alec made a good point.

Nely suddenly felt one of his funny turns come on and really wanted to excuse himself to visit the hospital.

"Is it possible we could have reversed in time, and everything has to happen again? And what of Captain Valmak? Did he die or not?" Denny was becoming confused with the whole situation, and he was frightened, to say the least. *Where was it all going to end?* "I just don't like the idea," he added.

"Tom, what do you think?" asked Adam. He still had his own doubts but knew they had to follow this through.

"I do agree we have to act, Adam. But go down to the surface – really?"

Adam realised Tom was the one crew member with a true logical head on his shoulders. His comments made sense. *But now what?* he thought. Logic surely didn't apply in these circumstances. The universe was not acting in a natural way, they were experiencing erratic fluctuations in the timeline, and somewhere unnatural forces were at work. It made no difference in the end to Adam's decision. He was going down to the surface and said so.

"Then I'll go with you, Adam, and I volunteer Nely as well," said Tom.

"Why me?" Nely couldn't mask the petrified quiver in his voice.

"Because, my dear friend, you're the one person with the least logical brain, and we might need that kind of thinking," replied Tom, adamant he was going.

"I want to do my thinking from the safety of the ship," Nely said, pleading not to go.

"Nely, I need you," Tom told him earnestly.

"But I don't want to be a hero," Nely said in frustration, his stomach churning up inside.

Alec put a gentle hand on his friend's shoulder for support.

"Nel, just think of your status when you come back from this mission. You know how much you fancy that Carol Harding. Do this, and she won't be able to keep her hands off you."

"Oh yeah! What if I come back in a body bag? Worse still, what if I come back alive? Have you seen the size of her brother?" Darryl Harding was twice his size and very protective of his sister.

"Nely, you're going. Tom is right, we need you," Adam confirmed.

It was time to fight back against these unnatural forces and put the universe back in order. He weirdly felt like a mercenary leading his men on a covert operation, and perhaps in some way it was. It was a strange time, but they had to do this. Someone had to deal with this catastrophe, but no-one else in the universe seemed to be aware of the enormity of the crisis.

*

The Avaans found it hard to concentrate, as they were fully aware of the disturbance going on around them. During many years in the wilderness of space the Avaans had honed certain skills, including levitation, teleporting, and disappearing. They could also now sense when something was imminent, and they knew their new friends were in trouble again and would need extra help.

However, another very important matter needed their attention. They were anxiously waiting on news from the hospital, where Evon was about to give birth. Niko had been told to be prepared for twins, but she'd found a new level of confidence with Sol by her side. He was proving to be a good replacement doctor, as he picked things up quickly.

He relished the idea of learning as much as he possibly could about alien anatomy and hospital procedures – it was a far cry from being a pilot in outer space. It felt good to have a new life skill, and he and his new love made a good team. His super hearing could be a little distracting at times, but it wasn't something he was able to switch off at will, and it wasn't always appropriate to listen in. He did his best to be discreet.

Kanon Garg let his mind drift away from the matter in hand. He knew Evon would be in safe hands for the birth. Sol would be there, and he was one alien Kanon Garg could rely on.

The sense of danger was strong; a force had awakened in the universe – a force which, if left unchecked, would destroy all life. It had to be quashed, but that was going to take a huge effort from all concerned. The people on Retriever-2 had to do this, but they would need help.

He felt Xander was ready. He had grown into the young man Kanon Garg had hoped for, and the humans could depend on him in a crisis. Xander would be the perfect secret weapon, and if it involved his friend Just Tom, he would not fail. Xander would do whatever was necessary to save his friends. As soon as Evon gave birth, Kanon Garg would speak to him.

*

Setting off in the shuttle to enter the upper atmosphere of Kangis-3, it was soon apparent that the air was different. It didn't have the same density as reported the first time, but the crew weren't too sure if that was significant or not. Captain Valmak had documented the mission in detail, but his data wasn't going to help the crew now. They had to do this alone.

Suddenly, on the descent, the dials and guidance system went crazy then stopped working altogether. The newly trained pilots, Erica Sotton and Danny Bowles, lost all control of the shuttle. They continued to descend to the surface in a controlled manner.

"Can you override the system?" asked Adam. He was annoyed at himself for not realising things wouldn't be easy.

"No, we're completely locked out. It must be an outside source operating the shuttle," reported Erica. She and Danny could only sit back and watch as they headed towards the surface.

"What do we do, Adam?" she cried out, worried they might actually hit the ground at speed.

"Just sit tight, guys," said Adam. He was seated behind Erica and had a good view of the planet surface approaching. He should have anticipated that the aliens, whoever they were, wanted full control. But they had managed it a little too easily for his liking.

"Best alert the ship and let them know what's happening," he said, trying to sound calm for the crew's sake.

Tom sat quietly behind Danny, and next to him at the rear was Nely, still unable to fathom how he had volunteered for this shit. *Getting no pay was bad enough, but putting his life at risk with no pay was out of order*, he reckoned.

"No good, Adam, can't get through to the bridge. All communication signals are blocked." Erica was starting to feel the pressure and was becoming edgy about the mission.

"I guess we're on our own then," said Adam. He could only wonder what these mysterious aliens wanted with them.

"Course now changing, Adam. Looks like we're being guided in," announced Danny.

"So, what now?" Tom hoped Adam had some sort of plan ready.

"We wait. Everyone have your phasic guns ready," Adam replied. He just prayed he was doing the right thing.

The shuttle gently touched down, much to everyone's relief. Nely was a complete bag of nerves; he had never fired a phasic gun before and wasn't sure he wanted to. He was just a humble pilot who lacked courage for anything else, and he would be the first to admit it.

Tom tried to reassure him. "Come on, Nely, you can do this," he said.

"You do know I might never forgive you for this," he replied, as Tom's hand on his shoulder beckoned him to move.

The misty horizon greeted the men as they stepped out of the shuttle. They knew they were expected, but what they could expect was a daunting prospect. All suited up, fully prepared for the rancid air, they soon realised their helmets weren't needed.

Adam lifted his visor to check. Captain Valmak's report had described a stench in the air, but that had gone. A very light mist hung in the air but even that didn't seem real.

Nothing was as the captain's report had described. It was like Kangis-3, yet it wasn't.

Because of the disruption in the natural timeline, Adam signalled to all the crew to be wary in case Doctor Forester in blob form had survived in the distortion in time. They could take nothing for granted. Everything about this place was surreal.

In the distance were the same black mountains, the same black soil beneath their feet, which they now realised was artificial. The boulders did appear real, though, which was strange. There was daylight, which was odd when the planet didn't have a star to orbit, and there was nothing to indicate where the light was coming from.

The black soil and mountains gave an eerie feel to the area, as if the planet was a barren wasteland, empty and forgotten. Perhaps that was the intention.

The silence was scary. The absence of even a light breeze made them wonder where the air was coming from. The crew almost forgot it wasn't a real planet. They were breathing just fine, so Adam took it to mean they were wanted alive – at least for now.

As the five of them edged slowly away from the shuttle, phasic guns at the ready, Nely stayed really close to the others. No way was he getting left behind.

Looking for signs of life was hopeless. There was not a single manmade structure in sight, which didn't come as a surprise if the aliens lived underground. So, there had to be an entrance somewhere. It was hard going underfoot, with heavy boots sinking into the soft soil, and Adam was beginning to regret his decision to come. He asked himself what Captain Valmak would do in this situation, but whatever happened they had to see it through.

Adam felt sure they were being watched, but there was no vantage point to spy on them. The mountains in the distance were the only structure with height, but they were way off.

"Okay, it's hopeless going on," he said. "Let's get back to the shuttle. I think we need to think of a plan before going any further."

Nely had never felt so relieved, and he was only too happy to turn back. He was first in the shuttle and strapped in, eager to leave. Erica and Danny followed him inside but immediately realised they couldn't take off because the shuttle was still out of their control.

"What now?" Danny asked, frustrated and scared they would be marooned on this dead planet.

"Ideas anyone?" asked Adam. He felt useless.

Tom answered, "I think we soon might meet whoever is here. They didn't bring us down without a good reason."

"Makes sense," agreed Adam. He started to wonder why Tom wasn't their leader.

"So, we just sit here and wait to be captured?" Nely was full of doom and gloom as always. He didn't like the way his stomach felt, but they had no choice but to sit and wait.

*

Stationary in orbit above Kangis-3, the crew desperately tried to make contact with the shuttle crew but had no luck. They couldn't even pinpoint their location as too much interference had started just after the shuttle entered the atmosphere. It followed the same pattern as reported in Captain Valmak's original report.

Frustration was boiling over on the bridge, with the crew fearing the worst. Retriever-2 had already lost men on this deadly planet, and they didn't want a repeat. With the timeline in a state of chaos, they couldn't be sure it wouldn't happen again.

"What the hell is going on down there?" yelled Alec, thumping his instrument panel. He was concerned for his best friend, who hadn't wanted to go in the first place. He wished he hadn't egged him on.

"Stay calm, Alec. I'm sure Adam has it in hand," said Cal, now in temporary charge of the bridge.

"I don't like it, Cal. They shouldn't have gone. Nely shouldn't have gone." Alec was angry with himself more than anything.

Privately Cal was just as worried as the rest of them. The silence from the intercom was killing them, and they didn't know how long they were supposed to wait. Adam hadn't given them a timeframe. Cal even pondered the idea of using the other shuttle to go after them, but he hoped he didn't have to make that decision.

*

Returning to the hospital after a short break, Niko headed straight to see Evon's new arrivals – a boy and a girl. The birth had been easy, and Sol had taken charge. Niko had never delivered two sets of twins before, but it seemed that twins were quite common with the Avaans. Xander was overwhelmed by the experience, almost bouncing off the walls. He was a very proud father, naming his son Just Tom after his best friend, and his baby girl Sola after Sol, who had kept Evon so calm during the birth.

Evon was sleeping, and the babies were in the makeshift beds once occupied by the other twins, Po and Levin, who were floating around the hospital causing all sorts of mayhem. It was hard to see them at times, as they were only four inches tall.

The latest additions were a welcome distraction for everyone – the Avaans, Sol, and their human friends. But the exuberance wasn't too last. Xander had to leave his babies sleeping, as he had pressing matters to deal with. Evon would understand he had to leave, but he made Niko and Sol promise to take great care of his babies.

After speaking with Kanon Garg earlier, he had been made aware that his friend was in trouble and knew he would have to go down to the planet to help. Niko and Sol, though, were understandably worried for the little guy. It was dangerous to go.

"I have to go, Niko. Just Tom needs me. I will be fine," he assured her.

Niko was really afraid for him, fearing there was little he could achieve, but Xander was adamant. Just Tom would do it for him – he had to go. Without another word, he vanished from the hospital.

"Oh, I wish he wouldn't keep doing that," said Niko.

"He will be just fine. I have faith in his ability, so should you," Sol replied, wrapping his arms round her waist and hugging her for comfort. "We will look after the babies," he said.

*

Inside the shuttle, everyone sat in silence, unable to come up with a plan to get them out of there. Tom was certain the aliens would show their hand sooner or later. They'd been waiting there for over an hour with no sign of anything happening, and it was getting frustrating. The shuttle had been brought down for a reason. *What were the aliens playing at?* Tom wondered.

Danny kept trying the controls, hoping for a spark of life from the engine. There was nothing.

Nely finally broke the silence. "How much longer are we going to sit here?" The uncertainty was breaking him, his nerves were shattered, and waiting around to die was definitely not on his bucket list.

"Nely, try to keep it together," said Adam. He could see the state Nely was in. Maybe it hadn't been such a good idea of Tom's to bring him along. Nely wasn't cut out for this.

"Just be patient," said Tom, changing seats to sit next to Nely. "We will get out of this, I promise."

But Nely didn't have the same confidence as the rest of the crew. He always felt out of his depth.

Suddenly they all jumped when a faint noise came from the rear of the shuttle, close to the airlock. All five swiftly stood up and pointed their phasic guns at the exit.

"What the hell was that?" cried Danny.

"I think it came from outside," said Erica, her hand shaking so much she struggled to grip her gun.

"No, it's definitely inside the shuttle," said Tom, the only one to approach the rear.

Another clatter of supply canisters brought him closer still. *Had something entered the shuttle without them realising?* "Get ready, guys," warned Tom, poised to shoot at whatever moved.

Then out of the blue came a tiny voice. "What a stupid place to materialise."

"No, it can't be, can it? Xander, is that you?" Tom, startled for a moment, put his gun away and moved the overturned canisters to help him out.

"Just Tom, hello," said Xander with a smile, his eyes everywhere as usual.

"Xander, what are you doing? I could have shot you," Tom exclaimed. The little guy was putting himself in danger just by being there.

"Sorry, Just Tom, I miscalculated my point of entry, and I'm very glad you didn't shoot me. I'm a new dad, you know. I have responsibilities now." He picked himself up while the others breathed a sigh of relief.

Tom was happy to see his little friend, but he shouldn't be there. "You have more important matters to deal with, Xander. Your babies need you."

"My babies are in very good hands, Just Tom, so I have come to help. There is much danger here. Kanon Garg sensed it and sent me to protect you all." He spoke with such confidence; he was sure he could do it. Kanon Garg had faith in him.

"What danger, Xander?" asked Adam. They needed to know what they were up against.

"What do you know, Xander? Tell us quickly," urged Tom.

"Someone is coming," he replied.

"Who?" asked Tom.

"I don't know yet, but they bring danger. I will protect you, Just Tom." Xander was gone in a flash.

"Where did he go?" asked Erica. "Surely he can't save us?"

"Good question, Erica, but I'm guessing he's gone outside," said Tom.

"Foolhardy idiot," muttered Adam. "Now what?"

"Well, if he has gone outside, then we follow." Tom was adamant they couldn't allow the little guy to go it alone. Adam still didn't have a plan, but Tom was sure Xander had one.

Outside, he called to Xander. He could have gone in any direction, and being invisible when it suited him was no help to knowing his whereabouts.

"So, which way then, Adam?" Tom asked.

"No idea," replied Adam, as he surveyed the area.

"What about heading for those mountains? Maybe they hold a clue," Erica suggested, trying to be helpful.

"I'm not walking that bloody far," declared Danny, indignant at the very idea of struggling any distance over the rocky terrain.

About to move off, Adam suddenly stopped. He felt the ground shift, the soil moving. "Please tell me you all felt that" he said.

"Sure did," confirmed Danny, lifting up his phasic gun.

Tom and Erica agreed; they had their phasic guns at the ready. Appearing out of nowhere, several deathly white alien beings rose out of the ground a short distance away. All had long white hair, were dressed in full length robes, and didn't seem too welcoming.

"Stand firm, guys, guns ready," Adam whispered.

The aliens stopped about ten feet away, looking rather stern.

"Who are you people?" asked Adam. He got no reply. *Did they not understand the language?* "What do you want with us?" he asked again, hoping for a response.

They didn't answer but simply beckoned for the visitors to follow. Tom counted five of them, which he reckoned they could handle.

"We want answers," demanded Adam. "If not, we will shoot." And he meant it.

One of the aliens turned round to face Adam. "Your weapons will not work. Now come with us."

Adam fired and so did Tom, but nothing happened. The phasic guns were indeed useless. Fear suddenly gripped them as they realised, they were defenceless.

"How the hell did they do that?" asked Tom, not expecting an answer from anyone.

"Come." The aliens beckoned again, but more forcefully.

"Do we have a choice?" whispered Danny.

Adam felt despondent. He'd let his team down, walking straight into a trap as he should have expected.

"I think we have to go," said Tom. He had a feeling Xander was close by and was up to something. But Adam stood his ground, determined it was not a good idea.

"Trust me, Adam, we should follow them," said Tom, and he winked at him as he walked past.

Adam couldn't make it out. *Had Tom a plan? And where was Xander?* He too realised they had no choice but to go. He signalled to Danny and Erica to follow.

"Where is Nely?" he said. They all looked round. "Nely, get your butt here now!" shouted Adam.

Poor Nely sheepishly appeared from behind one of the bigger boulders.

"You idiot, we stay together," said Adam. "Come on."

Nely stayed silent as he followed the rest. He had hoped he wouldn't be missed, though he had no idea what he would have done on his own. He hated every second of being there and feared they were all doomed, never to leave Kangis-3 alive.

A short distance from where the aliens had appeared revealed a flight of stairs leading deep into the ground. At the bottom a well-lit passage came into view. Three aliens led the way, with two behind.

Danny kept looking back, checking on them. They didn't appear to be armed. *Why were they allowing the aliens the upper hand? If he got the chance...* He clenched a fist ready.

Walking along the passage, Tom observed his surroundings and covertly tapped a wall. A metallic echo rang out, and he surmised the whole planet was built of metal with the artificial surface made to look real. *Clever*, he thought.

Behind them they heard the heavy sound of the surface trapdoor closing. Now they were well and truly trapped underground.

Nely was sick with fear, his stomach playing up again.

"What is wrong with him?" asked one of the aliens, as Nely doubled over in pain, ready to throw up.

"Take a guess, you alien freak?" snapped Danny.

Erica comforted Nely, while Tom and Adam watched in case the aliens reacted to Danny's remark. They were angry, but it mattered not.

"You ok, Nely?" asked Tom.

Nely nodded, but he wasn't really.

Adam could understand how Nely was feeling, as he felt just as sick. But he remained silent, still trying to think their way out of this hellhole. He wasn't having much luck; he could only manage to question his own leadership skills.

The aliens moved them on, and at the end of the passage a huge door opened, leading into a small room with the same look as the passage – metal walls, ceiling, and even the floor. Straight away they noticed how sparse it was, with no seats or furniture at all. It looked pretty grim.

"You will stay here until we are ready for you," said one.

"Ready for what?" demanded Adam. He didn't like the sound of that.

"You are here because we need you."

"Why?"

"You ask too many questions."

Without further discussion they were prodded from behind to enter the room, which quite clearly resembled a cell.

Danny, at the rear, was prodded a little too much for his liking. He didn't care for the poke in his back, and he turned on the alien and lashed out, hitting him hard between his two ugly, sunken green eyes.

The alien fell to the ground in pain, something he had never experienced before. The aliens were not used to retaliation.

Suddenly Danny dropped to his knees, screaming in agony, holding his hands over his ears. The pain in his head was unbearable. It only lasted seconds but felt a lot longer, and he was left numb, weak, and unable to pick himself up.

Tom and Erica helped him to stand, but he was very groggy and wobbly on his feet.

"What did you do to him?" yelled Tom.

"Disobey us again and you will see what we are capable of. Now get inside."

The fallen alien also got to his feet; his vision momentarily blurred. He felt dizzy, which was not an experience he enjoyed. He looked expressionless, unsure what to make of the pain.

He stared at Danny. "My name is Solomon, and I will make you pay for that." He wanted to inflict more pain on the visitor, but the other aliens pushed them all into the cell.

Adam gestured to Danny there should be no more antics like that. It was obvious the aliens had mental powers beyond their comprehension, so it was no wonder they didn't need weapons.

The door slammed shut. They were alone now, but for how long they had no idea.

Erica sat down with Danny, making sure he was alright, while Adam paced the floor, his footsteps echoing back and bouncing off several metal walls. Nely sat huddled in the corner, unwilling to talk to anyone, least of all Tom.

Adam broke the silence. "I think this whole place must be made of metal, the way it sounds."

"Do you know what I think, Adam?" said Tom.

"What?"

"That this isn't a planet at all, but a giant spaceship disguised as one. It would explain its movement through space."

Adam pondered the suggestion. "What about the atmosphere then?"

"Artificial. Probably for our benefit, I guess." Tom leant against the wall and slid down to his knees, his head in his hands. The feeling inside him was not a good one, and he truly felt he was the only one to get them out of this mess.

He looked across at Nely, his head resting on his knees. "Sorry, Nely."

"Go away." Nely wasn't in the mood.

Tom felt guilty now, but he was even more concerned for Xander. He couldn't understand why they hadn't heard from him and just hoped his little friend was safe.

Suddenly he felt a weight settle on his shoulder, then tiny little fingers running across his face. A familiar voice whispered in his ear, "It's me, Just Tom."

"Xander?"

"Don't talk, Just Tom, listen. Guards are outside the door. I came right past them, and they didn't suspect a thing."

Tom nodded, then gestured to Adam that he had company on his shoulder. He understood, walked over, and sat down close to Tom to pick up what was being said.

"Just Tom, I have been investigating. This planet is artificial, it's a giant spaceship."

Tom already knew that, but they needed to know more. He whispered to Xander, "What have you found out about the aliens?"

"Not much yet. I have to go now, Just Tom, but I will find out more about them and what they're up to. I will be back. You must hang on, trust me." In an instant Xander was gone.

Tom wasn't sure what his little friend could do. The Avaans were a unique species, but a single being against an entire race was asking a lot.

Adam hadn't caught much of what Xander said, but Tom told him it wasn't a lot. "He basically said to hang in there, then he left."

"Great," said Adam grudgingly.

It felt odd to put all their trust in an alien who stood only eighteen inches tall, with weird wobbly eyes on stalks. But it was all they had to rely on. Adam suddenly felt inadequate. For their size the Avaans had far superior mental ability than humans could ever hope to reach.

"So, we sit and wait?" he muttered.

"Guess so," replied Tom.

Minutes later the door swung open and in walked Solomon with a look of evil revenge directed straight at Danny. He pointed at him and Erica.

"You two, come with me."

Reluctantly they got to their feet. Danny now regretted hitting the alien and wished he had just strangled him there and then. It would have been worth the pain.

Erica clung onto his arm, more for her own comfort than anything. Neither of them wanted to go, but they didn't want to endure the pain.

Tom called out. "Hang in there, guys."

The door slammed again.

"I just hope Xander returns soon, before it's too late," he said quietly.

"So do I, Tom. So do I." Adam sounded subdued.

Nely was still huddled in the corner, shaking with fear, his stomach doing cartwheels. This was not how he had thought his life would end. He had plans, dreams, none of which were going to happen now.

He envied the Avaans with their families; he had none. He glanced over at Adam and Tom, but neither seemed to be coming up with a plan. *Just how had their lives come down to this, to die in a prison cell on an unknown planet, and six months into their own past? What an epitaph*, he thought. He supposed he could be sitting in a prison cell back on Earth, but at least there he would get fed.

*

Danny and Erica were led along the passage they'd first entered. Erica made a mental note of every inch of the way, with the forlorn hope that they could at least make it back to the others if they managed to escape.

They were eventually ushered into a room which couldn't have been more different. It was clean, brightly lit, and almost clinical looking.

Suddenly the awful truth dawned on them. Two operating tables stood in the centre of the room, along with a side trolley bearing multiple surgical instruments.

They glanced quickly at each other in disbelief. They had stumbled on the elusive space pirates, the ones responsible for hundreds of deaths across the galaxy and beyond – the aliens guilty of illegally harvesting vital organs from their victims.

"Oh god! Please tell me this isn't happening, Danny." Petrified at the sight in front of her, Erica was too frightened to let Danny's arm go. *How had they allowed themselves to fall straight into a trap?* It seemed they were next for organ donation, whether they wanted it or not.

"This is where you will be prepared for surgery," said Solomon. His manner showed no emotion or remorse for what was about to happen. He stared at Danny with evil intent.

His face was still sore, and he was determined to make the human pay for what he had done. There'd be no anaesthetics for him.

He swiftly turned and left, leaving two guards outside the door. Danny and Erica were alone.

"Got any last request?" said Danny, trying to make light of their plight.

"Don't talk like that, Danny. I'm scared enough as it is."

"Well, I don't know about you, Erica, but I'm not getting on that bloody operating table without a fight," he replied defiantly.

"No, Danny, you already know what they can do to you. Don't be stupid."

"Sorry, but they are not cutting me up for spare parts."

"Alright, so what's your plan then?" she asked.

"Just give me a moment," he muttered.

"You haven't bloody got one, have you?" Erica was annoyed, but she knew Danny was right. They had to do something – anything was better than doing nothing. She walked round the room, tapping the walls, listening for different sounds.

"What are you doing?" he asked.

"Checking for weak spots. We need an escape plan."

Danny put his ear to the door. He could hear the aliens outside, so that route was out of the question.

"Well?" said Erica.

"Nothing."

They waited.

*

Tom, Adam, and Nely sat in silence, waiting for Xander to return, and wondering what had happened to Danny and Erica. Adam prayed their fate hadn't already been sealed. He would never forgive himself if he lost them. He was really worried about Danny; he had been a bit of a hothead earlier.

Nely still sat in the corner of the cell, head resting on his knees, doing his best to block out the nightmare. He wasn't the bravest crew member and he'd be the first to admit it. He was a humble pilot. Right now, all he wanted to do was get out of this hellhole and go home. Then he realised he couldn't go home. He'd settle for decking Tom for getting him into this predicament – except he wasn't even brave enough to do that.

Eventually Xander returned as promised, coming to rest on Tom's shoulder again, still invisible, his fingers running across Tom's face.

"Xander, you're back, are you ok? You've been ages. What have you found out?" Tom was full of questions. Time was running out and they needed to act soon.

Adam looked up when he heard Tom talking and guessed Xander was back.

"I have plenty of news," whispered Xander.

"Well, what have you got? Erica and Danny have already been taken, and no doubt we're next."

Adam moved closer to listen.

"I found out the aliens are actually a unique genetically engineered species, created many centuries ago. They, however, soon discovered they cannot reproduce, and now they are in danger of dying out. That's why they need to replace their body parts, in the hope it will prolong their lives. Human organs are the most compatible. They just want to survive."

"Xander, you almost sound sorry for them," said Tom frowning.

"No, Just Tom, I do not. They are evil people."

"What else, Xander?" asked Adam, leaning in to listen better.

"I found out they are not from this universe. They come through the rift from a parallel universe when they need more organs, then return home to hide."

"So, they're helping to distort the timeline in the process. I sense the universe is not happy," said Tom.

"And that's why no-one has ever found them before. They do a raid and then disappear," added Adam.

"It's all beginning to make sense," Tom agreed.

"I also heard other conversations. They didn't go to the surface when your captain first landed. Something about a blob monster. I have no idea what that is, but they couldn't control it with their minds."

"It's ok, Xander, we know," said Adam.

"Well, as soon as they realised it was safe, they came for you. They were very pleased you killed it."

"Well done, Xander, but what now?" asked Adam. They still hadn't come up with a plan to get out of here.

"They think they are superior beings, really smart, but not as smart as me," said Xander, giving a little snigger in Tom's ear. He was so pleased with himself.

"Xander, what have you done?" asked Tom. He was trying to stay composed but was worried Xander had done something reckless, and he wasn't going to like it. He realised it was just the little alien's youthful nature, but this was serious, their lives were at risk.

"How do you say on your world, Just Tom? I put a scanner in the works."

"What? How?" Tom gasped.

"Please tell us you haven't done something stupid," said Adam.

"Well, I went deep in the planet, or should I say spaceship—"

"Get on with it, Xander," pleaded Tom.

"I am, I am," he said. "I went straight to the workings, sort of disconnected a few cables, and reprogrammed their whole computer system. That's all."

"Phew! Thank goodness for that," breathed Tom.

"Oh, and I rigged the planet spaceship to explode," he added proudly.

His snigger was loud enough for Nely to overhear. "What's going on?" he asked sleepily.

"No! No! Xander, what have you done?" yelled Tom.

Nely guessed the conversation was not going well. He moved closer to listen in. If something was happening, he wanted to know. "Tom, what is it?" he asked again.

"It appears Xander has rigged the planet to explode," explained Tom.

"Shit, that's a bit drastic." Nely didn't like the sound of that.

"Let me finish, my friend," said Xander. "It won't blow just yet, as it's on a time delay. I'm not stupid," he said indignantly.

"Sorry, Xander. So how long have we got?" asked Adam.

"Oh, plenty of time. The spaceship will be back in its own universe by the time it blows... hopefully."

"Hopefully?" questioned Tom. "That didn't actually sound very convincing, Xander."

"No, but how long, Xander?" asked Adam. Time was seriously running out, and they didn't want to still be on the planet when it exploded in the parallel universe.

"Two hours, give or take..." Xander was a bit vague. He couldn't calculate the exact time, so it had to be a guess.

"Shit, that doesn't give us a lot of time. And we still have to rescue Danny and Erica, if they're still alive."

"They will be fine. It's all been taken care of," Xander assured them. "These beings are not as powerful as they think; they need machines to control others. They relied on the machines for centuries, but now they have lost that ability after I pulled out the cables." Xander was full of joy, sniggering away. "I disabled the machines, so they cannot hurt you, Just Tom. I will never let anyone hurt you, ever."

Adam laughed. "Xander, you are a class act." He really liked the little guy's enthusiasm.

Suddenly Xander was visible, sitting on Tom's shoulder cross-legged, his eyes swaying frantically and with much confusion.

"Is that a good thing, Just Tom? Do I want to be a class act? What is it?"

Adam smiled. He couldn't help admiring the little guy's naivety.

"It's fine really, Xander," nodded Tom, who couldn't help smiling either. "Definitely a class act, but does it get us out of here?"

"Patience. Wait for it," said Xander, deciding to stay visible now that the danger was past.

"Wait for what?" asked Tom.

Suddenly they all felt a violent rumbling from deep inside the planet. Things were happening at the core.

"What was that?" Nely cried out. He certainly didn't care for the floor vibrating.

"Ah, the mechanics of the inner workings of the spaceship. And right on time." Xander was confident everything was going to plan.

"It feels like an earthquake," said Tom, as more tremors were felt.

"Xander—"

"It's alright. Two seconds and—"

The doors opened unexpectedly.

"Now we go," declared Xander. "Everything is unlocked."

Nely headed straight for the exit. "Are you coming or not?" he said, not hanging around for anyone.

Xander stayed on Tom's shoulder. It was comfortable there. "Let's go, Just Tom, we must make our escape."

They ran out the door behind Nely and along the passage, Tom recalling the layout as they went. The exit to the surface couldn't be too far.

Halfway along they were greeted by Danny and Erica, just as another explosion rocked the structure, some of the metal walls buckling.

"Boy, are we glad to see you guys," said Adam, thankful they were both safe. "What's happening? Our door just flung open, and the aliens took off," said Erica, bouncing off the wall as another explosion was felt.

"With any luck, it's all-out pandemonium," said Tom. "And if we don't hurry, we'll be part of it."

Xander alerted them that aliens were coming.

As they proceeded further, they were confronted by several aliens, appearing out of nowhere, very distressed that their prisoners were escaping. They were becoming hysterical at the demise of their spaceship. They were also experiencing emotions they had never felt before and were confused how to deal with them.

"You must not leave, you cannot. We need you," said one, holding his arms out to gesture for them to stay.

Though the aliens were all dressed in the same long robes and had similar features, Danny recognised Solomon. His face was still looking a bit red and swollen.

Danny boldly approached him. "Solomon!" he declared.

The aliens were trying to control their captives, but the thought command in their brains failed to relate to their instructions. They had no hold over them anymore.

"Solomon, remember me? You said you were going to make me pay for hitting you."

For the first time in his life Solomon was frightened. Intimidated by Danny in his face, he had no idea what he was supposed to do. Then a huge fist hit Solomon square in the face, knocking him to the ground for a second time. This time Solomon was really hurt, and the other aliens took a step back, just as frightened.

Danny stood over Solomon, satisfied by his actions. "Well, consider that a refund, you ugly worthless creature."

"Nice one, Danny," said Erica, patting him on the back.

"Okay, guys, it's clear they are no match for us now, but we need to go. We have less than two hours to get Retriever-2 out of here," said Adam, leading his team along the passage and brushing aside the aliens who were pitifully standing there.

"Let's hope the exit has opened for us," said Tom.

"It has," answered Xander.

"What about the shuttle controls, Xander?"

"They will work also."

The aliens were crazily rushing about aimlessly and disorientated, having lost all power to think for themselves.

For the first time in centuries, they truly had no idea what to do. They had always been in control collectively, so the mayhem was confusing them. *How could they survive without thought control? How could they survive without new body parts?*

Another tremor shook the underground structure. The passage was rupturing so they hadn't much time to get out before it was impassable. The steps appeared and a shaft of light shone down; they were close.

When they made it safely to the surface, they all breathed a sigh of relief. Aliens followed them up the steps, seeking guidance but unable to function without computer input, thanks to Xander.

Being genetically engineered, created centuries ago but without full capability to act alone, they had lost that quality of independence. They could no longer transfer thoughts to each other, which was something they needed to survive. Helpless, some were calling for help from the humans they had once held captive.

Ignoring all the aliens' pleas for help, the crew dashed hard for the shuttle. Xander held on tight to Tom as they raced over the boulders with the shuttle in sight. He was pleased his work was done and he had saved Just Tom and his friends. Kanon Garg would be so proud of him. Once off this spaceship, they would all be safe.

Xander felt at ease, relaxed even; maybe a little too relaxed.

Another tremor from deep within shook the ground with such force that Tom lost his balance, falling hard into the black soil. Xander went flying from his shoulder. Unprepared for such a jerk forward, he hit the ground hard and knocked himself out cold on a rock.

Tom, unhurt, scrambled back to his feet straightaway. He saw Xander half buried in the soil, not moving.

"Xander, Xander!" he cried out, rushing to gently pick up his limp body. There was a huge lump on the side of the little guy's head, his eyes dangled down and showed no sign of life. "Xander, wake up, please."

Tom was almost hysterical as he entered the shuttle and the doors closed swiftly behind him. Danny and Erica were quickly checking the controls, hoping everything would work.

"Xander has been hurt, I think he's stopped breathing. I don't know what to do." Tom had always dodged the first aid training programme that Niko had set up. Now he regretted his decision.

Nely was nearest. "Give him to me, Tom. I've had a couple of stints in the hospital." What he really meant was that he was always in the hospital for one complaint or another.

Reluctantly Tom gave Xander to Nely, who laid him down. He had seen enough in the hospital to pretend to know what he was doing. Xander's tiny body wasn't going to be easy to practise CPR on for the first time, but Nely was willing to try with two fingers doing compressions on his chest. Kissing an alien, even if it was Xander, was not exactly on his bucket list, but he did that, too.

Tom sat motionless, feeling it was all his fault. He felt wretched that he could not help.

"Engines okay, we're good for lift off," called out Erica.

"Let's get airborne then. This planet, spaceship or whatever, is about to light up the galaxy. Danny, can you contact the ship?" asked Adam.

"Already done," replied Danny.

"Tell them to be ready to go hyperdrive as soon as we dock," said Adam. By his estimation they had about ninety minutes to leave the sector, though Xander had said Kangis-3 would be back in its own universe when it really blew.

Adam wasn't sure how that was going to work. The rift would have to be open, and there was only a small margin for error. He watched Nely working on Xander on the floor of the shuttle, impressed with the pilot's skills.

"He's breathing!" Nely cried out, surprising even himself. "We need to rush him straight to the hospital, Adam."

"Right, Danny. Inform the ship we'll dock at hangar two, it's nearer the hospital," Adam instructed.

The bridge crew were relieved to hear voices again. The silence had been unbearable, not knowing what was happening down there, and it had been more alarming when the explosions registered on the scanners.

Nely held Xander gently in his arms, rubbing his chest and hoping he would respond. His sagging eyes looked pitiful. Tom sat next to Nely in tears, watching his friend, praying for Xander to pull through.

"Hurry up, guys," shouted Nely. "Xander really needs urgent medical help."

"We're doing our best, Nely. Two minutes," said Danny.

Suddenly Tom completely went to pieces. Blaming himself for the accident, he left his seat and sat at the back of the shuttle. If Xander died, he couldn't live with the grief, so he sat on the floor at the rear, thinking how unfair life was. Xander had saved their lives time and again, he didn't deserve this.

Danny and Erica were rushing the shuttle back to the hangar and hoping for a smooth landing. In their haste they hadn't dropped the speed enough and there was a slight bump on landing then the outer doors closed. They'd made it.

Immediately on landing in the hangar, Nely shot out of the airlock carrying Xander and hurried to the hospital. "He'll be alright, Tom, trust me," he shouted back.

Tom was slow to leave the shuttle.

"You okay, mate?" asked Danny. "Come on, let's go," he urged.

Tom left with Danny and Erica by his side, supporting him. Even though Erica was well over a foot shorter than him, she wanted him to know that no-one blamed him for Xander's accident.

"We're all safe, Tom, and Xander will be fine," she assured him.

Adam immediately returned to the bridge. Cal had activated the hyperdrive minutes earlier and Retriever-2 was quickly on its way. At the same time, they could see Kangis-3 in the distance, moving away, hopefully towards the rift it had come through. Explosions from deep at the core of the planet intensified as they watched the long-range scanner, praying Kangis-3 didn't completely disintegrate until it reached the parallel universe.

Alec informed Adam they were still experiencing random fluctuations in the timeline. At present it was hard to calculate even what year they were in. Space itself was behaving so erratically, with star systems disappearing only to reappear in another sector with a different timeline. The dimensional fallout was having a devastating effect on the universe.

Adam realised the ship was not moving away as quickly as he had hoped. "Never mind the timeline, guys, we need to go now!" he demanded.

Alec pressed the button and Retriever-2 shot into the darkness at a velocity never achieved before – a present from the Avaans, and a good time to test its capabilities. A reconfiguring of the ship's energy source, combined with the now safe solardrive generating increased engine capacity, proved successful. They could worry about what the date was later; the major concern was where their next destination would be.

*

In the isolation room, Niko sat with Xander. His vital signs were stable, thanks to Nely. Training some of the crew in certain procedures had obviously paid off, although she couldn't remember ever teaching Nely first aid at all, especially CPR. For now, however, Nely was getting all the credit.

Xander was asleep, joined by his wife Evon, with the newborn twins nearby. She couldn't leave them in her quarters but couldn't stay away from Xander either. She sat close to him on the huge bed, holding his hand. She looked forlorn, her eyes drooping down on her cheeks.

Turning to Niko she asked, "You will save my husband, won't you?" Her little voice trembled with worry.

"Evon, he will be fine. He's just sleeping so his body can heal. The lump on his head will go down, but I still know very little about your anatomy. I promise you, though, he is fine, and Nely did a good job to restart his breathing." Niko wanted Evon to relax a little. The stress wasn't good for her when she had the babies to care for.

"I must thank Nely when I see him. But where is Just Tom? Xander would want him here."

"I will find out, Evon." Niko knew that Tom had gone straight to his quarters, so upset by the whole incident. She decided a man-to-man talk would be best, so sent Sol to see Tom and persuade him to visit the hospital.

As Xander was just in a light sleep, Niko left the isolation room, needing time to think about her own dilemma. With everything else going on she'd had little time to think about herself. She hadn't even spoken to Sol. She had a big decision to make, and it wasn't going to be easy.

CHAPTER ELEVEN

The Earth space rescue ship Retriever-1, now back in operation after extensive repairs and a major upgrade, patrolled the galaxy as per its official duties. This tour of duty the captain was given had the added task of searching for the renegade ship Retriever-2, and to report its location to mission HQ immediately. Federation space police had also been deployed in numbers to its last known position, with orders to liaise with Retriever-1 if necessary. All patrols were given orders to detain and arrest Captain Valmak and his entire crew, and to bring back the hospital ship.

The arrest warrant had been amended to include the murder of an entire race of people and the wilful destruction of their planet Kangis-3. Bizarrely, the incident had been reported to mission HQ some two months before the actual event, and by an unknown source. Earth authorities were totally in the dark about what was going on in deep space. They hadn't even realised Kangis-3 didn't belong to this universe and that the inhabitants were actually the space pirates.

There was now a major problem happening right under the noses of mission HQ. Distortions in the natural timeline were affecting the very existence of life in the universe.

The crew of Retriever-2 seemed to be the only people to realise the universe was in trouble. They had to put things right, but outside forces were thwarting their efforts.

Mission HQ had deployed the gunships three months earlier but failed to notice for some time that all had vanished without a trace. No contact had been made once the ships left Earth, so more gunships were sent out to investigate. It couldn't be proved, but Retriever-2 was getting the blame, nonetheless.

It was unclear how Captain Valmak and his renegades had managed to evade the authorities for so long. Somebody had to have seen the ship. But little or no information was being sent back to Earth, and there was only limited contact available, mainly due to the universe repeatedly having a hissy fit. Fluctuations in the normal timeline were becoming more frequent, occurring without warning, which meant many of the messages sent from Earth got nowhere, while others bounced back into space. Any messages getting through to Earth arrived before actually being sent. There was so much confusion in the universe.

The distorted timeline affected many worlds, but Earth stayed constant, so they noticed nothing out of the ordinary. Only the crew of Retriever-2 understood the complexity of the situation. And they were powerless to stop it.

*

Aboard Retriever-1, Captain Marc Westler was alerted to a distress call from the edge of the galaxy, from an unknown planet. The signal was patchy at best, and a communication link could not be established. This detail, for some reason, infuriated Captain Westler. It was out of his way, for a start. He would rather continue heading in the opposite direction, searching for the elusive Captain Valmak. He had no wish to answer mysterious distress calls in some forgotten corner of the galaxy. He desperately wanted to bring Valmak in to face the multiple charges against him, as Westler detested the man with a vengeance. Arresting him would bring him so much satisfaction.

Second officer Stuart Kranley, though, pointed out that their first duty was to answer all distress calls; it was their primary function. It made Westler annoyed to have the rule book quoted to him, but he reluctantly gave the order to proceed to the distress call. With the upgrade to the engines now enhanced, and way more advanced than any other hospital ship in the company, Retriever-1 would reach the unknown planet in a matter of hours.

Probes sent into orbit failed to deliver any data. Westler was puzzled by that fact, and the silence from the planet was even more strange. The fact this planet was off course and seemingly heading for disaster, getting too close to the sun, made this mission time critical. It hadn't been established if the inhabitants were still alive or not, but the signal had most certainly come from this sector of the galaxy, and this was the only planet in the vicinity.

It was feared it might be another trap, like the one that had cost the lives of Retriever-3's crew, found some months earlier, and also the attack on Retriever-4. So, everyone was on edge waiting for Westler to make a decision.

The captain requested more data before descending to the surface. It didn't matter to him that the first probes came back with nothing, then Stuart Kranley pointed out further protocol that they could not descend to the planet without making contact. This time Westler ignored Kranley. More probes were quickly dispatched into the atmosphere, but disintegrated almost immediately, the intense heat having disastrous effects on the hardware.

Helm crew Aaron White explained, "Surface temperature is three times the normal level for sustainable life, Captain. There is extreme heat radiating from the nearby sun, and it's pulling the planet closer. It could be what's causing the interference."

Westler ignored the helm. He wanted information he didn't know, not the obvious data he could see. *There was something strange about this planet,* Westler thought, *but he just couldn't put his finger on what it was. And that sun? How could anyone survive that heat? What was it about that sun?*

Westler ordered the ship into a lower orbit while he pondered the situation. "Heat shields up, helm. We don't want to overcook from here," said Westler sternly.

Retriever-1 moved into a lower orbit with still no clues to who or what was down there. None of it made sense. A distress call had been received then nothing after that.

Westler made the sudden decision to investigate, but he was going fully prepared. All hospital ships in the fleet were now equipped with new advanced weaponry, and Westler had every intention of using it if necessary. Phasic guns had been made obsolete years ago, and each crew now carried powerful sonic-laser guns. They made the old phasic guns seem like water pistols.

Tired of sitting around, Westler wanted this mission done and dusted. He wasn't happy being stuck out on the edge of the galaxy. It was a prime location for space pirates, in fact an ideal hideout for any space rebels, and not where he would expect to find Captain Valmak.

"Helm, instruct the shuttle crew to prepare for immediate launch. Heat suits required and be armed. Kranley, you will join me. Let's not waste any more time," he bellowed, jumping up from his control seat. "I want all monitoring procedures maintained, no slacking in my absence, and send more probes out. One of them must give us something to go on."

"Yes, Captain," said White.

"Then jump to it, man!" snapped Westler as he left the bridge.

Kranley followed behind, feeling a bit sorry for White. There was no need for the captain to speak to the crew in such a manner, but he was obviously in a bad mood – again. Since arriving in this sector his bad temper seemed to have got worse. Kranley wasn't sure if he'd done something wrong, but he couldn't think what.

"Time to put this to bed, I think, Kranley," said Westler, as they proceeded to the hangar deck.

Kranley was almost at a trot to keep up. *Why was the captain in such a hurry?*

"Sir?" said Kranley, puzzled by the remark.

"I want this mission wrapped up swiftly, then we can get back in operation and continue the search for Retriever-2."

"But, sir, it isn't actually our mission. Besides, the federation police are all over it, and they don't really need us," he replied. Kranley liked things less complicated and to do things correctly by the book. He was a stickler for company protocol, but Westler was not.

"On the contrary, Kranley, the federation police haven't found Valmak in nine months of searching. He's hiding out there somewhere. I will find him, mark my words."

Kranley suddenly didn't like the way his captain was behaving; it wasn't healthy. He had heard about the vendetta between the two captains, all because Valmak had been given Retriever-2, the fastest ship in the fleet, which had really irked Westler. But all that was in the past and had happened years ago.

Now Retriever-1 had been given its upgrade and was the fastest ship by far. But still Westler harboured a deep-seated grudge against Valmak. There was talk about them having come to blows once at mission HQ, all brushed under the carpet much to Westler's annoyance.

Kranley decided there was no point in arguing while the captain was in this kind of mood. He would do his job diligently as always but keep an eye on his captain's irrational behaviour. He needed to keep him in check.

*

When the shuttle touched down on the unnamed planet, there was still no data forthcoming from the probes. Most just burned up in the atmosphere. Kranley didn't care for the lack of knowledge about this place, guessing he would have to wing it. But he felt something was off; weird even.

He had one eye on Westler all the time, feeling certain the captain would slip up sooner or later. The man's mind was not fully on the mission, so Kranley had to stay alert.

Immediately the crew felt the intense heat, the sun burning down relentlessly and getting closer all the while. The gravitational pull was taking effect.

"Regulate your suits, men. It will keep your body temperature down, and keep your visors down," Kranley instructed the two pilots.

Westler was already out of the shuttle, flipping his visor down. The sun's glare was nearly as bad as the heat.

"Captain, don't you think there's something very odd about that sun?" asked Rob Fenwick, the co-pilot. He had concerns about its intensity but also the white glow. A sun that extreme could have serious consequences.

He felt the captain should have warned them prior to landing. But it was more than that. Fenwick had done a thesis on supernovas as his specialist subject at the academy, so he knew enough to realise there was imminent danger.

Westler, though, was more interested in the landscape, or lack of it. The ground was hard, barren, and scorched. One sight, however, did catch his eye – a dome-shaped building situated high on a nearby mountain, with steps leading up to it. It was the only structure worthy of a look.

Kranley had no choice but to follow in hot pursuit. He wasn't losing sight of the captain at any cost.

Fenwick and his pilot Philip Hesslein were slow to follow. *Why rush?* they thought. They were uncertain they would find anything, as this place looked deserted of life.

Tugging at Hesslein's arm, Fenwick said quietly, "Leave them to it. I think we need to investigate over there." He pointed over in the distance.

"What is it?" asked Hesslein. He hadn't noticed anything, and the horizon looked empty.

"I swear I saw movement just now. We should check it out, as it could be survivors," replied Fenwick.

"And it could just be your eyes. What about Westler? He'll go mad."

"Screw him, he's an idiot, hell bent on doing what suits him. He's not even interested in the mission."

"Are you sure about that?"

"Of course, everyone knows what Westler is really like."

"No, I didn't mean that. I meant are you sure you saw something?"

"Yes, come on, Hesslein." Fenwick was sure if there were survivors they could help.

Hesslein, on the other hand, was reluctant to disobey orders, but he couldn't let Fenwick go alone.

"Okay, we'll go and check it out. Be it on your head if Westler goes bananas."

Reaching the top of the steps, the dome structure appeared much bigger than Westler had first thought. It looked solid enough, a building of immense opulence. He approached a large entrance door which he found locked when trying it.

"Now why do you suppose it's locked? Surely, they should be expecting us," he scoffed.

Westler was so eager to get to the building that he had raced up, even with his protective suit on. Kranley struggled with his, wondering how the captain had managed it so fast.

The captain had the perfect answer for the locked door, taking out his sonic-laser gun and blasting a huge hole in it. The door fell apart and clattered to the ground.

"You could have tried knocking first, Captain," commented Kranley, taken aback.

"No time," came the terse reply.

At that point Kranley realised the pilots hadn't followed them up the steps. This was not a good sign. "We've lost Hesslein and Fenwick, Captain," he announced anxiously, expecting Westler to blow his top.

The captain glanced down the steps, but there was no sign of them at all. "I'll deal with them later," he said casually to Kranley's surprise.

Stepping over the mess caused by the sonic-laser, the pair entered the building. What greeted them was totally unexpected. A quick glance round said sheer opulence, and the interior décor suggested a palatial residence. Gold and sparkling gems adorned the walls and furniture. *It seemed so out of place to have a place like this sitting atop a mountain,* they thought.

Kranley called out, hoping for a response. "Hello, anyone there?" His voice echoed back and there was no reply.

Westler strutted about the room before realising there was a slight downward slope in the ground. He surmised the building went deep into the mountain and the outside structure was probably a fake façade. *Did the inhabitants live inside the mountain, perhaps shielding from the sun?* There wasn't much else to see except the overindulgent use of gold. *How did such a barren-looking planet have so much of the stuff?* he wondered.

Kranley continued to call out; somebody had to answer soon. Westler, though, was getting impatient and moved on. Another locked door. He was about to blast it when Kranley reached out.

"Try this panel first, Captain," he said, pushing a square patterned block in the wall that looked totally out of place. The door opened.

Westler didn't like being made to look silly, so Kranley felt a little smug but did his best to keep a straight face.

"Aha, the control room, I believe," said Westler, as if he had discovered it all by himself.

"Wow!" Kranley gasped, astounded by the elaborate but complex computer system. There was floor to ceiling intricate machinery. "Impressive technology, what do you suppose it's for?" he asked Westler.

"Don't know, but it's still operational," answered Westler confidently. He could hear the inner workings whirring round inside. "It's very sophisticated, whatever it does," he added. It pointed to a superior level of intelligence.

"I wonder where the people are who constructed it?" Kranley said, then suddenly realised Westler had wandered off.

"Captain. Captain," he called out.

"In here," came Westler's voice from nowhere.

Kranley went in the direction of his voice, behind a large heavy black curtain, and found a much smaller room, sparsely furnished, not like the outer room.

"What do you make of this, Kranley?" Westler was standing over something covered in a dark robe of some kind. He lifted the robe to reveal the body of an alien.

"Oh Christ!" yelled Kranley, instinctively reaching for his sonic-laser.

"It's okay, he's dead," declared Westler, not in the least perturbed by the sight of the shrivelled head of the alien.

Kranley, however, was shaking. The fact that he had drawn his weapon on a dead alien was not good for his nerves. "I wonder if they're all dead then?" he spluttered.

"We're not going to get answers here. This guy has been dead quite some time," said Westler, oblivious to how queasy Kranley was feeling.

"Can you not just cover him up again, Captain?"

"Yeah, right. Pull yourself together, man." It was not in Westler's nature to show sympathy. He turned to leave. It was clear no-one was alive, or they would have shown themselves by now.

Yet as they turned to leave, footsteps could be heard in the distance and getting closer. All of a sudden, an alien stood in front of them, blocking the way out of the chamber of the grandmaster. The alien was startled for a moment but also annoyed at the intruders in a place of sanctity.

"Who are you? What are you doing here? It is forbidden," he demanded loudly.

"We ask the questions," said Westler, annoyed at being interrogated. "We received a distress call asking for assistance, so who are you and what is it you need?" he asked angrily.

The alien was becoming agitated, shocked at these beings barging into the palace and causing such damage. It was not acceptable.

"My captain is waiting for an answer. Who are you?" Kranley tried a softer approach, his voice not so harsh.

"I am Zumus, high priest of the Naasook people. You have violated the inner sanctum of the grandmaster."

"Look, pal, just tell us what you need," said Westler. "Then we can get out of here."

"I can assure you we sent no distress call. Now, will you please leave us alone."

Westler wasn't happy at the response. *The alien was holding something back, something they wanted to hide from outsiders,* he thought. He was still angry at the inconvenience of having to come to this hellhole in the first place, taking Retriever-1 out of its way. This sector was not even in the designated patrol zone, and he'd only answered the call because mission HQ had ordered it.

"So just tell us what's going on," tried Kranley.

"I ask again, who are you and what are you doing trespassing in the palace of the grandmaster? You have destroyed property and entered the forbidden chamber." Zumus was rattled at the off-worlders interfering in the Naasooks' plans, although at present those plans were falling apart.

"Well, I think you might want to check on your so-called grandmaster. He's back there – dead," Westler announced bluntly.

Zumus was shocked. "That cannot be true," he said. "You're lying."

"Check it out, why don't you," said Kranley. Even he was getting fed up with this conversation.

Zumus brushed past them in a hurry.

"Time to leave, Captain?" asked Kranley.

"Yes, I guess they don't want any help," replied Westler, relieved he didn't have to stay any longer. His protective suit was getting uncomfortable and a little too warm for his liking. "Let's go then."

They left Zumus to discover the truth. But Zumus didn't want to believe them; they had to be lying. The grandmaster couldn't die, the people of Naasook needed his guidance and wisdom in the coming days. Deliverance was coming.

Westler and Kranley exited the building, walking over debris from the once ornate palatial door. Kranley thought his captain's actions had been way over the top, but Westler didn't seem to care about the consequences.

"We better find Hesslein and Fenwick and get off this godforsaken planet. I can't stand the heat any longer," said Westler, striding down the steps with purpose. "And when we get back to the ship, arrest those two for gross dereliction of duty."

Kranley didn't like the idea, but he could tell the captain meant it. This mission was making him bad-tempered and crazy. He'd been unbearable to work with since entering the sector, as if there had been a switch in his brain.

Kranley still worried for the people. Somebody had asked for help and that sun was going to kill them all. He wanted to help, if only he knew where they were hiding.

Reaching the bottom step, they were greeted by Hesslein and Fenwick. Struggling behind them were about twenty or so rather dishevelled men, mostly humans, some barely able to stand. All were suffering from sunstroke and dehydration.

"What the—" cried out Kranley. "Where did this lot come from?"

Westler was not happy. This development meant they had to stay and sort things out.

"We went to check on something, out over that ridge, and found an underground prison full of these men. Some are apparently from Retriever-3," explained Hesslein.

"They said they were captured by hypnotism and brought here to do slave work," said Fenwick, as he started to usher the men to the shuttle to get them out of the heat.

"Slaves? Why?" Westler demanded to know.

"Apparently to build spaceships. We haven't worked out what for, but I'm guessing to get off this rock before it gets sucked in by the sun."

"You're not paid to guess, Fenwick. Get them loaded," snapped Westler. He was raging that this was going to cause extra paperwork he could do without.

"I think that guy back in his palace needs to answer a few questions, Kranley. Go and get him, and don't take no for an answer," he ordered bluntly. He was appalled at the state of the prisoners, and someone was going to pay for it.

Kranley rushed off, racing back up the steps. This was one arrest he did agree with, and for once his captain had made a proper request.

The prisoners collapsed around the shuttle, tired, exhausted, and very thirsty. They'd had very little to eat or drink for days. Fenwick handed out water. It wasn't much but would help until they got them to the hospital.

Hesslein left him to it and approached Westler. "Sir, we found two of the Naasook people willing to speak to us, especially after we persuaded them with a gun to their heads."

"Where are they now?" asked Westler. His rational trail of thought had gone, and he was getting angrier by the second. The whole situation was out of control.

"I believe that's them coming now," replied Hesslein, pointing to the small ridge.

Westler strode over to them, fuming at the mess he had just walked into. *How could any world operate modern day slavery – and for what purpose? This was going to have intergalactic repercussions.*

Hesslein went back to help Fenwick. "The captains in one very bad mood now," he said.

"Yeah, and I think we might be in trouble later as well. Better keep our heads down," replied Fenwick.

"Well, for now we better contact the ship to send down every shuttle we have and get these poor guys to the hospital."

"Good idea, I'll do it and inform the hospital to be ready on standby."

In the meantime, they comforted the prisoners as best they could, reassuring them their ordeal was over. Unfortunately, some were still disorientated by the brainwashing and weren't too sure what was going on. Dehydration was also having awful effects on their minds.

"I think you're right about that sun, Fenwick, it's getting closer by the hour."

"We need to leave pretty soon."

"Yeah, so long as Westler stops messing about. I think he's losing the plot."

"You only think, Hesslein. I know he is."

Having taken a good drink of water, one of the prisoners spoke to the men. "So glad to see you guys. I'm Officer King, assigned to Retriever-3."

"Good to see you. We'll have you aboard Retriever-1 very soon," assured Fenwick.

Westler ordered the two Naasooks to the ground, his sonic-laser pointing at them menacingly to ensure they obeyed.

"I want answers out of you two. You have five seconds to talk, or I might just blow your brains all over the place." He'd lost all patience now.

"Please don't hurt us," pleaded a tiny hunchback alien, cowering up close to his friend for protection.

"We tried to help in the end," said the other one. "I am Oston and this is my friend Qrotei. We sent the distress call. We need help."

"You sure do," smirked Westler. "You're in deep trouble with the federation police, and that's after I've finished with you."

"But we did it to help. Our high priest didn't want off-worlders to come," revealed Oston, putting his arm round Qrotei to comfort him. They were both visibly shaking with fear at the gun waving in their faces. "This galaxy is not safe. We had to send out the distress call so you could help us."

"What are you talking about?" Westler asked, but he really didn't care much for these worthless aliens. Still, if he had to make a report, he'd need answers.

Oston tried to explain. "Our planet arrived here after being knocked out of orbit in our own system. We experienced a strange time warp, then somehow catapulted here. A corridor opened to your universe, and Naasook came through. We are being pulled towards a sun that isn't ours."

"And we believe it will explode very soon," added Qrotei. "That's why we asked for help."

"A supernova," Westler muttered to himself. That would explain the intense heat and the fact the planet hadn't been on the star charts when he'd first checked it. *Maybe these two idiots weren't talking drivel after all.* It didn't stop the gravitational pull towards the sun. That was inevitable.

"Go on, what else?" Westler asked, still waving his gun at them.

"We just want to get back to our own universe before it's too late," said Oston.

"So, you kidnapped other beings as slaves, to do what exactly?"

"It was to build our spaceships so we could escape the sun, but unfortunately someone disabled our robot ships. We cannot complete our mission now. It's too late," Oston explained in a pitiful voice.

"We are doomed," said Qrotei.

"That's why we sent out the distress call, hoping someone could help us. Zumus knew nothing of what we were doing." They appeared genuinely remorseful for everything, but Westler wasn't buying their sad story.

"You do realise it is an offence to kidnap people to use as slaves," he told them. "I should shoot you right here and now." Westler was angry at the pitiful sight of these two morons.

"Please, please, won't you help us?" pleaded Oston.

Westler simply walked away. As he did, he saw Kranley returning, dragging Zumus with him. The alien was showing reluctance at being manhandled in such a way.

"He's not being very co-operative, Captain," said Kranley.

Zumus had been disturbed at finding the body of the grandmaster, and wrongly assumed the off-worlders had killed him. It hadn't occurred to him that the grandmaster had been dead for weeks, extreme old age being a major factor. He and the Naasooks had always deemed their illustrious leader immortal, so never expected this to happen. They had all sheltered inside the mountain waiting for deliverance, certain the grandmaster would save them at the right moment.

Only Oston and Qrotei had stayed with the prisoners to do what they could to help them.

"You killed the grandmaster, you murderer. I will make you pay for that," squealed Zumus.

Kranley was just about choking him with his own robe, and he wasn't letting go.

Westler had seen and heard enough; he was already seething from the sight of the prisoners. These aliens weren't worth saving.

"No, Zumus, I think you will pay for it." Westler raised his weapon and shot Zumus where he stood. The sonic-laser burned a huge hole in his torso, and Kranley had to release his hold as Zumus slumped to the ground, his robe smouldering.

Stunned, Kranley stepped back in horror. He was aghast at his captain's sudden action.

"Captain, what the hell are you doing? He was unarmed." *This time the man had gone too far.*

Westler thought differently, though.

"Doing what needed to be done, Kranley. Less paperwork. Now locate where the rest of these aliens are hiding. They are all under arrest," he ordered dispassionately.

Oston and Qrotei remained sitting on the ground, petrified they would be shot too, while Kranley remained motionless staring at Westler. *There was no reason to kill anyone, these people were defenceless,* he thought. *Yes, they needed to be dealt with – but not like that.*

"Kranley! Snap out of it, man, and do your duty," shouted Westler. "We need to move now."

Kranley couldn't move his legs, he was rooted to the spot. *How did he allow Westler to do what he did? To kill, regardless of who they were, wasn't right; it was against everything he believed in.*

He felt guilty for taking his eye off the captain, he should have realised he was not behaving rationally. This went against all regulations and was certainly not what he signed up for when he applied for first officer aboard a hospital ship. He walked away. He could not be a part of it any longer.

"Kranley, do you want putting on report as well?" yelled Westler.

"Go to hell!" his first officer shouted back.

Fenwick wandered over, having seen the alien fall to the ground.

"What just happened, Kranley?" he asked.

"I do believe Captain Westler has just committed murder," declared Kranley. If he hadn't felt sick to his stomach before, he did now. "How long before we get help from the ship?"

"Five minutes. They're sending everything down," replied Fenwick.

"Good, well done."

"What are you going to do about the captain?" he asked.

"I guess I have to arrest him." Kranley could hardly believe what he was saying, but he had no choice.

The remaining three shuttles touched down simultaneously, and Fenwick and Hesslein wasted no time getting the men aboard out of the blistering heat. It was going to be tight to fit them all in, but they calculated they could take everyone in one trip. The last few stumbled through the airlock, grateful to be rescued.

"Get them to the ship as quickly as you can," said Kranley. "I will leave in the last shuttle."

"Yes, sir, will do. What about him?" asked Fenwick, pointing to Westler, who hadn't moved an inch. The captain still stood next to the body of Zumus with his sonic-laser in hand.

Kranley looked at Westler, then glanced toward the two aliens still sitting on the ground, scared to move. They'd asked for help, but they hadn't banked on a psychopath turning up. He walked over to them, feeling genuine sympathy for them.

"Where are the rest of your people?" he asked.

"They fled inside the mountain. They were afraid and will not come out until the grandmaster says so," explained Oston.

"Well, that isn't going to happen," Kranley told him bluntly.

"We are afraid, too. That's why we asked for help," said Qrotei.

"You're not going to get it sitting there. Besides, we have our own problems to deal with." Kranley didn't go into detail, but he knew there was trouble ahead.

Without Westler's knowledge he had been doing covert monitoring whilst on route. He had grave suspicions about a time distortion in the universe, something which the science crew had failed to pick up. He didn't fully understand the dynamics and couldn't confide in anyone, but he felt a mysterious force had awakened in the universe and was soon going to kick off.

"Do you two want to come with us?" Kranley asked.

Qrotei looked up to his friend. "I want to live wherever it is."

"I do, too," said Oston.

Kranley waved them to the remaining shuttle. "No funny business, ok? Technically you're under arrest."

"We understand," they said together and hurried to the shuttle before he could change his mind.

Now Kranley had to deal with his captain. Still watching the smouldering body of Zumus, Westler looked a pitiful sight, but Kranley had no sympathy for him.

"Captain, time to board."

Westler didn't answer. He had nothing to say.

"I have to place you under arrest, Captain Westler, and you are relieved of duty. Do you understand?" Kranley tried to stay calm as he spoke. He'd lost all respect for his captain; the man's career was now over.

"You do understand, don't you, Kranley, that I just got angry? All I really wanted was the chance to chase down that renegade Valmak and bring him to justice. To wipe the smirk off his face. Coming to this godforsaken outpost prevented me from the search."

He sounded pathetic now, and Kranley wasn't interested in his excuses.

"Anger has a nasty habit of clouding one's judgement, Captain." Kranley took Westler's sonic-laser, then took him by the arm and led him into the shuttle.

Back on-board Retriever-1 Kranley took charge, having confined Captain Westler to his quarters for the duration of the journey. The planet Naasook was being pulled towards the sun and getting too close for comfort, so he instructed the helm to get out of there fast.

Kranley already suspected the sun was in danger of turning supernova, and he was extremely worried that if the star's core survived the initial explosion, it might end up as a neutron star or, worse still, a black hole and the ship would get sucked in. The effects would have devastating consequences across the galaxy.

Engaging maximum engine power, Retriever-1 suddenly found itself caught up in the distortion in the space time continuum. As the ship hurtled across the galaxy, the on-board time clock went crazy. Their destination was Earth – but it was uncertain whether they would arrive in the past or the future

Kranley feared that if they arrived on Earth in the past, had Captain Westler actually committed the dreadful deed? And, worse, could Kranley prove it?

In anger, the universe blinked again, the natural order had been disrupted once more. Two aliens not of this universe had come aboard Retriever-1, causing an imbalance.

Fluctuations in the normal timeline spread across the universe and cracks split open in every galaxy. Retriever-1, on course for Earth, carried on relentless, oblivious to the perils ahead. Kranley and his crew had no idea what to expect. A major distortion was detected directly ahead, and going round it was not an option, but getting back to Earth was imperative. Kranley ordered his helm crew to proceed at full speed – then they prayed.

CHAPTER TWELVE

As Retriever-2 entered yet another star system, the crew pretty much expected the same routine. They found nothing of any importance, nothing to help them in their quest for a new life. It was becoming disheartening to think that no worlds existed out there in the darkness that could sustain life. It had to be a world where they would never be found, but that quest was looking forlorn. Rebuilding their lives had been put on the back burner while they roamed the universe searching for something that wasn't there.

Long-range scanners suddenly detected a huge explosion of galactic proportions, some ten parsecs behind them. It made everyone sit up and take notice, as it was the most excitement the crew had in a long time. Incoming data was inconsistent and therefore could not be relied on.

Ripples of the aftershock stretched across space, reverberating beyond the star system, coming into contact with Retriever-2 before petering out. Luckily no damage was done to the ship. The crew could only speculate what would have caused such a devastating destructive wave to go beyond the perimeter of the galaxy.

It was feared another unnatural force was at work in the universe – one they could not control. A strange anomaly must have occurred. Something was making the distortions in space react badly, causing major rifts to open up, worse than before. The parallel universe had caused all the problems in the first place, so it was possible somebody had entered from the other side again.

The crew were right to fear a backlash from the universe, but they also realised they could not solve the problems or seal up so many rifts. How anyone could stop the chaos was beyond the knowledge of Cal, and even Tom. They'd exhausted every avenue and were totally out of ideas. It was quite obvious Retriever-2, and its crew were powerless against the forces of nature. All they could do was concentrate on themselves, but they had to admit they were simply running away on a journey to an unknown destination.

Several messages were intercepted from Earth mission HQ, but it was uncertain which timeline the messages referred to. The crew were certain some of the information they received hadn't actually happened. Then again, they had been away from home almost seven years – or at least they assumed they had. It was difficult to know for sure. Retriever-2 was so far away from Earth's solar system that it was impossible to know the true facts or even the real dateline.

Several days earlier, Paul had had a complete meltdown at the helm and smashed the timeclock in sheer frustration. It was doing his head in to watch it keep changing from the past to the future, and he couldn't cope with it any longer.

Everyone was frustrated by the events unfolding. It was hard to stomach the fact they had been branded renegades, wanted on numerous charges, including murder. And they couldn't defend themselves without alerting the Earth authorities to their whereabouts.

Further charges kept being added to the list of crimes, which alarmed the crew even more, particularly as several events hadn't taken place. Now they questioned themselves what course of action to take and whether they should change their own future. It was a difficult choice that no-one wanted to make.

Mission HQ hierarchy persisted in its ludicrous demands that Captain Valmak immediately surrender, hand over the hospital ship, and return to Earth to face the charges against him. They were still unaware that Captain Valmak and eleven other crew had died quite some time ago.

Adam and the others couldn't even report the deaths to their families, so they were never going to know the truth. And there was no way they were handing over the ship. It was their home now, the only one they had. They had to forget their previous life and somehow find a new world to create a new life where they couldn't be found or persecuted. It would be a life for themselves, the ever-expanding Avaans, and Sol, who was now a permanent member of the crew. None of it was going to be easy.

Time and time again the universe appeared to hinder any progress Retriever-2 tried to make. Strange fluctuations in the timeline seemed to send them back months in the past and in another galaxy, then shoot forward years into the future. It was hard to avoid the distortions. Many of the rifts appearing were suddenly turning into huge cracks in the universe, any one of which would take Retriever-2 into a parallel universe, the one place they didn't want to go.

Finding out who or what was causing the disparity was impossible, and they couldn't get involved anymore. They'd done all they could to bring harmony to the universe and it had been thrown back in their faces.

So, Retriever-2 sped across the vastness of space, doing its best to avoid the potholes the universe created – or at least the thing that created them. The universe blinked every time there was a distortion, its continual hissy fits making life hard for all creation.

Adam sat in his control seat, doing his bit to assist the others in monitoring each sector of space. They were continually searching for a possible planet; while also watching for irregularities so Retriever-2 could avoid the rifts. They feared slipping through one then not being able to get back to their own universe, which would only make the problem worse.

All seemed quiet for the time being. Helm maintained a steady course, things had calmed down a little, and Retriever-2 was alone again in the universe.

Cal was keeping himself busy trying to calculate a new timeline after Paul's earlier antics. He understood the frustrations of the crew, but smashing vital equipment up did nothing to help the situation. In the meantime, everyone did their duty as best they could to keep on top things.

Staying alert was paramount. They couldn't afford to run into anyone, least of all the Earth authorities. The ship had no defence against federation police gunships, which were heavily armed. Besides, they didn't want to fight – not anymore.

Looking up from his monitor for a second, Adam noticed a certain crew member was missing.

"Where is Nely?" he asked, realising he hadn't seen him for some time. "Shouldn't his shift have started by now?"

Paul swung round in his seat, quick to reply. "He asked me to cover for him, he's on a date with Carol Harding. She heard about his life-saving skills with Xander and thought he was rather cool after that."

"I bet it's once round the hydroponic gardens then back to his quarters," came a quip from Denny, smirking as he spoke.

"Anyone know how Xander is doing?" asked Will, changing the subject.

"Recovering well apparently, and enjoying his twin babies," said Cal. "But he does have a wonky eye," he added, taking a break from his screen for a moment. "Something about nerve damage, or so Niko said, but it was difficult to say if it's permanent."

"What about Tom then, Cal, have you seen him lately?" asked Adam. He had taken Xander's accident very hard and was keen to know about everyone's welfare, especially Tom's.

"He's buried his head in engineering, not wishing to talk much to anyone, not even Xander," reported Cal. He felt really sad for the man; the remorse and guilt Tom was feeling was immense. Cal had tried a couple of times to snap him out of his depression, but nothing had worked. Tom just wanted to be left alone.

Adam sat a few more minutes then decided he should do something. "Okay, guys, I'm going for a stretch of the legs. Maintain a full alert as usual. I need a break."

"Would that be anywhere near engineering by any chance, Adam?" asked Cal, with a wry smile and a wink at Adam.

"Possibly," replied Adam as he left the bridge.

*

In the hospital the Avaans were enjoying life to the full. The adults were fussing around the new babies, and the proud parents, Evon and Xander, could not hide their joy and sheer enthusiasm. Evon was happy her husband had finally grown up and had proved himself to be a hero. For a while she had thought she might lose him on that dreadful planet, but Kanon Garg had assured her this was his moment of glory, and he would not fail in his mission.

Xander was happy, but he wanted more. He wanted his friend Just Tom to visit the hospital. He'd named his son after him, yet Just Tom hadn't once come to see him. Xander held no malice towards his friend; it had been an accident, no more. Life, Xander said, would always have accidents, and he should know. He'd recovered very well and hadn't suffered too badly, though one eye still drooped down his cheek. He had little control over it because of the nerve damage, but his sight was fine as long as he didn't mind looking at the ground most of the time.

Mayhem continued in and around the hospital as Po and Levin, the older twins, were literally running amok, knocking things over and crashing into furniture, including the odd wall. They still hadn't mastered their levitation skills yet and were no more than babies in Niko's eyes, yet they were floating around the place as if it was normal.

The one astounding fact was that the new offspring could levitate and vanish without the use of a utility belt like their parents. They had evolved so well in their new environment and got into all sorts of mischief. It was a welcome distraction, especially for Niko, who still had a big decision to make about her own life.

Taking a breather from the hectic lives of the Avaans, who were quite obviously doing well, Niko walked over to the couch near her desk to contemplate her future. It was only marginally quieter there; the Avaans talking all at once could get a bit loud at times. She knew they would soon return to their quarters, then the hospital would be rather quiet.

A decision about her life was about to come to a head, and the very thought terrified her. For a moment she drifted away in deep thought, worried about what was happening on the bridge. She wondered if they would ever be able to find peace. It was a way of blocking out her own dilemma, just thinking about the lives of everyone on board other than herself. But that wouldn't make her own problem go away.

Anguishing over what she should do, her trail of thought was suddenly interrupted by a familiar voice calling out. Her long-time friend had a little free time and had decided to visit and enquire how Niko was coping with life in general. The situation was hard on all the crew, so they had to look out for each other. But Niko was the one true friend who had kept Mike sane throughout the long tour of duty, otherwise he would have spoken to no-one. Originally, half the crew had had no idea he was even on board.

"Hi, Niko," he said, sitting down next to her and giving her a quick peck on the cheek.

Niko was suddenly brought back to reality. "Oh, Mike, how are you doing?" She tried hard to raise a smile to hide how she was really feeling, but it wasn't as easy as she'd hoped.

"Where's lover boy?" he joked.

"Mike, I've told you before—"

"Sorry." Mike put a hand on hers, seeing his words had upset her. But he felt sure there was more, as she looked sad and not her usual self. He hoped she hadn't fallen out with Sol. That could be awkward.

"What's wrong, Niko?"

"Nothing. I'm fine, thanks, Mike. Why do you ask?" she replied, holding her emotions back with a façade of a smile.

Mike didn't believe a word. "Don't kid me, Niko, I've known you for twenty years. You're my best friend, so you can't lie to me."

He put an arm round her shoulders. Something was wrong and he wasn't leaving until he got the truth out of her. "Tell me, Niko," he urged.

She sighed heavily. She had to tell someone, and maybe her best friend would understand her dilemma. "Okay, Mike, there is something, but I don't know what to do about it." She started to get a little emotional, everything was just building up inside.

Mike was growing anxious. He feared she was seriously ill. "Niko—" he began nervously.

"Okay, okay. Well, it's like this, Mike… I mean, oh hell, here goes, I'm pregnant." She announced it quite abruptly in the end but was glad it was out in the open.

"Bloody hell! Niko, he's an alien, for Christ's sake." Mike didn't mean to be so direct, but her statement was such a shock that the words just slipped out.

"Oh, thanks for that, Mike. Just when I need support." She began to cry uncontrollably. Her hormones were all over the place, and she didn't know how to deal with it.

"Sorry, I didn't mean to sound so harsh, it's just, well, what are you going to do?" Mike asked, trying to be more sympathetic. "What I mean is, how far along are you?"

"Six weeks, I think," said Niko, through the tears.

"I guess popping out for the morning-after pill is out of the question then," said Mike, trying to raise the mood. "You have to tell Sol."

"He knows."

"Christ, Niko, this is a big one. Have you thought about the consequences of having an alien baby?"

"I've thought of nothing else, Mike. I don't know what to do. I'm worried. Is this the right environment to have a baby? Then do I want one at my age? It's not as if we can ever go back to Earth. I'm really struggling, Mike. Everyone turns to me for help, who can I turn to?"

"Me," he replied, cuddling her tight. Comfort was all he could give her right then. "You'll work it out, girl. Besides, forty-one isn't old."

"Thanks, Mike." She hugged him back, her tears making his uniform wet. "You're a real help."

*

Staring anxiously at the viewing screen, the bridge crew watched the four federation police gunships which were in hot pursuit. How they had managed to locate Retriever-2 and catch up with them was a mystery. But they were on their trail, and it looked like they had the speed to match.

The crew were stunned into silence. It suddenly struck them this was their destiny, to be hunted down as criminals, outlaws running from their own kind.

It didn't feel good.

"Get the hell out of here fast!" yelled Cal, who was in temporary charge of the bridge. He'd seen enough; they needed to escape pretty damn quick. There was no time to hang around and exchange pleasantries. He guessed the federation police wouldn't want a discussion anyway.

"What direction, Cal?" asked Paul. "We have spatial distortions on both sides, and now a major crack just opened directly ahead. I don't fancy our chances with any of them."

The situation looked dire. It appeared the ship was trapped between a rock and a hard place, and Cal was desperately trying to think of a solution. He wished Tom was there, but everything was going to be down to his decision making. He could only think of one option.

"Do you know how to do a U-turn, guys?" he finally asked.

"What?" Paul swivelled round in his seat with a look of total disbelief.

"Are you crazy, man?" Will was as shocked as Paul. "It's never been done," he added.

"No, that's why they won't be expecting it," declared Cal. The more he thought about it, the more he liked the idea. They just had to get away somehow.

"Listen, we come to a stop, they get close, then we hit maximum engine power and do a U-turn straight back past them. Trust me, guys, it's our only chance." Cal sounded confident, but he wasn't persuading the others.

Paul and Will exchanged looks, neither liking the idea.

With another glance at the oncoming gunships in the distance, Cal went on, "I know it's a crazy idea, a ship this size, but we have to try. We're running out of options, and time." Cal pointed to the viewing screen.

The others considered their options: captured by the federation police, or the ship possibly disintegrating trying to turn around.

"We don't have a lot of time, guys," Cal pleaded.

Denny had already received an ultimatum from the lead gunship to surrender immediately or they would shoot. Even he wanted helm to make a decision now.

"Look, ask yourselves," he said, "do we go forward into whatever that is out there, or backtrack and try another escape route?"

"Some choice," grumbled Will.

"Well?" urged Cal again.

"Engines already stopped," said Paul, making the decision against his better judgement. He didn't like either option but couldn't see what else they could do.

"Good," said Cal gratefully. "Now, let the federation ships think we're surrendering, then we go for it. Yes?"

Paul and Will nodded reluctantly. Denny just shrugged his shoulders and waved his hands in the air, more in despair than anything else. He was glad he wasn't in charge.

Just then Adam returned to the bridge, having finally found Tom hiding deep in the engineering deck away from everyone. Adam had taken time to deliver a good reality check, telling Tom to snap out of it and go and see Xander. Adam rarely exercised his authority as elected leader, but this time he ordered Tom to go and visit the little alien. It was the only way to help Tom, particularly as Cal and Sol had failed to get through to him.

Immediately Adam was aware of something going on. "What's happening, guys?" he asked, taking his seat.

"Federation police," replied Will bluntly.

Adam looked at the viewing screen. "So why have we stopped then?" He watched the gunships closing in fast.

"Better ask brains over there," said Paul, pointing in Cal's direction.

"Cal?" Adam swung round in his seat.

"We can't go forward, as it appears the universe is working against us every time we try a new escape route," replied Cal.

"So, what's your big plan then?" Adam was puzzled. It looked like they were giving up.

"We're about to do the biggest U-turn in history. If it doesn't come off, we're done for. But if we stay, the result is the same."

Cal could see by the look on Adam's face that he was extremely sceptical. A manoeuvre as bold as that was deemed impossible.

"We can't do it, Cal… can we?" asked Adam.

The Retriever fleet of spaceships were a minimum of three thousand feet in length; Retriever-2 was over four thousand feet, to accommodate extra facilities like the hydroponic gardens and the archives. It also meant the ship could sustain itself much longer away from home, which was an experiment that was originally planned to pay the crew a big bonus on their return. Nely, like some of the others, had been banking on that bonus.

Adam didn't like the odds of coming out of this situation alive, but he didn't have a better idea.

"Adam, we don't have much time," urged Cal, as he watched the gunships closing fast.

"What are our chances?" asked Adam.

"Less than zero if we hang around here any longer. We can't chance the rifts or that crack in the universe dead ahead."

"Okay, U-turn it is. Cal, you take charge of this then. I'm going to have to trust you," Adam replied reluctantly. He was scared at the thought of getting it wrong; they could all end up dead – or captured. Neither option was acceptable, so he had to get it right.

*

News spread fast around the ship that Niko was pregnant. She had wanted to keep it quiet for a while, at least until she'd made a decision on whether to keep the baby, but it seemed Sol was having none of it. Unable to contain his excitement, he told everyone he met.

Mike didn't help the situation either. He was genuinely happy for his best friend and reckoned she and Sol would make great parents. Indeed, everyone was happy at the prospect except Niko, who still couldn't decide what to do. Having a baby while on the run from the authorities was not ideal, and being so far from Earth was really hurting Niko. *How could she give birth hundreds of light years from home and not be able to tell her family?*

Knowing Niko was unsure about having the baby, Sol finally persuaded her when he said they would make a great family. That one word said it all for Niko.

*

Several months had passed since Cal's heroic and spectacular U-turn. It had been a great success, running Retriever-2 straight through the middle of the federation police gunships – a manoeuvre they were definitely not expecting. The two lead ships had failed to notice the crack in the universe directly ahead and disappeared without a trace.

It was surmised the crack was possibly the result of another hissy fit by the universe's natural forces. *Or did it blink again in frustration?* Maybe this time it really did have something in its eye. Whatever the black void was, nowhere was safe. Space was a very dangerous place to be.

Adam feared they would be blamed for the loss of federation property. Denny had picked up a transmission a few weeks earlier about police gunships, missing presumed destroyed, and these were added to the list of charges against Captain Valmak and Retriever-2. He didn't relay the message to the others. It would do no good to morale.

Cal had finally constructed a makeshift timeclock, if only to keep an eye on what the date was on any given day, and he warned Paul to stay well away from it – period.

Mission HQ had made it virtually impossible for them to return to Earth now. Denny picked up another transmission, but this time he decided to inform Adam what was being said. The warrant for their arrest had been amended yet again, accusing Captain Valmak and his renegade crew of mass murder and the wilful destruction of three police gunships. It seemed more charges were being trumped up at every opportunity.

The company was not interested in the facts anymore and had issued orders to shoot on sight. They were not bothered with the return of their hospital ship, which was obsolete now. If it was destroyed, the company wouldn't have to bring it back to Earth. Profit was always their primary objective.

*

The hospital was even more chaotic than usual. The Avaans seemed determined to survive and were growing in numbers at an alarming rate. Ke Tegan was now the proud mother of two sets of twins, another boy and girl. Evon was also expecting her second, probably twins as well, as twin births seemed more common than they'd first thought.

Learning about the Avaan babies certainly gave Niko insight to her own impending birth, but she hoped it was only one. Rumours floated around the ship about other pregnancies, including Carol and Nely.

They all realised it was not the ideal situation to be in, starting a family in the furthest depths of space. And some questioned how long they should go on running away. Earth had given them no choice, but finding a suitable world for all of them, where they could hide away from reality, was proving futile. *Was the universe holding out on them? It certainly felt like it.* For now, they had to make the best life they could inside a metal prison in outer space.

It didn't sit too well.

*

Federation police would never give up the pursuit. More heavily armed gunships were deployed, others kept going missing. A bonus was added for anyone who found Retriever-2, but there were no death threats.

The order was given under a different timeline, as the company wanted Captain Valmak and the entire crew alive to stand trial back on Earth. Retriever-2's crew were well aware of the circumstances, but it was difficult to know which timeline to believe. Their own was registering something completely different, and Cal had to use a lot of guesswork.

They had to stay one step ahead of the authorities no matter what time they came from. At least Retriever-2 had alien technology to assist with increased velocity – something Earth were not aware of.

Distortions in space continued to happen on a regular basis, and the parallel universe was having a devastating effect everywhere. Every time a rift appeared; a different timeline registered on the timeclock. Cal had to watch over Paul each time in case he smashed the clock again. But secretly Cal wished he hadn't bothered with it. The damn thing was causing so much confusion that it was better off not being there.

Huge fluctuations in space were always a danger if the ship got caught up in another flux, so the crew tried not to let the changing date worry them too much. They had no control over what the universe would decide to do.

Apart from the timeclock going haywire every five minutes, inside Retriver-2 the crew appeared immune from any effects from the outside disturbances, but it was the outside that worried them the most. Perhaps the universe was finally trying to protect them, not impede their escape. It was, however, a very fine line.

After escaping the federation ships, the crew were weary of travelling an erratic route across the universe looking for a new home. Until now they had managed to avoid any confrontation, but they were sick of the solitude. It wasn't all it was cracked up to be.

Suddenly that loneliness was shattered when Retriever-2 was alerted to several warlike ships on their tail. Computers were going nuts, and so much data poured in all at once – something that hadn't happened for months. This was the first contact the crew had received in a long time, and it caught them unawares. It was an unwelcome sight.

"Can you identify them, Alec?" asked Adam, jumping out of his seat, concerned about the ships closing in. *Why now?* he asked himself.

"Cynturian warships. I recognise them from our first encounter," replied Alec.

"Do we fight again?" asked Nely, who didn't relish the idea at all. He didn't want to die. Now he was going to be a father, he felt he had something worth living for, a reason to be strong for Carol and not be such a wimp anymore.

"Not unless we have to, Nely," replied Adam. What he meant was they only had the one phasic blast, and it wouldn't be enough against a fleet of warships.

"Should we perhaps try to negotiate with them?" enquired Denny. He thought it might be a viable option.

"We killed their leader, so what do you think?" Adam said. "Besides, the Cynturians don't negotiate, they just murder."

Suddenly a warning shot came across the bow, but not from the Cynturians.

"Where the hell did that come from?" yelled Adam, attempting to pinpoint its origin.

"Oh Christ!" screamed Alec, almost making Nely fall out of his seat. "Just detected federation gunships off the starboard."

"Now what do we do, Adam?" called Cal. "Cynturians probably want revenge, but what about the federation police? We can't deal with them all."

Adam froze for a second then sat down in his seat. He had no answers. *What was he supposed to say?*

Denny announced the federation police were ordering a complete surrender. The warning shot had been a courtesy call, they said, but the next one would not be. They had orders to shoot to kill if necessary.

It was a daunting prospect which nobody wanted to hear. Suddenly, appearing on the portside were armed hospital ships – new additions to the fleet and given orders to take no prisoners. They had arrived under a different timeline and were acting independently from the federation police.

Retriever-4 fired a shot, hitting Retriever-2 and causing damage to the cargo hold, which ripped open the hangar decks. Unpressurised, the shuttles drifted out into open space. The unknown ship picked up over a year ago and Sol's ship, however, inexplicably stayed put.

Thinking the shuttles were being used for escape purposes, a gunship fired continuously until both ships disintegrated. Retriever-2 was left with a gaping hole.

An entire fleet of Cynturian warships were not going to be outdone. They began their own attack, seeking revenge for their illustrious leader.

"Adam, what are we going to do?" pleaded Nely. "We can't defend ourselves. We're under attack from all sides."

Alec then shouted at Adam for some kind of response. They had to act now. But Adam couldn't answer. He had withdrawn into himself.

"Distortion directly ahead, just appeared. I think it might be a rift about to open up," Cal announced. "We could go through it, Adam. We might have a chance."

Still Adam stayed silent.

"More problems, Cal," interrupted Alec. "Twelve degrees to port a huge black hole just appeared – at least, I think it's a black hole."

Computers didn't register the data. It was a black void that simply didn't exist.

"Adam! What do we do?" Cal raised his voice further, but still Adam didn't speak. He couldn't ask his crew to carry on anymore; this was the end of the road. Everything they strived for gone. It was pointless. He'd had enough.

Call took the only option left. "Alec, Nely, Denny, black hole or through the rift?"

"Rift," said Denny straightaway. That void he could see didn't look very inviting, so he didn't fancy their choices there.

"Black hole," said Nely.

"Me, too, black hole. What have we got to lose?" added Alec.

"Our lives," muttered Nely in his usual way.

That was it. Cal took the decision to head into the black hole, whatever it was. He suspected it was something other than a black hole, as it had appeared so suddenly and so close by. *Was the universe offering them an escape route? No,* he shook his head, *that was too ludicrous to be true.*

The rift wasn't an option in case it led to the parallel universe. They had tried that once before and it hadn't ended well, with Captain Valmak losing his life on the other side.

And there was no way they were going home to be tried for crimes they didn't commit, nor did they want to be blown to pieces.

But with the uncertainty of the black hole being genuine or something else the universe had created for them; they were certain they were not coming back.

Closing in on the blackness, the gravitational pull grew stronger, too strong for Retriever-2 to pull away even if they wanted to. The Cynturians, the federation gunships, and the newly armed hospital ships opened fire from all sides, and huge explosions ripped through the stern and lower decks. The attack was relentless.

Sol sensed Niko was in danger and he was nowhere near the hospital. He raced to get there, but another hit on the ship rocked it sideways. He crashed against the metal bulkhead, hitting his head hard, and fell to the ground dazed. Instinct told him to get up, but he felt dizzy, and his sight was blurred slightly from the bang to his head.

Part of the inner bulkhead had buckled in the ensuing explosion and partially blocked the route to the hospital. As Sol staggered to his feet, two blurred images were coming towards him. He couldn't see clearly but was sure they had just walked through solid walls. The dizziness he was experiencing meant he wasn't thinking straight, so he wasn't sure of anything at that point.

As the images approached, he was sure he didn't recognise them. Though his vision improved, it was obvious they were not part of the crew; they were very young and wearing strange clothes. They began heaving some of the twisted metal out of the way.

Sol was perplexed by their presence. *Who were they? What were they doing?* He wanted to know but couldn't find the words.

"Go!" they said.

Sol went. He couldn't think about them when Niko needed him. The way along the corridor was clear now and Sol stumbled past the rubble, falling over a couple of times and picking himself up. He had to get to the hospital.

"Do you think he recognised us?" said one of the young strangers.

"Of course not, how could he? The timeline is so distorted in this universe that we haven't been born yet. But we must return home."

"Yes, we can't risk a paradox occurring if we are trapped in this universe. We must go."

They left the same way, straight through the solid wall, a portal to their world.

In the hospital, panic had set in. Niko had gone into early labour, there were complications, and Sol was nowhere to be seen. As the darkness engulfed them, many questions remained unanswered. No-one was going to know the real truth.

THEY WENT IN.

www.ingramcontent.com/pod-product-compliance
Lightning Source LLC
Chambersburg PA
CBHW030518310726
48979CB00010B/1712/J

9781803819969